Emilia has tried to quit her addiction to oxycodone and alcohol many times before, but has never lasted more than a day. Now she's been off them for three days, but her body is in rebellion and her withdrawal symptoms are about to drive her back. She knows she must do something different this time and goes to a *SMART Recovery* meeting.

Even in her state of withdrawal, she's drawn to the tall handsome Mosi, who runs the meeting. But a man like him could never look at a woman like her. Could he?

This is her story. Her successes and failures on her road to a new life. Even as she struggles to remain clean and sober, a strange artifact from the ancient past of her people drags her unwillingly into provincial politics. Can she maintain abstinence through it all? Will her hopes be dashed . . . again? Or will she finally find healing from her addictions and the hope of genuine love?

Emilia's Hope
Copyright © 2019 Sofía T. García
ISBN: 978-1-4874-2509-8
Cover art by Martine Jardin

Published by eXtasy Books Inc or
Devine Destinies, an imprint of eXtasy Books Inc

Look for us online at:
www.eXtasybooks.com or www.devinedestinies.com

Emilia's Hope
Mestiza Book 2

By

Sofía T. García

DEDICATION

To Leah M. Beta reader extraordinaire and powerhouse of a poet.

A special note of appreciation to the SMART Recovery® board of directors for allowing me the use of the SMART Recovery's name and recovery tools in this novel. In particular to board member Timothy Eddy for patiently reading each draft and his support for the novel before the board, as well as the current president, Bill Greer, for important input on SMART Recovery®.

If you or a loved one wishes more information on recovery from addictive behaviors, go to smartrecovery.org.

And I must express my gratitude to my editor, Jon and the proofreader Amber who both keep me on track, and the artist, Martine Jardin.

CHAPTER ONE

Smack! Emilia plowed face-first into the steering wheel of her car. She shoved herself back and looked around. *Where the hell am I and what just happened?* She ran her left hand over her face, then looked at it. *No blood at least.*

With a mist-filled mind she looked around and realized she was in a parking lot. *I must have hit the curb block.*

Hard.

She shut down the engine and tried to think. Thinking wasn't easy, especially not today. In fact, not for the last three days. Her head felt like it was being bludgeoned, her eyes were hard to focus, and her attention span was that of a gnat. She shivered.

It's not even cold out. It's spring and the sun's still up. She looked at the clock on her dash. 6:45.

I'm scared as hell. What if I never get my life back? God, my brain's so slow, it's like a slug on downers. My hands are shaking like I have palsy and every muscle feels like they're being torn off my bones. Oh God, I think I'm going to throw up again.

She threw open the door and hurled, but there was nothing left to come out. She pulled herself back into the car.

What am I doing here?

Finally, she remembered.

The meeting.

My God, I hope I get help here. She looked down at her palsied hands. *I can't even remember how many times I've tried on my own, but it never worked. If this doesn't help it'll be the end of my*

1

dreams. I'm not even thirty and I'm on the brink of death.
All her hopes, her ambitions, her being, lay in this meeting.

CHAPTER TWO

Emilia hauled open the stiff self-closing door with a struggle and ground to a halt on the threshold. The room was dim, which suited both her mood and the pounding inside of her skull. *Should I even be here? Can this really help? Maybe I'm lost for good. This is scary as hell. Should I go in or get the hell out of here? Yep, I'm gone!*

Even as that thought ran through her mind, the heavy glass door banged into her butt with enough force to propel her weak body eighteen inches further into the room. By some minor miracle she remained on her feet, though she wobbled where she stood.

A face appeared before her, looking deep into her eyes, and a warm hand was placed under her arm.

"Are you okay?" a stranger asked.

"Not really," she answered with atypical candor.

"I think you need to sit down," he said and took her elbow.

Without inquiring what *she* wanted, he guided her to a table and the nearest empty chair, with a gentleness to which she was unaccustomed. When she didn't sit down, that same warm hand which in that moment, seemed to be approximately the size of a subcompact car, pressed down on her shoulder. It wasn't hard or forceful, but in her weak state she couldn't withstand the soft push and thumped onto the chair. The stranger gave her a brilliantly white smile, left her side, and went to sit down.

They're laughing and chatting, but it doesn't seem like they're laughing at me. How could they be so happy? I'm scared and shaking and they're enjoying themselves. Is there something here for me?

Emilia looked around, now that she could see in the dimness.

Very informal. Two tables pushed together, long edge to long edge. She reached down and touched the chair she sat in. *Comfy. Not a recliner, but comfortable. How many people are here anyway? I could count them, which at least would distract me from my shaking hands.*

One, two, three, that guy looks really tall. Damn it, where was I? One, two, three, four, five, six, seven. Wow, her hair is totally pink and blue. Crap! Where the hell was I . . . eleven, twelve, thirteen, fourteen. Fourteen, that's it. Damn, did I count myself?

She was about to restart the tedious process of counting when the stranger who'd helped her to the seat spoke.

"Welcome everyone. It's time to get started. I'm Mosi, your facilitator this evening. This is an open meeting of *SMART Recovery.* For any newcomers, *SMART* stands for *Self- Management And Recovery Training.*"

My brain's just not working, I can't even keep up with what he's saying. Ah, at least I get that. It's anonymous. I wouldn't want the boss to know. She gave a soft sigh.

"We're going to check in," Mosi said. "Tell us your name and a little about how your week went. If at any time you don't want to share, just say pass. Let's start . . . here," he said with a warm smile, pointing at the person next to him on his right.

Is it his smile that's lighting up the room? Or the warmth and tenderness in his voice? Maybe it's his white teeth shining out from his ebony face. Jesus Emilia, get a hold of yourself. Though she was born and raised on the west coast, just outside of Vancouver British Columbia, and there were people of every ethnicity imaginable, she'd never seen a person with skin as black as Mosi's.

The man Mosi had pointed to spoke, and Emilia tore her

gaze from his ebony face to look at him.

"Hi, guys. I'm Josh. Last Saturday I completed two years clean."

The place broke out into clapping and there were congratulations from several around the table. Josh smiled and continued.

"It's been a great week, a lot better than last week when my car was broken into. I'd chosen the minimum deductible, which I wouldn't have done when I was using. Mostly because I'd have been too broke. My car's fixed and my wife and I are doing well. I was a lucky guy that she stuck with me and I'm trying to make up for all the lost time I missed with her and the kids. She's happy, the kids are happy and most of all, I'm happy."

"Thanks, Josh," Mosi said and nodded to the woman beside him.

"Hi, I'm Caryn. I'm just a little over two months clean from *OxyContin* and booze."

Emilia sat straight and listened wide-eyed to the middle-aged woman in disbelief. *Every word about the lady's past sounds virtually identical to what I'm going through. How can I feel encouraged and terrified at the same time? God, my body's shaking and the cravings are overwhelming my head. I have to super focus on what Caryn is saying.*

She tried not to listen as her addiction tried to persuade her. *Just one more time. You can quit tomorrow. You're not really addicted, you can quit anytime you want.*

Except I can't, not on my own, I've already tried many, many times and failed.

Emilia didn't hear much after that and before she realized it, Mosi said to her with a nod, "Go ahead, we've all been where you are today." He gave her a smile.

Trying to shake the thick cobwebs from her head, she began.

"Uh—I'm Emilia and I'm addicted to alcohol and

oxycodone. I haven't done any in three days and I'm trying to quit. I've tried a bunch of times before, but always went back. It's destroying my life and I have to stop, but I just can't do it on my own."

"Way to go, Emilia!" Caryn cried.

Others clapped and called encouragement. It really wasn't what she'd expected, though she wasn't sure exactly what she *had* expected.

"That's a tough one," Mosi said. "Have you seen a doctor or counselor?"

"Uhm . . . no. This is the first thing I've done besides trying to stop on my own."

"There are drugs that can ease the withdrawal symptoms if you need them. It's your recovery, but a good doctor that specializes in addiction might be helpful and they have some awesome counselors here at *Sources Community Services*. I'll give you some numbers to call after the meeting and when we're finished with check-in, we can find out how others have managed what you're going through."

When he smiles at me it feels like the whole room warms, and talking about my addiction seems to ease the powerful cravings. Maybe after years of trying I can finally quit.

Maybe.

The check-in continued, but Emilia couldn't focus on what was said. Her world seemed to revolve between Mosi's brilliant smile and the relentless urges, which had driven her back to alcohol and painkillers over and again. Even sitting, Mosi was almost a head taller than anyone else at the table. He was slender and lanky and she admired his skin. *Mine's mocha, but must look nearly white in comparison. And God that round face and those dark eyes. He's gorgeous.*

"Emilia has three days clean from oxy and alcohol," Mosi said. "What strategies did some of you use in early recovery?"

"As I said during check-in," a man who looked to be in his early fifties said. As he spoke he folded his hands, leaned forward toward Emilia. His blue eyes flashed with compassion. "I've got six months sober. For me, the *CBA* worked really well."

"*CBA?*" Emilia mumbled.

It didn't go unnoticed.

"*Cost Benefit Analysis,*" Mosi said. "That's a great tool and we'll do one on the whiteboard in a few minutes."

"For me," a younger man, no more than twenty or twenty-two, Emilia thought, said, "the first week was an hourly struggle. I just kept telling myself I wouldn't use for this hour and then the next hour I'd say the same thing. It was a bitch, I'll tell you, but one of the reasons I stay clean is 'cause I never want to go through that withdrawal shit again."

Damn. It's so hard to pay attention! The shakes and the foggy brain keep distracting me.

When the crosstalk stuttered to a halt, Mosi took three markers from the table in front of him and stood. Two he placed in his shirt pocket. The shirt was square cut on the bottom and he left it untucked. *It's a guayabera, like Dad wears on less than absolutely formal occasions.*

Mosi stood facing the whiteboard and divided the board into four quadrants with a black pen. He turned and looked at the group with his white smile.

"Josh, would you please take the *CBA* worksheets and pass them around? They're on top of the pile." He pointed to a stack of file folders on the table where he'd sat.

Josh nodded, flipped open the top folder, took the stack of paper, placed one in front of himself and then passed them on.

Mosi wrote in the top left quadrant.

What did my addiction do for *me?*

He turned and looked around the table.

That makes no sense at all. There was nothing good about my addiction. All it did was bring me pain.

"It gave me a buzz," someone said.

Another spoke. "It helped me cope."

"Numbed my feelings."

"Pain relief."

"Social lubricant."

"Helped me sleep."

"Helped me stay awake."

There was laughter around the table and Emilia found herself smiling at the familiar banter.

"We could go on and on," Mosi said. "But let's take the next step."

He wrote in the top right quadrant.

What did my addiction do to me?

"Kept me broke," Josh said.

There were nods and murmurs from all around the table.

"Jail."

"Destroyed my relationship with my wife."

"And my kids," someone else added.

"Ruined friendships."

"Lost my job."

"Shame."

"It made me someone that I didn't like."

"Made me lazy."

"Very good," Mosi said. "Let's move on." He wrote in the bottom left quadrant.

What do I think I will like about living addiction-free?

"No hangover," Emilia blurted before she could stop herself.

"Very good," Mosi said, endowing her with one of his glowing smiles.

That distracted her and she missed the next few additions. When she came back to herself, as well as the horrific urges allowed, she continued to listen with interest. *This is what I desire, this is my hope. To be free from my addictions.*

"More money in the bank."

"Better health."

One young woman said, "Self-care."

"Yes," Mosi agreed, "that's very important. Would anyone like to expand on that?"

"Well, bathing and brushing your teeth."

"Yeah, and eating healthier."

"Hell!" a tall, lanky older gentleman said. "Eating at all! I barely weighed one-forty when I quit the hooch. I'd been living on a liquid diet for two decades."

There were some chuckles at this confession.

"Exercise."

"Proper sleep."

"I don't know if this should come under self-care," a buxom gray-haired lady said, "but I have a better relationship with my husband, kids, and grandkids, as well as more sex. Well, at least I remember *having* sex." She finished with a sly grin.

Some around the table laughed and clapped.

"I like myself," another said.

Mosi looked at the speaker. "That's very important. What do you like better about yourself now?"

The man, who looked to Emilia like he might be in his mid-thirties, leaned back in his chair and was quiet for eight or nine seconds. "I'm a good dad and husband now. I help pay the bills, I spend time with my two girls and they're not afraid of me anymore." Tears oozed out of his eyes and he wiped them with the back of his hand. "I just had no idea of the harm I was doing to those precious creatures. I'm so lucky Sharon came back and gave me one last chance. I can't fuck it up this time, they're just too important to me." He sobbed and the

Rubenesque grandmother, who sat beside him, leaned over and gave him a warm if awkward hug.

Emilia realized that she also had tears rolling down her cheeks. She pulled a tissue from her purse and dabbed at her unmade-up face.

Mosi smiled. "Anything else before we move on?"

"I'm not as selfish."

"I don't have to lie."

"Great," Mosi said. "We could go on and on, but let's get to the last part." And he wrote.

What will the difficulties be in my recovery?

"Dealing with boredom."

"Dealing with urges and cravings."

That caught Emilia's attention. *That's what I'm trying to do right now!* She tried to super-focus on what was being said.

"Handling social situations sober."

"Feeling feelings."

"Oh yeah," someone said with a groan.

"Learning to budget. I'm trying to figure that out and it isn't easy. I started drinking when I was thirteen and using coke, heroin, and crack before I was twenty. I never learned to handle money. I got it and blew it on drugs and alcohol."

Mosi smiled at him. "Thanks for that. Recovery's not an easy road. What other difficulties might one have?"

"I have a war going on in my head," Emilia said. "I really don't know if I'm strong enough to win this battle."

"Been there," the well-endowed grandmother said.

"Oh yeah," Josh said.

"None of us is strong enough, not on our own, but with the tools we learn here at *SMART*, we can win that battle by changing how we think. Battles are won by strategy and determination, not by being *strong*," the tall older man said.

"Good input everyone. I'd like to get back to Emilia in a moment if she agrees, but let's look at the *CBA* we just finished," Mosi said. "What do you notice about the things your addiction did for you?"

"All short term." Josh said.

"That's right, what about what your addiction did to you?" Mosi asked.

"Most of that's long term," Grandma said.

"Spot on. How about the difficulties?"

The tall lanky man leaned forward and spoke. "Most of that is short term. I mean they're things you have to learn. It's kind of a skills deficit list, I think. But for me at least, they're things I'm learning."

"Very good point," Mosi said with his ubiquitous smile. "And how about what you'll like about living addiction free? What do you think of that segment?"

The young woman with pink and blue hair leaned her elbows on the table and looked at the whiteboard as if seeing something on the other side. "Those are my hopes. Part of what keeps me clean. The bad stuff, too, that reminds me of where I came from. A friend of mine was clean for six months." She stopped and sobbed into her hands. "He . . . he must have called his old dealer and scored some smack. I hadn't heard from him all day, so I walked over to his place and banged on the door, but he didn't answer, so I tried the door and it was open. He was lying on the floor of his room. I yelled at him to get up and ran over, but he was cold. Then I realized that he wasn't breathing. I think I passed out, but when I came to, I ran out into the hall screaming for someone to call an ambulance. People poured out into the hallway and I felt like I couldn't breathe. I don't remember anything else until I woke up in the hospital. They told me he'd OD'd. He was like a brother, you know. Crap, I have one more reason to stay clean now. In his memory." She wiped the tears from her cheeks with the back of her sleeve.

Emilia found that her eyes also overflowed. *I'm not the only one.* In fact, Mosi, too, was tearing.

"I used so I didn't feel the pain," Mosi said in a shaky voice. "To kill my feelings. But you see what Miranda did? She felt the pain of her loss and directed it to good. And the pain of loss will go away. Nothing lasts forever, whether good or bad. Everything comes to an end."

She could hear herself breathing for what seemed like an hour, but was probably closer to a minute.

"Hey, Mosi," Josh said. "How long have you been clean? You don't talk about yourself much."

"Eleven years tomorrow," Mosi choked out.

After a few more seconds passed, Mosi looked at Emilia. Emilia felt his eyes bore through her. His dark eyes shone with compassion and kindness. *Here is a man I can trust. I've never met a man I could trust, not absolutely, but I'm certain he is that man.*

"You have a war going on in your head," Mosi said.

She nodded.

Mosi stood and returned to the whiteboard, erased the *CBA* and drew a cartoon-like head.

"We're going to discuss," Mosi began, "the science behind that war. We've all either gone through it or are going through it right now. You're not alone, Emilia."

He drew a semicircle near the bottom of the head. "This, represents the limbic system. It's the part of the brain that keeps us alive. The limbic system is all about survival, like breathing, eating, sex, fight or flight, and in there is our pleasure center. So, when we do something that promotes survival, it creates a neural pathway to our pleasure center.

"I had my first drink at the age of twelve. My mother was of the opinion it was better to learn to *handle booze* at home, rather than at a club. I liked it and a pathway was formed that connected alcohol and pleasure. This is a case where substances fool our brain into thinking something is good. Alcohol and other drugs of abuse produce increased levels of dopamine, which make our brain *think* they're good for us. Most of you have seen this drawing before. Tell us what happens to this pathway over time."

"In my experience," the grandmother said, "that pathway gets stronger and stronger until it takes over your life and all you care about is feeding the addiction. That's the way it was for me anyway."

Josh gave her a thoughtful nod. "I have to agree, as I became heavily addicted, nothing else mattered but getting and using my drug of choice. I ended up using just to feel normal, or at least what I thought was normal."

Mosi drew a dot in the limbic system and a line to it. "This dot represents the pleasure center and this line the neuropathway that we created by using. As Josh said, when we're addicted, we can actually get physically ill if we don't use. Remember, our brain thinks we need our drug of choice for survival. That's why it's so hard to quit." He looked around the dim room. "How can we weaken that pathway?"

"*SMART* is based on science, which has proven that abstinence is the easiest and best way to weaken that addictive pathway," Josh sputtered, barely able to articulate the words. "After two years clean, I know that pathway's still there, and even though it has no power over me, I still have thoughts. And sometimes I have using dreams. So for me, abstinence is the easiest. I believe if I picked up a bottle again, I'd soon be back in that gutter of addiction in a few weeks if not days."

"If I understand correctly," Miranda said, "that addictive pathway weakens with lack of use, but if I used again, it would light right up."

"That is exactly right everyone and that, in short, is the science behind *SMART Recovery*," Mosi said.

Emilia looked around the room. *Even with my addled brain, this all makes sense.*

Then the world began to go black and she felt herself falling.

Chapter Three

M osi felt a warm glow at the way things had gone and it was time for checkout, make sure everyone was grounded and find out what they'd gotten out of the meeting. He turned to Doris to begin, when Emilia, the new young woman, collapsed.

Mosi shot to his feet and ran the few steps to where she lay. On his knees he leaned close to her mouth and felt her breath on his cheek.

"She's breathing," he said.

"Here's your cell phone," Josh said, holding it out to Mosi.

Mosi took it, then checked Emilia's pulse. "Her heart's racing like it's going to explode. I'm pretty sure she's in severe withdrawal." He punched 911 on his phone. Even as he dialed he called to Josh, "Make sure everyone's safe. We'll have to end the meeting without checking out."

"Nine-one-one, what is the nature of your emergency?"

"I have a woman who's around thirty years old who fell unconscious during a meeting. She's breathing and her heart rate is extraordinarily fast," Mosi said.

"What is the location of the incident please?"

Mosi gave her the address.

"What is the number you are calling from?"

He gave her that information, too.

"Can you please stay on the line?" the operator asked.

"Yeah, no problem," Mosi said.

"I've dispatched an ambulance. Is there any bleeding?" The dispatcher spoke in an extraordinarily calm voice.

"None visible, but I'll check," Mosi said. He laid the cell phone on the floor and put the speaker on as he slid his hands under her body to see if there were any sign of bleeding. "Th-there doesn't seem to be any bleeding," Mosi stuttered.

"What do you know about the woman's history?"

"I've never seen her before, but she did say she was addicted to alcohol and oxycodone and has been clean three days. She *is* acting like she's in severe withdrawal, but that's only an educated guess," Mosi said, puffing.

"Thank you," the dispatcher said. "May I ask who I'm speaking to?"

"I'm Mosi."

"Thank you, Mosi, the ambulance will be there any moment."

"I can hear the sirens," Mosi said as he looked up. He saw only Josh, and Doris.

"We're staying," Doris said, narrowing her eyes at him.

Mosi nodded and placed his fore and middle fingers on Emilia's carotid artery. *Crap!* "Her pulse is not only fast, but irregular now, too."

At that moment, Emilia began to moan and move her head. The instant the paramedics arrived, wheeling in a stretcher, her eyes popped open. Mosi jumped out of the way and stumbled back. A moment later he began answering questions one of the attendants asked while a lady paramedic knelt beside Emilia.

"What's your name, miss?"

Emilia gave her a blank look.

"How long was she unconscious?" the lady paramedic asked.

"Ten minutes max," Mosi answered, wiping beads of perspiration from his forehead with the back of his hand.

"Do you know where you are?" the medic asked Emilia.

Emilia shook her head and mouthed *no*.

"The gentleman here says that you're withdrawing from alcohol and an opioid, is that correct?"

Emilia nodded and held up three shaking fingers.

"Said she was three days clean," Mosi said, fidgeting with his collar.

The lady medic checked Emilia's temperature with an infrared tympanic thermometer and then pulled out a blood pressure cuff and after checking her brachial pulse, placed the cuff, put the stethoscope on her arm and inflated the cuff.

"One-eighty over one-eleven," she said to her partner, whose eyes widened at the numbers.

That's crazy high!

"We're going to take you to the hospital where you can detox safely and make sure there's nothing else wrong with you. Do you think you can get up with some help and sit on the gurney?"

Emilia gave what looked like a shrug.

"Can you all clear out of the way?" the other paramedic asked in a soft tone that belied his burly stature.

His eyes were level with Mosi's, but he looked like he had thirty pounds on him. *None of it's fat.* Mosi slipped over to the window to leave room for the stretcher to pass. The two paramedics helped Emilia up and sat her on the gurney. They helped her lie down and strapped her in. She was trembling as they wheeled her to the ambulance.

"Thanks for staying with me, guys," Mosi said with a sad smile

"I need to call my husband. He might think I was triggered at the meeting and stopped by a pub," Doris said while she rummaged around in her large purse.

"I'll wait while you call in case you need confirmation," Mosi said.

"I'm going to call my wife, too," Josh said. "It's only eight o'clock and it would be nice to meet at the coffee shop for a cup of tea. She might even leave the kids at home," Josh said with a grin.

Mosi spoke to Doris' husband. "It was good of her to stay. It was a young woman who'd collapsed. Having a matronly lady here was helpful."

After they'd separated, Mosi sat in his car and thought for a few moments. He made a decision and pulled out of the parking lot.

I have a new mission. I won't let what happened last time take place again . . .

CHAPTER FOUR

M osi rolled his eyes when he punched three hours into the parking meter. Ten-dollars-twenty-five cents, *outrageous*, but he unlocked his phone and touched it to the meter. It was a short hike from there to the emergency room.

Maybe I'll be able to help her in some way. We SMART Recovery Facilitators don't usually get directly involved in the recovery of participants, but I'm going to be as supportive as I can this time.

This time.

Nine months ago another young woman had come to his recovery meeting still in withdrawal from severe alcohol addiction. He'd given her numbers to call and she did come back once more. But she'd gone back to her old habits within two weeks. She'd called him once while she was clearly intoxicated and he found out the next day that she'd driven while under the influence. She'd wrapped her car around a telephone pole at ninety miles an hour without a seatbelt, and even the airbag wasn't enough to keep her from being thrown from the car. Julie had died in the ambulance on the way to the hospital.

I know it wasn't my fault. Everyone's recovery is their own responsibility, but it still gnaws at me sometimes. Times like now. Emilia may never recover from her addiction, but if she doesn't it won't be because I didn't go the extra mile . . . or three.

"Hi," Mosi said to the nurse at the ER reception. "I'm looking for Emilia. She arrived a few minutes ago in an ambulance."

"What's her last name please?" the nurse said in a bland tone.

She looks like she's had a long shift. "Sorry, I just met her at a meeting this evening. She passed out at the end of it and only gave her first name."

"I'm sorry, sir, I can't help and if you're not related, I can't let you in."

Mosi was about to object when he heard a familiar voice.

"Mosi! What are you doing here?"

Mosi turned and saw the forty-something year old doctor — *Reshma* — he remembered. She'd attended the recovery meeting for two full years. He hadn't seen her in quite some time, but that was the *SMART* way. Recover from your addiction and go on your way living your life.

"Hi, Reshma, I'm trying to visit a lady that passed out at her first meeting. I think that she was detoxing on her own," he said.

"Would her name be Emilia?" Doctor Reshma asked, with a warm smile, a tilt of her head, and a glint in her eye.

"Yeah, that's right." *How does she know?*

Doctor Reshma chuckled. "She's asking for a tall black guy that saved her life. She's quite agitated and she does seem to be having withdrawal symptoms. We'll know shortly when the blood tests are in and I've ordered X-rays as well as she seems to have had a fall."

"Isn't it a bit odd for the doctor to be looking for someone on behalf of a patient?" Mosi asked.

"Yes," she agreed, "but Emilia was insistent and all the nurses were busy, so I thought I'd take a quick look out here. I understand how she's feeling about now." Reshma narrowed her eyes and pressed her lips together. "Come with me." She put her arm though his elbow and hauled him to the door of the ER treatment area.

The nurse buzzed them in, but not without a glare for Mosi.

Mosi hadn't even been aware that he'd been tense, but the instant the doctor ushered him through the door, he blew out a great puff of air. He chided himself momentarily for his lack of mindfulness, but disputed that thought a second later. *I'm human and imperfect as is all of humanity.*

It was at that moment he smelled the chemical bleach-like odor he connected to a hospital. It was mingled with other smells less identifiable. *Death and dying.* Doctor Reshma pulled aside a curtain and touched him on his shoulder. He stepped inside and there lay Emilia.

She smiled at him and it warmed him, though it made no sense at all. Her black hair was stringy and matted. Her chocolate eyes were lit with delight, but jaundiced and sunken into her gaunt face. The white sheet looked like it covered a skeleton. *She can't weigh more than eighty or ninety pounds on the outside.*

"Hi," he said for lack of being able to think clearly. *And I pride myself on my quickness of mind.*

"Hi," Emilia answered. "I'm so glad you're here. Did the doctor have to call you? It seemed that you got here really fast."

Mosi chuckled. "No, I was already in the emergency waiting room trying to get in to see you. The doctor found me there."

"Oh, I'm glad," Emilia said.

It seemed obvious to Mosi that she was confused. He, too, had been where she was. "This is a good place to detox."

"I'm not really sure how I got here," Emilia said, with a frown.

Mosi sat in the lone chair, which was situated in a convenient spot beside the head of the bed. "You came to our *SMART Recovery* meeting and told us you'd been clean from booze and oxy for three days. You collapsed at the end of the meeting and I called an ambulance."

"Thanks," she said and reached her left hand out from under the sheet in his general direction.

Her hand was trembling. *One of the signs of withdrawal.* "If you're serious about quitting, you need to stay here until the doctor releases you. It might be good to get into a residential rehab center. There are a number of them locally that are gender specific. If you like, I could set you up for something like that. It usually takes a few weeks to get in as there are waiting lists."

Emilia looked at him with furrowed brows and pursed her lips. Mosi knew from personal experience, as well as from years of working with individuals suffering from addiction, that her mind would be slow to react. In fact, during detox and early recovery, her thinking would be foggy at best.

After three minutes of quiet she nodded. "Yeah, I think I need something. I've tried to quit lots of times, but always went back. This time I have to do something different or I'm going to kill myself."

"I'll schedule you for an interview."

"Yeah, thanks. That'd be great," Emilia said, then scowled and sucked her bottom lip under her teeth.

"Is there anyone I should notify you're here?"

"I told them not to call my parents, but maybe you could call Sissy. I mean my sister, Lupe," she said with a shudder.

"Certainly." He reached over and took her trembling hand. "What's her number?"

"It's on my phone. I think it's in that plastic bag." She pointed with her right hand, which shook like a leaf in a stiff breeze.

Mosi looked over at a small wheeled table where there sat a sturdy-looking plastic bag with a drawstring. He released her hand and got up to retrieve the phone. He pulled open the drawstring and dug around until he felt a hard rectangular object. He pulled it out and handed it to Emilia.

She tapped at her phone in series several times.

"Damn thing!" Emilia huffed. "I can't even hold my hand still and I'm not sure what the password is. Crap! My mind used to be so sharp, now it's a gooey mess."

"Alcohol and drug abuse damages the brain. That's why you're having trouble thinking straight. I'm sure it didn't just start," he said.

"No," she agreed, shaking her head. "It's been going on for a while now and getting worse."

"That's normal with heavily addicted people."

"I've destroyed my life, my body and now my brain. I might as well get it over with and OD on *Oxy* and vodka."

"No," Mosi said, then his jaw tightened. "The brain and the body have a great capacity to heal themselves if you give them a chance."

"How do I give them that chance?"

"Abstinence." He looked directly into her sunken, jaundiced, but somehow lovely brown eyes.

"I don't know if I can do that."

"If you really want to you can."

"Of course I want to."

"Don't speak lightly. You have to really, really want to. You have to be willing to change your lifestyle, even your friends if you have to. It's hard and will take a lot of work, but you have to remember that you're worth the effort."

"That's the problem, I'm *not* worth it. My life is garbage. I made it that way and now I have to live with what I've created," Emilia said in a tone of absolute resignation.

"You don't understand, Emilia, you're a good person, you're not the bad things you do and have done. You're not your behavior," Mosi said. *I always feel a powerful rush of emotion when I think about that.*

"How can you possibly separate the two?" she asked.

Mosi was quiet for a moment as he gathered his thoughts. *Recovery's too important to simply blurt out my thoughts and*

Emilia's mind can't be clear right now, but I want to get my point across and help her understand.

"I was addicted to alcohol since I was about thirteen or fourteen. I mean using it because if I didn't, I felt like shit. And I'm not just talking hangover. I skipped school because I was flunking anyway. I'd shoplift from corner stores, snatch ladies purses and I got to be a very good pickpocket. See?" He lifted his hand and showed her the watch he'd removed from her wrist while they were talking.

Her eyes went wide.

"All the money went to buy booze." He continued. "By fourteen I was drinking vodka straight up. I was seventeen when I was caught holding up an elderly couple with a fake pistol. The judge wasn't impressed with me and I got eighteen months in juvenile detention. Even inside I was able to get a hold of booze or any drug I wanted. When I got out I went right back to my old life, but I now thought I'd learned to be more careful from the juvie cons I'd been imprisoned with.

"By the time I was twenty-four, I was totally lost to my addiction and ended up in the hospital from alcohol poisoning. An older lady had found me. She'd realized I'd passed out and was choking on my own vomit. She'd turned me on my side and called a neighbor to get an ambulance.

"Once I detoxed in the hospital, I realized I was alive by sheer accident. The doctor got me into *MRTC*, a rehab center for men and after six weeks there, I came back to the real world. It was tough and I went to *Daytox*, an outpatient program, and they gave me more tools and the various options available for support groups. I tried several, but liked *SMART Recovery* best and after two years, I took the Facilitator's course and have been holding meetings once a week for almost nine years now.

"You see, while I was addicted, I did some awful things and caused many people a lot of pain, but underneath that addiction was a good person waiting to come out, all I needed was to get clean. Just like you, there is a good person inside screaming to be free. Only you can free that good person and the way to do it is to quit using. You won't be alone and can call, text or email me at any time."

At that point the doctor returned.

"Well hello, Emilia, and I see you're still here, Mosi," Doctor Reshma said, giving them both a pleasant smile. "Your blood tests are back and you're dehydrated, anemic and have both vitamin B and magnesium deficiencies. Your kidneys are only slightly damaged, probably from chronic dehydration, and lucky you, your liver's still in relatively good shape. The saline drip you're on should take care of the dehydration, and a nurse will be by shortly with the mineral and vitamin supplements you need as well as a glucose solution to add to the IV."

"How long do you think Emilia should stay here?" Mosi asked.

Doctor Reshma sighed and leaned over Emilia, holding onto the bed rails with the hand not occupied with her phone, which she constantly referred to as she spoke to Emilia.

"You need to stay here until your blood tests show you're completely detoxed. When you're done, I'll see about getting you into a women's residential rehab center. There's *Hannah House*, but they're twelve step. That might not suit you if you've chosen to go to *SMART* meetings."

"Uh, yeah, I wanted something based on science. *AA* seemed like hocus pocus, depending on some un-seeable, un-knowable higher power," Emilia said with a grimace.

Mosi spoke in his normal soft voice, but sadness clouded his features and there was firm criticism in his tone. "Remember, Emilia, *AA* has helped a lot of people, even if it's not for you or me."

Emilia gave him a blank stare.

"You're in luck," Doctor Reshma said. "I talked to the

intake coordinator at *Ellendale Treatment Center* for women and they expect an opening in four or five days. It's science based and they owe me a few favors, so you're in, if you *really* want."

"Thanks," Emilia said. "I need something for sure."

"It's an excellent program." Mosi said, with a nod and warm smile.

"Ah, here's a nurse with your meds," the doctor said. "I'm off to do my rounds. It looks like it's going to be a busy night."

Doctor Reshma held the curtain open for the nurse and then rushed off.

"Hi, Emilia," the nurse said with a warm if tired smile. "I'm Bahvya, your nurse while you're in the ER. You're in for a bit of a rough time over the next few days, but Doctor Reshma has prescribed *Valium* and an anticonvulsant, as well as a glucose drip with a series of vitamins and minerals you need."

The blonde nurse looked to be in her late thirties, but her deep olive complexion gave great doubts as to the natural origins of her hair color.

"I'm not sure I want any more drugs. They've given me enough problems already," Emilia said.

"Don't worry," Bahvya said. "You're taking these under the care of a medical team, and I'll add, we've had very good success with them over the years. Without them, you might not make it through detox." Bahvya then proceeded to add them to Emilia's drip. She checked the monitors, took her temperature, then checked her pulse and blood pressure. "Press the call button if you need me or feel any distress." She then slipped out through the curtain.

CHAPTER FIVE

"This is an open meeting of *SMART Recovery*," Mosi began, using the exact words he'd been using for nine years. He ran the meeting by rote, at first, still distracted or perhaps haunted by Emilia. Her recovery was her own responsibility, not only by *SMART* doctrine, but for one's own mental health. *Ultimately, everyone's responsible for themselves.* He'd stopped by to see her after work today—for too few minutes. She was already looking healthier and less drawn-out and was excited about going into rehab Tuesday morning.

It was during check in that he came back to himself. The third person to check in was a well-dressed man that looked like he might have been forty. *Age can be difficult to determine with persons abusing substances. Drug abuse tends to prematurely age the body.* Though the gentleman had no tie, he wore an expensive suit. He was Caucasian, perhaps five-foot-ten or eleven, with blond hair styled in a Modern Caesar, which Mosi frankly thought was intended for a much younger man.

"I'm Charles," he said in a sulky tone and pouting lips. "I just got my third Driving Under the Influence and my *father* decided he wasn't going to pay for my lawyer this time unless I got *help*. I went to a couple of *AA* meetings, you know, Alcoholics Anonymous, but they're a bunch of losers throwing all their problems on some imaginary higher power."

"I'm sorry," Mosi interrupted. "But in *SMART Recovery* we don't criticize other recovery modalities. *AA* didn't suit you and that's why you're here, searching for something you think'll work for you. Good on you, but remember that *AA* has helped a lot of people over the years and still does. We even have people here that attend both."

"Yeah, that's right," the tall slender man who was a regular at Mosi's meeting said. "I go to a couple of *AA* meetings every week and to *SMART* every Monday. It's all good, at least it is for me."

"Ya gotta do what works for you," Josh interjected.

"Maybe I should just leave," Charles said in a huff and stood, pushing the chair away with the back of his knees.

"That's entirely up to you, but you're welcome to stay if you like," Mosi said, keeping the frown from his face.

Charles turned as if to leave, but hesitated and looked to where Mosi sat at the head of the tables. "Does *SMART* give attendance verification?"

"Yes, I keep a few sheets in my briefcase," Mosi said, giving Charles his usual warm smile.

"I think I'll stay then," Charles said and plopped back into the chair without ceremony.

Mosi nodded and asked him to continue, but he would keep a close eye on the spoiled rich boy. *Daddy can't buy your recovery, my friend.*

CHAPTER SIX

Emilia entered the small but cozy office and sat in the chair the counselor gestured her to. From where she sat, the window overlooked a gorgeously landscaped and perfectly manicured lawn with a duck pond in the background and what looked to be a forest beyond it.

"So who did you kill to get in here?" the lady counselor said. But her eyes twinkled with mirth and her face held a warm welcoming smile.

"Uh, Doctor Reshma . . ."

"Oh goodness no!" the woman cried in mock terror. "You haven't killed Doctor Reshma. We're very fond of Doctor Reshma here at *Ellendale*."

"I mean, well, Doctor Reshma . . ." Emilia stuttered.

"Enough said." The lady raised her hand. "Doctor Reshma is a huge supporter of *Ellendale Recovery Center* and in addition to the money she donates each year, she comes over once every month with naloxone and other drugs she gives us for our patients and treats anyone who needs her help while she's here. At *Ellendale*, she's virtually a goddess. So, tell me how you met our doctor."

"I was at a *SMART* meeting in White Rock. I was three days clean and in severe withdrawal. I passed out, according to Mosi."

"You know Mosi then?"

"I met him at the *SMART* meeting. I didn't remember anything about it at first, but some things are coming back. I remembered him though and asked for him when I was in the

Emergency Room. He was actually at the hospital looking for me and Doctor Reshma went to search for him and brought him to me. She was my doctor during detox. Do you know, she even came to check on me when she was off shift?" Emilia finished, shaking her head.

"I *did* tell you she's a goddess, did I not?"

Emilia smiled and nodded.

"My name is Gavenina and I'll be your counselor while you're with us. Everything you tell me is confidential and while the normal stay is about six weeks some may stay longer if there is need. You're young and sharp. I think you'll do well here if you are truly committed to staying clean," Gavenina said as she flipped her hand, which Emilia took to be a habitual gesture.

"I *do* want to stay clean," Emilia said with fervor. "My life has turned to crap. I'm about to lose my job, I'm not allowed to see my nieces and nephews, my family'll barely speak to me and don't even invite me over for dinner on holidays, not to mention that I can't keep a decent guy around. In this week that I've been clean, I realized how much I'd let myself go, with bad hygiene, no exercise, horrible diet when I remembered to eat at all, so I also feel like shit."

"How are the cravings? It must be difficult quitting two addictions at once," Gavenina asked.

"Oh man." Emilia put her face in both hands for a moment and then looked up at Gavenina. "I can't stand them, they're too strong."

"I thought you said you'd been clean for a week now," Gavenina said.

"Uh, yeah, I have," Emilia said with a frown.

"Ah, so then you have withstood the urges and cravings for a week now. What makes you think you can't continue to say no to them?"

"Now that I think about it, I don't know," Emilia said.

"Are they getting stronger?" Gavenina asked.

"No, not at all. Now that I think about it, they may be getting weaker."

"So, why do you think you can't continue to stand the urges?"

Emilia slumped down into the chair where she sat. "I've never really thought about it like that. I've withstood the cravings for one full week. I've never been clean that long."

"I'm proud of you," Gavenina said. "And getting through withdrawal is a big step. You should feel proud of yourself. Many people don't make it this far. Do you think you can continue to be abstinent with some support and counseling?"

"I hope so. I want to. It just seems so intimidating, you know, never to have another drink or another pill."

"That's normal, Emilia. Everyone feels that way when they first get clean. Give that fear a little vacation so you can get to know what you're capable of. You're stronger than you realize." Gavenina smiled.

Emilia sat up straight and looked at Gavenina with new intensity. "Were you ever an addict?"

"Labels are for jars, Emilia. We don't use terms like *drunk, crack head, junkie, drunk* or *addict*. You are a good person with a substance abuse problem. You're worth the effort to stay clean."

Emilia was about to speak, but Gavenina lifted a finger and continued. "To answer your question, I was addicted to heroin. I even hooked to get money to buy my smack and like you, I ended up in the ER. With a peer group for support, counseling, and treatment, consisting of buprenorphine combined with naloxone, I was able to kick the habit. That was ten years ago and why I chose to counsel others suffering from substance abuse."

"So, I guess you understand what I'm going through right now."

"Yes." Gavenina nodded. "And I can assure you that it gets easier, as long as you maintain abstinence."

"Mosi said something similar. He visited me every day when I was detoxing in the hospital and talked about *SMART Recovery*. They also accept the science that abstinence is the easiest and best way to a healthy lifestyle. What I found most interesting was the use of *Rational Behavioral Therapy* to change the way we think about our addiction. That, he explained, is what changes our behavior," Emilia said.

"Sounds like you have it all figured out," Gavenina said with a wry smile.

"I think I'm beginning to understand the basics, but I'm here to actually learn how to do all this. Mosi said that it takes a lot of patience, mostly with yourself, tons of practice and mountains of persistence."

"Mosi was right," Gavenina said with a thoughtful nod. "So, Emilia, what do you think was the root cause of your addiction?"

Gavenina asked many more probing questions, many that Emilia had no answer for, but which forced her to introspect, as she had never done in her twenty-nine years.

CHAPTER SEVEN

"This is a closed meeting of *SMART Recovery*," the slender, pale, freckled, redheaded woman said. "I'm Neala, your facilitator this afternoon. *SMART* stands for *Self-Management And Recovery Training*. Everything said at this meeting is confidential, so whatever is said here stays here in this room. Breaking this rule could get you removed from *Ellendale*. We use *SMART's* four-point program.

"One, to build and maintain motivation for abstinence.

"Two, to cope with urges and cravings.

"Three, to manage thoughts, feelings and behaviors.

"Four, to live a balanced lifestyle.

"We're going to check in and I want to know how you're feeling and how yesterday went or the last few days for the two newcomers. In open meetings participation is voluntary, however, while you're here at *Ellendale*, I expect each one of you to take part. Ultimately, it is your recovery and only you can make it happen. We're here to offer you support and tools to help you on your journey. Let's start on my left." Neala nodded to a middle-aged woman with bright green eyes and streaks of gray running through long wavy auburn hair.

"Hi, everyone, and especially welcome to the two new ladies, I'm Anne. I've been clean for thirty-two days now and though I'm feeling good and had a great day yesterday I'm feeling a little anxious because I'm being kicked out next weekend." She gave the group a wan grin. "I think I'm ready, but real life is going to be a challenge. My husband is waiting for me, but made it very clear that if I don't return a changed woman, he's going to file for divorce. For the last ten years of our thirty-eight-year marriage I wasn't really a wife to him at all and no mother to our kids or grandmother to our grandkids. This is my second time in residential recovery and my family is at their wits end with me."

"Do you have a plan to stay clean, Anne?" Neala asked.

"Yes, I've been working on that," Anne said. "Don, my husband, has found a *SMART* meeting not far from our place in White Rock and I plan to go there as well as get more counseling at the *Sources Community Services*. They also have a food bank and I plan to volunteer. I'm going to keep working out and walking everyday as well as start to cook healthy meals. That will help fill in some of the time I spent stoned on *Oxy-Contin*. I'm also hoping to try to restore my relationship with my son and three daughters."

"Sounds like you're going to have a busy schedule," Neala said with an encouraging smile. "Thank you, Anne." And then she nodded to the next woman.

"My name is Sheila. This is my first week at *Ellendale* and I was clean for one week before I got here. This is the longest I've gone without a drink in twenty years. Yesterday was hard. The urges were really crazy. I think if I'd been in the real world, I would have made a beeline for the liquor store and have been pissed drunk by noon. It seemed like everything triggered me from group sessions to counseling. We did a *SMART* tool a couple of days ago and one of the things it suggested was surfing the urge, so I finally started to sit and feel the urge, just let it be and wash over me. It actually helped and they came less often and were shorter, or at least felt like it. I'm looking forward to learning more tools and trying them out."

"Good job, Sheila," Neala said and then nodded to Emilia.

"Hi, I'm Emilia and this is my first day here. I detoxed in the hospital in White Rock and was helped by the *SMART*

Recovery Facilitator there." Emilia glanced over at Anne, and gave her something close to a smile. Anne's eyes lit up. "I was very lucky to get into *Ellendale* so quickly but I'm nervous . . . well, more like scared as hell that I won't be able to stay clean. I feel devastated actually, because I feel like I've just lost my best friend."

"Has anyone else felt like that?" Neala asked.

A young woman that looked to Emilia to be virtually a teenager spoke. "I still feel like that. Crack solved all my problems. If I needed energy, I smoked crack. If I wanted better sex, I smoked crack. Well, I think you get the idea. It was my friend and never let me down, or so it seemed."

"Thanks, Dina," Neala said. "Please continue, Emilia."

"I learned the *CBA* from the White Rock *SMART* Facilitator, and it's helping me, but the urges are still really strong. I've been told that it gets easier with time and I think it does and may even be starting after only one week. I want to learn more of the *SMART* tools and put them into practice. I'm hoping that this time, I can stay clean."

"Thank you, Emilia," Neala said and then nodded to the woman beside her.

"Hi, everybody, my name's Aysha. This is my fourth time in a residential recovery program, but I'm hopeful this time I can stay clean."

"What gives you hope that you can stay clean this time?" Neala asked in a soft tone.

"Well, the first three programs I was in were twelve-step. There's nothing wrong with that and I know they've helped a lot of people, but I'm an atheist. The whole powerless thing and surrendering myself to an imaginary higher power didn't work for me. Actually, it gave me an excuse to pick up again. I felt like if God was actually there, it was his or her responsibility to keep me from using."

There were a few chuckles from around the circle and

Emilia thought that they were laughing at Aysha's reference to a deity being either male or female. At least that's what *she* thought. She smiled while Aysha continued.

"*Ellendale's* program is science based and makes it clear that my recovery is all on me. But what I'm getting from it are tools to help me change the way I think about my *DOC*."

"What does *DOC* mean?" a woman blurted.

Emilia understood her to be the other newbie. Without a heartbeat passing and not intending to interfere with Neala, the words slipped off Emilia's tongue. "*Drug of Choice*."

Neala didn't seem the least put-out with her and simply smiled and said, "That's right, Emilia, where did you hear that from?"

"Oh, I learned it while I was detoxing in the hospital. Mosi, the White Rock *SMART Recovery* Facilitator, dropped by every day to see me and we talked about *SMART*. He and Doctor Reshma were the ones that got me into *Ellendale* so quickly," Emilia said and reddened, which would be barely noticeable under her olive complexion, she knew.

Neala looked over at Aysha.

"So you're hoping that *Cognitive Behavioral Therapy* will be your stepping stone to staying clean, Aysha?"

Aysha nodded.

When check-in was complete, Neala stood and walked over to a whiteboard. As Emilia's chair in the circle faced away from the front of the room, she turned in her chair without moving it. Others did the same, she noticed.

Neala wrote *HOV* on the board with a broad crimson marker.

"Does anyone know what *HOV* stands for?" Neala asked.

"High Occupancy Vehicle lane," a woman dressed in a blouse that was very close to the same color as the marker Neala was using at the white board quipped.

Neala frowned at the woman, but there was mirth in her eyes.

"Uhm, no. Any other guesses?"

The woman with gray streaks in her auburn hair spoke. Anne, Emilia remembered, though her memory was not sharp these days.

"*Hierarchy of Values*," Ann said.

Neala gave her one short nod. "That's correct. You've been through this tool before, if I'm not mistaken. Why don't you help me out?"

"Sure," Anne said.

"Tell me what the most important thing in your life is."

"Uhm, I would have to say my relationship with my husband," Anne said.

Neala nodded to the woman beside Anne. "How about you?"

"My health."

They continued around the circle and Neala wrote each value on the whiteboard.

"Family."

"Friends."

"Being in control of my life."

"Happiness."

"Financial stability."

"My kids."

"A clear head," Emilia said when it was her turn.

"You know," the lady beside Emilia said. "I was going to say money, but when that was said, I thought about it and realized that I want to have food on my table, to feel safe and sleep properly. And the sleeping bit is something I haven't had in a long time. I would drink until I passed out, but I was always tired."

"That's because being unconscious is not the same as sleeping," Neala said. "Very good, everyone. Now, we'll pick out the top five from all the choices on the board." She wrote the numerals *one to five* on the whiteboard from top to bottom.

"I thought of another one," the woman in red said.

"Save it for next time," Neala said in a quiet, firm tone.

"If this is in order of importance," another participant said, "I would have to say family."

"No, not in any particular order, but who thinks family should be on the list?" Neala asked.

All but one raised their hands. Neala eyed the older lady who had not raised her hand, but wrote *Family* down beside number one.

"I don't get along with my family," the woman who'd not raised her hand said. "They're a bunch of religious nutcakes. Their addiction is their faith."

"Fair enough," Neala said. "Which other would you pick to add to the list?" She looked around the room, meeting the eyes of each person.

"I would say happiness. One of the reasons I used drugs was to hide from myself, you know, from my feelings. I've never really been happy and that for me would make not using easier," another said.

Neala wrote *happiness* beside the numeral two.

"Being in control," Anne said.

"I think," a woman said that Emilia thought was about her age, "that financial stability could fall under being in control."

"What do you, ladies, think?" Neala asked.

There was a significant amount of crosstalk on this point and it was during that discussion Emilia realized that Neala didn't care what was on the board at all, but simply wanted each woman in the meeting to think about what was important to her.

Emilia wanted something to write on and with, but her purse was in her room. There was, however, a small round coffee table in the middle of the circle, which held paper and a cup full of pens. Not certain what Neala or the others might think of the interruption, she slipped over to the small table and snatched a sheet of paper off the top of the small pile and slid a red pen out of the dented metal cup. Sitting back down in her seat she glanced down at the paper and realized it had writing on it.

HOV, was printed on the top in a bold typeface with the numbers *one through five* underneath in point form, just like Neala had written on the board. She took a quick and she hoped, surreptitious glance around the room. The others were still discussing the *HOV*, but the talk had turned to what else might be grouped together and whether it would be useful to decide what was *the* most important value in one's life. Emilia, with her head still looking down at the sheet of paper, pen poised to write, lifted her gaze towards Neala and found that she was looking directly at her.

Neala's lips held a tight smile and her eyes blazed. Then she winked.

After the *HOV*, the meeting ended and the women gathered their things. Each took one of the *HOV* worksheets, talked to Neala or went to leave.

Emilia talked to Anne for a few moments and the subject of Mosi and the White Rock *SMART* meetings came up. After, she headed for the door, but there was a considerable back up. She could see over the ladies heads that the rain was coming down in chaotic sheets.

Ah, the southwest coast of BC, four seasons in one day. Then another thought came. Its root was in her childhood. Emilia was born and raised with the completely confused and disorderly weather of the Vancouver region and as a child had often sought the rainstorms to play in, to the consternation of her mother.

"Excuse me, excuse me," she said as she pushed her way

through the waiting crowd, tucking her well-folded paper under her bra, for all the good *that* would do. The instant she reached the door, she stepped out into the flood that fell from the sky and ran for her dorm. With every footfall a huge splash of water danced from beneath her feet, filling her sneakers with cool summer rainwater.

Emilia laughed.

Then she heard more screams and laughter, and even without looking behind her, she knew that at least some of the others were following. When she reached the dorm house, her hand slipped on the knob and she thought for an instant that it was locked, but a second try released the catch and she pushed the door open and jumped inside.

With the knob still in hand and the door wide open, she turned and looked. Every single one of the other women was running towards the dorm while Neala held the door and stared out at them from the meeting room. Neala's eyes were wide and her lips turned up at the corners.

A few moments later the women all piled through the door and huddled in the entry with water pouring off their clothes and creating a near flood on the laminate flooring.

"Off with those wet clothes!" a voice boomed from the hallway that led to the common room. It was Bernadette, the housemother, who was their god while they were in the dorm.

One of the ladies thought to ignore this bear of a woman and started to walk towards the hallway that Bernadette guarded. Bernadette stepped in front of her and she bumped to a halt against that huge chest. She stood staring at Bernadette with wide eyes.

Not one to be disregarded, as Emilia already knew, Bernadette undid the top two buttons on the ladies blouse and pulled it over her head. "Are you going to remove those slacks?" she asked. "Or shall I?"

Emilia giggled and began to strip down to her bra and panties. The others, realizing that they had little choice in the matter, peeled off soaking outerwear as well.

"Will this do?" Anne asked when she was down to her underclothes.

"I suppose it will have to," Bernadette grumbled. "But you will choose three of you to mop this floor and my hallway after you get changed."

Feeling recharged, Emilia smiled at everyone, Bernadette in particular, and padded down the hall to her room, barefoot. Once in her dorm room, Emilia stripped off soaking bra and panties, dug a towel from her tiny closet, dried herself and put on dry clothes. *Most of the others will want to shower, so rather than wait in line, I'll see about mopping the entry.*

One week clean and my mind is already healing itself and my thinking's clearer. I have a long way to go, but it's starting to feel good.

CHAPTER EIGHT

HOW Emilia looked at the still damp page, reading and re-reading what she'd written during the *SMART* meeting.

One-love
Two-family
Three-health
Four-work
Five-travel

Love. *What does that mean to me?* When she wrote it, she'd been thinking of romance, a man in her life who cherished her and whom she could treasure. Mosi had also passed through her thoughts when she wrote that simple but profound word.

Family. *That's going to take a lot work for sure. As well as some clean time. Mosi said that it often took years for family, friends and loved ones to trust you again. That sucks!*

Health. *That most definitely needed investigation. Diet and exercise come to mind, though I'm not sure where to begin.*

Work. *Her boss had given her a couple of month's hiatus to work out her recovery, but from his tone, it was with great reluctance. So, that is still something of an unknown and it worries me. Mosi counseled me to try not to worry about it and concentrate on staying clean and educating myself about recovery and substance abuse. I'll try, but damn, it's hard.*

Travel. *That's a dream. My addictions have kept me flat broke, usually late with my mortgage payment and bills. But Mosi told me that dreams are good.*

Mosi. He kept coming into her thoughts. He was her black-skinned knight with shining eyes and effervescent smile. She really liked him, but knew that he would never see a woman like her who was still struggling with addiction. *I'm simply not good enough for a man like him.*

Emilia was one week into her stay at *Ellendale*. She now walked several times every day, sometimes alone, but most of the time with a companion. To her surprise, Bernadette often accompanied her. The stout block of a woman, who was the only person she knew outside of Mosi, with skin so black she would disappear in the night, could easily outdistance her and was surprisingly and perhaps alarmingly spry. At first Emilia was uncomfortable with Bernadette's company, but soon discovered a soft motherly underbelly to her outward veneer of cast iron.

"That makes one full week for you here today," Bernadette said. "So how are the urges coming?"

"A little less often and usually not quite so strong, but sometimes they're still very powerful," Emilia said.

"The urges are a physical reaction of your body while it heals itself. It wants that dopamine hit from the drugs and booze. It gets better as I know well, but the first while can be quite horrific," Bernadette said. "The walking helps. I walked a lot when I was first clean. It gives a dopamine spike, though not like drugs do. But it's normal and the body gets used to normal with time."

"Time," Emilia sputtered, breathless from trying to keep up with the older woman. "Everything takes time."

"Yeah, it takes some getting used to this waiting thing, especially when you're used to the instant hit from the booze and drugs," Bernadette said.

"How long have you been clean?" Emilia asked.

"Five years now. Best five years of my life. Well, that's a bit of an exaggeration as I wasn't addicted to booze as a child or young adult, but five great years of learning about myself."

"I don't think I want to learn about myself," Emilia said with verve.

"That's just the addiction talking. If you don't learn about yourself, you'll never change and change is what recovery's all about. If it's just about not using, you'll either relapse or live an unhappy life. I want a full life. I want to enjoy living not be miserable wishing I could use again."

"It's hard to think about the future and being abstinent forever," Emilia said.

"You're right, it's hard at first and you need to concentrate on one day at a time," Bernadette said.

"Yeah," Emilia said, "in fact, my first week I had to do one hour at a time."

"It sounds like a cliché, but it actually works, especially when you're new to recovery," Bernadette said, without breaking stride.

"It worked for me," Emilia puffed, still breathless from keeping up to Bernadette.

"You'll need a hobby or hobbies," Bernadette said. "At least most people do."

"Do you have a hobby?" Emilia asked.

"Yeah, I do. I skydive," Bernadette said, in a matter-of-fact tone, her face bland.

Emilia was astonished and couldn't picture this stout mass of muscle doing any such thing. She had expected something like quilting, knitting, needlepoint or some other craft. She realized her mouth was hanging open.

"You sound like you don't believe me," Bernadette said, narrowing her eyes.

"It's not that I don't believe you," Emilia said, looking everywhere but at Bernadette.

Bernadette stopped instantly and a surprised Emilia took

three more steps before she could come to a halt. Bernadette smiled and took two long steps toward Emilia, reaching into the pocket of her hoodie as she did so. When she drew up to Emilia, she hauled her cell from the pocket and opened her photo gallery. She touched the screen and then handed the phone to Emilia, who took it with great interest and watched what turned out to be a homemade video.

It showed a clearly jubilant Bernadette wearing a helmet and showing what could well be the door of an airplane in the background. This turned out to be the case when the door and the plane appeared entire in the video for a moment and then shot away at high speed. It was then that Emilia realized that Bernadette had jumped out of the plane and was now in free fall.

"My God!" Emilia exclaimed, "You just jumped out of a plane. Was that your first jump?"

"Hell no!" her companion said. "I've been skydiving for over four years. I wanted something that gave me a real adrenaline rush to take the place of my addiction. I tried it once and was hooked."

"That is too cool!" Emilia said.

"I see you believe me now," Bernadette said with a single nod, taking back her phone, tucking it back into her pocket and turning to head up the path.

Emilia laughed and nodded, but decided to save her breath to keep up with her new friend.

The moment Emilia and Bernadette got back to the dorm house, Bernadette headed for the kitchen and nodded for Emilia to follow.

"I have a surprise for you. Open the door," Bernadette said, pointing to the fridge.

Unable to stop the friendly smile that filled her face, Emilia did as she was told. On the top shelf at the very front, was a package of corn tortillas. She took them and looked closely at the bag. They were white corn, which was the best maize for tortillas and the ingredient list showed zero additives. Though it was a brand that she'd never seen before, she could tell that they were fresh and pliable.

"This is so good of you!" Emilia said with clear passion. "And they seem very fresh and from best kind of corn, too!"

"Well, you did say that you were craving them and I looked it up online and then asked for them with today's grocery order," Bernadette said.

"Maybe I could make some tacos. Enough for everyone." Emilia smiled, and her mind went back to childhood family gatherings and breakfast with eggs and tortillas. She knew there must be a tender smile on her face.

"Sure, what do you need?"

"A frying pan with oil, some kind of meat, ground will do in a pinch, lettuce, tomatoes, green onions, cilantro, chili peppers and some spices."

"What kind of spices will you need?" Bernadette asked, opening her spice cabinet as she spoke.

"Just salt, black pepper and cumin and of course chilies."

"Looks like we have everything you need, but only dried crushed chilies, if that works."

"I'd rather have fresh ones," Emilia said, with unbroken enthusiasm, "but they'll do. How about meat?"

"As they just came back from shopping, we have ground beef, ground pork, chicken breasts, chicken thighs and various sausages."

Barely letting Bernadette finish, Emilia answered with a grin as wide as a house. "Chicken thighs would be perfect! Mom would stew them, but we could roast them and then I'll add the spices."

"I knew you liked tortillas and Mexican food, but had no idea that it was so important to you. I mean, the way you talk about cooking it, is like someone who just walked into a candy store and the angelic look on your face, makes me think I'm right," Bernadette said.

"You know, I hadn't even thought about it until you mentioned it. I grew up with Mom cooking homemade Mexican food all the time and I really love it. Right now, it reminds me of the times before I was addicted," Emilia said in a joyful tone.

"Well, you'll be my angelic chef for dinner with that look of ecstasy on your face, and I'll be your sous chef," Bernadette said with a grin and wink.

Emilia's counseling session with Gavenina in the afternoon had been her toughest yet, as her savvy counselor had helped her strip away years of excuses for her addictions and helped her to discover the root causes. *I still have still tons of work to do in that area, but one thing Gavenina left me with was the indisputable fact that I'm responsible for my addiction and just as solely responsible for my recovery. I understood that from my conversations with Mosi and Doctor Reshma, but there's clearly a difference between understanding something superficially and actually getting it.* She was thinking about this as she entered the large industrial kitchen that was housed in the lower floor of *Ellendale's* solitary dorm building.

"Ah, here you are, my dear," Bernadette rumbled in clear pleasure the moment she entered. She held out a white full apron with the logo of *Ellendale* sewn near the top in small, cursive, red letters. "Here, put this on. We don't want you making a mess of your clothes."

"That's okay, I'm just wearing jeans and this is an old top," Emilia said and made as if to brush the apron aside.

"You'll wear it or you won't be working in my kitchen," Bernadette said in her housemother's growl.

Emilia was about to argue the point, but thought better of it for several reasons. Reasons that passed through a mind that was clearer than it had been two weeks ago.

Bernadette was the housemother and in charge of the kitchen.

She'd been clean for over five years and *her* mind *was* clear. She probably had good reasons for her request.

Bernadette had become a friend.

Emilia took the apron, slipped it over her head, spun on her heels and stopped. She took the apron strings and pushed them behind her. Bernadette tied the apron and pulled her hair out from under the top strap.

Emilia turned around again and smiled at Bernadette. "Thank you."

"You're welcome, my dear. Let's make some tacos."

Everything Emilia had requested was on the counter and the vegetables were in the process of being washed by another of the patients, a chore she'd done herself in this very kitchen. Emilia turned on the oven, washed up and then prepared the chicken thighs on a baking sheet.

The lettuce, tomatoes, green onions, cilantro and radishes were minced finely on her instructions while the thighs baked. In a separate oven, she blistered the skins of half a dozen large tomatoes to loosen the skin and give them a bit of a smoky flavor. When they cooled, she had one of her helpers peel them while she prepared the remaining ingredients for the salsas in the blender. The tomatoes wouldn't be added to the mixer, rather be minced super fine and along with chopped cilantro and minced green onions, combined with the chilies, garlic and spices from the blender. There would be one mild and one medium hot. Emilia wasn't one for fiery hot salsa.

While Emilia would have used lard, they didn't have any nor, according to Bernadette, was it something they ever kept in the pantry. They did have olive or peanut oil and she chose the peanut as she was told it had a high smoking point. The moment the chicken came out of the oven, she turned the burners on medium low to heat the oil. Using two forks she deboned the thighs and then added salt, pepper and cumin to it.

Looking at the clock she saw that dinner would be served in less than ten minutes and so she turned up the heat and then prepared an assembly line to get the tacos out to the dining room as quickly as possible. Moments before lunch was to be served, she dipped three tortillas into the three frying pans of oil, flipped them once after a few seconds and then lifted them out onto a plate layered with paper towels. Her first assembly line worker patted the excess oil off and handed it to the next woman, who placed a small mound of meat in the center of the tortilla and folded it over, passing it to the next in line. The final assembler waited until there were three tacos on each plate, then she garnished them with a large amount of lettuce, green onions, minced cilantro and diced tomatoes. When four plates were thus prepared, the lady who was serving wheeled a laden cart into the dining room and served the four people at the farthest table.

Twenty minutes later, everyone had been served and a few were asking for seconds. Two had not eaten the tortillas but everything else, the mild salsa was gone and of the medium there were only a few spoonfuls left. While eating her own tacos, Emilia felt a great deal of satisfaction. *We did a good job and I spread a little of my culture.*

Cleaning up had become less of a chore and more of a self-help group and therapy session. As it was Emilia's turn to help with the pots and pans and put away the leftovers, she joined in that evening with an excessive amount of glee. In part, this was because after two weeks clean she was beginning to feel better and also making dinner had been a victory as it were. It was a reminder that her life had not always been one of addiction and there had been simple joys and thrills in her life like this evening. She laughed and joked with the two other ladies while Bernadette sat at the island counter immersed in some sort of account book. She was just washing up and thinking about a shower before the evening group therapy when the phone rang. Bernadette picked up the cordless receiver from where it lay on the counter.

"Hello, this is *Ellendale Recovery Center*, Bernadette El-Hadidy speaking."

There was a short pause and then Bernadette smiled. It was unlike any smile of hers that Emilia had seen and it might be said that she radiated pure joy.

"Of course!" Bernadette cried. "Come right over. See you in fifteen minutes."

Emilia grinned to herself. *Bernadette has a boyfriend!*

CHAPTER NINE

Group counseling had been exceptional, in Emilia's mind, as it had helped to show her how important it was to accept others as they were. She'd never realized how often she had used other people's behavior as an excuse to use.

Unconditional Other Acceptance was also a scientific tenant of *SMART Recovery*, she knew, and was now beginning to understand why. The intensity of her thoughts consumed her and when she felt a tap on her shoulder, she jumped.

"In another world were we?" Gavenina asked with that twinkle in her eyes that meant she had said or was about to say something she thought particularly funny. "Bernadette has requested your presence in the kitchen, after the group counseling."

That was formal in the extreme. "Thank you, Gavenina, did you stay late just to tell me?"

"Don't be silly, I stayed for a client who needed some extra time, but Bernadette saw me before I left and asked me to tell you on my way out."

"Did she tell you what it's all about?" Emilia asked as Gavenina was turning away.

Gavenina turned back with that same flash in her eyes. "In fact, no she didn't."

Emilia was uncertain, but thought that she heard Gavenina chuckle.

What in the world is going on, and why such a formal invitation? Unless Gavenina is having fun with me. Well, I'll soon find out.

She returned to the dorm, but rather than go to her room

51

as she'd planned, she went to the kitchen as requested. Bernadette was seated at her normal perch at the island and was looking toward the corner, which wasn't visible from the doorway where she stood.

"Here you are, Momma," a deep voice she would recognize under any conceivable circumstances said.

Emilia ran five steps until she could see and there was Mosi pouring tea from a pot that she'd never seen. "Mosi, what are you doing here!"

Mosi smiled that smile that could defrost Antarctica, with his teeth looking like rows of tiny icebergs, then picked up a tray that contained three formal teacups with a matching cream and sugar set. With exaggerated care, he moved over to the island and placed it in front of Bernadette.

"I believe you know my son, Mosi," Bernadette said with a proud smile. But the smile was all for Mosi, she saw. "Sit," she said, apparently to them both, waving to the two high stools that were on the rounded corner of the island to her right. "I told Mosi about your progress over the last couple of weeks, but he wants to hear for himself. It's the facilitator in him I guess." She gave them a wide grin, but her gaze was mostly meant for Mosi.

"You're . . . you're Mosi's mother!"

"Yes, that's right. Didn't you think he had one?" Bernadette said, then clacked her tongue as she tended to do when she was pensive.

Mosi poured the tea and then put the tiniest smidgen of sugar in one teacup with a large dollop of cream, stirred it and passed it to his mother. "How do you like yours?" he asked with a look at Emilia.

"Uhm, just black please."

"A girl after my own heart," Mosi said with that luminous toothy smile.

He passed Emilia a cup of tea, picked up the last one off of the tray and took a small sip. She followed suit, unaware that Bernadette was still beside her or in fact that anything else existed, as for a moment, she found herself swallowed by his radiance.

"How are you finding the urges?" Mosi asked in a soft voice.

"They still come," Emilia began, "but it's less often now and as I'm surrounded by people supporting me, it's easy to say no. I'm also learning new tools and a little about my past and the root of my addiction, or at least what made me more vulnerable."

"I'm glad you're doing well," Mosi said. "Mom seems to think that you're quite determined to stay clean."

"She certainly shows every sign of it," Bernadette said with a clack of her tongue.

"I really feel a lot better. My mind is clearer and I'm told that it'll get easier," Emilia said.

"It *will*," Mosi said. "It takes a couple of years for the mind to completely heal itself, but it starts soon after we quit drug and alcohol abuse. That's why you already feel different, even have a clearer mind."

"That seems like a long time to wait, but as it's starting already and I can feel it, I guess that's not *too* bad."

Bernadette wasn't certain what it was that she saw. It most certainly didn't match what was being said between her son and Emilia. What she heard were simple niceties, but what she saw were sparks shooting from two sets of dark brown eyes. Side glances and upturned coquettish lips, and an all-consuming focus on each other. *I'll just have to be sure to take more time to get to know her and make sure that she's well-grounded before she leaves. Well, at least Mosi has more brains than to get involved with a woman who's been clean for only a couple of weeks.*

"I best get going," Mosi said. "I have an early day

tomorrow."

"Okay, it was great to see you. It's an encouragement for sure."

"Bye, Mom." He gave Bernadette a firm kiss on the cheek, smiled once more at Emilia and strode from the kitchen, a man on a mission.

Emilia looked over at Bernadette as if seeing her for the first time since she came into the room. "It was so good to see Mosi," she said.

"Yes," Bernadette agreed, "I'm glad we had a good chance to chat before you finished therapy or I wouldn't have been able to speak two words with him." She clucked.

Emilia was unsure if Bernadette was implying something. Something that had no basis in fact, if she was teasing her or was upset that she had spoken with Mosi for a few minutes. Bernadette's face was an unfathomable blank mask.

Chapter Ten

M osi climbed into his *Volvo* wagon and buckled the seat belt. He knew he could drive a *Mercedes* or even a *Porsche* if he chose to work for a private firm rather than his job for a nonprofit, and in fact had been offered such a position as recently as two months ago. *But as a lawyer heading this NGO I have opportunities to reach out to the helpless, weak and abused, not to mention to those suffering from addictive behavior. In addition, this position gives me the ear of high officials, both elected and non-elected.* In short, he was happy with his work and the connections that it gave him to do what was important to him in life. And that was more important to him than an extra one hundred or so grand a year.

As he eased out of the *Ellendale's* driveway to begin the tedious drive through the city of Surrey back to his home in White Rock, he thought about his short meeting with Emilia with wonder. In spite of the fact that she was still severely underweight, she must have put on seven or eight pounds in the last week or so. Her complexion no longer held the sallow skin and sunken dull eyes of heavy addiction. Her hair was also beginning to take on a healthier look and was well-kept with a slight wave he was certain was natural and left to simply hang down and tucked behind one ear. It was attractive, in part by the sheer simplicity of its style. In addition, he could tell by talking to her that neuroplasticity was already taking hold and though her brain was still clearly damaged from her drug and alcohol abuse, the healing had just as evidently begun.

And her eyes.

Her eyes, even at this early stage of recovery, hold a certain brightness that hints at intelligence well above the norm. All this is good news and gives me a sense of accomplishment, though all the decisions about Emilia's recovery have been her own and no one can take that from her.

However, one thing gnawed at him. He felt an attraction for her that was unhealthy. He wasn't even sure why he felt the way he did, but imagined that he might be visualizing a woman that he hoped she would become or rather the person she was before addiction took over her life. The real Emilia. That in itself was a harmful way to begin a relationship of any kind, including even a simple friendship. She was also barely three weeks clean, and relapse was still a real possibility. He had to maintain a professional and proper facilitator-to-participant friendship. For her well-being, that of the group, for *SMART Recovery*, and naturally, for himself.

I'm going to have a bitch of a time with that.

Mosi sighed.

"Good morning, Mister El-Hadidy," the slender woman behind the reception desk said, without looking up from her computer monitor.

"Good morning, Caroline," Mosi said to his secretary.

Caroline had recently turned fifty, Mosi knew, but looked closer to her early forties, except for the head of gray hair, which she wore bobbed at her shoulders. Caroline felt long flowing hair was for young women. His secretary was like that. She had ideas of how things should be, and could be adamant. She was also intelligent, resourceful, organized, witty, charming, and knew him like he was one of her children, of which she had four. All boys, men rather, and the second oldest and his wife were about to have her first grandchild. Caroline was sure to keep him abreast of everything to do with the pregnancy.

After organizing himself in his office, he buzzed Caroline. He didn't say a word to her over the intercom, but she was in his presence in less than thirty seconds.

"Wanda just entered her third trimester," she said.

Mosi smiled and nodded to the comfortable seat in front of his desk, which Caroline took with a warm smile before speaking.

"Warden McFarland called again. He's been trying to get a *SMART Recovery* group going in the prison, but still can't find a facilitator. He wants to know if you might be able to help."

"If I'm not mistaken, he has three or four inmates who have considerable clean time and aren't happy with the *AA* meetings. Surely one or two of them could take the *SMART* Facilitator's course," Mosi said. "If that doesn't pan out tell him I'll see what more I can do."

"I'll speak to him myself," she said as she rose, graceful as always.

Mosi didn't actually work for *SMART*, but for the *CCSA*. The *Canadian Centre on Substance Use and Addiction* was created by the Canadian government in nineteen eighty-eight, but was actually an NGO, or non-governmental organization, and Mosi was the CEO as well as the Director of Public Affairs and Communications. He could have made significantly more money as a lawyer in the private sector, but loved the fact he had the ability to help people with substance abuse problems. His impact was often powerful and could, at times, be immediate.

Until one year ago the *CCSA* spent a significant amount of time and energy fundraising. Today, with the severe opioid crisis, which began in Vancouver but had now spread throughout Canada, the US, and even into small towns in both countries, the Canadian government as well as some non-profit agencies were pouring money into the *CCSA* and other organizations involved in treating drug abuse.

Mosi knew that in part, this was to assure Canadians that the federal government was on top of the present crisis. For they would point to all the services *CCSA* offered to reduce drug and alcohol abuse as if the government itself had started the programs.

Mosi grinned to himself at this thought as he plopped his briefcase onto the stand beside his desk and flipped it open. He now had at his disposal funds that he had been using for something the government wished to keep at arm's length.

Safe injection sites.

He understood many Canadians as well as Americans, felt safe injection sites encouraged illicit drug use. And in a manner of thinking, they could be construed as such. Mosi, however, didn't involve himself in those discussions, but explained with facts and statistics that individuals who used the safe sites lived longer, used up less of the BC provincial heath care budget, had a higher probability of entering into recovery and lower rates of recidivism when they did.

There were some, he knew, who'd never give up their addiction, but they were still human beings and deserved to be treated with dignity. And that was the way he saw it.

Caroline knocked on his door. He knew it was her as there was a specific timbre to it. She made a habit of rapping near the jamb, which gave a distinct and lower tone than tapping on the center of the door would. This was his first appointment of the day.

He stood.

"The Honorable Marion Dubois, Minister of Health," Caroline said, in her throaty contralto.

"I'm pleased to see you again, Minister," Mosi said, stepping out from behind his desk with his hand extended with the warmest smile he could muster on his face.

"It's good to see you again as well, Mister El-Hadidy," the minister replied, taking his hand and shaking it with a firm grip.

"Thank you, Caroline," Mosi said and nodded to her.

She gave him one curt nod in return and left, softly shutting the door behind her.

"Please sit, Minister," Mosi said, pointing to the corner opposite his desk where there were situated four comfortable leather chairs and a cocktail table, overlooking the ocean view through a wall of glass.

The minister strode over to the window and hovered near one of the chairs, but didn't sit. Rather, she gave Mosi a stern look and spoke in a scathing tone. "I'm not sure my ministry should be paying for you to have a view of the White Rock beach, Mister El-Hadidy."

"No, Minister, I completely agree," Mosi replied with a kind smile. "Five years ago when I took this position, the offices were located in downtown Vancouver, and the rent, with no beach-front view, was over ten times what we pay here. And I will add, that five years ago this was the only office space in the city of White Rock that suited our needs. So you see, Minister, ocean view or no, I saved thousands of dollars in rent, which *your* ministry tried to claw back, but I was able to keep and utilize for other programs, including teaching BC school children the facts about drugs and addiction as well as to fund the needle exchange program. That was all before you were minister, of course."

Minister Marion Dubois dropped into the chair behind her with a puff. "Well, I'm very pleased to hear that, sir," she said as she squirmed in the comfortable seat.

Mosi was about to ask if she wanted a different chair, when the minister reached into a pocket of her skirt and pulled out a set of keys, which she threw into her purse, on the floor beside her, with something of a huff.

"Sorry," she said in a peeved tone.

Mosi smiled again. He was observant enough to know this usually had a calming effect on people and it worked particularly well with women. Even on his middle-aged secretary Caroline, who was less subject to such male machinations because of both her age and disposition.

The minister took a deep breath and visibly calmed. She looked up a Mosi and her eyes followed him as he sat in a chair across from her.

"Would you like tea or coffee, Minister?"

"Yes, a cup of tea would be delightful on such a cool rainy spring day."

Mosi pulled his cell phone from his pocked and used it to text Caroline with the request. Her answer was nearly immediate. *7-1/2 minutes.* Caroline knew exactly how long it took the kettle to boil and walk the short distance to Mosi's office with a tray.

"It'll be here in a few minutes," he said with a smile.

The minister only nodded with a confused look on her face.

"So, Minister, I'm curious to know what brought you here in the middle of a session of the legislature."

The minister cleared her throat. It looked to Mosi as if she was gathering her thoughts.

"As I'm sure you know, the Finance Minister will present the provincial budget in two weeks' time," she said.

"Yes, I'm aware."

"Our glorious leader, the Premier," Ms. Dubois said in utter sarcasm, "wishes to cut your budget by thirty percent and put that money into policing and groups she feels will be more effective."

"We already know *that* doesn't work!" Mosi slapped his thigh.

"Yes, we know that already." Her brows wrinkled, her lips pursed.

"My NGO alone has saved your department an estimated three hundred million dollars in hospital, ambulance, drug, and other costs. Cutting our budget will mean higher health care costs for the province," Mosi said, with a shake of his head and a slap to his temple.

"Yes, I know and I agree, but the Premier is resolved to cut your budget."

"Can you tell me why?" Mosi asked slowly with clenched teeth.

"There are certain *groups* lobbying hard to close down the safe injection sites."

"But why? I don't understand. They're not only keeping people alive, but out of the hospital. Not only that, they're incredibly cost effective with estimates of between two and a half to five dollars saved for every dollar spent, never mind the lives they're saving."

"The groups that are lobbying have pooled their resources and are spending that money to pay lobbyists and open new rehab centers," she said.

"Well, I'm happy they're starting new rehab houses, but why do they want to cut the funding to a proven resource for addiction?" Mosi asked.

"They believe the only way to permanent recovery is through . . ." She paused and cleared her throat. "Through their churches."

"That is incredibly ignorant and narrow minded." Mosi shook his head and raised both hands heavenward. "We have solid evidence and masses of statistics to prove our system works."

"Yes, but you don't save their souls." The minister's face cracked and a slight smile showed through.

"No, we don't and neither do we capture unicorns or inspire fairies to stop using drugs."

The minister laughed. "Indeed you don't. I understand

your family's from Myanmar and came to Canada to escape the Muslim persecution at the time."

"Yes, that's true."

"So tell me, Mister El-Hadidy are you a Muslim?"

"I was raised a Muslim, but I'm a non-believer," he said.

"Oh, somehow I thought you were Muslim, the same as your parents and family."

"And what difference would that make?" he asked, narrowing his eyes at her.

"Well, legally none, of course, but there are strong anti-Muslim sentiments among many Canadians because of Middle-Eastern terrorist groups."

Mosi looked deep into the minister's eyes. "How do *you* feel about me?"

"To be honest, I immediately suspect any Muslim I meet, though I know it's wrong and I shouldn't judge an entire religious group because a comparatively small fraction of them are terrorists. But I feel the way I feel and that's all there is to it. And I confess that I feel better about you knowing you're not a Muslim. But if you have *no* faith, where do you get your moral standard?"

"Before I answer your question, I'd like to point out that you *can* change the way you feel. About virtually anything."

"And how can you do that?" the minister asked, narrowing her eyes at him.

Mosi gave her his most winning smile as he noticed it often helped to soften people up for facts they might not otherwise be open to. "By changing the way you think."

"And how does one do that?" the minister asked, setting her hands in her lap and sitting up straighter.

"By using the tools of *Rational Emotive Behavioral Therapy.*"

"What's that?" she asked, her shoulders sinking and the seeming ubiquitous frown reappearing on her face.

"That would need hours to cover, but I can tell you that if

we simply dispute our irrational beliefs, it goes a long way to help change our way of thinking about something. When we change the way we think, it affects the way we feel," Mosi said.

The minister's face went blank for a few moments and looked through Mosi, instead of at him.

"Okay," she said with hesitation, "but how can thinking differently about something change how I *feel* about it?"

"Because, according to Doctor Albert Ellis' studies, a person is rarely affected emotionally by outside things, but rather by our perceptions or internalizations about outside events."

"If that's true, then how, for example, can I change the way I feel about Muslims in general? I already know that most of them are as peace-loving as me."

"Minister, you know I'm a lawyer, not a psychiatrist, but I think you understand that most Muslims are peaceful in theory, but probably don't actually believe it. May I make a suggestion for you to try?" he asked, with his warmest smile.

The minister frowned. "You've intrigued me, Mister El-Hadidy. Yes, tell me and I'll try it."

"Every time you hear, read or see news about Muslim terrorists, look up what the Muslim community says about it."

"That seems like a tall order."

Mosi grinned and shrugged. "That's why you have staff. Then repeat that point of view five or six times for every time you hear the opposing information. You see, our minds tend to think what we hear the most, as if it were true. So, try it and let me know how it goes."

"Hmm, yes I'll do your little experiment and see where it leads. But now I want you to answer my original question. Where do you get your moral compass?"

"From myself." Mosi gave her a cheeky grin. "It all goes back to what the Bible calls the Golden Rule, which I feel the need to add, goes back at least to Hammurabi and perhaps much earlier."

"Do unto others . . ." She trailed off and nodded. "Fair enough."

"Getting back to the matter that brought you here. Is there something you think I can do to stop these cuts?" Mosi asked.

With her eyes ablaze, the minister gave Mosi a smile that he could only think of as a cross between malevolent and mischievous.

"I do indeed, and the plan could save your government funding, which I know constitutes over forty percent of your NGO's income, perhaps even increase it. If the Premier can't get her cuts through, she will most likely be forced to step down and you may find yourself with a new provincial leader who understands the importance of the work you're doing."

"I see," Mosi said. *Oh my God, I think I do understand.*

Though Mosi thought of himself as a non-believer and even sometimes as an atheist, those words were just tags and didn't explain the depth of his personal belief system. *I'm about to be tested to the upper limits of my belief system. Will my beliefs survive? Will I?*

Minister Marion Dubois never actually said that she planned to use the provincial budget and the cuts to the *CCSA* in particular not only to topple the Premier, but to become leader of the province of British Columbia. But Mosi saw exactly where she was going with her plan. Mosi recognized the plan was brilliant and if it worked, she would surely become Premier, and it was highly likely that she would fulfill her promise not only to stop the cuts to the *CCSA*, but increase funding. Ms. Dubois was a dedicated supporter of decriminalization of drug abuse and treating it as a health issue. This he believed on account of any number of speeches she'd made on the subject and because she had successfully championed the cause in both the party caucus and in the Provincial Legislature.

64

In spite of the clear benefits for the *CCSA*, Mosi felt uncomfortable with her underhandedness, deceitfulness, pure political maneuverings, and the fact that he would find himself indebted to Ms. Dubois.

Damn politics!

CHAPTER ELEVEN

"How do you feel about the fact you're leaving *Ellendale* next week?" Gavenina, Emilia's counselor, asked during one of her last counseling sessions.

"A little nervous," Emilia confessed, wiggling in the comfortable chair where she sat as she dabbed perspiration from her forehead. "Actually a lot nervous." She gave Gavenina a tight-lipped frown and a forced laugh. "*Ellendale's* been a safe haven for me while I learned the basics of overcoming urges and cravings, but I do honestly feel that my mind is healing very quickly."

"I have to agree with the assessment of how quickly your brain seems to be rewiring itself, which is why we think you're ready to get back out into the *real world,*" Gavenina said softly with a slight nod, a warm smile and a fathomless look in her eyes.

"Bernadette said she'd never seen anyone show signs of mental healing so quickly," Emilia said.

"I've been counseling people with addictions for over twelve years, and I have seen neuroplasticity work this fast on a few individuals. They, like you, were fairly young and though heavily addicted, didn't have decades of abuse behind them. That's likely the reason you've healed so quickly. And of course everyone heals at their own rate for reasons we don't yet understand."

Emilia gave Gavenina a nod, but said nothing, lost as she was in her own thoughts.

"I hope you plan to continue counseling once you get

home. I feel it would benefit you to figure out the reasons behind your addiction in the first place, and we are simply running out of time to explore that aspect. That knowledge can be very healing." Gavenina gave Emilia a warm smile.

I hadn't thought about counseling after I leave Ellendale, but I think Gavenina's right and I'll need professional physiological help. Mosi told me they have counselors at Sources. I'll look into that.

CHAPTER TWELVE

Emilia plopped the suitcase down in the small foyer of her condo, flipped the deadbolt shut, and looked around the living room, which was visible from where she stood. It was completely and utterly disgusting. In addition to the dust that must have accumulated over the last six weeks, it was littered with dirty bras, panties, tops, jeans, skirts and dresses and not a few red wine stains on the beige carpet. The mirror over the small gas fireplace was broken with one shard missing, the lamps on both sides of the cheap sofa were not on their end tables, but she could see part of the base of one of them on the floor. At one time she'd had a lovely comfortable leather sofa, but sold it to buy more vodka and pills, then replaced it with the piece of crap that now sat on the wall close to the balcony door.

"Shit," she muttered. "God, there's a lot of work to do."

At least her extended medical leave from work had given her enough to pay the mortgage while she was at *Ellendale*, otherwise she'd be in dire straits right now. Though during her medical leave she was only paid 60 percent of her wages, she still had almost one thousand dollars in her checking account, which was more than she'd had to spare in several years. *That feels good. Another benefit of being clean.*

Sissy had been kind enough to pick her up from *Ellendale* at 8:00 that morning, had dropped her off, then rushed away to get to her part-time job as a cashier for one of the local grocery stores for nine-thirty. Emilia pulled her phone from her purse and checked the time. 9:11 in the morning. *I'll need to do a grocery run first and then start cleaning and do laundry.* She imagined a tidy condo again and smiled. *It feels good already.*

She rolled her suitcase to her bedroom and chucked it onto the unmade bed where it landed on another pile of dirty clothes, and for some reason, which she couldn't remember, a dried up spruce branch, a blackened banana peel and a Chinese take-out container. *I sincerely hope the thing's empty.* As there was no smell of rotten food, she believed that it had nothing much in it. She went directly to the en-suite bathroom to pee and wondered why the door was closed. The moment she opened it, she understood the reason, for the smell made her gag. Well, after picking up a few groceries and cleaning supplies as needed, this was the first room she'd scrub.

She began to make a cleaning plan the moment she left the bathroom. She checked to see what she'd need in the way of cleaning supplies, then strode out the door into the hall with a light step. *It's delicious to feel this good.*

Emilia hadn't needed any cleaning supplies, as she'd found a cupboard full of them. She had a vague recollection of buying supplies, perhaps several times, with the intent to clean her condo, but the addiction had always won out and anything more than a cursory tidy-up had seldom happened. She'd have a drink before she started and then add a few pills into the mix and before much could be done, she'd stumble over to the rickety torn sofa, collapse onto it, and turn on the TV to rest for a few minutes. She always had a bottle of vodka on the coffee table with a few extra oxycodone tablets and would rarely get up except to stagger to the bathroom.

Emilia had just completed scrubbing, wiping, and mopping the bathroom walls, floor, sink and tub and scouring the water stains from the toilet bowl, when she heard the video-door phone buzz. She shucked her rubber gloves and scooted into the living room where the intercom was located and answered.

"Hello, who is it?" Emilia asked.

"My name's Doris, is this Emilia Robles?" Came the disembodied voice.

"Yes, it is. How can I help you?"

"Mosi suggested you might need some help to organize your place after being away for six weeks," Doris said.

Not sure she wanted anyone to see the state of her condo, Emilia's first impulse was to send the woman away. But for some reason, the woman's casual invocation of Mosi's name changed her mind.

"Sure, that'd be great. I'll buzz you in."

"Thank you," Doris said, "but I'll need your apartment number, all Mosi gave me was the call number."

"Seven-oh-three. Take the elevator to the seventh floor, go right, then turn the corner. It's the first door on your left past the turn."

Less than five minutes later, Emilia heard the expected knock and answered the door. She'd half expected an adorable young thing, but instead a slightly plump middle-aged lady with a pleasant face and large bosom stood before her with a warm winning smile on her face. She held a beaten up galvanized pail in her left hand and a mop in the other. The pail brimmed with bottles of cleaners and rags.

"Please come in," Emilia said and found herself with a smile on her own face as if smiling was contagious. *Which it might actually be.* The woman's face was vaguely familiar. "Have we met?" Emilia asked.

"Only once. I was at the *SMART* meeting you came to a couple of months ago, where you collapsed," Doris said in a matter-of-fact tone. "I'm just five months clean myself and am still working at keeping myself busy to avoid cravings. Mosi knows that, of course, and that's why he suggested I come over if I had some free time today. And we'll have a chance to get to know each other. It's always good to have friends in recovery 'cause they understand what we're going through."

"The place is quite the disaster zone," Emilia said, with a vague wave toward the living area, and then confessed. "I didn't keep house much when I was using, I always started to clean up, but would begin to drink and pop pills as I went, so I would end up too stoned to actually do much of *anything*."

"Yeah," Doris said in an understanding tone, "it was like that for me, too. My husband would pitch in and get the laundry done, tidy up a little, maybe vacuum and mop the kitchen and bathroom floors, but he told me after I got clean that he'd felt he would enable my bad behavior if he simply took over all the chores. He was right, of course. He'd been going to the *Family and Friends SMART* meeting in Langley to help him learn to cope with my addiction. That's where he learned about not enabling a user."

"You don't know how good it feels to realize I'm not the only one that couldn't even manage to keep my place clean when I was in full blown addiction."

"Yes, Emilia, I *do* know how it feels. I know *exactly* how it feels," Doris said, then gave Emilia a glowing smile. "So, where'd you like me to start?" she asked, as if they'd not just had a moment of intimate conversation.

Emilia stepped over to Doris and hugged her neck. "Thanks so much for coming over, I really could use the help, and the company is very welcome right now."

"Yeah, it takes a bit of time to get used to the real world again when you've been in a safe place like a rehab facility."

"Maybe you could start in the living room. There's a laundry hamper in my bedroom for all the dirty clothes." Emilia turned and strode to her bedroom. She opened the door to the small walk-in closet and encountered another disaster of unspeakable proportions. She struggled through the strewn clothes, shoes, coats, sweaters, purses, and paraphernalia to get to the hamper, of which only one corner could be seen. "Crap," Emilia muttered, "the damned thing's already over-flowing."

"Not to worry, Emilia. I'll get a plastic garbage bag or two and use them to collect the clothes. I'll sort them and get a load of laundry on right away," Doris said in a completely un-frazzled, even cheerful tone and another glowing smile.

"Thanks so much, Doris, that'll really help. I didn't remember how much of a mess I'd left behind," Emilia said, shaking her head, rolling her eyes, and lightly slapping her forehead.

"Emilia," Doris said, "we've all left the paths of our lives strewn with physical, emotional and mental debris. Losing our driver's license, bar fights, destroyed relationships, and we usually hurt the ones we love the most. This" — she swept her arm around to encompass the entire condo — "is easy to fix. Relationships on the other hand are a totally different story."

Emilia took a deep breath and then exhaled slowly. "You're right, this is just a matter of cleaning up, and no one was hurt."

The two women smiled at one another and set to work.

"Wow," Doris said, looking around from where she sat with her legs crossed at the now clean though dilapidated *Arborite* kitchen table with chromed skirt and legs. "I can't believe how clean the kitchen is. Two hours ago it would have qualified as a UN disaster zone."

Emilia guffawed. "It would have at that. What I can't believe is not only did I used to live like this, but it didn't make me desperately ill."

Doris' face took on a frown and she pressed her lips together. "It probably did make you sick, but sometimes our using covers our illness up."

"I didn't know that. Oh God, I still have so much to learn!"

"That's good." Doris knew her face took on an expression her husband called angelic. "It's all about the journey. That's how I stay clean. I'm enjoying the journey."

The video-door phone buzzed and Emilia jumped up and ran to the living room.

Doris laughed. "I wish I had that much energy."

"It's awesome," Emilia cried over her shoulder.

Doris smiled warmly and shook her head.

Why do I like this girl so much?

Emilia punched the button on the video-door phone and saw Mosi's smiling black face. "Hi," she said, not even trying to keep the excitement from her voice.

"Hi," he replied, and his grin got wider, if that was possible.

"Doris is here, I'm so glad you suggested I might need the help and she's also a great person just to have around, I mean, you know to talk about recovery and things. My place is such a mess, you wouldn't believe it and we've been scrubbing and mopping all morning and Doris has already done two loads of laundry and put on a third . . ."

"Whoa, whoa!" Mosi laughed. "It'd be nice if you told me everything in person and not with me standing here in front of your building."

"Oh, I'm so sorry, I'll buzz you in."

She pushed the *door* button somewhat harder than absolutely necessary and then rushed back to the kitchen and skidded to a stop in front of the tattered table.

"Mosi's here," she said. "I'm a mess. Damn, my hair must be a tangle. Crap. Look at these frazzled worn-out shorts and ratty top."

Doris laughed and jumped to her feet. She wrapped Emilia

in a bear hug with tears of laughter flowing from her blue eyes like a raging creek.

"Don't worry about it. Your being clean and sober will be more important to him than your old clothes." She spun Emilia around to face the door to the entry, and pushed her like a tugboat might maneuver a barge in a contrary current, to the recently cleaned mirror in her tiny foyer. "You look fine. We'll just fix your hair a little." With that, Doris pulled a comb from one of the deep pockets of her housedress and ran it through Emilia's hair.

There was a knock on the door.

Doris gave Emilia one last hug, spun her ninety degrees, and gave her a gentle shove in the direction of the door before she strode back to the kitchen. Emilia had seen the wide grin on her face before she turned away.

Emilia found herself a few feet from her door with her mind a nebulous mass of sticky goo that refused to work properly. She stared at the door for a few moments before her sluggish brain reminded her to open it. She stumbled the three steps over, grasped the handle, pushed it down, and pulled open the portal.

There stood Mosi in all his glory, towering over her and wearing a slightly rumpled pinstriped business suit, with a tie loosened at the collar. His glorious smile caused the fog in her brain to thicken, but in spite of this, she managed to step aside.

"Sorry," she said before he could speak. "I'm having a bad moment." Emilia put her left hand to her face while her right continued to hold the door open.

Mosi rushed in and then with great care dislodged her fingers from the door handle and closed the door. "Don't worry about it," he said as he put his hand under her elbow. "It's still early in your recovery. You're bound to have bad days and moments. It's quite normal."

It doesn't feel normal. Is this because of the healing that's taking place in my mind, Mosi's presence, or some of both?

Mosi said, "Oh here, I brought these to cheer you up. It's always a tough transition getting out of rehab and back into the real world."

Mosi held a huge bouquet of mixed flowers and she'd been so taken by his presence that she hadn't even seen it.

"Oh my God, they're beautiful! I have to put them into a vase right away. Come on, Doris is at the table. Maybe you'll sit with her for a few minutes while I get them into water."

Emilia stepped into the small kitchen and Mosi followed. The tiny battered table was in clear view and he swept by Emilia to sit by Doris. That slight brush of clothing gave Emilia goose bumps. This was not how she normally reacted to men she felt attracted to. Maybe it was something to do with being clean and sober, she thought, as her heart raced.

"It's good to see you, Doris," Mosi said as he sat at one of the old chrome and vinyl chairs that must have seen much in its day. "I'm pleased you stopped by to help Emilia get her place cleaned up. It'll do you both good."

"Is it normal for a *SMART Facilitator* to get so involved in the lives of their groups participants?" Doris asked in a soft voice and with a sly grin.

"No," he said quietly as he shook his head and looked away.

"She's very beautiful." Doris grinned.

Mosi only nodded as he saw Emilia gliding over to the table with a simple clear glass vase held in both hands. It overflowed with the wild bouquet.

Mosi felt the heat rise into his face and was happy his black skin would hide the flush, but was careful not to show any other signs of embarrassment, so he was sure not to look away and looked directly into Emilia's eyes. This turned out to be something of a mistake, he realized, for the first thing he noticed was their clarity and the deepened brown her eyes had taken on as she regained her health. They'd lost the sunken, jaundiced look of addiction. He forced his gaze away from hers and with a warm smile, examined her face, which was now clear and without the splotches that had affected her in early withdrawal. Her deep olive skin now held no blemish and the face he'd thought might become attractive with abstinence was now stunningly beautiful. She was still underweight, but filling out and doing so in a manner he could only think of as scrumptious.

"Glad you like the flowers," he said as he could think of nothing else, for his mind had wandered, absorbed by the beauty of this woman, who only a few weeks ago had been a physical wreck.

Emilia beamed back at him, which caused his heart to race until he thought it might explode. *She must be the most beautiful woman I've ever seen.*

"They're gorgeous. It's the most wonderful bouquet of flowers I've ever gotten, the brilliant colors and simplicity of the wild stock is amazing. Again, thank you so much," Emilia said with glowing eyes and a smile so wide it seemed to absorb everything in the room. Maybe the universe.

"How are you feeling now that you're out of *Ellendale*? It must be a shock," Mosi said as he crossed his legs. *I hope I look normal and not like a schoolboy.*

"Yeah, it was when I first got home, but when Doris knocked on the door all the crazy thoughts about how badly I needed a couple of pills followed by a shot or three of vodka vanished. I'm *so* glad Doris came by to help. It feels great to have someone with me who understands what I'm going through right now and it acts as a distraction having her here and I can talk to her."

"The studies are clear. One of the important things people all have in common who have successfully recovered from addiction is staying connected. And thank you, Doris, for coming over. It'll do you both good, I believe."

"You're right, Mosi, I've only got five months clean myself, so being here helps me to occupy my time. Boredom is a killer for me," Doris said. "Besides, I've taken a liking to this striking brunette." Doris grinned at them both. Her eyes flashed with—

Emilia plunked the vase onto the chrome and laminate table, then leaned over and gave Doris an awkward bear hug where she sat.

"You're great," Emilia said with glistening eyes.

"Looks like you'll be good friends," Mosi said, as there was something about these two that said they would get along super well, in spite of their age difference. That was good. Being connected through *SMART* was important, but to stay clean, one needed other connections like new friends, and a new lifestyle.

Mosi finally realized that Emilia wore a t-shirt that was well past its day and tattered and worn jean shorts, which hung on Emilia as if she still needed to fill out to her normal body weight, which was likely. However slight she was, he was aroused by her figure and perhaps, by the promise of what was to come as she filled out.

I have to stop thinking about her like that. She's a participant in my group and needs me to act professionally. She needs me to be there for her as a facilitator, not her lover. She's vulnerable right now and needs protection, not to be taken advantage of—but maybe in time. Two or three years down the road. I'll leave it at that—for now.

"I'm off, ladies, be good to yourselves," Mosi said, as he stood and then gave them both his ubiquitous smile. It was clear to Mosi that his smile was well received by both women, and that pleased him.

Emilia ushered him to the door and then thrust her hand out at him. He couldn't tell for sure because of her olive complexion, but he thought she blushed. He took the proffered hand, shook it with gentle firmness, turned and offered Doris another warm smile and left.

"Well, that was interesting," Doris said.

"What was interesting?" Emilia asked, as she sauntered back to the table.

"That little visit from our local White Rock *SMART Recovery* Facilitator," Doris said with a warm smile for Emilia.

"It was nice of him to drop by," she agreed, feeling the warmth flood her face and hoping her skin would hide her flush.

"Do you think he visits all the people who come to his meetings?"

"I . . . didn't think about it much. I thought maybe he did."

"I know of nobody else he's visited when they were brand new. I know he and Josh have started hiking together sometimes, but Josh had close to two years clean when they started. Don't get me wrong, I don't think he's hitting on you, or going to. He's too smart for that."

This time the heat in Emilia's face was from anger. "Too smart? What do you mean by that?" she growled.

Doris laughed. "I don't mean that you're bad or anything like that. But he knows if a romance goes south when you're in early recovery, it often leads to relapse. In fact, I wouldn't be surprised if virtually every man at the meeting will want to date you. Don't be surprised if you get a lot of invitations for coffee after the meeting tomorrow."

"Why would they want to date me? I only have a little over six weeks clean."

"Honey, you're gorgeous. You're beautiful, sexy and intelligent. You are in every way desirable. Granted, you looked like hell when you came to that meeting . . . uhm, six weeks ago, but you're lookin' good now."

Emilia covered her mouth to hide her smile, but burst out laughing instead.

Doris laughed with her, but then cautioned her. "I don't think now's the time for you to get involved in a romantic relationship. You need to concentrate on healing. You still have lots to learn and there'll be plenty of temptations. Give me your number and I'll add you to my contact list."

Emilia told Doris her phone number and seconds later her phone rang.

"There, now you have my number if you need to talk."

"That's great," Emilia said. "And call me any time you want to talk as well. We can get together after work and do coffee or something, maybe once a week or—whatever."

"That'd be good. My husband's okay, but he really doesn't understand why I can't *just have one*."

"I know *I* can't."

"Yeah, me neither. Been there, you know what I mean?"

"Unfortunately yes, I know exactly what you mean."

Doris had left to make dinner for her husband and an exhausted Emilia plopped onto her old couch. She had no cable, having not paid that bill for some time, but felt good about herself, finding a new sober friend and the amount of cleaning they'd done. The place still needed work, but was almost respectable. The dryer hummed in the background, drying the fourth load of laundry, which put quite a dent in her dirty clothes basket. *I'll walk to the grocery store and buy a few things for dinner tonight and to take for my lunches, which I'll need starting tomorrow, as I'll be back to work. After dinner I'll write up a budget. That's something I haven't done for years. I'm not looking forward to my first day back at work and don't know how I'll explain my time off to my co-workers. The boss knows, of course, but no one else. Maybe I'll just be honest. That'll be a nice change.* Emilia smiled.

CHAPTER THIRTEEN

Emilia awoke before her alarm sounded. She turned over and looked at the bedside clock. 6:10. She felt rested and awake and though it was earlier than necessary, she got up, put the coffee on and went about her morning routine. It was a new routine she'd learned in *Ellendale*.

Self-care.

It was something she'd only had memories of when she was using. Regular showers, brushing her teeth twice a day, keeping her hair clean and tidy, nails trimmed and filed, and then the importance of a good diet with lots of fruit, vegetables, healthy fats and protein.

She still had memory lapses, but her brain was healing very quickly.

She was happy that the worst of her addiction had only lasted about five years, which was likely the reason, she was told, neuroplasticity was working so quickly for her. That and the fact she was not quite thirty. *Youth has its advantages.* As she had no Internet — another bill left unpaid — she sat at her table and read the news on her phone. She'd always paid her phone bill, as it had been her conduit to her dealer to get her oxycodone pills, or the street variation at least. Little had she realized at the time how dangerous it was to use those street drugs, not really knowing what was in them. It wasn't exactly like buying from a pharmacy, which she also did, but used up her prescription faster than her doctor permitted refills. *I'm alive! I didn't kill myself and now have a chance at happiness.*

"A real chance," she said out loud to the air. Emilia smiled.

Whatever happened at work, she would accept it and take it in stride. And, she decided in that moment, she'd inform her co-workers about her addiction.

That brought a frown—but she was determined.

"Good morning, Mister Douglas," Emilia said, as she stood outside her boss' office.

He looked up from his computer. "Hi, Emilia. Glad to have you back." Then he turned back to the monitor.

Emilia shrugged and headed to her office, set her purse on the stool to the left of her office chair, as that was out of direct sight of the doorway and sat in front of her computer. *I'll leave my office door open, contrary to the old Emilia's custom.*

As her computer was up and running, as it always was when she arrived, she checked her emails and discovered her inbox had been kept up-to-date as there were only recent emails waiting. That was good. She dealt with the mail first, and then checked the lab results that were out of the ordinary to be sure everything had been done according to proper protocols. She was really getting into it and absolutely absorbed, when Mr. Douglas' voice broke in on her concentration.

"Sorry, I was occupied and didn't catch what you said," Emilia said, as she lifted her gaze to the open door.

"Wendy, the team leader, called in sick and I'm already short-handed in the lab. I'd like you to step in and do five hours on the floor—if you think you're up to it."

Emilia gave him a large warm smile. "I most certainly am up for it."

"Good, that'll help. Thanks," he said with a bland face. He slipped back to his office.

At twenty-one, she had graduated from the University of British Columbia—UBC—with a management degree. Normally the course took four years, but she'd completed it in three by taking on an extra heavy course load each semester. She'd always hold off drinking until after she was nearly done with her studies each evening, which helped keep her on track. There were few management positions available when she graduated and as she had an interest in the health care industry, she took a one-year technicians course to get into the company she most wanted to work for. BC Medical Labs. As they were desperate for technicians when she graduated, she was snapped up and began lab work. Within two months, she was regularly on the weekly list of top ranked technicians and after one year, she was untouchable as the best, most consistent lab tech with highest productivity record and lowest redoes. This meant when a sample came in that was especially small and an additional test would not be possible, it would be passed to her.

In just under two years, a vacancy came on the management team and as was the company practice, it was first posted to existing employees. The head of the local management team had left for a position in the head office in Ontario. The managers were each bumped up a grade, which left a position open at the bottom. She applied and was their first choice as she had all the necessary management qualifications on paper as well as having acted as team leader on the floor for more than six months.

Emilia was now on the management team, and exactly where she wanted to be.

Emilia donned her white lab coat, which she kept for when she did inspections on the floor, went through the Clean Room process and once decontaminated, stepped onto the floor of the company's local, central lab.

Her first thoughts were for Shelley, who'd be in a controlled panic without Wendy, her supervisor. She found a clearly flustered Shelley at the distribution station, trying to organize and triage blood and urine tests. She'd never liked Shelley, and thought of her as a bit of an air-head, though she was a good enough tech. However, Emilia realized in that instant that she'd possibly been mistaken and decided to try something out.

"Hi, Shelley. Let me show you a little trick." Emilia took the next vial in line for examination, lifted it so both of them could see, and pointed to the code line. "I look at the last three letters on the line. See, this one says LS-five. I think of L as standing for life, S is the speed it needs to be done at, five is the speed. A numeral one is the most important, ten is the least important, so this one is average. What I do is lift the vials and check the code real quick and pull all the LS-one's out first, then I check the others as they come in."

Shelley looked at her with wide eyes. "Why didn't anyone show me this before?"

"That's a good question, Shelley. I'll look into it tomorrow," Emilia replied with a warm smile.

"So what are you doing on the floor?" Shelley asked.

"As Wendy's sick I'll be helping with the tests."

"Oh, are you going to take over here?"

"No, you'll do fine," Emilia said, believing it to be true now Shelley had some simple information to be able to do the job properly. "I'm just going to work on doing tests. I'll get Wendy's station set up and then come for some vials."

"Sure, sounds good," Shelley said, as her shoulders fell. She sighed and smiled.

Emilia strode toward Wendy's workstation and booted up the computer, then turned on the equipment so it could warm up while she prepared everything for use. As she logged onto the computer, she heard the whirring of helicopter blades and when the sound didn't diminish, she knew a sample was arriving which needed emergency testing. She hoped Shelley would assign it to her, but decided not to interfere, as that would undercut Shelley's authority, even though it was only temporary.

At least for now. *Wendy's close to retirement and someone will get a promotion. I wonder why Wendy hasn't passed on some of the information her successor would need.*

I'm acting so differently than I would've six weeks ago. My brain's clearer and I actually feel compassion for fellow workers. The only thing that used to matter were the pills and vodka. I like this new feeling.

The moment she turned to go for blood to test, she saw Shelly rushing toward her with a test tube in hand. She grinned in pleasure. Her first test would be an emergency. The flush of delight felt better than the rush of oxy and vodka, because she knew it was a real feeling and not artificial.

"This tissue sample just came in, and well, I thought you'd be able to get on it right away. It's tiny and don't think we'll be able to do a second test if this one fails," Shelly said in a composed tone, but her brows were raised.

"I'll do it right now and make sure it's done right."

Emilia read the surgeon's instructions and realized that someone was likely on a table at that moment and a surgeon was waiting for the results. As every hospital in the region could perform tests on biopsies, it must mean St. Catherine's had an equipment failure and that might also account for the small sample. She deduced all this as she prepared the sample for testing, checking and double-checking her procedures. The lab here at BC Medical was much closer to St. Catherine's than any of the other hospitals. Once she had the vial in the centrifuge, she read the rest of the paperwork that came with the sample. *Yep, St. Catherine's.* The moment the tests were done, she emailed the results to the hospital. There was an immediate reply.

Thanks, we owe you one.

Someone had pancreatic cancer. She hoped it wasn't too advanced. It hit her that she cared that this anonymous individual would get well. What a difference from her using days when she'd lived in a bubble of one and in a fog that lacked any kind of feeling. This was so much better. *Well, feelings aren't always good.*

She went back and took the tray of samples Shelly had put

in front to be tested first and returned to Wendy's station and worked until the lunch buzzer sounded. Emilia checked the equipment to be sure what was running could be left for half an hour and went to the lunchroom.

She pulled her lunch out of the large fridge the company kept for its employees, took her water bottle and refilled it with cold water from the water cooler and sat at a chair which was both empty and she thought, unused. This would be the first time in a few years she ate in the lunchroom. But of course, this was part of her plan.

Bailey, one of the floor staff, said with a wide grin, "Hey haven't seen you around in a bit. At first I thought you was hidin' out in yer office, but I heard you were on vacation or something. Where'd you go?"

Blustering ahead before she could change her mind, Emilia said, "I was at *Ellendale*."

"*Ellendale*?" Shelley asked. "Where's that?"

"It's in north Surrey. It's a rehab facility for women."

"Holy shit." Emilia heard someone say in *sotto voce*.

"Oh," Shelley mumbled, then said in a normal voice, "Well it seems to have helped, you certainly act differently, if that's a sign."

"It can be," Emilia said. "I still have a lot of healing to do, and I'm learning to react more thoughtfully to people."

"Do you mind if I ask what you were in rehab for?" Tara, another of the floor staff, asked.

Emilia felt her heart race. This was the moment of truth.

"I was addicted to oxycodone and alcohol," she said in such a firm tone that it surprised her.

"That sounds dangerous," Tara said.

"Yes," Emilia agreed, "very dangerous. I'm lucky to be alive and my mind and body have some serious healing to do."

"I'm sure you can still pound back a few at the Christmas party," Bailey said with the grin he tended to use when speaking to any female employee.

"You're an idiot, Bailey," Shelley said.

"Yeah," Tara agreed. "I think we should support Emilia. I'm sure it's been hard."

"Yes, and it still is and will be for a while, I understand." Emilia noticed Mr. Douglas leaning on the doorjamb of the lunchroom, but continued. "I went to a *SMART Recovery* meeting three days after I quit, but ended up in the hospital from withdrawal symptoms, from there I went to *Ellendale* and tonight I'll be going back to our local meeting and plan to do so for a *loooong* time."

"Is that like *AA* or something?" an unseen person whose voice she didn't recognize asked.

"It *is* a self-help group, if that's what you mean, but it's science-based. In *SMART* you don't depend on a higher power, but are in control of your recovery and responsible for both your addiction and recovery from it," Emilia finished. She exhaled softly.

"Well I for one am proud of Emilia," Mr. Douglas chimed in, to the evident surprise of many who'd not been aware he was listening in. His words, and the fact he was proud of her, certainly surprised Emilia.

Lunchtime chatter continued around Emilia's time in *Ellendale*, *SMART Recovery*, and addiction in general. Emilia found that the more she discussed her problems and addiction with the others, the more comfortable it became. It was also, she realized, a valuable tool to deter her from using again as now all her co-workers knew. It was something she'd learned and discussed at the *SMART* group meetings while at *Ellendale*, and it was having a positive effect. *For me at least.*

For the last hour of the day, Emilia returned to her office to catch up, as much as she could, on her workload. She could tell her mind was not what it used to be, but it *was* improving and there was that hope. She'd take some work home tonight, but only do what she was able to and still get to the SMART meeting. She had lots to learn and knew she needed the fellowship of others in her condition. That was one of the many important things she'd learned so far. Staying connected was critical to maintaining abstinence.

The buzzer had gone a few minutes before, but Emilia was still working on something and wanted to stay for a few more minutes to finish it. As she typed furiously, she heard something and looked up. Mr. Douglas was at her open door. He glanced down the hall, looking both ways, then stepped inside and closed the door behind him.

He fidgeted and cleared his throat. "Just wanted you to know how pleased I am you're back." He rubbed his neck, then ran his hand over his face. "I . . . my . . . my brother, my little brother's hooked on crack. He . . . he's been trying to kick it for over a year. It's scaring the hell outta' me. He's on the verge of living on the street and only has a place to crash 'cause I usually pay the rent for him. He keeps going to *Narcotics Anonymous*, but only lasts a few days and then it's back to smoking up. I'm at my wits end and don't understand why he doesn't just quit."

"I'm no expert on crack, but a lady at *Ellendale* had been on it and said the high was better than sex. That can't be easy to get off of," Emilia said with a direct look. Her eyes were wet.

"Do you think this *SMART Recovery* might help him?"

"It might. I can give you the address if you like. We meet tonight from seven to eight-thirty. He'd be welcome."

"Yes, please. And I see you're more like the woman I hired." He smiled, but his eyes never once met hers.

"Thank you."

Emilia wrote the address on the sticky-note pad she kept

on her desk, peeled it off, got up and handed it to him.

He thanked her and left. Emilia finished her work and prepared what she wanted to work on after the meeting tonight, saved it, packed her things and headed home afoot. It would be a while before she could afford to insure her car again, but the walk felt good, even though there was the threat of precipitation. She lived on the coast after all and virtually everyone carried an umbrella. Her step was jaunty and she could smell the sea air, even from here on top of the hill. She looked forward to the meeting tonight. Doris would be there and of course, Mosi.

She smiled.

CHAPTER FOURTEEN

Emilia walked the six short blocks from her condo to the *SMART* meeting and arrived fifteen minutes early. What a difference from the last time she'd been here! It took a moment for her eyes to accustom themselves to the dim intimate lighting and she had several surprises when it did.

Mosi was at the head of the table where he always sat, but Josh sat beside him. She saw Doris and on the way to sit beside her, she had a momentary shock to see Mr. Douglas. Then, just as quickly, she realized it was a younger version of him and must be the brother he spoke of at work. Though this man's hair had no gray, his face was thin and sallow.

She smiled at Mosi. "Hi," she said.

"Glad you made it," he replied.

"You're Josh, I think," Emilia said.

"I am glad you're here." He smiled at her.

"Haven't seen you since ... my God, yesterday," Doris said as Emilia approached, then stood and gave her a bear hug.

Both ladies sat and chatted in a private conversation, many of which were occurring around the table. She'd only been sitting for two minutes when a figure she would know anywhere strode in with the confidence of many years addiction-free. Bernadette rushed over to Mosi and hugged him from behind, then came directly to where she sat, pulled her to her feet and hugged her with intense ferocity, then stood on tip-toes and kissed her forehead.

"Good to see you, dear," Bernadette said and then plunked

herself down onto the empty chair beside Emilia.

"That," Mosi said, with something between a grin and a look of consternation, "is my mother."

Bernadette waved to the group with a grin and gleaming eyes.

"And — she was my housemother at *Ellendale*," Emilia said, with a smile. She was enjoying both the shock and the playfulness the group displayed.

"Looks to me like she does a lot of mothering, but I'm not sure if that's a rational belief or not," a young woman with pink and blue hair and platinum blonde roots said.

Miranda, Emilia remembered.

"I have no idea if she did much mothering before, but when I was at *Ellendale* she was most definitely very much a mother to me. How about you, Emilia?" Anne asked.

Emilia smiled and waved to Anne and when she glanced at Bernadette, saw sparkling eyes and a gleaming smile.

"Well, I plan to do my talking during check-in," Bernadette said, then winked at Emilia.

"Having said all that, it's seven and time to get started," Mosi said. "You'll notice Josh is sitting here with me and that's because he's signed up to take the *SMART Recovery* Facilitator's course. I'll let him open and then tell us what he plans. Go ahead, Josh."

"My name is Josh and I'm co-facilitating with Mosi this evening. *This is an open meeting of* SMART Recovery. SMART *stands for* Self-Management And Recovery Training.

SMART's *four main objectives are.*

One, to maintain motivation for abstinence.

Two, to learn to cope with urges and cravings.

Three, to manage thoughts, feelings and behaviors.

Four to live a balanced lifestyle.

SMART *sees addiction as a learned, unhelpful behavior. At the core of* SMART *is the principal that I am largely responsible for my thoughts, feelings and behaviors, including addictive behaviors. If I want to change the way I feel, I can start by changing the way I think.*

SMART also believes that often at the core of addictive behaviors are many unhelpful thoughts and beliefs about my worth as a person. SMART encourages me to move toward thoughts, feelings and beliefs that support Unconditional Self-Acceptance.

These changes will take Patience, Practice and Persistence. At this meeting we support one another in learning and practicing the principles of SMART so we can make the changes we believe will improve our lives.

If this is your first time at a SMART meeting, welcome! You are invited to participate as much or as little as you want.

When he was done he began the check-in himself. "Mosi asked me to consider taking the Facilitator's course, in part because he has no back-up if he goes on vacation since Jessica moved to Vancouver Island. I thought about it for a few weeks and figured that it would be useful for my recovery and it would feel good to help others. With that, let's continue with the check-in. Tell us your name and how your week's gone and if at any time you don't wish to speak, just say pass. Let's start on my left."

The young blue-haired blonde, Miranda, had a good week and so did the tall slender gentleman she remembered from her first meeting. Anne, who she'd met at *Ellendale*, was still clean and sober in spite of temptations. Bernadette was next in line.

"I'm Bernadette and I have five years clean. I'm happy now, and do a good job as housemother at *Ellendale*, but I was never a good mom to my son, Mosi. I was too busy getting high and plastered to keep him on track, or even in school. So, instead of keeping him clean and being a good mom, he got clean, then worked on me. Five years ago his gentle pressure and good example took hold and I will be forever grateful to this amazing young man I'm proud to call my son. He's driving me to the Vancouver airport after the meeting as I'm going on vacation to Peru where I plan to do some skydiving as well as see some of the Incan temples. I have never been so happy in my life and to have a son like mine is a Godsend. If possible, Emilia, I'd love your company for the ride as well . . . if Mosi doesn't mind." She grinned.

"Whatever you like, Mom," Mosi said, with a slight tremble in his voice and without a smile on his face.

She and Doris checked in and then it was the turn of the man who looked to be a younger, but poorly kept version of her boss.

"Hi, I'm Steve and I'm a crackhead. I've been in and out of *NA* since the late nineteen-nineties, but it never seems to stick. I'll get clean for a couple of months and relapse. I can't say *NA's* bullshit, 'cause other guys have been helped, you know? I lost my wife and kids years ago because of my addiction and we don't even keep in contact. I keep meaning to, but then I crave the next high and nothing comes of it. In *NA*, they tell me I'm not doing the steps properly or not giving myself over to the higher power. I just wanna be fucking clean God fucking damn it!"

"Is this your first time at a *SMART* meeting, Steve?" Josh asked after a quick nod from Mosi.

"Yeah, my brother, who's a bigwig at BC Medical told me about it this afternoon and even drove me down. I figure it can't do me any harm."

After another nod from Mosi, Josh continued. "In *SMART*, we don't use terms like drunk, junky, or crackhead, because they have no positive value for your recovery, they just make you think that's what you are and that there's no escape. Instead, I see in you a good person with an addiction to crack. Deep inside of you the real Steve is crying to get out and that's why you're here. And I want you to know that you're very welcome and I'm pleased you came."

Mosi clapped, and then everyone with the exception of an

apparently stunned Steve, and the man who sat beside him, did the same.

After the clapping ended, the man next to Steve spoke. Emilia didn't recognize the man, but he had on an extravagantly expensive suit, though it looked rather rumpled and he wore no tie.

"I'm Charles," he said in a clearly bored tone. Slumped as he was in his seat, he looked to be the essence of boredom to Emilia.

"I'm good. Dad's going to pay for my lawyer as I'm attending these meetings, so you'll be seeing me for a while yet." He glanced over at Emilia with a look that reminded her of a lion stalking prey. "Hey, and it's not all bad after all." He smiled, exposing a perfect set of teeth.

Screw you, Charles.

The check-in finished and there were two other new individuals in addition to Steve. Seventeen in all, Emilia counted. It seemed a comfortable-sized group to her.

"Given what was said during check-in, I'd like us to go over the *Stages of Change*," Mosi said. "Would you do that on the whiteboard for us, Josh?"

Josh nodded and stood, erasable marker in hand. "I'm new at this, so if I screw up I'm hoping for some latitude."

Charles grumbled under his breath.

Doris frowned at Charles, then spoke. "You'll do fine and *I think* you'll be a *great* facilitator, Josh."

I like Doris better every moment.

Josh drew what looked like a spring standing on end. Emilia had never seen this tool before and leaned toward the front, super curious about how this worked. At the bottom of the spiral, Josh wrote a capital *P* and circled it.

"What's the first stage of change?" he asked the group.

Obviously some have done this exercise before.

"Pre-contemplation," Doris called out in a firm clear voice.

"Right," Josh said. "What does that mean?"

Miranda of the colorful hair spoke up. "It's like when you don't think you have a problem with your *Drug of Choice.*"

"Good." Josh nodded and gave her an encouraging smile. Next, a little higher up and on a line of the spring, he printed a capital *C* and circled it.

Without waiting for Josh to ask, colorful Miranda called, "Contemplation." Then she grinned at Doris, who smiled back and nodded.

"A definition please?" Josh asked.

A tall slender man who looked familiar to Emilia replied, "That's when you start to think you might have a problem. Can I continue?" he asked Josh.

"Sure, please go ahead."

"I know for me, I went back and forth between pre-contemplation and contemplation for years. I've learned here at *SMART* that it's not uncommon."

"That's right," Josh said, "and thanks for sharing that."

Higher up the drawing, Josh printed another *P* and again circled it. "What's the next stage?"

"Preparation," another man Emilia didn't recognize said.

Again without prompting, Anne, the lady she knew from *Ellendale*, spoke. "This is where I began to plan and prepare myself to get clean. I'd already decided to do it, but needed a plan. I'd gone through residential treatment before, but I'd relapsed. And I mean relapsed badly. So in my preparation or plan, I included what I'd do after I left rehab, which is why I'm here."

Josh smiled. "That's exactly right, Anne. Next stage please," Josh said as he wrote an *A* on the board, higher up yet again.

"Action." It was Mosi who spoke up this time. "But I'll let someone else define it." His smile lit up the room, to Emilia, who had to tear her gaze from it to hear what was said next.

"This is where you put the plan into action and start

actually *doing* it," another young man said.

"This is where others begin to see a difference in your behavior. Is this making sense to you so far?" Josh asked, nodding to Steve and the other newbies.

They all nodded back.

Next, Josh drew an *M* with a circle. "What's the next stage?"

There was a few seconds of silence before Doris spoke. "Maintenance."

"Good," Josh said. "What does that mean to you?" He waved his arm to encompass the whole room.

"I haven't done this exercise before, but it seems self-explanatory," Emilia began. "This must be the stage where I keep practicing the things I've learned. I guess I'm at the beginning of this stage, so I'm also planning on gathering more tools to help me."

"I like that," Mosi said. "Adding tools, especially early in maintenance, is very valuable to changing the way you think, which is how we stay clean." He nodded to Josh, who continued.

Josh then drew an *S*, circling it as he'd done with the other letters. "This doesn't represent a *Stage of Change*. What is it?" Josh smiled and looked around the room.

Emilia glanced around the table and saw she wasn't to only one in attendance who had no idea where this was going.

Miranda, however, had obviously been through this and spoke up at last. "That's a slip or lapse."

This time Josh didn't wait for more of an explanation from the group. "While not a part of the *Stages of Change*, slips and lapses are so common that most everybody has one and most have several and some have many before they are able to completely maintain abstinence."

"And a very few never slip at all," Mosi said with a warm smile directed at Josh. "You've got over two years clean and haven't slipped to the best of my knowledge, Josh."

"Yeah," Josh agreed, "but mostly by dumb luck and lots of fear."

"Fear of what?" Mosi asked.

"Of losing my family."

"Oh," Emilia said, not realizing at first that she was speaking aloud, "the *Hierarchy of Values*."

"You got it, Emilia," Mosi said and then grinned.

"I understand your point, Mosi," Josh said. "We can't use the fact that most people do slip as an *excuse* to lapse or even relapse."

"That's right, do you want to go ahead and finish the exercise?"

At the very top of the spiral, Josh drew a line with an arrow that extended to the edge of the whiteboard. On the line he printed an *E*, which he circled. Instead of asking what it meant, he told the group himself. "This is the final stage and is where we Exit recovery. At this point we've changed the way we feel and think and simply go on with life. I need to mention here that in spite of the drawing, most addicted people don't go through a clean linear journey like we depicted, but go back and forth, similar to what was mentioned earlier. As for me, I consider myself in the maintenance stage. How about you, Mosi?"

"I definitely think of myself as having exited recovery, but want to say that there is some discussion as to whether or not an exit actually exists. I've come to the conclusion, and this is my *opinion*, that for some there's an exit and for others there's not," Mosi explained as he leaned back in his chair and smiled.

It was quarter after eight by the time they finished the *Stages of Change* exercise and Josh called for checkout. "I would like to know if you're safe and tell us one thing you got out of the meeting."

They went around the table and when it was Steve's turn, he broke down in sobs and stuttered through his checkout. "I-I just never knew any of this stuff. God ev-every time I'd slip they'd say I wasn't doin' it right. No one ever told me — crap! Never told me that slippin's normal, and I'd just say to myself I'm a fuck-up and might as well smoke another pipe, then another and another. I-I can't believe no one said nothin' to me. This time I'm gonna make it, and if I do fuck up, instead of beatin' myself up, I'm gonna get up an' climb back onto that damn horse like someone here said at check-in. Thanks, Josh. You may be brand new at this, but I feel like you saved my life, both of you, in fact, all of you."

Emilia pulled a tissue from her pocket and dabbed at her eyes. She wasn't the only one she saw. After the meeting, she went over to Steve and hugged him.

Emilia felt torn between her desire to tag along with Mosi and Bernadette to the airport and to stay and attack the work she'd brought home. Even as she contemplated this, and did a quick *Cost Benefit Analysis* in her head, Charles stepped in front of her.

"That Steve guy's quite the loser don't you think?" he asked with a smirk.

"He's addicted to crack, but underneath his addiction I'm sure there's a good man," Emilia replied, in a less than cordial tone. *Go away.*

"Enough about him, how about a Latte or Mocha at the coffee shop on top of the hill. We could talk . . . um, you know, about recovery or something."

"I have work at home and Bernadette wants me to go with them to the Vancouver airport, so either way I won't have time."

"That's okay, we'll make it tomorrow. What time would you like me to pick you up?"

What an ass! Just assuming I'll go out with him like he was God's

97

gift to womankind. "How about you pick me up never." And she strode away from him and over to where Bernadette stood talking with Anne. While she waited for them to finish their conversation, she felt a tap on her shoulder. She spun around prepared to face Charles once again, but it was Doris. "Maybe we could do tea after supper on Wednesday, if you don't have any other plans?" Doris asked.

"I'm not sure if I'll need to do work at home yet, but I'd love to if I can. Is it okay if I let you know Wednesday after work?"

"That's fine. We don't do much during the week, so I'll be free at any rate."

"Perfect," Emilia said. "I'll call you either way, probably around five-thirtyish."

"That works," Doris said, then hugged Emilia around the neck.

That felt good, a hug from a friend with no expectations other than to enjoy each other's company. She added a reminder to call Doris to the calendar on her phone.

Bernadette was beside her moments after Doris left. "I promise to be difficult if you're not willing to accompany me to the airport. We leave in a few minutes, so you won't get back too late, as I assume you're back at work."

"I really want to go, but I also have work I'd like to get done. I spent most of my day on the lab floor so I didn't get a lot of my stuff finished and brought it home. I'm debating with myself on how important it is to finish it tonight. It was my first day back and my brain's still slow," Emilia said.

"Maybe you should give your brain a rest," Anne interjected.

"Is there science to back that up?" Emilia asked with a smile.

Anne shook her head. "I don't know, it just seems intuitive—to me anyway. The body needs exercise *and* rest, so it must be the same for the brain."

"I really would like to go and spend some time with you, Bernadette, and even if Anne's theory's wrong, I'll have time to catch up with the paperwork the rest of the week, so I'm just going to go," Emilia said.

"Thank you," Bernadette said with a satisfied smile. "It'll be good to have you along and you can keep Mosi company on the drive back."

Emilia felt her face flush but tried — she hoped successfully — to avoid any other signs of embarrassment.

Chapter Fifteen

Everyone else had left. Bernadette watched while her only son, Mosi, set the alarm and locked the door of the meeting room.

"We're ready to go, I think," he said. "Do you need anything from home before we go?" Mosi asked Emilia.

"I wouldn't mind a bottle of water, but we can pick one up at any corner store," Emilia said.

"Sure, and can you think of anything you've forgotten, Mom?"

"No, I'm ready to go. Don't forget I've been planning this trip for almost a year," Bernadette said with a smile. *My eyes must be glowing.*

When Bernadette saw Emilia pull open the rear door of Mosi's *Volvo*, she shot her arm out and grabbed Emilia's wrist. "Sit in the front please," she said, with an unfathomable look in her chocolate eyes.

"But you should sit in the front with your son." Emilia's eyes went dark.

"Not today." She smiled and wrangled Emilia through the door until she plopped into the front seat.

Let's see what happens. God I'm so satisfied with myself. What the hell am I thinking? Ah, young love. But will you be good for my boy?

Mosi drove up the steep hill using a route that took them through White Rock's quiet downtown core and an almost straight run to the freeway, which led to the city of Richmond where Vancouver's International Airport was located.

Mosi asked his mother about her plans and Bernadette fig-ured this was for Emilia's benefit as she'd discussed her plans ad nauseam with Mosi. As the conversation waned Berna-dette spoke up in what she thought of as her housemother's voice.

"I'm not entirely sure what's going on with you two, but I'm going to give you unrequested, and perhaps unwanted, advice. First, my dearest and beloved only child, you've spent nine years as a *SMART* Facilitator and you're very good at it. But right now you need to beware not to complicate Emilia's recovery. I'm not telling you anything you don't already know, but if you two begin to date and something goes side-ways, she could not only slip, but relapse. She's at a very vul-nerable stage of her recovery.

"And you, my dear Emilia, I would be delighted to see you and Mosi get together, but right now you need to concentrate on yourself. And another point I'll add is that I don't think it would be wise for you guys to date as Mosi's the facilitator and you're one of the participants. That reeks of coercion, even if it's a consensual relationship. Besides, you never know how it might affect others in your group." Finished, Berna-dette sat back in her seat.

"Mom, nothing's happening and nothing's going to hap-pen," Mosi said in an almost indignant tone.

"It's true," Emilia, said, "nothing *is* going on between us."

"I believe you both," Bernadette said. "But there's an in-tense attraction between you and you're both trying to ignore it. Emilia's new to recovery, but you know better, son. I'm talking about mindfulness. Living in the present and being *aware* of your thoughts and feelings."

"Shit," Mosi mumbled and slapped the steering wheel. "Mom, it's true and I'm aware of the attraction I feel for Emi-lia, but I also know that it can't be, right now and maybe never."

"We're both grown-ups. We should be able to do whatever we want," Emilia griped.

"You *can* do whatever you want," Bernadette said as she leaned over the back seat, fanning her elbows out while leaning her chin on her hands. "You could pick up a bottle of vodka tomorrow and buy a bottle of painkillers, but you choose not to because you know the consequences and aren't willing to pay the cost. You two dating could also be unhealthy right now, but most important, it's now in the open and you can deal with it. I love you, Mosi. I was never the mother you needed and I guess I'm trying to make up for it, even though that's impossible. And I've learned to care for you as well, Emilia, even though we've only known each other for two months. You're a special young woman, so I'm mothering you as well. You both know how the other feels and what you need to do so you can talk about it," Bernadette said.

Mosi mumbled something under his breath.

"What was that?" Bernadette asked.

"Nothing."

Emilia chuckled. "It didn't sound like nothing."

"He knows it's the truth, that's why he's mumbling. He does that when he agrees but doesn't want to concede the point."

"Okay, I'll discuss it with Emilia if she's willing," Mosi said, speaking softly but clearly.

"Well yes, I guess we need to talk about it, then. Because I need to stay clean and sober for sure," Emilia said in what sounded like a thoughtful tone to Bernadette.

"Good, I'll enjoy Peru much better knowing you two are going to do what's best for yourselves, the group, and for *SMART*," Bernadette said with a grin neither could see.

When they arrived at the airport, Emilia hopped out to see if she could give Bernadette a hand. The International Drop-off zone was crazy and over-crowded with vehicles stopping helter-skelter, scooting in, and then trying to bull their way back out. By the time she got to the trunk, Mosi and Bernadette were already there. Mosi was hauling out a medium-sized suitcase and Bernadette was shouldering a daypack.

"Thank you, son," Bernadette said, gave Mosi a peck on the cheek, then spun to face Emilia and gave her what Emilia could only describe as a bear hug, then a light kiss on the cheek. "See you in three weeks," she said, then sprang onto the sidewalk and strode inside, hauling the burgundy suitcase behind.

"Let's get out of here!" Mosi called over the noise and bustle, then sprinted to the driver's side and jumped in. Emilia was seconds behind.

Emilia kept her peace. She had two specific reasons for this. The first was she wouldn't want Mosi to be distracted while wrangling his way out of the departure area and the second was she had no idea where to start the upcoming conversation. She'd barely been willing to admit to *herself* that she had feelings for Mosi, and in fact was sure those feelings were kept close and that she'd not allowed them to be seen. But even Bernadette knew. Whether or not Mosi had known before, he most certainly did now. *We really know how to deceive ourselves.* She remained quiet, hoping for Mosi to speak first. She really wanted to know what he thought.

In ten minutes, they were back on the freeway heading for White Rock. Still Mosi was quiet. She considered opening the conversation, but truly wanted to hear what came out of Mosi's mouth without any suggestions or input from her. Waiting became tedious to the point she decided to pull her earbuds from her purse and listen to some music on her phone. As she rummaged for them in her purse she realized how juvenile she was behaving. She slipped her fingers from the bag and turned in her seat to speak.

Mosi spoke first. "Sorry, I was waiting for you to talk first, but just now realized that was childish. I like to think I'm beyond that type of thinking, but it's clear I'm not."

"I was waiting for exactly the same thing. In fact, I was just rooting around in my purse for my earbuds when it struck me how silly I was acting."

"Good to know I'm not the only adult here that can act like a kid." Mosi gave her a wry grin as he glanced from the road.

"Most definitely true," Emilia said, with a shake of her head.

"How about I tell you a little bit and then you tell me a little?"

"Works for me." *I'm much more relaxed, but wouldn't exactly call it at ease.*

"This may sound really strange, but when I saw you at the hospital when you were still in withdrawal I thought you were beautiful."

"That's hard to believe." Emilia furrowed her brows.

"I can understand your skepticism. I don't understand it myself, though I've thought about it a lot. But even at that low moment of your life, there was some incomprehensible beauty about you. Anyone can see it now, but two months ago it was more hidden."

"I — don't know what to say."

"That's okay, it's still my turn." He grinned, turned to her and winked. Then he returned his attention to the road.

Emilia smiled back, lost for a moment in the power and depth of his smile.

"But I also knew I couldn't date you. You needed hospital care and then rehab at *Ellendale* and even now, you're very vulnerable and a bad romance could cause you to relapse. And I would be to blame. At least in part."

"Okay, I think I understand," she said as calmly as possible, but her mind was screaming, *No!* "At rehab they did caution those of us who were single to be very careful about dating until we were well established in our recovery." Emilia thought she sounded calm and almost normal. Mosi didn't seem to notice her inner turmoil.

"That's excellent advice. I went out with a woman who'd been sober for over a year when I only had a couple of months clean. It didn't last long and when she broke it off, I slipped and got pissed drunk. Happily it only lasted two days, but I was devastated by both the breakup and the fact I'd lapsed. If it wasn't for *SMART*, I think I would've relapsed," Mosi said with emotion.

"Did you ever slip again?"

"No, that was enough for me. After I got over the hangover, I realized how little I'd actually drunk. My body wasn't used to the amount of booze I used to pour into it and it didn't take as much to intoxicate me. I'm glad I made the decision never to drink again, because I know quite a few people who've slipped over the years and ended up in the hospital with alcohol poisoning. Some of them didn't make it."

"That's disturbing. I don't want to be one of them, especially not one that dies. So, you think it's too early for romance. How much is enough clean time before it's safe for me to date?"

"That's impossible to answer. Everyone's different. For some people two years isn't enough, for others, after a few months they're steady in their recovery and can easily withstand the pressures of a romantic relationship."

"Pressure of a romantic relationship? I can't say I ever thought of falling in love as being under pressure."

"Falling in love's easy." Mosi chuckled. "But yeah, maintaining a romantic relationship takes a lot of work and can be very stressful."

"If it's so stressful, maybe it's not worth the effort," Emilia said coldly and she frowned at the thought.

"I'm sure that's true sometimes, but many of the relationships we cherish are a lot of work and very stressful to maintain. An example, if I may?"

"That might be useful," Emilia said. *I really hate the path this conversation is headed.*

"I kept a relationship going with my mom for five years after I got clean."

"That's not a romance."

"True, but please give me a few minutes."

"Okay." She paused. "But I don't think it's relevant."

"I understand, but please be patient with me."

Emilia nodded and grimaced.

"So, when I got clean I wanted to fix my relationship with my mom. For five years, she was still abusing alcohol and other drugs, so it was tough to see her and to actually get to know her. For the most part she just wanted me to do things for her. I did get groceries and stuff like that, but I wouldn't bring her drugs or booze, which she usually wanted me to do. She'd say how I didn't love her and a *good* son would go to the liquor store for her and things like that. And it hurt me hearing her say those things even though I knew it was the drugs talking and not her. She did end up in the hospital quite a few times, and the last time, I didn't think she'd make it. Well, neither did she and that was the turning point. She went to rehab at *Ellendale* and eventually went back to work there. Even though it wasn't a romance, it was family and making it work was hard, almost as hard as getting clean myself. We had a lot of arguments over those years, but we came through in the end."

"I still don't see how that compares to falling in love and having a relationship. It's just not the same."

"It's not identical, no, but love is love. We have expectations in *all* of our relationships, but especially with the people we love. I really understand what you're saying, but with romance you add sex into the mix and that changes everything."

"I'm not trying to suggest all love is the same, just that there are similarities. Sex can bond couples, but it can also drive them apart," Mosi said, waving his right hand in the air like a windmill.

"I don't completely understand what you're saying," Emilia said, "but I have a friend, maybe *had* a friend before my addiction totally took over, whose husband was on some long-term meds that affected his libido so he was always tired and not interested in sex. It really upset her 'cause she wanted sex and he hardly ever felt like it."

"I know it can go both ways, but men tend to have higher sex drives, so that's more likely to be an issue."

"Yeah, and men not paying attention to what their partner wants and how to please her," Emilia said in a sardonic tone that brought a cheeky grin from Mosi.

"Yep," he said flippantly. "Love and sex are complicated and that's a good reason not to indulge in romance while you're in a vulnerable state like early recovery." Mosi glanced over at Emilia with a fleeting look she thought of as both knowing and sad.

"I understand—more or less—why I need to avoid a romance right now, but I do like you and appreciate all you've done for me. You and Doctor Reshma saved my life."

"I admit I've been attracted to you since I saw you at the hospital, and I think it must have been something I saw, sensed, or some other subconscious perception, because I saw beauty when you were in a very sad state."

"I sure was!"

"Having said that, there are two solid reasons we absolutely shouldn't date. The first and most obvious is you're very early in your recovery. You've said you agree with that."

"I didn't say I agree with it, just that I understand it. And,

I'm unwilling to put my recovery at risk. I've tried to quit so many times I gave up counting, but it never lasted more than a day or maybe thirty or thirty-five hours. When I went to your *SMART* meeting, I'd been clean three days and that was the longest I'd been sober."

"Now you have over two months."

"Yeah, and it feels good."

"So," continued Mosi, "the second reason we shouldn't date is because I'm your facilitator."

"What has that got to do with anything?"

"We simply can't know what might happen to others in the group. It could disrupt meetings, give a bad example to some who really want to be in a relationship, and because they saw *we* got together *they* could be willing to give it a go without thinking it through and slip or relapse. Does that make sense?"

"I understand what you're saying," she said, irked by the thought. She shook her head.

"But you don't believe it."

"It's not that I don't believe it, I just don't want to *accept* it." *Though I'm not actually sure if it's true or not. I'll do a* CBA. *The important thing right now's to stay clean.* "You act like it's so easy to say no to the things of the heart."

"You'd be mistaken if you thought it was easy for me to ignore my heart. However, I do have over ten years working the *SMART* tools and that does make it easier. But it's still not easy. Tell me, do you think it would be a good idea to date your doctor or teacher?"

" . . . Um, no, of course not." She wrinkled her brows as she spoke.

"Why not?" Mosi raised both brows.

"People who have power must also have high moral standards. They've been given a lot of power and we expect an especially high level of trustworthiness from them."

Emilia decided to be completely honest about her feelings and thoughts, so she spoke without hesitation before her courage failed. "I don't remember much about the first *SMART* meeting I attended, but I'll never forget your smile. It seemed to light up the room at a time when I was in the darkest moment of my life."

Mosi smiled, and she caught her breath.

"Then you came to see me every day while I was detoxing in the hospital. I got to know you, and every day my mind was clearer. I began to think about us becoming a couple, but knew you could have no interest in someone who had only been clean for a few days. I was hoping that in time we might, you know . . . get together, but you don't think that's a good idea because you'll be my facilitator." Emilia furrowed her brows, puckered her lips.

"It's a tough call, but it's safer for you right now anyway and while we can't foretell the future, there will never come a time when dating your facilitator would be a good idea."

Emilia looked at her feet and mumbled.

"Sorry, I didn't catch that," Mosi said.

"I said" — Emilia spoke up this time, but with a slight tremble in her voice — "that maybe we could be friends."

"I can think of a dozen reasons we shouldn't, but I believe there are many good arguments in favor, too," Mosi said with a grin. "We could get together for coffee or tea on Wednesday or Thursday if that works for you."

"As far as I know, that would be fine."

"Good. I'll text or call to make plans," Mosi said and gave her an earthy smile, which filled her stomach with butterflies.

After a few moments of silence, they arrived at Emilia's complex. Mosi stopped in front of the main entrance to let her out.

As she slipped the key into the deadbolt, she glanced over her shoulder and saw Mosi still waiting at the curb. She waved and stepped inside. She looked back again to see Mosi pulling away. *He must have been watching out for me. Very sweet.*

As soon as Emilia was safe inside her complex, Mosi pulled away. He took a long, slow, deep, breath. *Am I doing the right thing? Is this just as bad as dating her?* Mosi sighed and shook his head. *I'm convincing myself this is all to keep her safe from relapse, but damn it, I want to be with her.* She was the one who suggested they be friends and the more he thought about it, the more he liked the idea. He'd be able to spend time with her, and get close, yet remain aloof enough to cause her no harm or to relapse. So, that was what he'd do. He knew it would be tricky as he felt a primeval attraction to Emilia. While she was now stunningly beautiful, he'd felt that pull even while she was at her worst, so was certain it was more than her looks that held him and he wanted to know why.

I always want to know why.

Chapter Sixteen

"Good morning, Mister El-Hadidy," Caroline said, without looking up from the computer screen.

"Hi, Caroline," he said. "Anything I need to know?"

"Several things. They're in your inbox. I forwarded the important communications to your private email. Number one on the list is a *note* from the Minister of Health. Another is regarding your ten o'clock appointment with the Vancouver School Board Chairperson. She's going to be ten minutes late on account of traffic and hopes it's all right. I told her you'd work around her tardiness."

"That's perfect, thanks, Caroline. It'd be crazy hard to replace you. It's even tough when you go on holidays, in spite of the fact you leave detailed schedules and information for your temp."

Caroline smiled at him. "I'm glad I can be of help. Your work is very important to the province and our country."

"Yes, Caroline, it *is* important, and you make my job much easier."

"Thank you, sir." Caroline's eyes sparkled with joy. "I confess I'm pleased to work for you these past years. Your predecessor was overly conservative and mostly thought of this position as a job, but you see it as an opportunity to help people and I appreciate that. It makes me proud of my work."

Mosi gave her a grateful smile. "Thanks again. I'll catch up on my messages and calls. Please bring Miss Templeton in as soon as she arrives."

"Of course, Mister El-Hadidy," Caroline replied with a

nod.

Mosi checked his email, with particular attention to the ones forwarded by his receptionist. On the top of the list he'd formed in his mind after scouring his inbox, was the one from the Minister of Health.

Mosi opened that one first.

Dear Mr. El-Hadidy,
I hope this email finds you well.
Regarding the matter we discussed privately last week, I can say I have more information, which might be useful for our combined efforts. In your inbox, you should find several emails from a JD Langdon. Attached to them are documents you will find useful to our joint cause.
I would recommend saving the attached files to a secure USB flash drive or to a memory card.
Please delete this email after you've read it and then empty your computer's trash.
Regards,
Marion Dubois.

Mosi searched for emails from JD Langdon to no avail and wondered for some moments where they might be. It then occurred to him that it was unlikely Caroline had forwarded them to him. Feeling a need to *do* something, he got up and went into the reception area rather than email, call or text his receptionist.

"Excuse me, Caroline, I'm looking for some emails from a JD Langdon."

Caroline looked up from her workstation and raised her brows.

She's probably wondering why I didn't call or text.

"I'll look, sir," she said, with some apparent confusion. "Yes, here they are. I didn't forward them, as I had no idea they were important. I planned to look at them later this morning — okay, I've sent them to your inbox. Did you want me to forward anything else before I've checked it?"

"No, Caroline, that's good.

Mosi had felt there was little that could surprise him in politics, but when he opened the mail from JD Langdon, his shock was total. The attached documents showed the Premier had accepted large amounts of money from church organizations. To all appearances the money was being funneled into private bank accounts, not the Premier's political party's accounts. If this was true, which as of yet Mosi had insufficient evidence, it could indeed bring the leader of the province down.

The only thing he'd discovered through various searches on the Internet on JD Langdon was a ghost. There was most certainly no person in British Columbia politics or anyone in public service here in the province that he could find.

He was still working on who this source was when Caroline buzzed him on the intercom to let him know his first appointment of the day was here.

The door to Mosi's office opened and Caroline ushered in a well-kept woman of perhaps fifty years old. Her hair was bobbed at her shoulders, was thick and straight with two distinct shades of gray, which could have been real or highlights, Mosi thought. Her black dress was well-fitted to her body without being tight and hung two inches below her knees. It had short sleeves with a modest neckline, which somewhat minimized the size of her substantial bosom. Mosi approved as, in his experience, her attire generally spoke of a woman who depended on her mental faculties rather than sex appeal to do business.

"Good morning, Miss Templeton," Mosi said with his

warmest smile.

"Good morning, Mister El-Hadidy," she replied in a tight voice and downturned lips.

Mosi intuitively realized that Ms. Julie Templeton was onto his smile and was fighting the attraction most women felt when he used it. That didn't bother Mosi in the least, as that simply meant he was correct in his supposition he was deal-ing with an intelligent thoughtful woman and that could only be good. His plans for the schools were ones based on science and reason, so it would be best for his plans to deal with a thoughtful individual. Mosi's smile changed to his *real* smile, the one he used without affectation, the one he preferred to use.

"Can I get you tea or coffee?" he asked.

"No, but I wouldn't mind a glass of water," she said as she followed him to the comfortable chairs by the window over-looking the sea.

They made small talk until Caroline brought in two glasses of water and a small bunch of grapes.

"Thank you so much for coming. I hope you find your trip more than worthwhile," Mosi said, this time with sincerity in his smile.

Ms. Julie Templeton's shoulders slumped and Mosi knew at that moment he had a good chance to forward his agenda. It was a plan—he believed—that would benefit school kids under the Vancouver school board's jurisdiction and *might* be an example to all local school boards in BC and across Can-ada.

Ms. Templeton took a small sip of water, put the glass down on the coffee table in front of her. She eyed the grapes, but didn't take any. She returned her gaze to Mosi.

"Your email was tantalizing and I'm interested to know more, however, I warn you the Board has a limited budget and we can't afford to add costly programs outside of the regular curriculum."

"I can certainly understand your problem, Miss Templeton, and I may have a solution to your cost issues as well. But let me begin by explaining what we would like to offer your school district and why."

Julie slid to the edge of her seat, put her hands on her lap and looked intensely at Mosi. He kept the smile off his face, but was pleased he had her rapt attention.

"We have tools based on *Rational Emotive Behavioral Therapy* and *Cognitive Therapy* we'd like to give the kids a chance to learn."

"And what benefit would children get from this type of therapy?" she asked.

"They wouldn't actually be taking therapy, but learning cognitive tools to help them make good decisions. These tools help many people change the way they look at themselves, others, and the world."

"Of what use could that possibly be in a child's education?"

"That's a reasonable question and one answer is if a person is at peace with themselves, accepting of others and of the crap life throws at them, they will tend to find it easier to concentrate and to get along with others."

"That's one answer you said. What other benefits might there be?" Ms. Templeton asked.

"If one is mentally at peace, there's a better chance they will be a better student. Perhaps it would be better to say they could be the best they can be," Mosi said, with a sincere smile, as he, too, leaned toward his guest.

"Okay, that makes sense. So what kinds of *tools* do you offer them?"

"We would teach them how to do a *Cost Benefit Analysis*, for starters. This tool can even be used to make simple decisions like *should I do my homework* to *where should I go to college."*

"Or *should our company build this skyscraper in downtown New York,"* Ms. Templeton said. "Yes, this is a well-known tool in the business world and industry. It never occurred to me that it could be used in such a way. My curiosity's piqued."

"Good. Another tool would be *Disputing Irrational Beliefs."*

"Like—"

"Like my girlfriend dumped me, so I must be no good or unlovable or a bad person. I didn't get an A on this test, so I must be stupid."

"Unfortunately, many children think exactly that way," she said.

"Yes," Mosi agreed. "And it's not only kids. That's why it's good to teach them these skills when they're young so they can use them both now and for the rest of their life."

"Okay, I'll bite, but how do you get people to make these changes?"

"How does a baseball pitcher learn to throw a curve ball?"

"They would take instructions and then practice a lot, I imagine," she said, lifting her right hand palm up.

"*Exactly,*" Mosi said in triumph and with a warm authentic smile. "We'll teach them these skills and then they can practice them. Another example of an irrational belief might be *if I don't drink at this party everyone'll think I'm not cool.* To dispute that, I can remember that at other parties not everyone drank. Or some people acted as designated drivers and I could do that. Another way to dispute that *IB* might be many cool people choose not to drink to be better at sports or get better grades."

"It sounds a little simplistic."

"You mean like throwing hundreds of baseballs every day to improve your skills?"

"I don't think it's the same thing," Ms. Templeton said.

"What's the difference?"

"I'm not sure."

"When you repeat anything over and over, whether it's running, throwing a ball, shooting a puck or disputing irrational beliefs, you get better at it. It's how our brains work. As a member of the school board you actually know that."

"I suppose you're right, after you explain it like that. It certainly could be worth an experiment. But remember, we have no extra money in the budget to hire or train staff to teach this."

"I understand, but given the opioid crisis, *CCSA* presently has funds available to pay teachers both to take the training course and to instruct students, either during free periods or after school hours."

"You're making this all very easy, but I'm not sure how you can justify using funds dedicated to reducing the opioid crisis to teach kids these skills."

"That" — Mosi grinned — "is the easy part. You see, these are the same skills used to help people addicted to drugs, *including opioids*, as well as other addictive behaviors like gambling, to change their lives. My plan is to teach young people those same skills so they never become addicted in the first place, or if they do, to be able to recognize it early on and free themselves or get help."

"That is cleverly devious."

"I'm not quite sure how to take that."

"I prefer you take it as complement."

"I'll do my best," he said, tapping his chin with his forefinger.

Ms. Templeton stood and extended her hand.

Mosi took it and she gave him a handshake with a firm grip.

"I'll have my staff send you a contract and we will see if we can work this out," Ms. Templeton said.

"Oh, we'll make it work, that we will." Mosi smiled.

CHAPTER SEVENTEEN

Emilia's cell phone rang and she slid her finger across the button on the screen to answer the call. It was Doris.

"Hi, Doris."

"Hi," Doris said, in a strange tone of voice.

"Doris, are you all right? You don't sound well."

"My husband and I had a fight. He drove off to . . . who knows where. This is the first time we've fought since I've been clean. The truth is, Emilia, I feel triggered and I was wondering if maybe we could have coffee or something. I just need someone to talk to. I want a drink so badly right now," Doris said in a strangled voice.

"Yeah, no problem," Emilia said without hesitation. *I want to be there for her.* "Where would you like to meet?"

"There's a little coffee shop on top of the hill called the *Pelican Rouge*. It's close to both of us and they're open 'til nine, if that works for you."

"That works for me, I can be there in ten minutes."

"Great, I'll see you there."

Eight minutes later, Emilia strode through the doors of the coffee shop. As she didn't see Doris, she went to the counter and ordered two cups of *Earl Grey* tea. She already knew Doris enough to know she wouldn't want coffee this late in the evening. As she stood in the short lineup, Doris arrived. She pushed at the door then turned away, but turned around again and shoved it open. *She looks like she needs a smile.* She smiled and waved to her from where she stood to show her new friend the affection she felt she needed.

Doris smiled back, though it was a simple, and tentative upturn of the lips.

Emilia motioned for Doris to sit while she waited for the tea, then gathered the two ceramic cups and went to sit with her.

Doris wrapped her hands around her cup and closed her eyes. "Thanks," she said.

"It was nothing," Emilia replied with a nonchalant wave at the cup as she slipped into a chair across from Doris.

"No, not that, for coming to meet me."

Emilia gave her another warm smile. "I'll always be here for you. I'm worried about you. I've only been clean for around two months and already I know of several people who've relapsed."

"I don't want to be one of them."

"Me neither."

Doris looked Emilia in the eye. "One of the things Mosi has pounded into us is the importance of staying connected. I always thought of connections as something fun or *SMART* meetings and things like that, but right now, I know if I didn't have this connection with you, I'd be at the liquor store at this very moment."

"I understand. When I was in *Ellendale* I would have relapsed a few times if it wasn't for the support of others."

"Yeah," Doris agreed. "But abstinence sucks."

"But not as much as the alternative."

"Damn right about that." Doris shook her head, then took a sip of her tea. "I don't want to go back to where I was. I'd virtually lost my family. I wasn't even allowed to see my own grandkids and my husband was about to leave. And now I'm not sure if he's going to stay anyway."

"Whatever happens, you'll be able to deal with it better sober. You know that."

"Yeah, I do, but God damn it, we've been married forty-five years. He was my childhood sweetheart for God's sake. I've never been with another man and I honestly don't want to be. I just want my Blake."

It occurred to Emilia that if Blake didn't return or ended their marriage, it might mean relapse for Doris. Unsure if it was the best thing to say, she forged ahead, deciding to go with her gut. "What will you do if he divorces you?"

"I'll . . . kill him and then myself!"

"Really? What about your children and grandchildren?"

"No, I couldn't do it. I couldn't kill their dad and grandpa, but damn it, I'd feel like it." Doris sighed as she squirmed in her seat.

"You'd live through it. You'd make it and start a new life. That's what you'd do."

Doris sighed. "Yeah, I'd make it. I just don't want to have to."

"I didn't want to have to quit using booze and oxy, but I did it because it was the best for me."

"I really do feel better," Doris said. "I feel safe. I'm not going to lapse or relapse. At least not tonight." She gave Emilia a forced chuckle.

Doris' cell rang and she dug around in her purse for it but took too long and she missed the call. She checked the phone log. "It was Blake. I'm scared as hell to find out what he wants, but I'm going to call him right back and find out. I'd appreciate it if you stayed while I call. I could use the moral support about now."

"Of course I'll stay."

Doris' finger shook and she wasn't certain she could touch the button to call Blake. It was like she was in withdrawal again. She forced her finger to be steady—almost steady—and pushed the green phone icon. A few seconds later she heard his phone ring. Blake picked up on the second ring.

"Thank God you called back, I thought for sure you didn't answer the phone on purpose. You didn't did you?" he asked.

"No, I missed the call 'cause my phone was at the bottom of my purse. Sorry about that."

"It's okay, I'm just happy you picked up. Where are you? You didn't answer our home number."

"I'm at the *Pelican Rouge* with Emilia, the young woman whose house I helped to clean."

"Oh, good. I thought I might've pushed you over the edge."

"I *was* triggered but met up with Emilia instead and we've been talking."

"I'm really sorry. I've been thinking about what I said and well—why I said it I guess. The thing is, I'd gotten used to taking care of you and cleaning up after you when you were drunk. I know it sounds stupid, but I guess I felt like you didn't need me now, 'cause you can do it all on your own."

"But I *do* need you. You're my guy, the love of my life. I want to be with you and *do* things with you. I want us to be fabulous grandparents. I want it all," she said.

"I think I'm afraid because you're becoming the woman I fell in love with and I'm falling for you all over again. I don't want to be hurt again."

"You and your love are too important to me now. I didn't realize how much I'd hurt you and the kids. But now I understand and that is all the motivation I need to stay sober."

"I love you, Doris."

"I love you, too, my dearest Blake."

"I'm at Jen's place. I'll be home in fifteen minutes. Do you want me to pick you up?"

"No, I'm good. I want to walk home and get some fresh air."

"Okay, love. Bye."

"Bye, dearest. We'll talk some more when we get home."

"Well," Doris said after she hung up. "That went very well. I think we'll be able to work things out. He's just over at our oldest daughter's place and coming right home. I should get going. I can't tell you how much I appreciate you meeting me. I really needed that connection."

"I'm glad for you," Emilia said with a compassionate smile. "I could use an early night myself. I thought I might try some meditation before I go to bed. It seemed to help center me when I was in rehab."

"Thanks again," Doris said.

Emilia hugged her. They left the coffee shop, and parted ways.

"Good morning, Emilia," Mr. Douglas said with his head stuck in the doorway to her office. "I saw my brother last night. He said he was very impressed with the *SMART* meeting he went to the other night. He's been clean since that night. It's been a while since he hasn't smoked crack unless he was out of money or in jail. I hope it works for him."

Emilia thought for a moment about some of the things she'd learned at *Ellendale*. "Mister Douglas, from what I've been taught, crack is a very insidious drug and very hard to quit. According to the best studies, most addicted individuals slip several times on their journey to living addiction-free."

"Are you saying I should just tell him it's okay if he uses again?"

"I'm not an expert in this, but from what I understand, if he does slip, it would be more helpful to point out that he had been clean for X amount of days and you have confidence he could continue to stay clean. I remember while I was at *Ellendale*, one lady slipped and when she told the group about it, the group leader asked what had triggered her and helped to figure out how to avoid that trigger in the future rather than condemn her."

"So, this group leader showed the lady that lapsed how to use the slip as a stepping stone instead of putting her down," Mr. Douglas said, rubbing his shaven chin with thumb and forefinger.

"Yes, that's exactly it. You've explained it better than I could." Emilia gave him a cheerful grin.

"It's just what I understood from what you explained."

"That's also what *SMART* teaches. It's just the facts. Not that slipping is good, but it's common, and I can use it to prevent further lapses rather than beat myself up over it."

"I've always berated him when he used. Maybe I wasn't helping," Mr. Douglas said.

"Probably not, but I'm not an expert. I know when my family refused to see me or even talk to me I'd use drugs and alcohol to forget the pain of that rejection. So, for me at least, it didn't help. I think Mosi said there's a *Family and Friends SMART* meeting locally. They'd have more and I'm sure better information for you," Emilia said, as she twirled a black lock of hair between thumb and forefinger.

"Thanks, I'll look into that. I do want to see him get better."

"I'll get you that information."

Mr. Douglas nodded, gave her a sad smile and left her to work.

Tonight was Monday and it was Emilia's second *SMART* meeting since she'd gotten out of rehab. She was looking forward to it for a number of reasons, one of which without a doubt was to see Mosi. But there were others she wanted to see, including her new friend Doris and to get to know Anne from *Ellendale* better. She also hoped to discover if Steve

Douglas had been able to maintain abstinence from crack cocaine. In addition she found Josh's two years of abstinence an encouragement. She *needed* to stay connected in order to remain clean, but she also delighted in the 1-1/2 hour meetings. It was a place one could be completely open and share both the best and worst of one's week. It was a place where even men opened themselves up and bared their souls. It was unlike anything she'd experienced in her life outside of rehab, which had been all women at any rate.

She'd cancelled her car insurance when she went into rehab. Money was still scarce and she considered the car a luxury rather than a necessity so she still hadn't insured it. Work was a five-minute bus ride from the bus stop, which was a block from where she lived. Doris lived within easy walking distance and even the *SMART* meeting was fifteen minutes from her condo afoot. The walking was healthy and she continued to run in the mornings. That was now done on the beach a few blocks from home. Running on the beach turned out to be much harder than on the hard-packed paths she'd used while at *Ellendale*. The sand dragged at her feet and it took a lot of extra effort, but it was worth it, as with the exercise, good diet, and total lack of booze and oxycodone, she was feeling better and stronger all the time. And she'd put on weight as well, though she was still severely under what the doctors told her was healthy for her body type and height. At least she wasn't skeletal anymore.

Showered and dressed-down to jeans and a three-quarter sleeve printed top with a modest neckline, she put on lip liner and called herself ready to go. The short walk to *Sources* was heady with an offshore breeze bringing the scent of the sea and her body feeling stronger and her mind clearer every day.

CHAPTER EIGHTEEN

Doris was already at the *SMART* meeting when she arrived. They hugged and then Emilia sat with her. Mosi was chatting with Josh but stopped when she arrived and gave her a smile.

"How are you feeling, Emilia? Doris?" he asked.

"I'm good," Doris replied.

"I'm doing really well," Emilia said with a warm smile for everyone there, but in particular for Mosi.

More people came in, including Anne, who she waved over and patted the empty chair next to her. Anne grinned and strode over and sat. The three women chatted about their day while they waited for the clock to roll around to seven.

"I love your hair," Anne said to her. "Is that slight curl natural?"

"Yeah," she answered, "and it usually gives me the devil of a time in the morning."

Doris and Anne both chuckled, and Anne said, "My three girls would kill for curls like that."

"I'm good with that as long as it's not me they target," Emilia said with a straight face.

The other two ladies laughed.

"Can I get in on the fun?" a familiar voice asked.

All three of them looked up, Emilia noticed. It was the young woman with pink and blue hair, who Emilia recognized as Miranda and thought was a regular.

"You certainly may," Doris said without a moment's hesitation.

"Thanks," she said with a twinkle in her eye and a soft smile on her lips as her cheeks dimpled.

"Thanks for coming, everyone. It's time to start. I'm Mosi your facilitator this evening. This is an open meeting of *SMART Recovery . . .*"

When he finished the introduction, he opened the meeting for check-in. He pointed to his right. "Can you start for us tonight, Charles?"

"Yeah, whatever," Charles said in a tone that sounded like disgust to Emilia.

She glanced over at Anne, who rolled her eyes.

"Four weeks without a drink," he began. "I'm not really happy about that, but my lawyer said it's best if I expect any kind of leniency from the court, *and* my old man's got someone checking me out at irregular times to see if he can catch me drinking. But I'm staying clean, at least until this whole thing blows over." He shrugged.

Mosi nodded to the next person in the circle.

"Hi, everyone, I'm Caryn and I've got almost four months clean under my belt now. I still get triggered when I pass the alley where I'd meet my dealer. I couldn't get enough prescription drugs to feed my addiction, so I'd buy them on the street, too. I used alcohol 'cause it enhanced the effect of the oxycodone, and I still want to go into the liquor store every time I pass one. For now at least, I'm avoiding going near that alley and near liquor stores. It's helped some I think."

Mr. Douglas' brother was next.

"I'm Steve, and I've made it a whole week without using crack. I can't remember when I went that long without a pipe."

"How're you managing to stay clean?" Mosi asked.

"Well, one of the biggest triggers for me is money. If I have it, I'm gonna buy a rock, so I followed your suggestion, Mosi, and found someone to handle my money for me. My brother's the one helping me there and the honest to God truth is, if I'd had the cash in hand or access to my bank account, I would've used for sure by now. He really surprised me with how much shit he's willing to put up with to help keep me from using.

"Oh, and by the way, he asked about where there was a *SMART Family and Friends* meeting around here. He's really backing me up and trying to find out *why* I use. I'm really lucky to have a brother like him and you know, I wanna make him proud."

"I'm Cam," the tall lanky man Emilia remembered said, though his name had escaped her.

"Gotta year behind me last Friday. Never thought I'd go that long without a drink. Thing was, there was a big temptation to *just have one*, to celebrate, ya know. But I remembered Mosi's drawing and how that old pathway would light right up and I figured it'd be no time and I'd be back where a was a year ago. Playin' it forward, I think you call it, Mosi."

"Yes, that's right." Mosi smiled and nodded to the next person.

Three more checked in and then it was Miranda's turn.

"Had another friend die of an overdose last week. Well to be fair, she wasn't a close friend, but we'd gone to rehab together, so we had that bond. She hadn't used in months but scored some pills. We think it was fentanyl, 'cause she was gone before the paramedics got there. It reminds me how vulnerable I am right now as I haven't used in months, so I'd OD for sure, 'cause my body's not used to the stuff like it used to be and I never used fentanyl anyway, but now it's in everything. Or at least it seems that way. Helps to keep me clean for sure."

"That's right, Miranda. When we begin to abstain from our drug of choice, our bodies start to heal. This also means we become more susceptible to overdose as our bodies lose their tolerance. I'm pleased and proud of your understanding of this problem," Mosi said.

"It's all your fault I know about this." Miranda grinned.

There were chuckles around the tables.

"I'm Doris. Had a bit of a bad week. My husband and I had a fight and it really triggered me. My brain kept saying *fuck it, I might as well get drunk*, but I held on and instead called Emilia here and we got together for coffee. That got me over the hump and I didn't have a drink. Blake called while Emilia and I were talking and we sorta' made up. That night we talked until late and decided we needed to go for couple's counseling. We start here at *Sources* this Thursday."

"Good for you, Doris!" Mosi said and clapped. The others joined in.

"I'm Emilia and I had a pretty good week. I found that being there for Doris gave me a real dopamine boost and it felt good. I still have lots of triggers and think I'll follow Caryn's example and try to avoid all the ones I can, and if I can't I'll call Doris or somebody. That worked for Doris and I'll try those things myself. Another thing I want to do is get the confidence of my family back. I'm not sure how to go about it or even if it's too soon, but I really want them back in my life."

"What if you can't get some of them back? What'll you do then? Do you have a plan so you won't relapse?" Mosi asked.

"No, I hadn't thought about that," Emilia said.

"Always good to have a plan," Josh said. "Try to prepare for the worst and hope for the best."

"Yeah, that's a great idea," she said. "I'll see what I come up with." *It just hurts so bad not to be with them, to talk to them.*

"I'm Anne, and I had a pretty good week. This time rehab seems to have taken. There are temptations, cravings and triggers, but now I have actual tools to keep me from using. I'm going to volunteer at the *Food Bank* starting tomorrow and then again on Fridays, so that'll be two days a week I'll be busy. I'm also walking a lot. I found when I was at *Ellendale* that if I felt a craving, a walk helped to take off the edge. That's working, too. The only thing missing is staying more connected. For me at this stage of my recovery, getting together once a week isn't enough, so I thought I'd see if maybe Emilia, Doris, and Miranda might like to get together for tea and chit-chat a couple of nights a week. Maybe Caryn, too?"

"I'd be happy to join with that group," Charles said with a smirk.

"Only if you're gay," Miranda growled.

There was laughter around the tables and Charles reddened. It looked like he was about to get up and, Emilia thought, perhaps leave, but he settled back into his chair with an unhappy glare for Miranda.

Finally, there was a small, short, very slender man who Emilia didn't recall seeing before.

"I'm Michael," he began. "I've been in *Narcotics Anonymous* and *Gambler's Anonymous* for years, but haven't ever been able to stop gambling and snortin' coke. I just started counseling 'cause I needed to try somethin' different and Raj, my counselor, told me about the *SMART* meetings here and I figured it sure as hell couldn't do me any harm. I lost my house, my wife and my kids as well as most of my friends 'cause I borrowed from anyone who was foolish enough to loan me money. I'll never get my life back, but if I can get clean and stop the gambling, I hope to at least get close to my kids again."

Mosi listened to each check-in intently, as he always did, for this was the time he decided which tool to go over with the group or if pure crosstalk would be more valuable. There were a number of indicators as they went around the room, but when Emilia checked in he lost track of his thoughts as she filled his world and pushed everything else into a tiny compartment in his brain that was aware of the other things happening, but barely, as he concentrated on every word that sallied from her lips. Happily he came to himself again when Anne spoke. Then the new participant checked-in, which confirmed in his mind what he'd already decided. He'd do what he knew many facilitators considered to be the most complex tool in *SMART*. It was the very one *SMART Recovery* was based on. Mosi would do an *ABC* with the group.

Mosi gathered three colored erasable markers, dropped them into his shirt pocket, stood and stepped to the whiteboard. He printed the letters *A, B, C, D, E* in large caps spread across the length of the whiteboard, then divided each letter into columns.

"Okay, some of you have done this with me before. What does A stand for?" he asked.

"Activating event."

"Good." He nodded. "What about B?"

"Beliefs, in particular, irrational beliefs."

"Right again, thanks, Cam. And C?"

"Consequences."

"Now, this may seem counterintuitive, but we're going to start here at the consequences. Can anyone, besides Josh, tell me why?"

"This is a new tool to me," Caryn said, "but I suspect if there was an activating event when I was using, my mind would blur through the irrational beliefs so fast I wouldn't even realize it and I'd be pulling into a liquor store without thinking about it."

"That's exactly right, Caryn. You've been paying attention." Mosi gave her a warm smile. "A and B happen very fast. Remember, our addiction is directly connected to our pleasure center, which is part of our limbic system, that we often call the *Lizard Brain*. Can anyone tell me why we call it that?"

"It's very old," Josh said. "Our limbic system evolved from the earliest types of brains and it helps us react without having to think about something, like eating, breathing or getting the hell out of the way if we're about to be hit by a bus."

"Right," Mosi said. "So we had a behavior that gave us pleasure and it became habitual. For me, as an example, when I was sad, I used, or to celebrate, I used, if I had a problem, I used so I'd forget about it for a while. Whatever I needed, my go-to method was drugs and alcohol. That neuropathway I'd formed in my limbic system became automatic. So, for consequences here we'll use the example of using, or gambling, whatever our unwanted behavior is or was."

Under C, Mosi printed *use or gamble* in caps, and then explained. "When you use this tool, it won't be as it's happening, it'll be before, like we're doing now, or after the fact, to figure out what went wrong. The plan is to slow down that virtually instant process from the time we were triggered until the time we used, so we can change the way our brain reacts. It takes a lot of time, patience, and practice. It's a lot of work, but remember, you're worth the effort.

"So," he continued. "What was the trigger, the *activating event*?"

"I woke up," Steve said.

This caused many chuckles and not a few nods of agreement.

Mosi also laughed. "I remember feeling that way, too, Steve, but let's use something more concrete for our example. Anyone else?"

"Boredom," Michael said.

"Okay, so that's our activating event," Mosi said. "Does anyone know what the number one cause of relapse is?" Mosi asked.

"Boredom?" Emilia suggested.

Mosi smiled and touched his nose with his forefinger.

"Bingo, you got it." He then wrote *boredom* in capital letters under A, for activating event. Mosi pointed at B. "What thoughts might have been going through my mind at that moment?" He wrote the answers down as they were given.

"I'll just have one," Josh began.

Others nodded knowingly.

"No one will know."

"I can't stand the boredom, I need that drink."

"I'll die if I don't light a pipe *right now*," Steve said.

"It's not fair for me to be bored, I shouldn't have to be."

"I've already lost everything," Steve said poignantly. "I might as well gamble. What do I have to lose? And at least I'll feel better."

"Okay, we'll stop there," Mosi said after several more suggestions, "or we'll never get out of here on time." He grinned. "So, what does the D stand for?"

Josh made a zipping motion over his lips and smiled. Mosi smiled back and nodded.

"According to the *SMART* Handbook, the D stands for disputing, as in disputing irrational beliefs," Anne said.

"Correct. So, the question is how do we go about disputing our irrational beliefs?"

"I read that but I can't remember," Cam said.

Josh raised his eyebrows. Mosi smiled but shook his head and continued to scan the group around the tables. After several long seconds, Doris spoke up.

"In many cases, you can turn a statement into a question."

"Sure, could you give us an example, Doris?" Mosi asked.

"Um, well the first one might be something like *will I just have one?*"

"Good," Mosi said. "How would *you* answer that, Josh?"

"For me, there's no evidence to support *I'd just have one*. My history is *I'd drink 'til I passed out*," Josh said.

A number of the others nodded.

"For the second one?"

Emilia answered without a moment's hesitation. "*Will* no one know? I always thought I was hiding it before, but everybody knew and even if I was really able to hide it, I'd know."

"Excellent. Number three?"

"Can't I stand the boredom, do I really need that drink?" Miranda said. "I mean there've been lots of times I was bored and didn't use, so I really don't *need* that drink, or crack or smack or whatever."

"Thanks for being so drug inclusive." Mosi teased her with a droll grin. "Next?"

"Will I die if I don't light up a crack pipe right now?" Steve answered his own irrational belief. "In fact, I know for sure I won't because there were lots of times I craved a rock, but didn't have any money. And dealers aren't known for their generosity."

"Well spoken," Mosi said. "How about the next one?"

"I think this one's a little different," Miranda said. "It may *not* be fair to be bored, but in life, shit happens. Like when my friend died last week or a few weeks ago when my best bud OD'd and I found him dead. None of those things are fair, but good things and bad things happen to everybody, so we just have to accept that life's not fair sometimes. In *SMART* we call it *Unconditional Life Acceptance.*"

"Thank you, Miranda. You've figured out something very profound at a very young age. Good for you," Mosi said. "Miranda understood, that a belief might be true, but if it's dysfunctional, it's irrational because it's unhelpful. How about the next one? *I'm an addict anyway so what the fuck?*"

"If I may?" Josh asked.

Mosi nodded and gave him a smile.

"In *SMART*, we avoid the use of labels like addict, crackhead, or junkie as they're not useful in recovery. In fact, they're often harmful. I'm a father and I can't undo that, it's part of who I am, so if I'm an addict, it also becomes part of who and what I am. In the minds of many that can lead to a sense of helplessness and stigmatization. Rather, we like to think of each individual as a good person, who has a substance abuse or behavioral problem. *SMART empowers* us to change our problematic behaviors by giving us tools, like the *ABCs* we're going over right now. These tools, through hard work and persistence, help us to change the way we think, which in essence, creates new neuropathways in our brain. That leads to changing how we feel, which can ultimately modify our behavior, which of course, is our goal in coming to *SMART* in the first place."

"Eloquently put," Mosi said. "Does that make sense to everyone?"

As Mosi saw no confused looks, he forged ahead. "How about this one." He pointed at the whiteboard and read. "*No one understands me, so I might as well use.*"

"Are there people who understand me?" one of the men who'd not spoken until now said.

"That seems like a no-brainer," Emilia blurted. "I mean virtually everyone here understands what the others are going through. I've never had an addiction to gambling like Michael, but I was every bit as overpowered by the oxy and booze as he was by gambling, so I get it. Anyway, that's how I'd dispute that belief."

Others nodded in agreement and Mosi smiled.

"As that last one was mine, I'd like to take a stab at refuting it, though I might need some help," Michael said. "Have I really lost everything? What things do I have left to lose? Will I feel better?

"So actually, my kids still love me, but they're angry with me for gambling so much we lost the house. It's possible to win them back if I prove I've really changed, at least I hope so."

"You're also still alive," Cam said. "So there's still hope.

And being alive is something for sure. Look at Miranda's friends who died from overdoses. There's no hope for them. I suggest you can add being alive as a reason to change."

"Yeah, I hadn't thought of it like that. Thanks, ah—Cam was it?" Michael asked.

"Yep, Cam's my name."

"Will I feel better?" Mosi read off the board, bringing the attention back to the tool.

"I'll feel a little better *while* I'm gambling, but as soon as I'm done I always feel guilty, and that's usually when I try to scare up some cash for coke, but then when I come down, I feel more guilty than ever," Michael said.

"Thanks for that, Michael. Now, what does the E stand for?" Mosi asked the group. No one answered so he nodded to Josh.

"Effective New Belief and Emotional Consequence," Josh said by rote.

"After disputing the irrational beliefs, what is the new belief?" Mosi asked.

Caryn said, "There's things I can do to battle boredom, like go to *SMART* meetings and visit with others in recovery, so one new consequence is I can battle the boredom."

"Another new belief, for me at least, is sometimes I'm just bored and that's life. I can live with it without picking up," Cam said. "Oh, and it won't last forever." He grinned at the others.

"How about the *New Emotional Consequence*?" Mosi asked.

"I'd rather not feel bored, but sometimes it just happens. I can surf it, find something to do, visit with family or friends, but it will pass just like everything does whether good or bad, so I can choose not to let it get to me," Doris said.

Mosi led them through checkout and only Charles was bored and negative. *What can I expect? He's here by coercion.*

CHAPTER NINETEEN

Tuesday after work Emilia went through her normal routine. Routines were good, especially new routines that helped her avoid thoughts of getting drunk and high. She'd learned that at *Ellendale*.

When she was done with her chores and had put on a small load of laundry, she sat at her computer. Her fingers hovered over the keyboard, but rather than type in the *SMART Recovery* website as she'd planned, her mind wandered back to the recovery meeting last night.

Charles had hit on her again after the meeting, and the only thing that had stopped him was when Cam, Steve, and Michael had rushed over when it became clear Charles wasn't taking *no* for an answer. Mosi had watched, but had been occupied with Doris who had a question relating to the *ABC* tool they'd gone over during the meeting according to what she'd told her. When Mosi was finished talking to Doris, he'd also come over.

"Is Charles still pestering you?" he asked in *sotto voce*.

"Yeah, but he finally left when Steve, Michael, and Cam *requested* he not bother me."

"Good, I'm glad others are defending you. That'll make your life a bit easier."

"Yeah, it was a relief for sure."

"If he continues, I may have to ban him from the meeting."

"I wouldn't want to be the cause of him not being able to attend the meetings."

"You wouldn't be. His bad behavior would be the reason."

Mosi gave her a soft stare. "Would you like to do coffee one Wednesday after work?"

"That'd be great."

"I'd like to invite the other ladies you plan to meet with as well," Mosi said.

"That would be nice," she said. *I'd rather have him to myself, but that's not to be. Certainly not this early in my recovery.* It was also good because she felt particularly triggered by the stress at work and her decision to try to work things out with her family.

What Emilia really wanted was to talk to her dad, but had decided the best person she could discuss it with was Sissy, her oldest sister. Sissy was eight years older than Emilia and the oldest of the three siblings. Her brother was two years older than she, and both of them had looked up to Sissy almost like a second mother. Sissy was the only one in her family she'd told about going into rehab. Emilia took a deep breath, picked up her phone and called her sister, Lupe.

Lupe answered on the third ring.

"So, how's your recovery coming along," Lupe asked in a strained tone.

"Actually, it's been going really well. I'm back at work and that's slowly getting better. Mister Douglas has been very supportive and I'm going to *SMART Recovery* meetings now that I'm out of *Ellendale*," Emilia told her sister.

"I've never heard of this—*SMART Recovery*. Is it like *AA* or what?"

"Kind of, but it's self-empowering and based on the latest science."

"Figures you'd go for something like that. You know how upset Mom was when you stopped going to Mass."

"I understand, but I can't make myself believe in something I don't. I mean, could I say anything that'd make you believe in fairies? What if I told you I talk to them and they guide my life and beliefs?"

"Really? You talk to fairies?"

"No, no, Sissy, I'm just using it as an example."

"Good, I was about to call UBC and have you put into the psych ward."

"So, believing in fairies would make *me* crazy, but you believe Jehovah God hears and answers your prayers and that's *okay*? Don't you see how they're exactly the same thing?"

"I think you really are sober," Lupe said. "You're actually making sense. Before you stopped popping pills, your lack of belief was just a mumbo jumbo of crazy explanations."

"Yeah, it's amazing how much better my brain works now that I'm off the oxy and vodka. And it's still healing."

"Well, I'm happy you're sober, but you've quit god knows how many times before and it didn't take, so it'll be a while before I can trust you."

"I understand, and it drives me crazy, but I learned it will take some time for my family to trust me again after all the lies and deceit you put up with from me. But it's my fault not yours, so I'll just have to keep on until I can regain your trust."

"Well yeah, you will. And I have two kids I'm responsible for, so they're more important to me than your feelings. I can't have you around them like you — were. What I'd really like is to have tea with you one evening. Just the two of us. I want to see you face to face and look into your eyes when you tell me you're not drinking and popping pills."

"That'd be totally awesome," Emilia said cheerfully.

"How's Wednesday?"

"I'm meeting some of the other ladies from my recovery group that evening, but if it's the only day you have free, I could beg off," Emilia said.

There was a long pause. "How's Thursday sound? Anything going on that evening?"

"No, nothing. That'd be great. I really appreciate this opportunity. It's a start and that's all I can hope for right now, especially after the way I treated you, Mateo, and your girls."

"Anywhere particular you want to meet?" Lupe asked.

"If you could come to White Rock that would save me a bus ride."

"What happened to your car?"

"I cancelled the insurance when I went into rehab. I was on medical leave and got paid something, but money was tight. Now, I'm going to wait a couple of months to get ahead financially a little and then insure it."

"Oh, I thought maybe you got a DUI."

"No, but that was only luck. To tell you the truth I could have on any number of occasions."

"Wow," Lupe said in obvious surprise. "You're being completely honest with me. That's a good sign, I have to admit, but I still have doubts."

"Of course you do," Emilia agreed. "That's perfectly normal, or at least that's what they explained in rehab. They said it would take time and I'd have to be patient. I'm not incredibly good with that, but it's something I'm working on. One of the many things I'm working on."

"I can be in White Rock at about seven-thirty. Does that work for you?"

"Oh yeah, that's perfect. Do you know where the *Pelican Rouge* coffee shop is?"

"Is that the one in the little mall on top of the hill?"

"Yeah, that's the one. That's an easy walk for me."

"Okay, Emilia, I'll see you then."

"Thanks, Sissy."

"No problem. *Hasta entonces.*"

"Yeah, see you then."

Emilia was close to ecstatic that she would meet with her

sister Thursday night. It was one more step forward in her recovery. It was one step closer to a *normal* life. In spite of everything she'd heard about how difficult it could be to prove yourself to your loved ones that you're going to stay sober. She was hopeful Lupe wouldn't be *too* hard to convince that she was *determined* to stay clean and was on the right road. But, she tried to prepare herself for the possibility she'd have to remain sober for an extended period of time before Lupe in particular and her family in general would accept her as rehabilitated.

Monday night Emilia didn't sleep well at all. Though surprised, she *had* been warned it often took three or more months for the body to readjust itself and get back into proper sleep patterns. Though this hadn't been much of a problem for her, she was aware it was normal and the knowledge helped to keep her from fretting about it. She'd managed with less sleep and when she'd felt more tired than she did right now. This was simply part of the cost of having been addicted to drugs and alcohol. And, her body was healing so she wouldn't have to live with it forever.

After one cup of coffee, she began to feel more awake and had a quick shower, then dressed in a soft brown skirt that hung just below her knees with a matching top. After checking the weather on her phone, she decided she'd not need an umbrella today and donned low-heel black shoes, grabbed her briefcase and headed for the bus stop.

She checked the time on her phone when she got to the bus shelter and was pleased she had five minutes to spare. In spite of her lack of sleep, she felt awake and even chipper. In fact, she was looking forward to work today. She decided as she waited for the bus, it would be a good idea for her to spend time on the floor doing tests as she'd done the week before. It seemed possible for her to keep up with her other work yet be able to do that, too. Possible with her brain beginning to function better at least. She looked down the street and saw the bus four of five blocks down the road. There was a bus stop on every corner, and the bus would stop at each one if someone wanted on or off. She knew it would still be two or three minutes before it arrived.

She tore her gaze from the bus and they settled on the opposing bus stop across the street, where she caught sight of some idiot driver coming around the corner way too fast and then crossing two lanes of traffic with no signals, cutting off two other drivers, one who blared his horn at him. The *BMW* convertible shot right into the bus pullout and screeched to a halt.

"Hey, beautiful, it's a nice day for a drive in the country. Hop in."

It was Charles. *Idiot!*

"I thought you lost your license," she called, without moving from where she stood.

Charles turned red. "Don't know where you got that idea," he lied — obviously.

"I'm on my way to work."

"I'll drive you."

"Thanks anyway, but here comes my bus."

The bus began to turn into the pull out, but had to stop well shy of the shelter as the *BMW* was in the way. The bus driver blared his air horn and Emilia chuckled behind her hand when Charles jumped at the sound. He frowned, booted the beamer and shot out of the bus pullout into traffic. Tires screamed as drivers hit their brakes to avoid hitting the *BMW* as it shot out onto the road.

"What an idiot," a deep voice behind Emilia said.

She turned her head and saw a black gentleman with a bright green and red fedora, sporting a spotty gray beard. "Agreed," she said.

"Do you know him very well?" the man in the fedora asked as they lined up to climb onto the bus.

Emilia was about to say she'd only seen him at a couple of *SMART* meetings, but remembered that would be against the group guidelines. *SMART* was anonymous. However, as she was reluctant to lie, she said," I've seen him at a couple of meetings, but I can't really say I know him."

When she sat in an empty seat, the older black man sat with her. "I think I've seen him at a couple of *meetings,* too." He stuck out his hand. "I'm Phineas."

She took his hand and he gave it one gentle shake. "I'm Emilia."

"I can't say where I saw him, but I attend *AA* meetings. I haven't seen you at any local meetings."

"No, nothing against *AA*, but I attend *SMART Recovery* meetings."

"Ah, so you're in recovery. Well, no need to discuss where we met him, but it's always good to talk to someone in recovery. So, where do they hold the *SMART* meetings?"

"At the *Sources Community Services Center.*"

"Oh yeah, they have counseling there, too, I understand."

"I'm seeing a counselor starting next week," Emilia said.

"Good for you. Counseling can be useful, especially if you get the right counselor. I've been sober fifteen years now. How about you, young lady?"

"Just a few months."

"Everybody starts somewhere." He gave her a wide, warm grin.

"Yes, indeed they do." She smiled back.

"Tell me, is everyone welcome to your *SMART Recovery* meetings?"

"To all the open meetings, yes."

"And the one at *Sources*, is that an open meeting?"

"Yes it is."

"When do you meet?"

"Monday evenings, seven to eight-thirty PM. You'd be very welcome I'm sure. Excuse me, this is my stop."

Phineas stood and moved out of the way. "It was a pleasure talking to you, Emilia. I'm looking forward to my first *SMART* meeting."

"I look forward to seeing you there." She extended her hand and he took it and gave it a gentle shake.

"Take care of yourself, Miss Emilia," he said, with a wide smile.

"You, too, Phineas," she said, reciprocating his smile and she hoped, its warmth.

Five minutes later she was sitting in her office.

At lunch, two young men who worked on the floor as technicians, sat at her table with clear deliberation. Within moments of siting down, Frank asked her a question.

"I heard you're going to *AA*."

His friend, Jordan, elbowed him, causing a few potato chips to fly out of the bag he was holding. "Careful, moron," Frank said.

"It's not *AA* she's going to, I heard it's a different group," Jordon said, ignoring Frank's insult.

"Whatever," Frank said.

"What's the name of the group you go to again, Emilia?" Jordan asked.

"It's called *SMART Recovery.*"

Jordan leaned forward with his elbows on the table and ignored his lunch. "What's the difference between the two?"

"I don't actually know much about *AA*, but *SMART* is based on science and is self-empowering."

"So — what do you mean, *self-empowering?*"

"It means they teach you tools based on *Cognitive Therapy*, and show you how to use them. So this empowers you to take control of your recovery," Emilia explained.

"I like that idea, but if it's science based they must keep updating it," Jordan suggested.

"That's true," Emilia agreed, "but I've only got a couple short time clean so I haven't had time to see any changes yet."

"Okay," Frank said. "We found out what we wanted to know, let's go outside and get some sun while we can."

"Go ahead, Frankie. I'm curious about what they do in these meetings?"

"Okay, but I'm outta here," Frank said.

Jordan *did* stay and asked Emilia questions until the buzzer went off and they all went back to work.

A few minutes after lunch, Mr. Douglas stuck his head into her office.

"Got a minute?" he asked.

Emilia tore her gaze from the computer and looked up. "Ah—sure," she said, though it was actually not a good moment. He *was* her boss after all.

He closed the door and took one solitary step into the room.

"I just wanted to thank you," he said.

"Thank me, for what?"

"For my brother, for Steve. He's still doing really well and he said you and some of the others were a real encouragement to him. So, I just wanted you to know I appreciate it."

"I think Steve's the one who's keeping himself clean, not me or anyone else. You should be proud of *him*."

"I am proud of him and I told him so. I—ah went to a *Family and Friends* meeting and well—it was a real help. They explained what he was going through, you know, like how the addictive brain works, and things like that. As well, we learned a bit about how *not* to enable friends and family to use. It was very helpful. Thanks for telling me about it."

"I'm glad you found it useful," she said.

Mr. Douglas nodded and left after giving her a wan smile.

Emilia was the last of the five women to arrive at the coffee shop that evening. Caryn, Anne, Doris, and Miranda were already sitting at a table that held six chairs. Miranda saw her and waved, the others looked up and smiled. Emilia pointed toward the counter and mimed drinking a coffee, then went and stood in the short line. She thought a cappuccino would be a nice treat and that was what she bought.

The moment she sat, Doris asked, "How'd your day go?"

"Actually, really well. Work went smoothly and I had no urges or cravings all day, which is unusual," she answered.

"Miranda was just talking about Charles," Anne said.

"Oh." Emilia wasn't sure she kept the look of surprise off her face. "What about him?"

"Tell her," Doris encouraged a seemingly reluctant Miranda.

"Well—he hit on me," Miranda said with a reddened face.

"He probably hits on any woman under forty," Anne said and then chuckled.

"You know what, I think Anne's right," Emilia said.

"Do you have some personal knowledge we don't?" Caryn asked, obviously curious.

"Well, you could say that," Emilia said.

"I saw him on Monday," Miranda said. "He was definitely trying to get Emilia to go for coffee with him after the meeting."

"Yeah," Emilia admitted, her gaze everywhere but on her friend.

"And when you turned him down, he came right over to me and asked me to go for *coffee* with him, as if I hadn't overheard the whole conversation he had with you," Miranda said.

"I don't think he understands there are things more important than money," Doris said.

"Yeah," Anne agreed. "Like sobriety."

"I don't think he actually has money anyway," Caryn said. "If he did, he wouldn't be worried about Daddy paying for his lawyer and other fees for his DUI."

"Speaking of which," Emilia interjected, "I saw him this morning on my way to work."

"Where?" Doris asked.

"I was at the bus stop."

Anne chuckled. "Reduced to taking the bus now is he. How apropos."

"Actually, he was in a *BMW* and asked if I wanted to go for a drive in the country and when I told him I was on my way to work he offered me a ride."

"I hope you didn't take him up. That kind has expectations if they do you a favor," Doris said.

"No, I most certainly didn't. He's full of himself and only comes to the meetings so he can get his lawyer paid for," Emilia said.

"Yeah, he's not at all happy to be abstinent," Anne said.

Caryn said in a thoughtful tone as she tapped her chin with her forefinger, "Honestly, I don't even like him coming to the meetings and I most certainly wouldn't want to spend time with him alone."

"I don't think Mosi would ban him from coming," Caryn said.

"I believe he would, but Charles'd have to do something disruptive," Anne said.

"Hitting on two women right after a meeting's not disruptive?" Doris asked with a frown.

"If you two are upset, or think you won't come to meetings if he's there, then we should talk to Mosi about it," Caryn said.

"Yeah, I agree," Miranda said. "It should be up to those of us most affected, which as far as I know, is Emilia and me."

Emilia took a sip of her decaf cappuccino. "I'm good—I mean as long as he doesn't touch me, I can handle him, but if he does, I'll ask to have him banned. How do you feel about it, Miranda?"

"I like your idea, and I think that's a good boundary to set. I mean, I don't think it's appropriate to hit on us after a meeting, but what if I meet a guy I *would* go out with? Like, I wouldn't want *him* banned for talking to me," Miranda said with verve.

Anne and Caryn laughed. Doris nodded her head.

"So, for now, we'll leave it at that," Emilia said in a decisive tone.

"Next order of business," Anne said.

The others laughed.

"I didn't know we were here on business," Emilia said, then chuckled.

"Well, maybe not technically, but I was thinking we could get together for an outing one Saturday. No drugs, no drinking, just the five of us," Anne said.

"Might be fun," Doris agreed.

"Anybody have any ideas?" Anne asked.

"I thought you had an idea and that's why you suggested it," Miranda said.

"I do have a thought, but I don't want to act like I'm in charge. We've all had people telling us what to do for so long, well at least I have, so I think we should discuss it and come to a consensus," Anne said.

"I like your way of thinking," Emilia said. "I'm tired of not being able to make up my own mind. I mean, I couldn't think straight enough before, but now my mind's clearer and I want to make decisions." She laughed. "But I don't have any idea what we could do as a group."

"I like the idea, too, but I just heard it, so haven't even thought about it until this minute," Caryn said.

"I say you tell us what you have on your mind, Anne," Doris said with a wink.

"Okay, I just didn't want anyone to think I was trying to take control," Anne said.

"Yeah, yeah," Miranda said with a hearty guffaw. "We got it, just tell us what you've got in mind."

"I thought we might do a day trip downtown. There's lots to see, like the *Art Museum* or a trip to UBC to see the *BC Museum of Anthropology*," Anne said.

"I haven't been to the *Museum of Anthropology* since I was in high school," Miranda said.

"Me neither," Emilia agreed. "I'd love to go there one weekend."

"How about you, Doris, and you, Caryn? How do you two like the idea?" Anne asked.

"I think we have a group of geeks here," Doris said and then chuckled. "I think it'd be great. We could pack something to eat and make it a picnic."

"Well, if we're going to have a picnic, I'll go if just for the food." Caryn chuckled.

After much discussion, it was decided that the coming weekend was too short of notice and they agreed on the Saturday after for their jaunt.

A few moments later Mosi walked in, waved to the ladies and went to the counter. For tea, it turned out. He pulled over a chair and sat next to Emilia. Emilia didn't remember much about the conversations after that as Mosi's nearness took over her senses.

CHAPTER TWENTY

On Thursday evening at 7:18, according to her cell phone, Emilia walked into the *Pelican Rouge* coffee shop. She wanted to make absolutely sure she was not only on time, but early. When she was drunk and stoned, she was inevitably late. It would be difficult enough to win her sister back even if she did everything right. If she fell into old habits even though she wasn't using, it would tend to leave doubts in Lupe's mind. That she was even able to reason this out was a source of pride to Emilia as it was a sign her mind was continuing to heal.

She ordered decaf and was tempted to order chamomile tea for her sister, but as it had been over four years since they'd been relatively close, she wasn't sure her sister's tastes hadn't changed. Nevertheless, she'd try to surprise Lupe by buying, or at least trying to buy her tea, or whatever Lupe was drinking in the evening these days.

At 7:28, according to her phone, which sat on the small table in front of her, Lupe walked in, checking *her* phone as she hauled open the glass door. Emilia waved and gave her sister a genuine smile. Lupe was her big sister after all and before Emilia's addiction took over her life they had been close. And maybe they could be again if Emilia stayed on the path to recovery.

Lupe gave Emilia a tentative smile and pointed to the cashier, but Emilia mimed drinking something and pointing first to herself and then to her purse. Lupe came right over.

"Are you offering to buy me a decaf?" she asked in

astonishment.

"Yes. I mean you drove here from North Surrey and saved me a ton of time. It's the least I can do."

"I can't remember the last time you paid the bill for anything, even when you said you would."

"I know, and I'm ashamed of it. I have a little money now that I'm not spending it all on alcohol and pills. I owe you and it also makes me feel good to do something for you even if it is just a little thing."

"Okay," Lupe said. "Do you remember how I like my coffee?"

"One cream."

"Yep, that's right."

"You guard mine and I'll be right back with yours." Emilia smiled.

A few minutes later Emilia was back with another decaf. She placed it in front of her sister and sat across from her.

"So how long did you say you've been without drinking and popping pills now?" Lupe asked with raised brows.

"A little over two months."

"That's the best you've ever done, as far as I know, but it's not very long."

"I know. I'm not asking to come for dinner or see the girls yet, but I still need you."

"Oh—need me how?" Lupe's eyes narrowed.

"I need you to talk to. Actually, it would be better for me to say I *want* you to talk to and I want to be able to at least *hope* I can become part of the family again. And I think you're the most likely to give me one more chance."

"Don't you have people you can talk to? Like that group you told me you were with last night."

"Oh yeah, I don't think I'd be able to stay clean without them. And they've been through the same thing as I have so they understand how I'm feeling and what I'm going through, and that's great, but you're family. I'm the one that broke the connection, it wasn't you or Mom and Dad, and I'm the one who's got to fix it. I'm starting by staying clean and I hope with time, to show you guys it's real. What I'm hoping right now, is for you to see I'm on the right track and to tell me if there's anything I can do to let you know for sure I'm serious."

"You know what," Lupe said. "There *is* one thing I want from you. I have to know you'll do this for me or you'll *never* be part of my life or my family's again."

"Whatever it is, I'll do my damnedest to do it for you." Emilia took a deep breath.

"I'm going to call you."

"Sure."

Lupe put her forefinger to her lips. "I'm not done."

Emilia nodded.

"As I was saying, I'm going to call you at odd times of the day or night. You'll never know when I'm going to call and you *have* to answer. If you can't answer, I'll give you ten minutes to get back to me. You know I can tell if you're sober or not just by talking to you."

"Oh yeah, I used to try and fool myself that you couldn't, but I was just lying to myself." Emilia shook her head.

"So, if I call and you're not sober, that's it, no more chances. Got it?"

Emilia sighed. "That's tough, but I get it. I've screwed you over so many times you have no trust left to give me. It's my own fault. I don't like it, but I don't blame you. The thing is, I'm determined to stay clean. I went to rehab for six weeks, and I'm following the *SMART Recovery* doctrine and using the tools, and they're helping me overcome the cravings."

"You're right about one thing, I don't get the whole cravings thing."

"It's hard for me to explain, but by abusing drugs and

alcohol, I've created a very strong neuropathway to my pleasure center, to the point my body didn't function well without it and if I didn't use, I'd get withdrawal symptoms, which is the body and brain basically demanding the drug it's used to. From what I understand, this all takes place in the limbic system, which is part of the autonomic nervous system, so the brain thinks it needs the drug for survival. It's like . . . I don't know, you try to prick yourself with a needle and you haul your finger away. You don't think about it, you just do it automatically. It's about survival. It's a lot more involved than that, but that's what happens."

Lupe furrowed her brows, then said in a thoughtful tone, "So how can you get through the withdrawal symptoms if your brain thinks you're going to die without your drug?"

"I can only speak for myself, but I just kept saying no for three days and thinking of how it was ruining my life. Then I went to my first *SMART* meeting and I passed out. They sent me to the hospital and the emergency doctor had experience with treating persons with substance abuse and she kept me in the hospital until the withdrawal was over. She gave me something to reduce the cravings and pumped me full of vitamins. Then she got me into a ladies rehab center in Surrey and if she hadn't spoken for me, I'd have had to wait three weeks. So anyway, I had a lot of help and I still have support with *SMART* by going to the meetings, doing the tools, and meeting with some of the others on our own time as well. In fact, next weekend we're going to the *BC Museum of Anthropology*."

Lupe laughed. "I can't believe you're going to a museum. That's not like you at all."

"In high school I loved history and science, you know that."

"Yeah, but that was over twelve years ago."

Emilia was silent for a few seconds. "You're right. Basically

I've lost twelve years I could have been doing productive things I loved 'cause I was hooked on booze."

"Well, you can't get those years back."

"No, I can't change the past, but I'm only twenty-nine and I have the rest of my life ahead of me. Sissy, there are people in the *SMART* group that've wasted most of their lives thanks to substance abuse. I'm actually quite young, by comparison, so I'm glad I've started working on it now instead of when I'm fifty or sixty, always assuming I didn't get some bad dope on the street and die of an overdose."

Lupe threw her hand over her mouth. "Holy shit! It never occurred to me that your habit could have killed you," she choked out.

"I didn't think of it either until I quit."

"Well, little sister, you've got me half believing in you already, but the proof will be you picking up the phone every time I call."

"I'm going to ask you to try not to call on Monday nights between seven and eight-thirty. That's when we have the *SMART* meeting."

"And if I do?"

Emilia shrugged. "I leave the room and answer the call. That's the bargain."

"Well," Lupe said with a grin, "I'm not going to guarantee I won't call at that hour."

"Okay, I'll let Mosi know so if I leave the room, he'll know why."

"Who's Mosi?"

"He's our *SMART Recovery* Facilitator."

"Facilitator. Has a nice ring to it."

Lupe stood, stepped over to Emilia, and gave her a hard hug, which surprised her.

"We'll talk soon," Lupe said. "Very soon."

On the short walk home from the coffee shop, it occurred to Emilia that Sissy had just, and quite possibly without realizing it, become another mooring line in her battle to overcome addiction.

Emilia smiled.

Chapter Twenty-One

"Good morning, Caroline," Mosi said as he strode over to his receptionist's desk, head high and a broad smile on his face. *I feel great. It's Monday and I have a SMART meeting tonight. Emilia will most certainly be there. But that's not the reason I feel so good I'm sure*

"Good morning, Mister El-Hadidy." Caroline's voice was distant and she pursed her lips.

Mosi frowned *as* his cheerful disposition took a distinct beating.

"What is it, Caroline?"

"There are a number of emails here I'm unsure if I should forward to your private inbox or not."

"You can always ask, or just forward them all to me."

"There's over fifty I'm unsure of."

"Fifty — you're unsure of?"

"At least."

"Have you opened any of them?"

"Most of them, yes. As per protocol."

"Okay, so why're you unsure if they should be forwarded to me if you've seen them?"

"The majority of them contain, what seems to be, very damning information on our Premier, the leader of our province.

"Damn Marion Dubois!"

"The Minister of Health?"

"The very one. I didn't tell you this, but according to Miss Dubois, certain evangelical church groups have the ear of the

Premier. They want to close down the safe injection sites and other facilities they consider *sinful,* and have the grant moneys that are presently used to fund *CCSA*, to be transferred to said church groups so they may use it to pay for their faith-based rehab centers."

"But many churches already have rehab centers and fund them privately."

"Yeah," Mosi agreed. "But these groups want to use public funding to support faith-based rehab, which our governments, both provincial and federal, have absolutely rejected up 'til now in favor of science-based programs, which have evidence-based track records."

"And the Health Minister wants to help us keep those funds?"

"So she claims . . . but she also wants to be Premier."

"The Premier is just the leader of whichever party's in power in a parliamentary democracy like Canada," Caroline said. "So she must plan to push the Premier out as head of the party."

"That's seems to be her plan, and she wants me and *CCSA* to help implement it."

"But we're an NGO, and completely unassociated with politics or any political party," Caroline said, wide eyed, then her mouth hung open.

"It doesn't appear the Minister cares."

"What are you going to do?" Caroline raised both hands palms up as she shrugged her shoulders.

"I'm not sure yet, but if you come up with any clever ideas, be sure to share them with me," Mosi said, putting what he was afraid was an unconvincing grin on his face.

Caroline frowned.

"This is all disturbing, and I still have my original dilemma about which emails to forward you," Caroline said.

"I think I'm going to need to look at all the ones that are

doubtful. Your judgment is impeccable, so if you're undecided, I'll need to see them."

Caroline grimaced and nodded. "That's going to add a lot to your work load today."

Mosi rolled his eyes and sighed. "Yeah, it is."

Tuesday Mosi was to meet with the entire Vancouver School Board, and he needed to prepare *today*.

Mosi pushed himself back in his desk chair and snorted. After going through what he considered his most important emails, he'd begun reading the emails that had stumped Caroline. He'd just finished the fifth one, and according to his email program, had forty-six to go. The anonymous information clearly showed the Premier taking bribes of both cash and gifts. One of the *gifts* was a trip the Premier took to Pensacola, Florida for an illegal drug use reduction forum. Mosi recalled a request from the Premier's office to *CCSA* to pay her airfare and hotel bills. Caroline had had severe doubts about the request, as it would have been more usual for the province to pay her expenses. He'd rejected the request outright, as it was not an application he considered directly useful to his mandate. Caroline's suspicions were a secondary reason he'd turned down the request. *You were right as usual, Caroline.*

His thoughts wandered to the evening *SMART Recovery* meeting and by extension, what tool he might present. He tended to have several topics prepared and the tone of the meeting and the needs of the participants that night would ultimately guide his decision. In spite of some resistance on his part, his mind then strayed, inevitably it seemed, to Emilia.

Her night-colored hair always had a gentle wave. He was unsure if she had straight hair she curled slightly, very curly hair she straightened half-heartedly, or if it was her hair's natural state. Two months ago it had been a little past her shoulders, but had now grown out somewhat and hung down her back. These days it looked bright, healthy, and well-cared for. Her olive skin also had a healthy glow, very unlike her pocked skin probably brought on by picking at itchy spots when she was abusing oxycodone. She was also filling out and her figure began to draw his attention as did her eyes. Once dull and bloodshot, they were now clear as crystalline pools of water. She was, he thought, the most beautiful creature he'd ever seen in his thirty-five years. But there was more to Emilia than a beautiful face. Though she was still in early recovery, her mind was beginning to show intelligence well beyond the norm. *I wouldn't be surprised if in two years of sobriety, she proved to be a genius.*

Mosi forced his mind back to work. *How am I going to counter the Minister's efforts to force me into becoming political? As head of* CCSA *she must know I can't outwardly take political sides. Ah, yes! She knows I can't do or say anything directly, but* – an idea was beginning to form. *I'm a bright guy, but I'm going to need some help. Brainy help.* SMART *help, yeah. Some of those recovery participants are virtually brilliant* – *damn and I'll bet Emilia's one of them. Yes, her and Josh,* mmm, *Anne, Doris, Cam and of course, Mom. I'll have to be sure none of them is triggered. I'll talk to them all, first. Just to be sure. Especially Emilia. I can't have her relapse because I've put her into a bad situation.*

Mosi took a slow, long, deep breath and focused once more on the remaining emails to see what he might glean, to both keep the *CCSA* and his *SMART* group's participants safe from government manipulation and keep science in publicly funded recovery.

Emilia's phone rang. She pulled it out of the side pocket of her large purse where she kept it for ease of access. The moment before she slid her finger over the answer button, she glanced at the time on the screen. 6:51. It was Sissy.

"Hi, Sissy," Emilia said in a jaunty tone.

"Something sounds a little weird, where are you?" her sister asked.

"I'm walking outside. I'm on my way the *SMART* meeting."

"You don't take transit?"

"No, on the way there it's all downhill and one of the ladies always gives me a ride home."

"Is it windy there or something?"

"Yeah, a little, it's just a block off the beach, so it's usually a little windy here."

"Okay, I was just calling to check up on you, but you sound fine."

"Yep, sober as a raccoon."

"Sober as a raccoon?"

"Yep," Emilia quipped again. "Sober as a raccoon."

"Is there something I need to know about raccoons?" Sissy asked.

"Well, one of the ladies from *SMART* just started volunteering at the animal rescue center and she brought a young raccoon that was drunk. Apparently it got into some fermented apple pulp they use at a nearby feedlot. One of the other volunteers explained that you never see a drunken older raccoon in the area. They try it once and never get into it again."

Lupe laughed. "Okay, I get it."

"There's actually more to the story if you've got a second."

"I'm all ears, little sister."

"Well, that same day, someone also brought in a drunk squirrel. The volunteer who works with my friend told her that this squirrel was a repeat offender and had been brought in several times already this season, but is quite the little devil to catch."

Lupe roared with laughter. It was so loud Emilia held the

phone away from her ear.

"That's a great story," Lupe managed to stutter between further bouts of chuckles.

"I thought so, too," Emilia said and then in a more serious tone. "You were the raccoon and I was the squirrel."

"I'm really pleased that you're sober at this moment," Sissy said.

"You and me both. Hey, Sissy, I'm just walking into the parking lot at *Sources* where the *SMART* meetings are held."

"Okay, I'll let you go. Talk to you later."

"This is an open meeting of *SMART Recovery*," Mosi began and then continued quoting the opening statement.

Twenty-one people. That's a few more than I like to have. Five newbies, too, but what is, is and I'll manage just fine I'm sure, especially with Josh and some of the others here. And what a surprise, Doctor Reshma is here.

After having Josh read the meeting guidelines, Mosi began the check-in. He was pleased with how Doris was doing this past week after struggling the week before.

"Hi, I'm Doris, and I had a pretty good week. One of the things that really helped was seeing some of the other ladies during the week and planning to do some things together. Having plans with others in recovery makes me feel more accountable, which makes it much easier for me to say no to cravings."

"Thanks, Doris," Mosi said with his usual warm smile, then nodded to Emilia who sat beside her.

"Hi, I'm Emilia. I'm nine weeks clean today. I know some of you don't really count the days you're clean, but for me it's useful 'cause I've never been clean more than one day before this time. So, for me at least, it gives me encouragement. I've gone this far, so I can make it all the way. I *also* found it easier to say no to cravings knowing I'm going to be seeing some of the others. And one last thing. I made contact with my older sister and we met for coffee on Thursday. She's giving me another chance, but plans to call me at odd times. This also makes me feel more accountable, as I never know when she's going to call and our agreement is I have to answer or call her back within ten minutes. For me, it's a good thing."

"Thanks, Emilia," Mosi said, not quite sure if he was able to give her a normal smile that didn't show too much of his feelings and his inner turmoil about her. He nodded to the next person, who was new to the group.

"Ah—hi. I'm Zachary, but everyone—well everyone but my momma—calls me Zach. I think I understood from the guidelines you read that *SMART's* anonymous?"

"Absolutely," Mosi said.

"The only one's here I know are Reshma and Charles and I'm pretty certain they won't tell anyone I'm coming," Zach said.

"I know you too well to do anything like that," Charles said. "You'd have me in a mountain of trouble overnight. Yeah, it'll never come out of my mouth that you're attending *SMART Recovery* meetings. Got that damned right."

Doctor Reshma smiled and shook her head.

Zach nodded and continued.

"Like I said, I'm Zach and I just got out of a private rehab facility—shall we say—in eastern Canada. The Minis—my employer had concerns I might let some—sensitive information slip while I was high. Probably rightly so. I was heavily into alcohol, but couldn't ever get drunk enough, so I started using cocaine to keep me from passing out so I could get drunker. This landed me in the hospital a number of times with alcohol poisoning. You'd think I'd learn, but no, I'm kinda' hardheaded and was stupid about my addiction. However, my last hospital episode and time in rehab really got my attention. My job's safe 'cause I know too much, but I definitely want my life back and though I know I can't do it on my own, I'm going to make it happen."

"Thanks, Zach." Mosi nodded to the woman next to Zach.

"Hi, I'm Jennifer. I'm very glad it's been clarified several times that *SMART's* anonymous, 'cause that's important to me because I'm a nurse for *Fraser Valley Health*. I'm addicted to amphetamines. I suffer from narcolepsy and my doctor prescribed methylphenidate, which is a stimulant and did help to relieve a lot of the symptoms, but I figured if a little was good, a lot was better, and I got hooked on it after using it according to directions — more or less according to directions for several years. I did like the euphoric feeling and that's what got me hooked in the end. I've been called before the BC regulatory board for misconduct for a mistake I made giving a patient her medication. They don't know I've been working impaired or *diverting* meds. But that was my wake up call. So, I quit using the stimulants two days ago and have an appointment with my doctor to go over what I need in the way of medication and some lifestyle changes to help me manage the narcolepsy. I start counseling here at Sources on Thursday and plan to continue coming to these meetings. Not being high while I'm on the job should help, but I'm on a medical leave-of-absence right now as they assumed my error was caused by stress and overwork. That should give me time to get over the worst of the withdrawals and get normalized . . . kind of. At least that's what I'm hoping."

"Thanks, Jennifer," Mosi said with a compassionate smile. "You're going to see your doctor about changing your meds, I assume, because you'll still need medication for the narcolepsy?"

"Yeah, I'm hoping we can figure out a different drug that I won't get addicted to."

"Good for you," Mosi said with a nod, then looked to the next person. Doctor Reshma.

"Hello, all, I'm Reshma and it's been several years since I've been to a *SMART* meeting. I've got over six years clean from narcotics and have *SMART Recovery* tools to thank for that. I will say I'm pleased to see Joshua, Anne, Emilia, and Zach here this evening. You're all relatively new to recovery and I take a tiny bit of credit for getting you all here. However, I'm not here to brag about the ones I've helped in their early recovery, but to announce my new plans. I'm taking the *SMART Recovery* Facilitator's course. I'm about halfway through it and in around three weeks should have my certificate. I then plan to open a new *SMART Recovery* meeting here in White Rock. However, it will be a closed meeting and open only to health care professionals. I hope to have this group's and especially, Mosi's support."

"You will most certainly have my support and any help I can offer," Mosi said. "It might be helpful to have Emilia and Jennifer at your meeting at least in the beginning, to help newcomers on their journey."

"But I've just gotten clean two days ago!" Jennifer cried.

Emilia chuckled. "That'll help keep you on the straight and narrow. Being accountable is good I think, and if you're accountable to Doctor Reshma as well as your regulatory board, it could be enough to tip the balance and keep you clean."

"Good point, Emilia," Doctor Reshma said. "But Mosi suggested you should be at my new meeting. I didn't know you were a health care professional."

"I work as a junior manager for BC Medical Labs," Emilia said. "Though I'm not sure that qualifies me as a health care professional."

"I think it does," Mosi said with a glowing smile for the whole room.

"Yes, I agree with Mosi," the doctor said. "And you'll likely have some very unique perspectives to share at the meeting when it starts."

Emilia nodded and said, "Okay then, I'll be there and it can only be helpful in my own recovery."

After check in, Mosi did the *Three Questions* tool from the *SMART* Handbook, writing them on the whiteboard.

One – what do I want for my future?

Two – what am I currently doing to achieve that?

Three – how do I feel about what I am currently doing?

He wrote a number of answers for each question as they were called out by the participants and gave each one a worksheet to do at home.

After the meeting, while most were mingling and chatting, Mosi signaled Emilia with his eyes and a nod that he wished to speak to her. She smiled and nodded back and then continued her conversation with Cam, Anne, Miranda, Josh, Doris as well as two of the new women. While he was trying to think of something intelligent to say to Emilia that didn't sound like he was hitting on her, which of course he absolutely wasn't, he heard someone clearing their throat behind him. He turned. It was Zach.

Zach leaned close and spoke in a whisper. "We need to meet soon. Tuesday's best. You're up shit creek without a paddle. I'm going to offer you a paddle."

Mosi's eyes widened as he wondered what the hell Zach knew and what he was talking about. "I'm meeting Emilia for coffee on Tuesday evening, so that won't work."

"Even better," Zach replied. "She's a bright one and may be useful in keeping you, the *CCSA* and *SMART* out of a crap load of trouble. What time will we meet and where?"

Mosi's mind raced. *Emilia's sobriety is more important than anything. She doesn't need any powerful triggers with less than three months clean. But this might not even be a trigger for her. I simply don't know.* "I'll have to confirm that with Emilia. Her sobriety is more important than anything else right now."

"Here's my card." Zach slipped a business card into Mosi's shirt pocket. "This can't wait."

Mosi collected one of his *SMART Recovery* business cards from the table where he put them during each meeting and then as an afterthought, pulled one of his *CCSA* cards from his wallet. "I'll call you no later than tomorrow."

"Good. I'll be expecting it. Don't text, make sure you call." He then slipped out the door.

While a stunned Mosi was greeting various participants and handing out his *SMART* business card to the other new-bies, he noticed Emilia was working her way to the front of the room where he stood. The look on his face must have been strange, he thought, from the frown on her face.

"Are you okay?" Emilia asked in a quiet voice.

"I'm not sure," he said, then grinned to give her reassurance. "Crazy things are happening. Can we talk for a moment after everyone leaves?"

"Sure." She gave him such a heart-warming smile he lost his train of thought for a moment.

The room was empty except for him and Emilia. She gave him an expectant look. There were a number of the others outside talking. Mosi motioned to Emilia to sit in a chair near his.

"I'm looking forward to coffee with you Tuesday," Emilia said the moment she sat and before he could collect his thoughts.

"Me, too, but there's a little glitch."

"You can't make it?"

"Oh no, I'll be there, but someone else wants to join us."

"Oh—I guess that'd be all right." Emilia's face fell and she sounded disappointed.

"Not my first choice, and I want to be sure you won't be triggered if he comes."

"It's not Charles, is it?"

"No, certainly not. It's Zachary."

"I can't imagine why he might trigger me."

"There are some odd things happening in the Ministry of Health and the Premier's office that look like they'll affect *CCSA* where I work and our ability to battle drug addiction. I've been unwillingly plunked down in the middle of it. He says he has information that might help — he kind of said that. And I don't want you put in a position where you might relapse."

"I can't imagine anything he could say that'd affect my staying clean, but I'll tell you what, I'll let you know if I get triggered."

"How'll you let me know?"

"Um . . . I'll nod to my left, like this." She did as she'd explained.

He nodded.

Mosi thought about her reply until he could see Emilia was tapping her foot and decided he needed to answer her right away. "Yes, let's do that. I could drive you home afterwards and that would give us an opportunity to speak alone for a few minutes. Especially if you're triggered."

Emilia gave him a smile that lit up her face. "Sure, that'd be great, though I don't live far from the coffee shop."

I love her smile. Don't go there — don't go there. "Actually, the original reason I wanted to speak to you was just to offer you a ride home."

"I'd love that."

Mosi dropped Emilia off at her apartment complex after driving one of the other ladies home. The moment he stepped into his condo, he dropped his briefcase in the foyer and called Zachary to confirm time and place for their Tuesday night meeting.

He decided that if it were necessary he'd resign from *CCSA* to protect the NGO from government interference.

The phone rang three times before there was an answer.

"Hi, Dad," he said before his father could speak.

"Hello, Zachary, when did you get back from Ontario?"

"Got in Saturday late. I didn't call Sunday because I had a bad day. Don't get me wrong, I didn't pick up, but the temptation was bad and I didn't think I'd make it through the day sometimes. But I did make it and again today. It's a lot harder here in the real world than in the rehab facility. Today though, I got some relief."

"That's good," Mr. Robinson told his son. "So what happened today that was different?"

"I went online and read about a different recovery modality called *SMART Recovery*. They had a lot of information and science-based tools to keep from using and then I went to my first *SMART* meeting this evening."

"Where did you hear about this *SMART Recovery*?"

Zach chuckled. "From the Minister."

"The Minister of Health told you to try *SMART*?"

"Not directly, no. But part of her plan to become Premier includes getting the head of *CCSA* on board and he not only runs a *SMART* meeting himself, but advocates to get the *SMART* tools into schools and teach kids about addiction. I wasn't really happy with rehab, though they *did* use some science, but it was basically twelve step like *AA* and they rely heavily on a higher power and surrendering yourself to it."

Mr. Robinson laughed. "That wouldn't sit well with you at all. Your mom and I raised you to depend on yourself and put your trust in that which is scientifically verifiable."

"Yeah, it's a hard habit to break."

"Not a habit you should break."

"True enough, unlike the coke and alcohol. I think I've got what I need to make it through recovery this time. The rehab did get the drugs out of my system and got me through withdrawal. Now after just one *SMART* meeting I'm feeling very positive. This Mosi El-Hadidy knows his stuff and explains things well. He has the ability to read the group and give them exactly what they need."

"And you learned all this from one meeting? How long was this meeting anyway, ten hours?"

Zach chuckled. "I also went to the *SMART* website and found some tools there and Mosi's well known by the Minister, so I'm not only going by what I saw at the meeting, which was impressive by itself in many ways."

"Okay, what else impressed you?"

"You know I've never been humble about my intelligence. It's not that I brag about it, but I don't like spending time with people who are mediocre in the cerebral compartment."

"Yes, in fact you avoid them."

"In White Rock *SMART* group, there's a lot of brain power among them. Most seem to know about *AA*, but reject the whole spiritual thing. These are thinkers, Dad. I actually felt very comfortable among them. I felt like I was with my peers."

"That's interesting, very interesting," Mr. Robinson said in a hesitant soft tone.

"I wish I could give my brain more time to heal, but the Minister is bent on becoming Premier."

"She'd be better than our present master," Mr. Robinson joked.

"True enough," Zach said with a friendly chuckle for his father. "But I have a better idea and a better prospect."

"Who could that be?"

"Why, Miss Gillian Dyck, the Liberal Party's rabble rouser."

His dad laughed. "You'll never get her voted in as leader of the ruling party."

"I don't know, Dad. She's got a lot of popular support for

standing up to the Premier and if the Liberal Party wants to win the next election in just over a year, they're going to need that kind of grassroots leader. I also happen to know of quite a number of members of the Liberal caucus who are very worried about getting reelected, and would no doubt stand with her—with a little persuasion."

Mr. Robinson howled with laughter. "You're a good man, my son. I hope your recovery sticks this time."

"That's my plan."

"You've never said that before."

"I never cared before. Now I do and now I'm going to make it happen and while I'm at it I'm going to make Gillian Dyck Premier."

"I believe you, son. What do you need me to do?"

"I thought you'd never ask."

CHAPTER TWENTY-TWO

Mosi sat reading the evening newspaper's headline for the third time. *Impossible! What's going on?* He was so engrossed he didn't see or hear her until she quite literally spoke in his ear.

"Have you gone deaf, Mosi?" Emilia said, then chuckled.

A shocked Mosi started in his seat and then turned to look. His eyes met two deep pools so dark they absorbed all light and seemed to draw his eyes and even his being into them.

"Are you okay, Mosi?" Emilia asked with a frown and crinkle of her eyes.

Mosi pulled himself back from the brink of what he now realized were Emilia's eyes. "Sorry—I was concentrating on this article." He pointed to the newspaper sitting on the table. *Wow, I've got to watch myself.* He stood. "Please sit, I'll get you a coffee or whatever you're drinking."

"Thanks, just a decaf please," Emilia said, then sat, turned the paper around and read the headline.

Easton Robinson Sr. calls on Premier to resign after she pushed for government funding for religious rehab.

This is crazy! What the hell could the Premier be thinking?

Mosi returned as she was reading the account. She lifted the paper and shook it in the air. "The Premier's had a mental breakdown!" she said, rather louder than she'd intended and realizing it, looked around the coffee shop. Sure enough, there were a dozen faces looking her way. She forced a smile and shrugged.

Mosi chuckled. "Maybe this whole fiery Latina thing I've heard about isn't far from the truth."

"I can't speak for all Mestizos, but I'm a lot like that and my parents, too. If they haven't had a good fight at least once a month, they both look for some reason for a spat. Then they make up and you should hear the noises coming from their bedroom!"

Rather than the chuckle she half expected, Mosi had a confused look on his face. She was about to ask him about it, but he spoke first.

"You used Mestizo as if it was interchangeable with Latina. I don't understand."

"It is and it isn't. Mestiza is the feminine and Mestizo is the masculine form or may refer to both genders. You spoke specifically referring to the women, but I answered including Mestizo men. But to answer what I think you really wanted to know, Latina is not a word we use in Spanish. Those of us whose heritage is Latin-American, call ourselves Mestizos, or if we happen to be women, which you may or may not have noticed I am, Mestiza, which is the feminine form of the word." She grinned.

"Very interesting conversation," a third voice said.

She and Mosi both turned in their seats and looked up. It was Zach.

"Hi," Emilia said with a forced smile, though Mosi *had* called her the day before to confirm he'd be coming.

"Hi, Zach, please sit down," Mosi said, then gave him a warm, very Mosi smile, Emilia noticed. She tried not to grin.

Zach's already got a paper cup with the Pelican Rouge *logo, so he must have been to the counter while Mosi and I were discussing the newspaper article and talking.*

"You said something—strange to me at the end of the meeting on Friday," Mosi said, looking directly at Zach.

"Indeed," Zach said with a wry smile. "I'll repeat it for Emilia here, that is if you've not heard it."

His gaze darted over to hers. She shook her head.

"I told Mosi that he was up shit creek without a paddle and I was going to offer him a paddle."

"There's something going on I don't know about and you've both been less than frank. Please explain," Emilia said, trying her best not to let her exasperation seep out.

"That's what I'm here to do, but it must be understood that everything we discuss here *must* remain absolutely and without fail, between the three of us and any others I choose to bring in. What say ye?"

"If it's illegal or immoral, I'm out," Mosi said.

"Me, too," Emilia agreed.

"Illegal, possibly borderline and only if we get caught, which is highly unlikely. Immoral? Well, that would depend on your definition of immoral. If you believe it's immoral to make public figures accountable, then we can part company right now, but if you think accountability for elected officials is important, you're liable to have a more easy going attitude about what is moral and immoral. For my whole career, I've stood firmly for what I believe and will do so now. From what I overheard when I arrived, you've both read the headlines. I can vouch for the truth of them. If you know anything about politics at all, you know Easton Robinson doesn't tend to involve himself in provincial affairs. But this time he's spoken out. Clearly and truthfully. I know, because he got the information from me on Monday night and I've got documented evidence."

"And how do you know Easton Robinson?" Mosi asked, with obvious curiosity.

"Well, he's my father. I'm Easton Aubrey Zachary Robinson the second, but please call me Zach." He gave them a grin that wouldn't have looked out of place on a bear.

"How the hell did you get this evidence?" Emilia demanded. *I should probably be running out of the coffee shop right now, but I feel like a moth attracted to the light.*

"Please keep your voice down, Miss Emilia," Zach whispered. "I'm only meeting you here because it was what you two planned. I would have liked somewhere private. I work with the Minister of Health, the Honorable Marion Dubois and am a trusted aid."

"So your plan is to oust the Premier and put Miss Dubois in her place," Mosi said.

"Five weeks ago that was my plan, but it's changed recently."

"Whoa, whoa, just a minute," Emilia hissed. "Why'd you change your mind and what's in it for you?"

"Excellent questions," Zach said, placing a forefinger on his lips as he finally eased himself into a chair and continued in the soft voice he'd been using. "In short, I changed my mind 'cause I got clean. This was my fourth trip to a rehab facility, but the first three times were a farce. I never quit my addictive behavior at all, just faked it. But this time, though I went with the same intention of faking it through, some things happened."

"What *things* happened?" Mosi asked, with narrowed eyes and skepticism dripping from his tongue.

Until that moment Zach's tone had been virtually flippant, but now took on a seriousness that surprised Emilia.

"While in rehab, I got close to three guys, in part to be able to get coke when I got out, but they were bright guys, you know. Except for their addiction and state in life, people I could have hung out with in the real world. Two were getting off heroin. They called it smack or horse. The other had been hooked on fentanyl.

"The guy addicted to fentanyl—friend he called it—OD'd. And the assholes that ran the place didn't even have a naloxone kit on site. Said they thought it would encourage relapse.

He died waiting for an ambulance. The facility is quite a way out of town. I mean they gave him CPR, but they weren't trained for it very well I thought, and he didn't make it. Two days later, one of the fellows hooked on heroin got a hold of some, but it was contaminated, according to the coroner. It killed him and I mean fast. Two weeks into rehab, the third guy got some smack. Another OD and another case where a naloxone kit could have saved a life.

"First, I'll admit it scared the shit outta me. They were men I knew personally and we'd even made plans together for after we finished rehab, and then they died—just like that. Then I thought what might happen if I got some bad blow, you know, maybe mixed with fentanyl or something even worse. Poof, I'd be gone. I'm not a believer, you know, so death to me is permanent. This is the only life I've got and I figure I want to live it fully, be happy and do something useful. So, that's why I no longer plan to support Miss Dubois for Premier. We can't allow people who run rehab centers to decide it's all right to let people die rather than have a lifesaving drug on site."

"Millions wouldn't believe you," Emilia said in a light tone. "But I do."

"Do I hear sarcasm in your voice?" he asked.

"No, though you should, but I'm sold. However, I'll go with Mosi's opinion. He's got many years clean time and is— well brilliant."

Zach and Emilia both looked to Mosi.

"I do think you're sincere," Mosi told Zach as he gestured with his right hand, turning fingertips up. "But this will probably put a lot of strain on your recovery and cause you to slip or relapse, so I don't think it's a good idea to go ahead with your plan, whatever it may be."

"Honesty is rather new to me, except with my family, or at least my parents, but as I think it's going to be an important part of my recovery, I'm going to tell you the truth," Zach said. "When I'm running a game, I never drink or snort cocaine while it's going on, so it'll be afterwards I'll need extra support. And you can be sure I will look for it. But if you two will promise to be there for me when it's over, I can do this and stay clean. I'm convinced of that."

"Okay," Mosi said. "But I need to know your plan before I commit to it."

"Fine, but I need your word this will remain between the three of us, whether you work with me on it or not."

"Unless you kill somebody — or have them killed, I give you my word," Emilia said.

"Yes," Mosi agreed, "I can live with what Emilia said."

Easton Aubrey Zachary Robinson the second explained his plan in significant detail, leaving out only minor issues, Emilia figured. The last was such a surprise she choked on her decaf and sputtered for an entire minute. After slapping Emilia repeatedly on her back until the sputtering died down, Mosi spoke.

"How can you possibly imagine getting Gillian Dyck in as head of the Liberal Party, much less as Premier?"

"Within one month, she'll be the obvious choice. Everyone will agree — most everyone — that she's the best person for the job. And with a tiny amount of guidance she'll be so popular next year the Liberal party will shoot up in the polls and be shooed into power once again. But this time with an actual decent person in charge, who cares more about the good of the people of this province than power."

"And you'll be the power behind the Premier," Mosi said, with glowering eyes.

"Mosi, Emilia, the Honorable Miss Gillian Dyck has no need of me to tell her *what* to do. She needs me to show her *how* to get it done."

"Okay, I'm in," Mosi said.

"Yeah, me, too," Emilia agreed. *I can't believe I'm doing this.*

Zach stood and reached over first to Emilia and then to Mosi, putting one hand on each shoulder. "If anyone is triggered by this, just stop. Our individual sobriety is more important even than the state of this province or our country."

She and Mosi both nodded.

CHAPTER TWENTY-THREE

"Mister Easton Aubrey Zachary Robinson the second," her secretary announced, then shut the office door before the two even shook hands.

Zach shook hands with the Member of the BC Legislature Gillian Dyck. Three times in recent history she'd voted against her party's polices, most notably on cuts to the *CCSA* with the funding going to faith-based recovery groups.

The woman was no more than five-foot-four and slender with a figure that could easily be mistaken for a man's from behind if she dressed in slacks. Today, however, she wore a colorful spring dress, which hung just below her knees. It had a modest if not actually high neckline and short sleeves. It was no business suit by any stretch. Her straight dark hair was bobbed at the shoulders and her pale face, which either by genetics or design, held barely a wrinkle. She sat and examined him in silence over a pair of reading speckles and looked more like thirty-two than the forty-two he knew her to be.

"Thank you for seeing me on such short notice," Zach said.

"I believe I'd be a fool not to," she replied with a flash in her eyes.

Easton Aubrey Zachary Robinson the second gave her his most brilliant smile.

"You're aware I'm presently unemployed as the Minister of Health has resigned and may even be recalled."

"Yes, and the Premier will most certainly resign within the next few days. That will leave *my* party, the *Liberal* party in complete disarray. Few know what's going on or how the information got to the press, but I suspect you may have had something to do with it," she said, narrowing her eyes at him

"Now Miss Dyck, do you have any evidence I leaked any — *sensitive* — information?"

"I most certainly don't, nor would I expect to. In fact, none of the other Members of the Legislature believe you had anything to do with Miss Dubois' resignation nor the Premier's — *predicament.*"

"Very wise of them, wouldn't you agree?"

"Yes, it most certainly is," Ms. Gillian Dyck said. Her forehead puckered.

"With your permission, I'd like to get to the point of my visit."

"Please." Ms. Dyck gestured with both hands and a shrug as she fell back into her chair.

"When the Premier resigns, there must be a caucus meeting within a few days to elect a new temporary party leader. Then that leader will call a leadership convention for the very next month. The temporary leader will, without a doubt, be elected by the party members for she will have shown that she alone has the ability to raise the Liberal party in the polls and then win next year's election."

"*You've chosen* the next leader."

"Yes, Miss Dyck, I have."

"God help us when a drunk crackhead is picking our political leaders!" Gillian cried.

"I'm going to tell you a story, Gillian Dyck. My story —"

Gillian sat at her desk, contemplating the implications that this now apparently sober man, was to be her new Aide. Ms. Gillian Dyck, Member of the BC Legislature, representing the riding of Langley East, well-known rabble-rouser, speaker of her mind and shunned by her own party, might soon be the next Premier. If that indeed happened, and if Mr. Easton Aubrey Zachary Robinson the second proved to be the new man he seemed to be, she might, just *might*, lead the province of British Columbia into a new era. It was beyond anything outside of her wildest dreams. She took a long, slow, deep breath that filled her lungs until she thought they'd burst, then exhaled and called her receptionist, Jas.

CHAPTER TWENTY-FOUR

Friday's sun rose before six in the morning. The breeze wafting through her bedroom window chilled her the moment she brushed the covers off her warm body. Emilia jumped out of bed and slammed the window shut. *What an idiot I am! How stupid to leave the damned window all the way open all night. Now it's freezing cold in here.*

Her next thought was to pop an *Oxy* and she went to the bathroom cabinet where she kept them. She fumbled open the mirrored door of the medicine chest in an angry rush before she realized she had none in the house. Her mind began to race, trying to recall where she might have hidden a few tabs, but nothing at all came to mind, so rummaged around all her previous hiding spots. Under the loveseat sofa she felt a small plastic bag and with inordinate glee, hauled it out. It only contained crumbs. *Damn it!*

She felt like shit. She didn't every remember feeling this low in her life. She wanted an *Oxy*. She *needed* an *Oxy*. She needed that pick-me-up. She wanted that high so badly she could taste the bitterness of it as if she had a pill sitting in her mouth. She was beginning to feel giddy, it was almost like she'd just taken a couple of pills.

Then, something inside screamed at her. *What the hell am I doing? I've got 2-1/2 months clean! I can't lapse now. I might never get free again!*

Emilia ran over to her printer and hauled out a sheet of computer paper, grabbed a pen and ran, quite literally ran, to her small, battered kitchen table. She slammed the paper onto the table drew out four quadrants on the paper and feverishly began to do a *CBA*. Ten minutes later she was done. An instant after that, she realized the awful cravings were gone. Distraction, she realized, that and her determination to be sober.

Emilia then became aware that she was stark naked and began to laugh hysterically. When she'd calmed, she wiped her eyes and headed for the shower. *Goddamn that was close.*

As she showered she thought about the weekend. She and some of the girls were having an outing to the museum of Anthropology. They'd make a day of it, have a picnic and, she was certain, a great clean time together. She'd tell them about her close call this morning. Maybe they'd know something. Like why. Honestly, she still felt like death warmed over and her nerves felt like they were vibrating. They were the worst urges she'd had since her first days in recovery.

Emilia had just sat at one of the lunchroom tables at work when her cell phone rang. It was Sissy.

"¿*Que tal chica?*" Lupe asked.

"I'm fine," Emilia replied, while pulling her sandwich out of the brown paper lunch bag one-handed. "Are you okay? You usually go into Spanish when you're excited or upset. You sound upset."

"Don't *ever* have kids," Lupe said, in what sounded like disgust to Emilia.

"Oh, that sounds awful, what happened?"

"Your oldest niece has a *boyfriend.*"

"Okay — so are they — having sex or — something?"

"They better not be or I'll strangle both of them!"

"Well then what, Sissy?"

"She's only twelve for God's sake."

"You're starting to sound like Mom."

"What's wrong with that?"

"I recall you saying when you were about that age you'd never treat *your* kids like that." Emilia covered her mouthpiece so Lupe couldn't hear her laugh. Then she noticed her untouched sandwich in her left hand and gave it a forlorn look.

"I said nothing of the kind."

"Um, actually, yes you did, quite a few times, probably hundreds of times."

"Okay, maybe I did, but this is different."

"Of course it's different, you're the mom now."

"Mi," Lupe said, using the nickname she'd used for Emilia when they were growing up, "I hate it when you're right, I *really* hate it. One good thing came out of this call anyway."

"You mean you're going to start treating Clara like a young woman instead of a little girl?"

"Dream on! No, I mean you're clean—again and still. You're beginning to act like your old self again, and according to what I've been reading on the *CCSA* website, those are signs of a healing brain. It means you haven't used in a while. I'm proud of you, little sister, but don't think I'm going to stop calling."

"That's okay, it's one more stone in the wall I'm building against relapse, so your calls are welcome."

"Okay, we'll talk later."

"Okay, Sissy, bye."

Half her lunch break was gone! Emilia wolfed down the sandwich, then ate her apple. While there were curious looks from around the lunchroom, no one questioned her, which to Emilia, felt absolutely appropriate.

That evening after work, her phone rang and she snatched it from the vanity where it lay and looked at the display. Emilia was surprised to see Mosi's name on her cell phone's screen. She tapped the answer button and took the call.

"Hi, it's a nice surprise to hear from you," she said in a cheerful tone.

"I think you and some of the ladies are going to be busy tomorrow." Mosi's worried tone concerned Emilia.

"Yeah, we're going to UBC for the day. Is everything all right?"

"Not exactly. Would you have some time to get together on Sunday?"

"Of course, that'd be great."

"Okay," Mosi said. "I'll call you Sunday morning. When's a good time?"

"Any time after seven's good."

"That'll work. Talk to you then. Bye."

"Bye." *That was very weird. I wonder what's going on.*

Emilia was having trouble concentrating on the novel she was reading, so decided to surf the Internet to occupy her time. Boredom was the number one cause of relapse, according to Mosi and other information she'd learned from *SMART*. At this moment, she felt the truth of it. She still didn't have Internet reconnected to her condo, though she'd paid the overdue amount several weeks ago. Not wasting all her money on vodka and oxycodone certainly made paying the bills easier. But she'd decided not to reconnect her Wi-Fi quite yet and would get her car on the road first. Nevertheless, she did have her cell phone and had upped her data package. So, she set her phone up as a hotspot and connected her laptop to it via Bluetooth and surfed the Net trying to distract herself. She watched two short funny videos, but they weren't enough to distract her from the cravings. In fact, the urges felt as strong as they had during her first few days clean.

Emilia shoved herself away from her desk and jumped up. She'd go to the liquor store and buy a pint of vodka. Her body began to tremble in anticipation as she slung her purse over her shoulder. The moment her hand touched the door handle she remembered that Sissy could call at any moment. She yanked her hand from the handle as if it was red hot. Emilia stood before her door and shook. She hadn't felt such a strong urge since her withdrawal. What the hell was going on? She remembered to take slow deep breaths. In the words of the *SMART* handbook, this would pass. She could ride it out. Then she remembered her *HOV* and dug it out of her purse. The purse slipped to the floor as she unfolded the worn sheet of computer paper and re-read it.

One, love.
Two, family.
Three, health.
Four, work.
Five, travel.

Mosi! What would he think if I relapsed? And her family. Sissy! I'll call her right now.

Emilia picked up her purse from the floor, dug her phone out and speed-dialed her sister as she marched over to her battered kitchen table and thumped down into a vinyl-covered chair. The phone rang six times and she thought it was going to go to her sister's voicemail when Lupe picked up.

"Hey, Emilia." Came the cheerful voice of her sister. "How's it going?"

"Actually, very shitty."

"Are you drinking?"

"No and I'm not using *Oxy* either, but damn it, I'm close."

"What happened? You were doing so well."

"I really don't know what's going on, but I think I'll call Mosi after we're done. Maybe he's seen this before."

"Okay, Emilia, what I need to know is how you kept yourself from using."

"Two things, Sissy. The first was I didn't know if you'd call. Some days you've called me three times, so I never know when I'll hear from you. The second was one of the tools I learned from *SMART* called the *Hierarchy of Values.*"

"Oh—kay, so how does this *Hierarchy of Values* work?"

"I list five of the things I value most in my life. Then I remember that if I use my addiction takes over and it becomes the number one on the list. Everything else, all the things I value, all the people I love become second or not even important at all."

"And that stopped you."

"Yeah, it did. I want you guys. I want your family and Mom and Dad and Bartolomé to all be part of my life. *Dios sabe,* God knows, I love you all." Emilia sobbed.

"And God knows we love you, too, little sister." Lupe choked. "You've no idea how your addiction affected our brother."

"How's Bartolomé doing, anyway?"

"He's suffering from depression. The worse you got, the more deeply the depression affected him."

"Um—have you told him I'm clean?"

"Nope, not my job. That's up to you."

"Do you—mind if I call and tell him?"

"If you're going to make it this time, sure, tell him, but if you have any doubts, I think it'll just make him worse if you relapse."

"He really tried to get me into *AA* or *NA,* but I wasn't interested. Actually, I wasn't interested in *any* kind of rehab. I'm gonna make it, Sissy. I don't understand what happened just now or why, but I think our facilitator, Mosi, can help me. Then I'll call Bartolomé. He'll be glad I'm clean, even if he doesn't trust me yet. That's going to take a while I'm told."

"Who told you that?"

Emilia chuckled and when she did, felt a wash of relief pass over her. "Pretty much everybody I'm in contact with in recovery told me the same thing. I spent years proving to you all I was a liar and unreliable, you're not going to think I've changed in just three months."

"Yep, little sister, you got that right. Don't get me wrong, I'm on your side and I can tell you're definitely trying this time, but yeah, it'll take some time to have confidence in you again. Lots of time."

"Okay, thanks for picking up the phone and talking to me."

"That's all right. I'm glad you called instead of popping a pill or drinking yourself into a stupor. Take care, Emilia, I do love you."

"Me, too, Lupe. Love you. Bye."

"Good night, little sister."

After she ended the call with her sister, Emilia stared at her phone undecided if she should call Mosi or her brother Bartolomé first. After contemplating the phone's screen for an entire minute, she decided on Mosi for a couple of reasons, the first of which was he might have some insights into what was happening to her brain these last few days. The second reason was it simply felt good to talk to him. It was safe and he was both interesting and knowledgeable about recovery and many other things. She opened her contact list and dialed his number. The moment she hit send, she remembered it was Friday evening. Hell, he might be out, perhaps having dinner with some other woman. Then he answered and she realized she'd been holding her breath.

"Hi, Emilia," he said.

A chill ran down Emilia's spine, for in order for her name to pop up on his screen he must have added her to his contact list. "Hi, Mosi, am I interrupting your Friday evening?" she asked.

"Actually, I'm with a very special lady." His tone was cheerful.

Emilia's heart sank.

"I could call back tomorrow, I guess."

"Who's that you're talking to?" a familiar voice said in the background of wherever Mosi was.

"It's Emilia, Mom."

"Let me say hi before you hang up," the voice Emilia now recognized as that of Bernadette said. She gave a quiet sigh.

"Okay, will do," Mosi said to his mother. "So, Emilia, what can I do for you?"

"I've been having a bit of a hard time this last week. I don't know what's going on, but suddenly I get these super strong cravings. I think they're as bad as when I was in withdrawal."

"*PAWS*," Mosi said.

"*PAWS*?"

"Yes, *Post-Acute-Withdrawal Syndrome*. You're also at about three months clean, right?"

"Yes, just over three months."

"So, you see, Emilia, you're past the pink cloud or honeymoon stage."

"What's that about?" Emilia was curious now.

"When we quit our drug or drugs of choice, our brain and body realizes we need dopamine. When we were using, the drug was pumping us full of dopamine, and usually way too much. So, in short, the body begins to produce a whole bunch of it, but realizes after a couple of months that it's too much and it begins to taper it down to normal. For a while the brain is battling to figure out exactly how much is normal because we messed up our brains and its receptors with our substance abuse."

"So if I understand correctly," Emilia said, "I was feeling good because my body was over-producing dopamine, and now I feel like shit because it's trying to normalize."

"Pretty much, yes."

"That really sucks."

"Yeah, sorry about that, but it is what it is. We all go through it as part of the cost of recovery. Don't forget we brought it on ourselves by abusing drugs."

"Yeah, and I wasn't thinking about getting hooked, just that it felt good to escape, first the pain caused by the accident and then just escape from life. So what happens as my body normalizes to the amounts of dopamine it's supposed to get?"

"We'll never get the unnatural amount of dopamine we did when we were abusing our chemical of choice, but your body acclimatizes to the new state with time."

"So," Emilia asked, "how long does this *PAWS* last?"

"Two years on average."

"Oh my God! I've got a long way to go."

"Where you're at right now we call *The Wall,* and it's a high risk for relapse, but remember, from now on as long as you maintain abstinence, it gets easier and easier."

Emilia sighed. "At least I understand what's happening and I know I'm not alone and it *will* get better."

"Yes, it'll get better. And you're young, less than thirty, so it'll be easier on your body to heal itself. Some of the older people who come to *SMART* were addicted for decades and their bodies are older and well abused, so they don't heal as fast."

"So, do you want to discuss whatever it was you wanted to talk about on Sunday right now?" she asked.

"No, that's something we need to discuss in person. I'll call you Sunday AM as planned."

"Okay then, 'til Sunday."

"Have fun with the girls tomorrow," Mosi said. "I'll get Mom, she wants to talk to you."

"Okay, Bye, bye."

Emilia talked with Bernadette for five minutes, then they said goodbye. Emilia gave a great sigh. She liked Mosi. Liked him a lot. And liked his mom, too.

Emilia looked at her phone to check the time. *8:30, it's still early enough to call Bartolomé*. She opened her contact list, found his number and pushed send. It rang twice and then an unfamiliar female voice answered.

"Hello."

"Hi," Emilia answered, a little confused. "Is Bartolomé there?"

"Yeah," the voice said, clearly suspicious. "Who is this please?"

"I'm his little sister, Emilia."

"Oh yeah, the druggie."

Emilia had zero interest in speaking with this woman who didn't even know her. "Can you get my brother please?" she asked, doing a fair job of keeping the irritation out of her voice.

"I'll tell him you're on the line, but I can't make him talk to you."

"Of course you can't." Emilia wasn't sure how much longer she could be polite to this woman.

"Barty," the disembodied voice said. "Your sister the drug addict's on your cell phone. Shall I hang up?"

"Absolutely not! I want to talk to her. Here give me the phone and watch the barbeque for a few minutes. The kebabs are almost ready to turn."

"Whatever," said the same pouty voice.

A moment later, Bartolomé was on the line.

"Hi, Emilia, how are you doing?" he said with obvious concern in his voice.

"Actually, really well. I'm three months clean from the alcohol and oxycodone."

"Really?"

"Yep, really. Sissy's been keeping track of me if you want to confirm it with her. My *SMART* Facilitator and my boss can both vouch for my sobriety."

"Lupe didn't tell me a thing, not a hint."

"Yeah, I've tried to quit lots of times before, so she didn't want to get your hopes up, or her own for that matter."

"So, what'd you do differently this time to get and stay off the drugs?"

"Well, I went to a *SMART Recovery* meeting. I collapsed as I was in the middle of withdrawal, so they sent me to the hospital and I detoxed there. After that, the Emergency doctor got me into *Ellendale*, a ladies only rehab facility, for six weeks. Now, I'm back out in the real world and attending *SMART Recovery* meetings and working full time."

"Good for you. I'm proud of you. Forgive me if I'm still wary, but this *is* the longest you've been without a drink or your *Oxy*."

"Yes, and the booze and *Oxy* aren't who I am. They turned me into a liar and worse."

"That they did. What are your plans as far as Mom and Dad are concerned?"

"I'm not sure yet. I haven't even seen Sissy's kids yet 'cause Lupe's waiting until she's feels I'm safe with them. I think I hurt Mom and Dad the most, so maybe I'll wait a few more months before telling them."

"They're both hurt, but Dad's feelings manifest as anger. I don't know if you should wait to tell them or not. I guess it depends on how serious you are about quitting. What does Lupe say?"

"We haven't discussed anything about them yet, but I suspect she would prefer me to wait. I mean she hasn't even told her kids."

"Does her husband, Mateo, know?" he asked.

"Yeah, he knows and he's even more against me being around their kids until he feels I'm clearly not going to relapse."

"Yeah, well, I can understand how he feels. If I had children I'm not sure I'd want you around them until I was confident you're going to stay clean. I do have a question though."

"What's that?"

"You mentioned *SMART Recovery* and I've never heard of it before."

"It's a science-based self-help group. Google it. I think you'll find it interesting," she told him.

"I'll do that. Thanks for calling."

CHAPTER TWENTY-FIVE

"Good morning, Amer," Zach said to his father's secretary. Amer was an Iraqi Canadian who'd been working for his father for more than forty-two years. Amer's hair, once jet-black, had turned a silver-gray over the years and he now wore reading glasses, but he was as slender as in his youth. Though small in stature he was both brilliant and able. Zach knew Amer and his father not only worked well together, but had the same moral standards and had been close friends for most of that time.

Amer looked up over his reading glasses and smiled. "Good morning, Mister Zachary." He then stood and reached his hand over the low reception desk and offered it to Zach, who took it and received a warm firm handshake.

"Your father wants to speak to you but is in the midst of a meeting. Would you like to wait here in reception or in your office?"

"If you're not too busy I'd rather stay and talk to you."

Amer pushed his office chair away from the desk and sat back. "I'm never too busy to speak to you."

"Thank you, Amer. There are few people I really trust besides you and my father."

"I have to say you're forgetting about your mother," Amer said.

"True enough, but her interests lie elsewhere," Zack said and then seated himself in the comfortable chair nearest Amer's desk.

"Yes," Amer agreed. "Indeed they do. But I feel I must add

that her pastimes have had a large influence on you, your father, and even myself."

Zach smiled. "Yeah, that's for certain. I think she's raised more money for *The Red Cross*, *The Vancouver Island Marmot Society*, *The BC Children's Hospital* and many other worthy charities than any other person in Canada. Of course, my opinion may be slightly biased."

"Perhaps," Amer said with a smile. "But I would vouch for the truth of it. She's also encouraged your father to give large donations to her causes."

Zach nodded and smiled. "Yes, and she hits me up regularly, too, and I'm sure you're not immune."

"No, I'm not. But I will say I tend to agree with your mother on the causes she sponsors and raises funds for, so it's not a great burden for me to help out."

"My mother's an angel."

Amer grinned at him and then nodded in the direction of his father's office door. "Ah, Mister Robinson's done with Monsieur Guichard, go on in Mister Zachary."

Zach gave Amer a warm smile, then stood and strode toward his dad's office, nodding to Monsieur Guichard as they passed.

The moment he shut the office door, his father came around the desk and gave him an affectionate hug.

"I'm so glad you're in recovery, my boy. Your mom, sister, and I have all been worried for the last five years about the direction your life was taking."

"I can imagine," Zach said in a contrite tone, hanging his head.

"In spite of the fact you were very high-functioning, ultimately there could only be one end and that's what we all feared for you."

"I do appreciate the support—of all of you, and I include Amer in that as well. Especially after the first three times I went to rehab."

Mr. Robinson gestured at a leather guest chair for his son to sit. Zach sat and then continued.

"I lied to everyone those first three times and didn't actually make any attempt to quit. In fact I continued using most of the time I was in the facilities."

"I didn't realize it was that bad," his father said. "I thought you'd just relapsed after you came out."

"No, Dad, I never did try to quit. I just wanted everyone to leave me alone, so I went along with it."

"So, this time it'll be different?"

"That's my plan. Complete abstinence. I'm only forty, but all the abuse was catching up with me. Even though I was pretty high-functioning, I could tell my mind wasn't as sharp as it had been."

"And now you have big plans for the province. You intend to remove the Premier, to block the Minister of Health from becoming the party leader and ergo the next Premier, and then to install the premier of your choice, Miss Gillian Dyck."

"Yes. It's ambitious but that indeed is my plan," Zach said, with a thoughtful smile for his dad.

"And you need my help."

"Indeed, Dad, I do need your help. All behind the scenes of course."

"I approve of your plan wholeheartedly. The Premier has gone rogue and is trying to have her government fund faith-based recovery and if she gets that through, she'll be supporting the evangelicals to overthrow science, both in the classroom and in government run recovery houses. And the Honorable Miss Dubois, Minister of Health has plans to take over, but she, too, is toxic to the well-being of British Columbia and the rest of Canada.

"Miss Dyck, however, is a different species of politician altogether. She was virtually pushed into running by her local riding association, she's outspoken about the importance of science in the classroom and wants absolute separation of church and state, she's fiscally conservative, socially liberal, and in addition to all that, she wants the government to do something completely different to help with the opioid crisis and have those who are addicted treated as patients rather than criminals."

"That's right, Dad, she asks why should we continue with laws that clearly haven't worked and she's open to new ideas."

"So, yes, I will support you, both financially, emotionally and bring in other powerful people behind the scenes, but . . ."

"But what?" Zach felt his muscles contract. His eyes blurred, his throat tightened, and his heart pounded like it was trying to escape from his chest.

"But this time I have conditions."

"What kind of conditions?"

"The type of conditions that'll help keep you clean and sober," his dad said.

"Okay, so what am I to expect?"

"You can expect random urine, breathalyzer, and blood tests, beginning as soon as we're finished with this meeting. Tomorrow, every vehicle you drive will be fitted with a car Breathalyzer Interlock Device. We'll be testing you for alcohol and cocaine, but Amer suggested you be tested for other drugs as well, and they shall remain a secret from you. According to his information, which he got from a doctor who specializes in treating addiction, people suffering from addiction frequently trade one addiction for another."

"I see. I suppose I asked for this as I broke your trust over and over again. I don't like it, but I can live with it. It'll most certainly keep me honest."

"There is one additional condition."

"Oh—what's that?" Zach asked, narrowing his eyes.

"We'll be sending a personal *bodyguard* with you."

"A bodyguard? What the hell for?"

"I'm sorry, son, but the bodyguard bit is just a cover story. She'll be with you to be sure you don't even *bend* the rules."

"She?"

"Yes, she's transgender. She was in *The Canadian Special Operations Regiment* as a man, but when she retired from the Forces, she had the sex change operations done. She retains all the skills she learned as an elite Canadian soldier, so she *will* be able to act as a bodyguard if necessary."

"Don't lie to me, Dad. You think there's a possibility I'll need a bodyguard, don't you?"

Mr. Robinson sighed. "Yes, actually I *do* think that's a possibility, and my security people agree. You're getting deep into politics and aren't an elected official. If some people figure out how powerful you are, you could be a target for assassination."

"I hadn't thought of that, but you could be right. So when do I meet my bodyguard?"

"She should be in the reception area about now," Mr. Robinson said. "She'd gone to pick up some things she needed for your protection, but said she'd be back this morning."

Indeed there was a woman in the reception area speaking with Amer. She was very tall, six foot or a little taller, certainly taller than his five-foot-eleven. She had long very straight bleached blonde hair, a rather square jawline and broad shoulders for a woman. Her breasts were sufficient rather than large and Zach thought that would be a good choice as he supposed too much tissue in the chest area might cause some issues if she got into a physical altercation, though he didn't know that for a fact.

Zach strode towards her and after two steps she spun around and faced him. She had her hands in a classic karate attack pose. For a fleeting moment, she looked ready to take on the world, but that look was gone in an instant. He believed she knew exactly who he was.

"Good morning, Mister Robinson," she said as she dropped her hands and straightened up. "I'm Alexa, your new bodyguard."

She extended her hand, which he took in his. The handshake was firm and Zach was certain it was controlled pressure. He was sure she could crush his hand with hers. Zach felt very safe and completely certain he wouldn't be using or abusing drugs or alcohol any time in any foreseeable future.

Thanks, Dad.

CHAPTER TWENTY-SIX

Emilia woke to an early sunrise. The day was cloudy, though the forecast didn't call for rain. She stretched languorously, reaching for the headboard with her arms and pointing toward the footboard with her toes. Though she still felt crappy, at least she knew why. Her body would readjust itself. In the meantime, she'd do things that would release dopamine in natural amounts—like going to the Museum of Anthropology with her new friends.

Emilia threw off the covers and slid out of bed. After washing up and brushing her teeth, she went to the kitchen to prepare snacks and lunch. 3-1/2 months ago, she'd been skeletal, but now she was filling out. In fact, she knew if she wasn't careful she'd put on *too* much weight. She was pleased her hair now had a healthy shine, unlike when she was using. When she was abusing *Oxy* and alcohol, her hair tended to lack luster and she didn't care for it properly. She now liked the soft natural wave of her hair, and rather than straighten it or curl it, she simply brushed it.

She decided on one salmon sandwich on whole grain multigrain bread, cut up veggies, and two pieces of fruit. Eating a healthy diet was one of the things many people of the *SMART* participants claimed had helped them. *It only makes sense.* She checked her phone for the time and then glanced at the clock on the stove to see if its time was correct. Seven forty-five. Doris, Anne, and Miranda would be here at quarter to nine, with Doris driving. Emilia decided she had time to try something she'd heard about at several *SMART* meetings and quite a few participants had used with success.

Emilia kicked off her slippers, sat on her battered sofa and tucked her feet up under her in some semblance of the lotus position. The point, she understood, was to get comfortable. This done, she sat straight and put the palms of her hands on her legs. She closed her eyes — though apparently not everyone did — and listened to her breathing. She breathed in deeply through her nose and exhaled through her mouth. She felt her breath go in and then out again. After several breaths her mind wandered to the trip they were going to make this morning and she berated herself for not being able to concentrate. *It's normal for the mind to stray.* So she began again and each time her mind went off in another direction, she would gently bring it back and take more breaths and concentrate on the sensations. She stopped after a while and got up the check her phone for the time. She'd meditated for fifteen minutes. It seemed like a good start. She felt more relaxed and aware of herself. *I'm going to do this every morning.* It had been fifteen minutes well spent and she was curious to see what happened when she made a habit of it.

Emilia packed the lunch and snacks into a small ice chest, added three bottles of water and an ice pack, then went to change. As she was raised in the Vancouver area, she knew it could rain without warning and in fact usually rained about one hundred and sixty days a year on average, and today it was overcast. She'd take a daypack with her and pack a light rain slicker to wear over her hoody. It would also give her the option to put the hoody in the backpack if it got too warm. When done with this, she pulled on an old pair of stretchy jeans and as virtually anything goes with jeans, she added a black top with red, pink and blue flowers printed on it, a pair of sneakers to be sure she was comfortable on her feet all day, and her wallet, which would fit into the backpack, and she was set for the day.

Doris was a few minutes early, but she was ready and went down the stairs, eschewing the elevator, which she'd inevitably used when she was drunk and stoned. Her feet felt light and excitement ran through her. She knew it was the dopamine, a natural high from the anticipation of spending the day with friends at a super cool museum. It made her forget all the temptations of the last few days.

It felt good.

"I see I'm the last one." She grinned at the others through the open windows.

"I'll pop the trunk," Doris said, then smiled.

She put her backpack and the ice chest into the trunk which contained a small mountain of other supplies, then sat in the backseat beside Miranda, who was dressed in a pair of jean shorts and a pink blouse, which coordinated with her hair. Quite nicely, Emilia thought. They smiled at one another.

A twenty-minute drive later, they were at the Sky Train where they met up with Caryn, who'd chosen to take her own vehicle as she lived closer to the Sky Train than to White Rock. They boarded at the King George Station and travelled to the end of the Expo line to the Waterfront, which ended at Vancouver Harbor. They debarked and scurried across the street to board the bus conveniently called the forty-four UBC Route. They arrived at 9:55, which was perfect as the museum opened at 10 AM.

The five women began to explore the Great Hall together, but as they moved at mismatched paces, they were pulled to different aspects of the exhibits. Soon, they began to separate. Doris called their attention to this fact, and confirmed each had her cell phone. They decided to meet back at the foyer at 1 PM to lunch together. The five ladies then began to spread out, each to her own interests. However, Emilia found herself constantly encountering Miranda, and the two decided to continue together. Once past the indigenous totems, bent boxes and baskets woven from cedar roots or bark, they entered a small display from Mesoamerica, which fascinated Emilia as this was a part of her heritage, which she understood went back to before the Mayan civilization. Lost as she was in reading and seeing everything there was in the small exhibit, she thought she'd lost Miranda, but a few moments later, she jumped when she felt a soft touch on her shoulder. Miranda laughed quietly behind her hand as if afraid to disturb the figurines.

"Sorry, you startled me," Emilia said and then chuckled.

Still wearing a broad smile, Miranda asked, "Did you see the Peruvian artifacts? They go *way* back."

"No, not yet, but where are they? You've got me curious."

"This way." Miranda plucked at Emilia's hoody. "Aren't you hot in that thing?" she asked.

"I didn't even notice until you mentioned it. Yes, I'm burning up. Wait." She removed her backpack and dropped in on the ground between her feet, took off the now unneeded garment and stuffed it into the pack. "Okay," she said as she hoisted it back in place. "Let's see the stuff from Peru."

Miranda smiled and led her around a corner. Emilia noticed that behind the exhibit she was interested in was a room separated from the exhibits by glass walls. Miranda obviously saw her curious look and smiled.

"That's part of the Preservation Rooms. It's glassed in so the public can see what the Conservators are doing, or at least working on."

Emilia could see two men. One was an older man, perhaps a professor and the other was a younger man who she thought might be close to her own age. His skin was a dark mocha and he had a slightly rounded face similar to hers. *I wonder if his heritage heralds back to the Aztecs or beyond.* She was about to turn her attention back to the Peruvian display when the young man looked up at her. He smiled and nodded.

Maybe he's wondering if we have a similar heritage just like I was. Then his face changed and he looked—astounded. Emilia shook her head, not believing what she saw and turned back to the exhibit behind her.

"What was that all about?" Miranda asked, in a hushed but intrigued tone.

"What was—what all about?"

"You two, do you know him? He seemed surprised to see you."

"Never seen him before."

"You sure? He seemed to recognize you."

"He was probably looking at you in those cute shorts and revealing blouse."

"Um, no. He was definitely looking at you. I was off to one side and he wasn't looking anywhere near me. Do you really think my shorts are that cute?"

Hoping to divert Miranda's mind from the present conversation, which Emilia found curious, but embarrassing, she said, "Oh yeah, they're adorable and very sexy. Haven't you noticed all the looks you're getting from the guys?"

"Really?" Miranda did a little jump and clapped her hands like a child. "Who was looking at me?"

Unwilling to lie, as had been her constant habit during her addiction, she mentioned four instances when she *had* noticed men ogling young Miranda. This pleased Miranda excessively, Emilia thought, but found it made *her* feel happy to see Miranda in such a good mood. She knew from check-ins and other conversations that for a woman of only twenty-two, she'd suffered a lot. *It's no wonder she'd became addicted to try to escape the horrific reality that had been her life.*

Miranda glanced around surreptitiously, and by sheer coincidence, a young man of perhaps twenty-five or six was looking directly at them. He turned away red-faced and Emilia winked at her friend, whose face took on an unearthly glow and her broad smile widened even further.

"Well, I guess we should get going. It's almost one o'clock and I'm starving. I've got my stamp to get back in after we eat lunch, did you?" Miranda said as she pirouetted, then strutted back toward the main entrance, with her head held high.

Emilia nodded and held up her left wrist for Miranda to see.

"Awesome," continued Miranda. "And maybe after lunch we can find out about that guy who seems so enamored of you." She grinned at Emilia.

The other three had taken a different route but had stayed together and spent most of their time in the local indigenous exhibits. They told Emilia and Miranda of some of their discoveries. Miranda and Emilia took turns telling about what they'd seen and then, all of a sudden, Miranda took over their end of the conversation.

"And then," Miranda said, with something of a gleam in her gray eyes, "Emilia and I were like, looking at this glassed in area where the public can see how the Curators do their preserving and stuff, when this guy who looked like he could be Emilia's cousin or something, gave her the eye. Really, he acted like he knew her or something. Hey, Emilia, did you recognize the guy?" Miranda asked, as if the thought had just occurred to her.

"No." Emilia shook her head. "I mean he looked Mestizo, and maybe even like he had some Mayan blood, but I've never seen him before."

"Whoa, whoa, whoa!" Caryn shot her hand out in the universal *stop* signal. "Explain yourself, Emilia."

"Um — explain what?"

"This Mestizo thing. I've never heard that word. What does it mean?" Caryn rattled out the words like a machine gun.

"Mestizo means a mix, but that's just its literal meaning. In Spanish, those of us who are of a mixed heritage of white and indigenous, call ourselves Mestizos. It's become the name of our race."

"I thought you were like Latinos or something," Miranda said, with puckered lips and a scowl.

"Indeed, you call us Latinos, but we call ourselves Mestizos in our language. If someone says I'm Latina, I don't get upset, but Latino refers to where we came from geographically, whereas Mestizo speaks to our bloodline being a mix of the white Conquistadores and the native peoples of the Americas."

"It sounds like you're suggesting that Spanish is your native language," Doris said. "But I'm sure you said you were born here in Canada."

"Well, yeah, I was born here, right in White Rock at the Peace Arch General Hospital, but the language we spoke at home was always Spanish. My parents said we'd hear English everywhere, so to be sure we learned Spanish that's all we spoke at home. My folks felt a second language was healthy for the brain and possibly useful in the working world, as well as being an important part of our heritage. So my brother, sister, and I all grew up speaking both languages."

"But the language you spoke at home was always Spanish, so that's why you think of it as your mother tongue?" Anne asked with crinkled brows.

"You got it," Emilia answered, with a warm smile for her girlfriends.

"Looks like we're done with lunch, so let's pack up and get back inside," Doris said, though her tone suggested she was torn between the present topic and a desire for more adventure in the museum.

"Yes," Caryn agreed. "We can always talk more on the way home. I'm for looking at the South American exhibits myself."

"I'm with you," Caryn said. "Especially if that young Mestizo's around." She grinned.

The others laughed as they packed up and headed back inside the museum.

Emilia's plan had been to head directly to the local indigenous exhibition area, but she was waylaid by the other four, who begged her to go with them in a hope of seeing the young Mestizo, who Miranda had claimed was *quite gorgeous.* They were all laughing and as it was all in fun, Emilia didn't want to disappoint the others and so went along, though with some minor apprehensions. *I was probably just imagining his reaction anyway. It may have even been a flashback from one of my* Oxy *highs. I've been told those things happen sometimes.*

When the five friends got to the glassed-in Preservation Rooms, all but Emilia seemed disappointed that the only person they could see was an older man leaning over an object on a table as if doing some work on it. Emilia exhaled inaudibly and prepared to desert the others in favor of the native displays and in fact had taken six steps when Anne cried, "Hi!"

Emilia turned and looked. Anne was waving to the very Mestizo man she'd seen before like a school girl instead of a married women with three children and Emilia had no idea how many grandchildren. She spun on her heels. *I've gotta get outta here!* She almost ran into a little girl of no more than four, and to avoid the collision found herself obligated to come to an abrupt halt, nearly teetering over from the sudden change in momentum.

Once Emilia realized she wasn't going to crush or harm the child, she spun to her left and scooted around her, to the surprise of a bewildered couple with the same deep brown skin as the little girl. *Don't run, don't run.* She then scooted down the wide hall at a fast walk and headed for the Indigenous Exhibits. As she stepped into the doorway into the main Indigenous Gallery, she paused and took a deep breath. *I'm shaking. What's wrong with me?* She took several more deep breaths and soon found herself calm once more. *What was I trying to escape? A Mestizo guy who looked at me oddly? Really, get a hold of yourself, girl!*

Calmed by her reflections, Emilia began to peruse the artworks and read the documents that accompanied them. She was soon engrossed by the Chilkat tunic, which she read was made by sewing together pieces of a number of cut robes and had shown the high status of the owner. *Such a different life and way of looking at the world.*

She heard a hemming sound behind her and when she turned to look, it was the older gentleman she'd seen working in the Preservation Room.

She blinked twice to be sure it wasn't an apparition leftover from her using days. He was still there, looking like he was cut from stone.

"You are Mestiza, are you not?" he said abruptly.

She stared at him in disbelief, but said not a word, muted by her absolute astonishment. The man looked to be in his sixties and of obvious European decent. *What would he know of the Mestizo people? Then again, he must be a professor and have some knowledge of my ancestry. Maybe he knows more than I do.*

"Perhaps you didn't hear me," the old professor said in a gruffer tone. "I *asked* if you were Mestiza."

Emilia brought herself up to her full height and stood tall and proud. "Indeed," she said, lifting her chin, "I am, and my heritage may go back to before the Mayans."

"Yes." He nodded thoughtfully. "I believe you may be right. Please come with me. My assistant and I have something you should see."

He turned to go, expecting her to follow him, it seemed to Emilia. *He may be a professor, but I don't trust him. I don't know what it is, but I don't like him – not at all.* Emilia stood where he'd found her.

The man seemed to realize she wasn't following him. He

stopped and turned. He glared at her with a gaze as fierce as a wolf's on the hunt and his frown was like bullets.

Emilia scowled back. "I don't make a habit of following strange men at their command."

He nodded. It seemed no more than an acknowledgment that she'd spoken. He stood looking at her for an eternal ten seconds.

"I'm Professor Johansson, and I'm the Senior Conservator for Latin America."

"And why are you singling me out?"

"Ah, an astute question. My studies lead me to believe the Olmec were a rare and brilliant people. You may have inherited some of those genes and they would course through your Mestiza veins."

Was he claiming I might have Olmec ancestry? He used the feminine form of Mestizo when referring to me. What does he know? What's he willing to share? What might he know about my history?

"The answer to your question," he continued, "is you have certain physical traits I've come to believe are likely Olmec, just as my postdoctoral assistant seems to have."

The Mestizo man! Maybe he saw something like that in me.

"I have a celt that we've determined was Olmec. It's not on display, but I would be pleased to show it to you."

"I'm with friends. I can't leave them hanging."

"What time do you all plan to leave?"

"At closing time."

"Good, we have over an hour. It'll be well worth your time I'm sure."

"What will *you* get out of this?"

"Perhaps insights into Olmec way of thinking by watching one of their ancestors interact with a relic of their history." He gave her a grim daunting smile.

It wasn't a pleasant look, but Emilia's curiosity overcame her better judgment. *If at any time it looks like I'll be alone with this man, I'll run like hell.* She felt in her purse for the keys to her condo. *Keys can be and have been useful weapons in an emergency.*

"Okay, I'll go with you. I want to meet this assistant of yours."

"Ah yes, Julián. Smart, smart boy."

The professor pronounced it *hoo-lee-anne,* which was very close to how the name was properly pronounced in Spanish. *He must actually know this Julián fairly well.* "Lead on, Professor Johansson," she said.

CHAPTER TWENTY-SEVEN

Emilia walked beside the professor. He said not a word and only glanced at her when he made a turn. *To make sure I'm still with him.* He unlocked a door marked *Staff only* with the security ID card he wore around his neck and ushered her through. There were a number of — mostly younger men and women — at various stations doing a variety of tasks, she could only assume, having to do with the preservation of artifacts. The professor seemed to have noticed her curious gaze.

"That group is cleaning those glass artifacts." He pointed. "They" — he pointed again — "are consolidating those coins."

The professor, quiet and serious until now, smiled and nodded to different groups and individuals, even offering greetings, succinct though there were.

He's in his element.

They passed through another security door with the use of the professor's ID and entered a room with floor to ceiling drawers on both side-walls, with only enough room available for a door in the two ends. They headed for the other door, and, passing through it, came to a large open room that was lined by large windows on one long wall. Emilia could see other visitors on the other side, some stopping to look in, others passing by and small groups or individuals examining various displays. *I've seen this room from the other side!*

At a desk, not visible to the visitors on the outside, a Mestizo man who looked to be in his thirties, sat in front of a computer monitor. He must have heard them and turned in his swivel chair and looked up. His mouth was open as if he was about to speak when his eyes fell on Emilia. His jaw dropped and his eyes went wide.

The professor spoke.

"There, Julián. You see, I've brought the young lady you saw earlier."

"Are you okay?" Emilia asked. *I can't imagine what's going on in his head, poor guy, but I hope he's okay.*

"Come, Julián," the professor said with a chortle, "the young Mestiza is here. Can't you think of anything to say to her? Tell her of your vision, apprentice 'o mine."

"*Vision?*" Emilia asked, louder and with more emphasis than she'd intended. However, whether it was the loudness of her voice, the question itself, or the fact that she spoke at all, it broke the spell that had fallen on Julian and he shook his head, then blinked four times in quick succession.

"Sorry," Julián said, "It's just that I saw you."

Emilia huffed at his reply, and her voice took on a distinct tone of irritation. "Well duh, of course you saw me, I was standing in front of you."

"No, I mean I saw you before—I saw you."

"What the hell are you talking about?" Emilia began to feel an urge to have a few drinks and one or two *Oxy*. *It's the frustration.* She grimaced inwardly at the realization. Understanding that, the thought was easy to set aside. Especially as her mind was otherwise occupied. *This is a good lesson.*

"I'm a little overwhelmed right now and not explaining myself well," Julián said. "What I mean to say is I saw you, or a woman that looks just like you, in a—dream—or as the professor calls it, a vision."

"When was this?"

"About a year ago."

"And how did this come about?" Emilia rolled her eyes before she could stop herself.

"Yes, it sounds incredible and I'm not suggesting it was

supernatural, but it *was* something beyond my ability to understand. All I did was touch an Olmec artifact."

"And when you went to sleep that night you dreamt about me."

"Oh no, it all happened almost the instant I touched the celt."

"Okay, okay," Emilia raised her hand palm forward. "Just hold it a minute, so this all happened while you were awake?"

"No — yes — kind of — after I touched it I passed out. That's why I say I don't know what really happened. I specialize in Mesoamerican artifacts, so it's possible I saw what I wanted to see. Even my memory of you may be my mind playing tricks on me," he said.

"So why am I here? Why did the professor go looking for me?"

"For science, young lady," the professor interrupted. "I would like you to touch the celt to see what happens."

"Sure," Emilia said sarcastically. "So I can collapse and crack my head on the concrete floor. No thanks. How do I get out of here?" She moved toward the door that she'd entered.

Julián jumped to his feet. "Oh no, please don't go Miss . . . sorry, I don't even know your name."

"Robles, Emilia Robles. But that's a moot point 'cause I'm outta' here."

"We most certainly won't let you get hurt. We planned to have you sit on a comfortable chair before you handle the celt. That way you can't fall," Julián said.

"I don't think so. I'm not taking the chance of falling unconscious in the hands of two men I don't even know. That would be stupid and dangerous. Forget it."

"But we *need* you."

Emilia remembered some more of her *SMART* training. Word exchange. Substituting absolutes for more conditional words. "You may *want* me but you most certainly don't *need* me."

"Oh no," Julián insisted. "We have to have you."

"Will the world end if I don't stay? Will your studies come to a grinding halt? Are there no other Mestizos besides you and me in Vancouver?"

"Well no. Point taken." Julián shrugged and his shoulders sank.

"That may be," the professor interjected. "But imagine you being able to have an experience like Julián did. We can always get one of the lady post docs to be with you."

If I could find a way to do this so I felt safe, I'd try it. It really sounds interesting. "It would still be someone I don't know or trust." In that instant, Emilia looked over the professor's shoulder and glanced out the windows into the gallery proper when she saw all four of her friends pointing at her and talking among themselves. Anne seemed to be the first to realize that Emilia saw them and waved at her wildly, with a huge grin on her face. The others too began to wave and laugh.

"Actually, I've just found some people who I trust to be with me during your little experiment," Emilia said.

"Where are they?" the professor asked.

"They're standing just outside, there in the gallery. See the four ladies waving? Those are my friends. I'll do it if they'll be in the room with me."

"One of them, certainly, but no more," the professor said.

Emilia did an abrupt about face. As she strode toward the door they'd entered through, she called over her shoulder. "Fine, count me out."

Before she reached the door to the room of drawers, a hand took hold of her shoulder with just sufficient force to slow her advance. She stopped and spun, lifting the arm on which the hand rested straight up at head height. This had the desired effect of knocking the hand and accompanying arm away. "Get your hands off me!" Emilia snarled. She spun away again with her heart in her throat. *Oh God, I'm shaking.*

"Okay, Miss Robles, you win. All four may accompany you," the professor said grudgingly.

Emilia's legs slowed as the words began to penetrate and she ground to a halt, then slowly turned around. When she faced the two men, she noticed the ladies were still there. Doris was pointing at her wrist. *Right, the time.* She plucked her phone from her back pocket. *4:48, almost closing time!* "The museum's about to close," she told Julián and the professor.

"No matter," the professor said. "We're often here well past the museum's public closing time. Let's get your friends in here. Would you be so kind, Julián?"

"Of course, professor."

Julián disappeared through the door Emilia had been headed for.

Emilia decided to call Doris, so that her friends would be prepared when Julián invited them to meet her.

"Hi, Doris, a Mestizo man about my age is going to ask you to go with him. We're all going to meet and he's going to show us an Olmec celt."

"Oh, okay, but it's just a few minutes to closing time you know."

"Yeah, I know, but they don't work by the public's hours."

"As long as you're okay, I'm good with that. Let me ask the others."

Doris must have covered the phone's mic with her hand for all Emilia could hear was indistinct female voices.

"Okay, Emilia, were all in. Sounds like fun, a private showing, even. Oh, that must be him coming now. Olive skin, white lab coat?"

"I'm sure it's him. His name's Julián."

"Yep, he's coming right for us. We'll see you in a few. Bye."

"Thanks for coming. See you in a couple of minutes."

"Please follow me, we'll meet your friends in a more

private space. One that has a comfortable chair for you and room for your friends to sit as well," the professor said. He looked — *grim?*

Decidedly unhappy to be alone with the professor, she followed him nonetheless.

The room the professor took her to was on the small size. No more than ten by fifteen feet. It was however, replete with chairs and must be used for small meetings, Emilia imagined. This fact calmed her worries. In a small way at least.

After five minutes, she began to wonder where they were. She kept checking her phone for the time.

Six minutes.

Seven minutes

Eight minutes.

What the hell's going on?

Nine minutes.

The professor, too, was fidgety, so Emilia decided he wasn't the reason behind her friends and Julián taking so long.

Ten minutes.

Eleven minutes.

She decided to call Doris, and as Doris' phone rang, they walked through the door with Julián. Doris pulled her phone from her backpack, which she held in her hand, and looked at the screen. She smiled and winked at Emilia.

"Sorry we took so long, Professor," Julián said, "the ladies needed to make a . . . pit stop."

"You could have called," griped the professor with downturned lips.

"I didn't have my phone with me, it's in my desk," Julián said apologetically, but maintained eye contact with his senior.

"We're here now," Anne said, in a cheerful voice with both hands raised in the air and her purse sliding down her arm.

The ladies laughed.

"Yes, yes, well let's get on—that is shall we continue, ladies?" The professor's face held a forced smile.

He doesn't like to be kept waiting. Emilia kept the grin that so wanted to appear, off her face.

"Please sit in this chair here." The professor pointed to a cozy-looking executive chair. "And Julián, be so kind as to bring the celt."

Emilia sat and made herself comfortable and less than one minute later, Julián appeared before her with an object wrapped in white cloth. He also wore a pair of cotton gloves. *He sure seems to be going out of his way not to touch the celt and I wonder how he got it so quickly? The room's filled with banks of drawers. I didn't see, but it must have been in this room all along.*

"Here, Miss Robles," the professor said as he handed her a disposable wipe. "Be so kind as to clean your hands before you handle the artifact."

Without a word, Emilia nodded, took the wipe and scrubbed both hands as best she could. As she did so, her friends sat together on the edge of the chairs and leaned forward with their elbows on their knees.

Julián unwrapped the celt and held it out to her. She took it with both hands as she realized how ancient this object was. *A piece of history – of my history.* She expected nothing and that was exactly what she got. Sighing with relief, she ran her fingers over the etchings and a moment later, she saw the history of her people.

It began today and went backwards. The first stop on her journey was with the Conquistadores. She saw them interbreed with the indigenous peoples, and create a new race, the Mestizos. Then she saw what looked like an exact copy of herself. The same round face and hair like night, with just a hint of a wave to it. She desired to know more about that woman, but she was torn away, back, back, back to the Mayan empire and then to the times of the Olmec.

Emilia opened her eyes and realized she must have blacked out. The celt was now in her lap and when she looked over at Doris and the others, their eyes were wide. Julián looked worried and the professor looked smug.

"Tell us what you saw in detail," the professor demanded.

Emilia nodded. Unable or perhaps unwilling to demand respect from the professor in that moment, she told them everything she'd seen, heard, and felt.

Emilia was exhausted. The moment she arrived home she kicked off her sneakers, emptied her backpack, put things away, then collapsed onto the old couch. *I really should get a new one. This old thing's not only ugly, but uncomfortable. At the rate I'm saving money I should be able to purchase a better one within one month and still have a small fund for emergencies. Monday, I'll insure my car again, so I won't have to depend on others to take me home after the SMART meeting. I think I'll keep busing to work though. It's better for the environment and cheaper than fuel, car repairs and pay parking. Never mind finding an empty spot!*

Within minutes of sitting down, her phone rang. It was Sissy.

"How are you doing? Have fun at the museum?" her sister asked.

"Kind of — I mean yes, but the day ended strangely."

"What do you mean strangely?"

"You're not going to believe this."

"You're meandering. Get to the point," Lupe grumbled.

"Okay so, first I get a strange look from this guy who turns out to be an assistant Conservator for Latin America."

"Hold it! What do you mean *strange look*?"

"I don't know, he looked — astonished."

"Whatever. Go on."

"So the actual Conservator seeks me out and introduces me to his assistant, and they want to perform a strange experiment."

"An experiment," Sissy said in a monotone of disbelief.

"Yeah, so they want me to touch this adz. And it's old, like Olmec old and it's got engravings and stuff. But, I don't know these guys from Adam and refuse until my girlfriends appear outside the glass of the Preservation rooms."

"You were in the preservation rooms, with two professors?"

"Yeah, I guess I forgot to tell you that part. Anyway, they got my friends and I sat on a comfortable chair and felt the celt."

"Hold on, hold on, you said you touched an adz, now you say it was a celt, what is a celt and what did you actually touch?"

"The professor called it a celt, I thought it was an adz, so I think they're the same or at least similar. Do you want me continue or not?" She teased her sister and gave her an unseen smile.

"You'd *better* go on."

Emilia chuckled and continued. "I saw our history."

"I hope you plan on expanding on that."

"Only if you quit interrupting."

"Okay, not another word, *zzzzzzzip!*"

"I saw the history of our people, the Mestizos. From the landing of the Conquistadores all the way back to the Olmec. I saw a woman that looked very much like me, and another that was a spitting image of you. I saw a man that looked like the professor's assistant and many other people before the Mayans and as far as the Olmec. Then I saw all the children and children's children of the Conquistadores and their indigenous wives and concubines, all the way up to the present, where we are now a great race. It only took a few seconds according to the witnesses, but it seemed like I was there for centuries."

"Do you think it was a vision?"

"I don't know what it was, but Julián, the professor's assistant, told me that he saw it and when he saw me, he remembered me from the—vision or whatever it was. He also told me after that two other women said they saw the same thing, two Mestiza women, a mother and daughter. He said the mother is the owner of the celt thing and had used it for a *tejolote* for generations."

"They were using an historical object as a pestle?"

"Yeah, how crazy is that?"

"No crazier than what you just told me, little sister."

They both burst out laughing.

When Sunday morning rose it felt like Christmas, just like when Emilia was a child. The excitement she felt was a high better than booze and *Oxy* together. Or it seemed that way to her now. It wasn't because she was struggling with urges less, which was true, nor was it on account of finding she had a clearer mind and thinking came more easily, though that was also happening. All that was great, but the best thing, what was most in the forefront of her mind, was lunch with Mosi today.

At first it was to be coffee, but when they decided on eleven-thirty it seemed more appropriate to lunch together while they were at it, which suited Emilia just fine and seemed to please Mosi as well. It *almost* seemed like a date, but she knew it wasn't, nor could it be. At least not right now. But there was still hope for the future—as long as she stayed clean. Everyone at *SMART* told her she must do her recovery for herself or it wouldn't last and she knew it was true. But she also knew there were many other reasons for staying clean. The *HOV*—the *Hierarchy of Values*—had taught her that early on. She had the possibility of getting her family back and keeping her job, which she loved. Her mind was slowly returning to normal and functioning at a higher and higher

219

level. She now had time for herself, to cook proper meals and exercise. She could do things with friends and live life. And one day, she hoped not *too* far in the future, she'd be able to handle a real, close, romantic relationship. A love between equals. She knew she wasn't ready. Her addictions were still too real, too much a part of her. But that was all fading with abstinence. Right now, at this moment in time, she wanted that special significant other to be Mosi. She didn't know if that was how she'd feel in another year or eighteen months, or if those imaginary timelines were a reasonable goal. She had learned that it usually took a couple of years of abstinence for most of the brain's healing to take place, so it *seemed* reasonable and rational to plan on romance after that time. *I've spent over ten years in addiction. It only seems reasonable that recovery will take a while.*

It was 11:22 and Emilia hoped she wasn't so early she appeared over eager, or end up waiting twenty minutes for a Mosi running late. Of course there was always the possibility he'd be a no-show, though she was certain he'd call if that were the case. Dozens of possibilities ran through her mind, and they were all negative. She steeled herself at the glass door on the coffee shop and peered inside against the glare of the sun, with pupils shutting down to pinpoints from the sudden brightness. *I can't see anything dammit. Bloody sunlight.* She laughed at her own irrational thinking and shoved open the door.

As the door swung shut behind her, Emilia looked around the coffee house and saw a jet-black face with the whitest teeth she'd ever seen, bestowing a gleaming cheerful smile on her. On her alone. She felt she was alone in the coffee shop with that smile, with him for a few earth-shattering moments and then he was rushing toward her with arms open wide.

Emilia blinked, not believing her eyes, and sure enough, Mosi was there, but had only stood to welcome her and hadn't moved from the table. She wasn't sure if it was an overactive imagination, a holdover from her addiction, or something else her brain was doing. Nevertheless, Mosi's smile was overwhelmingly warm and her heart skipped a beat. She inhaled deeply and smiled back. She was both unable and unwilling to keep the glow of seeing him off her face. Without remembering the journey, she found herself in front of him.

"You look good!" Mosi said.

While her blush would have been hidden by her olive complexion, there was no way to hide how her eyes lit up at the very sight of him, she knew.

"Thank you, you look great too," Emilia replied, thinking he was the best looking thing she'd seen — ever.

Mosi extended his hand and took hers, giving hers a soft squeeze. Heat ran from the tips of her fingers to her feet and back. Though it was more a warm glow than an electrical charge.

"Thanks, but I think I didn't express that well. What I mean is you were a scarecrow when you went into rehab, but now you've — well, filled out." He looked away.

Emilia laughed to see him embarrassed. "I'm glad you approve."

Mosi chuckled, too, and Emilia was pleased he could laugh at himself. She'd spent way too much time around people who were unable to do that unless they were high on something.

"Can I get you a coffee or something?" he asked.

"That's okay, I'll get it." Emilia took one step toward the counter, but he reached his arm out, not touching her, but so she could see.

"No, I insist, and when it's time for lunch I'll get that, too. But only if you promise not to feel obligated."

"As long as I get to pay next time, I'm good with that," Emilia said with a broad smile on her face.

"That works for me," he said with such a warm smile her

heart fluttered. "So, what can I get you?"

That's almost as good as a promise to get together again "A medium non-fat Latte, please."

Mosi nodded and went to the counter. Emilia settled into one of the cozy armchairs at the table Mosi had occupied. She noticed at that moment there was no drink on the table and he must have either just arrived, been holding the table, or simply waiting for her arrival to order for himself.

When he returned, he carried two white ceramic mugs, from which clouds of steam erupted. He gently placed them on the table, pushed one toward her and then unceremoniously plopped himself into the armchair opposite hers, like a person who'd just ended a long fatiguing day at work.

Emilia pulled the mug closer and was about to pick it up when she realized her Latte had a design in the foam.

"Look, the barista did a fern on my Latte," she said with surprise.

"Mine has a design, too," Mosi said. "It's a tulip."

Emilia, who'd been coming to the Pelican Rouge coffee shop since she was ten with her father, twisted in her seat so she could see who was at the espresso machine. "It's a new girl, I've never seen her before."

"Her name tag said Jenny," he said. "I looked when I realized she'd just done two bits of coffee art on our Latte's."

"That girl's talented." Emilia dug around in her purse. "Ah, here it is." She pulled out her cell phone, unlocked it and took a picture. As an afterthought, she took another photo of Mosi's tulip. She dropped her phone back into the back and dug her wallet out.

"What are you doing?" Mosi said with his brows knitted.

"I'm going to give her a tip."

"I already did."

"It wasn't enough."

"I gave her five bucks!"

"I'll give her another five."

Mosi shook his head, but smiled when Emilia stood and with great determination, strode to the counter. Jenny was manning the espresso machine and she bypassed the counter and walked over to where the young woman was working filling orders.

"Hi, Jenny?" Emilia asked. Standing on tiptoes to be able to see over the tall machine. However, she saw no one, but could hear the hissing of steam as milk was heated.

"Hi," a disembodied voice replied.

A moment after the hissing of steam ended, a small sunken oval face peered around the espresso machine. "Can I help you?"

"Are you Jenny?"

"Yes."

"Did you do the art on our Lattes?"

"I must have if it was done here."

Emilia laughed. "It was a few minutes ago, so it must have been you."

Jenny nodded and called out, "One large chocolate Cappuccino!"

Emilia leaned over the high counter and passed Jenny a five-dollar bill. "My friend left you a tip, but I want to add this to it."

"Thanks," Jenny said with a pleased smile. "We share all the tips, I'll put it in the tip jar."

"The other girls must get a lot more tips since you started here."

"That's what they tell me." Jenny's face looked—hungry.

"You don't mind sharing all the extra tips with the others?"

"No, we're a team. Maybe I'll need *them* one day."

"I like your attitude and your coffee art is awesome." Emilia gave Jenny a warm smile and returned to sit across from Mosi. She looked at her coffee once more, then took a sip.

"It's also the best Latte I've ever had here," Emilia said.

"Yeah, mine's good, too. I've been coming here for about a year and it's only been in the last month Jenny started." Mosi leaned his lanky body over the small table until his face was no more than twelve inches from Emilia's and whispered, "Did you notice anything odd about her?"

"Actually yes," Emilia said back as quietly, and with a quick glance toward the counter. "Her face is very thin, almost skeletal and her skin has a sallow pallor."

Mosi nodded. "I've also seen her act erratically. I think she may be addicted."

"To what?"

"It's hard to tell. As you've learned, abuse of a lot of different drugs can have similar symptoms. Of course, she could have cancer or something else."

"I wonder if there's anything we can do?" Emilia whispered.

"We must each choose to deal with our demons—or not. But every time I've come since I first saw her, I wrap my *SMART* business card in a fiver and drop it in the tip jar." He smiled at her.

"That's a good idea. I mean if she's addicted, her co-workers must know."

"If she is, I'm sure they do."

"Holy crap! Maybe that's what she meant."

"What are you talking about, Emilia?"

"She said she'd put the money I gave here in the tip jar, because they were all a team, and she might need them one day."

"That *is* very curious. Anyway, I could eat a horse. A very small one, but a horse nonetheless. How about you?"

Emilia grinned at his playfulness. *Another thing to love about him.* "I'm famished."

"Do you want me to get you a menu?"

"Nope." Emilia smiled. "I would like a chicken and avocado on Focaccia please."

"I had that once or twice, it's pretty good. I think I'll do the Thai beef salad today, though, and get us another Latte, if you'd like. Do you want a glass of water?"

"Another Latte sounds decadently good, and a glass of cold water no ice for me if you'd be so kind."

"Sure." Mosi stood. "I'll be right back."

While she waited for Mosi to return, Emilia's mind wandered between the reason Mosi had asked her to meet him today and Jenny's possible addiction. She'd come to no certain conclusions on either matter before he returned to sit across from her.

"I'm really enjoying our visit, and I hope we can see each other again from time to time, but I think you had a specific reason for asking me here," she said.

"Yes, I did. I've been putting it off because it's not a topic I want to discuss, but how about I tell you while we eat?"

"Sure," she said casually and shrugged as if she wasn't dying to find out.

A few minutes later lunch arrived and she settled in to hear what he had to say.

After a few bites of salad, Mosi put his fork on his plate very deliberately, at eight o'clock.

Mmm, very formal.

"I'm not sure why—our mutual *friend*—wants you involved in this—*escapade.* But I'm concerned for your well-being."

"You mean my sobriety."

"Yes, that and your peace of mind."

Emilia began to feel hot. It was a moment before she realized it was anger. He was trying to *protect* her, God damn him. *How dare he!*

"It's *my* life and *my* recovery. You've *no* right to interfere."

"Of course I don't and I won't, but I *will* worry. Please," he begged, "be careful, be mindful, keep yourself as your first priority, or you could relapse."

Her anger faded into confusion at his words. "I know I'm at *The Wall*, but I understand what's happening and *will* wait it out. I'm not going to relapse. Besides, I've got my *HOV*, the *CBA*, and Sissy."

"And I'm going to give you a new tool, one that's not in the Handbook yet."

Emilia sat up straighter. "A new tool? One that's not in the Handbook? How do you even know about it?"

"*SMART* Facilitators are all connected online . . . if they want to be. And our Regional Coordinator keeps up to date on things *SMART's* working on. Probably giving input, too. I found out from her."

"Oh, that's cool. So what's this tool?"

"Pick up your sandwich, but don't take a bite," he said.

She picked it up.

"Close your eyes and feel the bread. Just touch it. Now hold it close to your nose and breathe in deeply. Think of the smells. How does the bread smell? What do you sense?"

"I feel the heat of the chicken, the Focaccia is crusty and I smell the sourness of the dressing."

"Take one small bite, but just hold it in your mouth." After one minute Mosi said, "Now chew it, but chew slowly. How does it feel? What do you taste?"

Emilia had never chewed so slowly in her life, but she did now and after twenty-five chews, she swallowed. "That was interesting. I've never tasted the food like I just did right now."

"That's because you were *mindful* of every bite. That was an exercise in *Mindfulness*. Another is to lie down, relax your whole body and then concentrate on each muscle group one at a time and relax them. You could also do a gratitude list and I think you said you meditate."

"Yeah, they taught us meditation in rehab."

"That can be part of it. It's all about being aware of yourself. If you're always self-aware, it's much harder to relapse."

"So you brought me here to give me a new tool?"

"In part, yes, but also to let you know you can call me at any time of the day or night and I'll answer as soon as humanly possible. I'll be here for you. I'm proud of how far you've come and how fast, but I still worry."

Emilia found herself content. Confused, torn, and frustrated, but content. *Maybe the future holds real promise. It's certainly worth staying clean and sober for.*

In the background, music had been playing, but Emilia hadn't even heard it until the moment she heard a Latin tune on the canned music. There was something about the juxtaposition of being clean, clear-headed, with Mosi and the salsa beat that made her body want to move. She popped up out of the chair and Mosi gawked.

"Wanna dance?"

"Dance?"

"Yeah, you know, one, two, three, five, six, seven."

"Salsa? Here? Now?"

"Yes."

As Mosi was taking far too long and the song could only have a few minutes remaining, she, without thinking about it, reached over, took his arm and tugged. In spite of the fact the force of her pull was trifling, he followed it and stood. This small success emboldened her to lead his willing body to an area between the tables large enough to dance if one took care.

Mosi took the proper stance, though he seemed hesitant, but a moment later he indicated to her the first steps, one, two, three, pause, five, six, seven pause. He continued, very slowly and clearly in her eyes a novice, but it was fun. Unexpectedly and with complete lack of finesse, he did an exaggerated J indication for her to turn. She loved this! She was no professional, but most certainly accomplished and even though her partner lacked practice and finesse, he seemed to have some abilities, but just needed practice. It occurred to her Salsa and Latin dancing might be a way for them to spend some quality and fun time together — if he was interested.

The song ended to scattered claps from other patrons and they went to sit back down and finish their Lattes.

"That was fun, but a bit embarrassing. I'm not good at the Salsa," Mosi said. "And I would have never thought of dancing spontaneously at a coffee shop."

"It's a Mestizo thing I think," Emilia said with a cheeky grin. "Anytime there's an opportunity to dance, *take it.*"

"Might I suggest it's more akin to creating an opportunity than taking one?" Mosi sucked at his bottom lip.

She laughed. "You may be right, but perhaps it's about perspective."

"And how you were raised. Was it common in your family to do things like we just did?"

"Now that I think about it, yes. I remember Mom and Dad breaking into a Rumba quite a few times while we were at the supermarket. I remember there was always a lot of room near the frozen food section and they'd just start dancing."

"Were you kids embarrassed?"

"Hell no, we'd usually join in. My brother would even dance with my sister and me at the same time. He really has some great moves. My dad used to sing sometimes too. Totally out loud and it didn't matter if we were at home or in the checkout at the grocery store. My sister, brother and I thought it was pretty cool, though my brother changed his mind at about fifteen and started to feel humiliated. Dad kind of backed off a bit when he was with my brother when he realized it bothered him."

"Is this normal among Latinos?"

"To some degree, I think, but my folks were the most extroverted Mestizos I know."

"I need to get going soon. I've got an appointment to play tennis this afternoon, but you've mentioned the word Mestizo and I'm not sure what it means. I assume it's another way of saying Latino, but I don't actually know."

"In a way it is, but in a way no. The word means a mix, and as we are mix of the conquistadores and Indigenous people of Latin America, and now form about ninety percent of the population, we've essentially become a new race. Others call us Latinos, but in our language, in Spanish, we're Mestizos."

"Ah, okay, I get it. Thanks."

"I was thinking it'd be fun to get together to practice the Salsa and maybe some other Latin dances. You have the basics."

"Yes, it would be and could be a *VACI* for you."

"*VACI?*"

"*Vitally Absorbing Creative Interest.*"

"I think I read about that in my *SMART* Handbook."

"With three months clean, it would be a good time to find things you love to do. They help replace old addictive behaviors."

"I'm in," Emilia said, and they laughed.

CHAPTER TWENTY-EIGHT

"You have an unexpected visitor, Mister El-Hadidy," Caroline informed him Monday morning as he worked in his *CCSA* office.

Mosi looked at the intercom Caroline seldom used, with a frown. To alleviate his bewilderment he asked, "Who is it?"

"A gentlemen who says you only know him as Zach and he has a young woman with him."

The only Zack, Mosi knew in any recent time was from the *SMART* meeting. He couldn't very well confirm this in front of Caroline, as *SMART Recovery* was strictly anonymous, at least for any who wished to remain so. Unable to simply ask if he was *that* Zach over the intercom, he decided to tell Caroline to bring him in. He turned off the monitor as what he was viewing was confidential information on volunteers, turned off his wireless mouse, sat back in his executive chair, and waited.

In less than ten seconds he heard Caroline's distinct knock and without waiting for permission, she opened the door and ushered Zach and the young woman into the office.

"Hello, Mosi," Zach said before Caroline could close the door.

This raised Caroline's eyebrows, of which Mosi caught a fleeting glimpse before she shut the door.

"Hi, Zach, you could have called me if you're having" — he eyes went back and forth between Zach and the young woman, and as he didn't know how much she knew of Zach's situation said — "issues."

Zach gave a throaty laugh. "This is Alexa, technically my bodyguard, at which I'm sure she's quite able, but she's also my — keeper — I guess you might say. My father has set her on me to make sure I don't relapse. To test my urine, take random blood samples, and keep me away from my dealer and the liquor store. I'm afraid I've lost my father's confidence, at least as far as my sobriety goes. However, I'll take this in stride as my mission is too important to be upset by such trivialities, and it will certainly add an additional barrier against relapse, which would be unfortunate at this time, given our plans."

"*Your* plans I think," Mosi said, in a vexed tone as he shook his head.

"In part, yes, but as they include keeping the funding for *CCSA*, keeping religion separate from the state and in particular, the continuation of publicly funded, science-based recovery, we are at least on the same team."

"Okay," Mosi grumbled, "I'll bite for now, but I don't want anything to do with the Minister's plans to take over as Premier."

"No to worry, that'll never happen."

Mosi's eyes opened wide.

"The Premier must be ousted," Zach said. "But the Minister of Health cannot take her place. *Will not* become Premier. No, for too long we've had politicians in power who are there for their own power and to better *their* peers, not the public whose trust they hold and whose money they spend."

"But you work for the Minister," Mosi said in surprise.

Zach gave him a smile that made Mosi shudder. "I *technically* work for the Minister, but I'm a man of the people."

"Who do you consider to be *The People?*"

"Ah, an astute question, Mosi," Zach said casually and with a crinkled smile.

I don't trust him. Not in the least, but what options do I have right now? Life, circumstances or possibly Zach himself has maneuvered me into this corner and all I can see to do, is whatever I have to do to keep CCSA *in the forefront of addiction rehabilitation and prevention. No! I don't* have *to do anything. I will do my best to keep* CCSA *going, but that's all I can ask from myself or of anyone.* "More importantly, do you have an answer to that question?"

"I do, but will you believe me?"

"I can't know the answer to that until I've heard it," Mosi said, calmly.

Zach nodded. "I'll grant you that. My position is all inhabitants of Canada are *the people*."

"Not just citizens?"

"There are many people who live here who aren't citizens. Some are permanent residents, others have work or visitors visas."

"What about illegal aliens?"

Zach shrugged. "At one time we were all illegal aliens. If you go back far enough, even the indigenous among us arrived here at one time."

"There was no country then, no law and no inhabitants," Mosi argued.

"That's exactly correct. There were no countries in existence at that time. Countries as we know them are artificial constructs, made so certain men can have power over other men of lesser intelligence, or perhaps less greed or hunger for power. It's most certainly not the wisest and best individuals that run our countries. But you're wrong claiming there was no law, for wherever there are Homo sapiens, there is law and suggesting the land was empty of inhabitants is claiming something we don't know for certain. In fact, there's some evidence there were other hominids here in North America long before our Homo sapiens' indigenous ancestors arrived fifteen thousand years ago. Is it possible our indigenous ancestors drove out other hominid species? I don't know, but it's possible. But my point is, the very term illegal alien is a human construct of a certain group of humans maintaining a form of exclusivity for a particular region."

"So you don't believe in the rule of law or the right of a country to defend itself against aggression?"

Zach gave a great sigh. "That is all we have. It's where we've come, what we've become. I simply think there's something better for humanity than killing one another over plots of dirt or globs of petroleum. I think we can be a better kinder race, maybe evolve into something better. Perhaps become a people who don't tend to kill one another or rape our planet."

"I confess that's a wonderful dream, but it also sounds a bit like anarchy."

"Not anarchy, rather organic law. One that comes from treating everyone around you the way you wish to be treated and doing so because our brains have been programed to do so by nature, or if you'd rather, by evolution."

"I don't think it's possible. Do you?"

"Let's say I hope it's possible. It's certainly not going to happen in my lifetime or yours, but I think it's a worthy goal and one early step is to begin to weed out the worst of the politicians and replace them with individuals of genuine conscience."

Mosi looked into Zach's eyes. He felt he could tell a lot from delving into the depths of the eyes. He could certainly not discover any deceit there. Zach, he was convinced, believed what he said. "That is all good, but my interest is to see the *CCSA* funded so we can continue to do our work to alleviate and reduce drug addiction and the harm it causes. Both to the individual and to society."

"Yes," Zach agreed. "We must return to the real present and not concern ourselves ever much with a hypothetical future. You're a good man, Mister Mosi El-Hadidy, and you have a good and worthy project. I myself was a victim of the drug and alcohol culture and am just now freeing myself of that pernicious addiction and lifestyle. And that's why I need you to make a speech to the lawmakers at the BC Legislature. *You* are how we will begin to change the future."

"A speech about what?"

"About the opioid crisis and *CCSA's* endeavors to lessen its impact. On your successes, dear Mosi. A *Cost Benefit Analysis*, if you will."

"And what does Emilia have to do with all of this? Why do you want her a part of it?"

"Ah, Emilia, yes. She may become more important than we know. Her heritage may go back into prehistoric Mesoamerican history. But I can't tell you what I don't know. I feel intuitively that we need her in this. Possibly simply as a testimony to *SMART Recovery*. That's all I can say right now, but perhaps she will become more in the future. I can't tell."

"I'd rather keep her out of this. I can't possibly know what might trigger a relapse in her."

"I think she's strong. Stronger than you realize. And let's not forget she's taken to the *SMART* training and tools very well. It's the tools that will save us, that and our desire to be free."

"It's helped a lot of people, yes, that's true."

"This is her decision, not yours. You can advise her, but she'll do what she feels is right. Rather, according to *SMART* doctrine, I believe she'll *choose* to do what she thinks is right."

"I'm afraid you're correct, but I still worry."

"Each individual is responsible for their own recovery, true?"

"Yes, of course. That's what self-empowerment's about. But I'm still concerned."

"That's because you're a good man, Mosi, which is why I want you to make that speech. Will you do it?"

"Understanding what's on the line, I will, but under protest."

Emilia knew what was coming and was pleased with the whole situation. When Mosi smiled at her, she gave him a warm smile in return and then looked over at Josh and gave him another smile.

"Hi, everyone," Mosi said. "I've got a surprise for you. A pleasant one." He grinned. "Josh has just finished the *SMART Recovery* Facilitator's course and received his certificate. I've asked him to co-facilitate with me again this evening."

Josh stood and moved around to the front of the table where, by some known miracle, there just happened to stand an empty chair beside Mosi.

"Thanks, Mosi. Even though I've co-facilitated with you before I'm nervous as hell, but I'll do my best," Josh said.

"You'll do great!" Emilia called and pumped her right arm in the air.

There was some spattered clapping.

Josh lifted a copy of the sheet that lay before each chair and began to read *The Opening Statement*.

This is an open meeting of SMART Recovery. SMART *stands for* Self-Management And Recovery Training . . .

"Thanks, Josh. Please go ahead and do the check-in," Mosi said and leaned back in his chair, which was unusual, as he tended to lean forward, often with his arms on the table.

"We're going to check in and for new people that means to give us your name and tell us a little about how your week went. If at any time you don't wish to speak, please just say pass. Let's start on my left." Josh pointed to Steve.

Steve doesn't look happy.

"I'm Steve," he began in a dejected tone. "On Friday night I relapsed. I spent all night and most of Saturday doing crack and blew over two grand. God, it makes me fucking sick. I worked *hard* to save that two thousand bucks and I blew it in one day. One fucking day. Anyway, I stayed clean Sunday and again today, so at least I didn't go into debt."

"I understand," a young woman Emilia hadn't noticed said, as there were so many people in the room and she'd been chatting with her girlfriends until the meeting started. "Crack's better than sex."

It's Jenny, the barista from the Pelican Rouge!

Josh interrupted her thought. "You had a slip, Steve, or you could call it a lapse, but at *SMART* we only consider it a relapse when you fall entirely back into your old behaviors. You used for one short period and then stopped and came back to the meeting, so good on you."

"Maybe you could explain the *Stages of Change* model after check-in," Mosi said, looking at Josh with a smile.

"Good plan," Josh said, with what looked like a worried smile, then nodded to Anne, who sat beside Steve.

Check-in soon came around to Emilia, who sat about one-third the way around the packed table. *God, there's twenty-five people here!*

"I'm Emilia and I had both a good and bad week." She smiled. "I ran into some tough cravings. I thought I was over the worst of them, but it turns out I'd hit *The Wall*." As there were quite a number of puzzled faces, Emilia expounded, "It turns out that as the body begins to heal and normalize, the amount of dopamine it produces often drops off at around three months, because it realizes it's been producing too much. It looks like my body went to the other extreme with me, which also turns out to be common. So, I was feeling depressed and the cravings got really strong. I almost went to the liquor store once it was so bad, and the thing is, I almost didn't realize what I was doing. If it hadn't been for *SMART*, I'd have relapsed for sure. I keep my *HOV* in my purse." She saw confused faces. "That is, my *Hierarchy of Values* worksheet, in my purse and pulled it out before I went out the door. Another thing that's kept me clean was having to answer to my sister, who calls me all the time and could call at any moment without notice. I've also found the *CBA*—the *Cost Benefit Analysis,*" she said to clarify for newcomers, "is useful to keep me on track. But there were good things, too, and some things I'm not sure if they were good or bad yet. But that's just life."

Zachary, the enigma, sat on her left and was next.

"Hi, I'm Zach. I've got six weeks clean and it's feelin' pretty good. Thanks to Emilia for bringing up *The Wall.* I'll know what to expect in a few weeks, and knowledge is power. As my employer lost her job in cabinet, I've taken a new position that I feel very good about. In my new state of *clean* I'll be working for one of the backbenchers of the governing Liberal party. Gillian Dyck. On account of my new position, I'll be away a lot, but will come back whenever I can. However, there are a few *SMART* meetings in our wonderful provincial capital, Victoria, and two fairly close to the Legislature. I'll check them out and either choose one or go to both, though from personal experience, I'd say they need a *SMART* meeting *inside* the Legislature buildings." He chuckled. "I do get cravings, and sometimes they're severe, but now I know they'll pass and I don't *have* to pick up. *SMART* taught me that. Thanks." He nodded.

A tall blonde with a perpetual frown and muscles like a steam engine, sat beside Zach, and appeared to know him. "Pass," she grunted.

A moment came Emilia'd been waiting for since she realized the *Pelican Rouge* barista was in attendance. It was Jenny's turn.

"Hi, I'm Jenny. I didn't know what to expect, but I decided to come here 'cause I wasn't comfortable at *NA*, and my employer told me I had to do something or I was fired. That wouldn't be new, I've lost—I don't know how many jobs because of my crack addiction. I wanted it to be different this time. I really like the people I work with and the others actually stuck up for me and asked our employer to give me one more chance. So, I've gotta make it work this time, and I'm hoping *SMART*'ll help. I think I owe Mosi a thank you. You left your card with us and the others showed it to me." She gave him a wan smile.

The last to check in was a man Emilia recognized from bussing to work. He was dressed in bright Bermuda shorts and a blinding Hawaiian shirt. He wore a large necklace that looked to be made of wood and glass beads with a large wooden cross hanging from it.

"I'm Phineas, and this is my first *SMART* meeting ever. I'd never heard of it until—a young lady—told me about it. I've been going to *AA* for seventeen plus years and been clean fifteen of those. Got my fifteen-year cake six months ago now. It never occurred to me that *AA* might not work for some people. I just figured they weren't working the steps. Like we say in *AA*, the steps work if you work the steps, but I'm thinking I might have been mistaken there after listening to some of the people here check in. I'll say I like the way the meeting's going and look forward to see what happens now, as I'm the last one to check in."

"Thanks, Phineas," Josh said.

"Here in *SMART*, we've stolen that *AA* saying and changed it to suit *SMART*," Mosi said to Phineas with his ubiquitous broad smile. "The *SMART* tools work, if you work the tools."

Phineas grinned back at Mosi and smiled.

Josh stood at a nod from Mosi, took a red erasable marker and went to the large whiteboard at the front of the meeting room. He drew a loose vertical spiral that ended with one long single line fading to the right.

"You'll find the *Stages of Change* model on page eleven of

the Handbook. There's also a handout explaining it that Mosi's passing around right now."

Once everyone had either opened their Handbook or taken a handout, Josh began.

"What's the first *Stage of Change*?" Josh asked, looking to the regulars.

"Pre-contemplation," Anne said, reading right out of the Handbook.

"Good, can somebody explain what that means?"

Zach lifted his new-looking Handbook and spoke. "Pre-contemplation is where I lived for the last ten years." He grinned. "I didn't think I had a problem. What I mean is I used coke and alcohol to relax or reward myself. I would often go for weeks without vodka and coke. My only problem was *other* people and *their* attitudes. So drinking and drugging was a result of others not myself. Ergo, I didn't have a drinking problem, but a *people* problem. So, that was pre-contemplation to me."

"Well said," Josh replied, then drew a large upper-case *P* at the bottom of the spiral and circled it. "What's the next stage?"

"Contemplation," Doris said.

"Right, what does that mean, Doris?"

"I think it's similar for most of us, but to me Contemplation was when I began thinking I — *maybe* — had a problem. I actually went back and forth between Pre-contemplation and Contemplation for years."

"Yes, and that's very common. Remember, recovery isn't a linear journey." He drew a capital *C* and circled it a little further up the spiral. "What's the next stage — Miranda?"

"Preparation."

"Will you explain it or should I ask someone else?" Josh asked.

"No, I can." Miranda's voice was as bright as her pink hair.

"Preparation is when you've realized you have a problem and decided you're going to do something and you're figuring out how to go about it or fix it. Like me, I went to *NA* and *AA* meetings, tried a *Women For Sobriety Group*, which was great, but too far for me to travel on the bus, and looked up *LifeRing*, but they didn't have anything local either, so I came to a few *SMART* meetings here, and this is working great for me. So my preparation, was looking into different things that were available and deciding what I figured would work for *me*."

"Thanks, Miranda, that was great. What's next?" Josh asked as he drew an upper case *P* further up the spiral and circled it.

The moment he turned to face the group, Phineas spoke, reading from the handout. "Action—I *like* that word—means I'm gonna do somethin' not jus' sit back an wait on the Almighty. Ya know what I mean?"

Josh and Mosi laughed. "Succinctly put, Phineas," Josh said. "Who'd like to add to that?"

"The Action Phase is when we put the plans we made in the Preparation Stage into—well, into action," Anne said.

"For me," Emilia said, "the Action Stage was when I came to my first *SMART* meeting. That didn't go very well in one way, in that I passed out 'cause I was still in withdrawal. But Mosi called an ambulance and Doctor Reshma treated me for the withdrawal symptoms and gave me an opportunity to get into rehab. So, my Action and Preparation Stages were kind of jumbled together."

"Good point," Josh said as he marked an *A* with a circle higher again on the spiral. "Always remember that the stages don't have to be linear or sequential."

"For me, it's where I went into rehab—for the fourth time, got counseling and started coming to *SMART*," Anne said.

"This's the first time I've seen this *Stages of Change* model," Phineas said. "But I'd have to say for my first couple a years in *AA*, I kinda' jumped from the Contemplation Stage right into Action, so didn't have a plan and I'd fail after a week or two every time, much to the disappointment of my sponsor."

Josh looked at Mosi and shrugged.

Mosi spoke. "That, Phineas, is a fine example of why the Preparation Stage is so important. Great point, well explained."

Josh gave Mosi a forced smile and continued. "What's the next stage?"

Glancing up from his Handbook, Michael said, "Maintenance."

"What can you tell us about Maintenance, Michael?" Josh asked.

"Ah, I'm not there yet?"

"Fair enough," Josh said and laughed. "Anybody else?"

"I would say I've just entered the Maintenance Stage of my recovery," Caryn said. "I'm just over four months clean and I struggled for a long time to get there, going back and forth. New situations pop up and I find I'm constantly learning new ways to approach problems and temptations. I still need a lot of support, which I get from *SMART* and our ladies group of participants, so Maintenance to me is continuing to build on what I've gained and to learn new things and ways of problem solving."

"Very good," Josh said, as he drew an *M* and circled it. "This all looks great up here on the board, but reality is very different for most of us."

"Sure the hell is," Phineas said. "It all looked a little too easy, going by what I went through."

"Indeed," Josh agreed. "Because most people lapse or slip several times before they're able to quit permanently." After the circled *M*, he picked up a black marker and drew an *L* further up the spiral.

"So, let's say I'm in Maintenance and I lapse. I get pissed

drunk, stoned, or lose a few hundred bucks at the casino. But I come to my senses the next day. Where do I go according to this model?"

"Back to the beginning," Phineas said, "or at least back to contemplation."

"Actually, in the *Stages of Change*, we never go backwards, so what happens?"

"I've done this before and as no one else is answering, I will," Cam said. "If it was me, I'd go to Preparation, but I wouldn't be moving backwards according to the *Stages of Change*, I'd simply be figuring out what I'd done wrong and why I lapsed. Once I figured that out, I'd modify my action plan, and re-enter Maintenance, always moving forward. I lapsed twice early on, but Mosi explained this and I was able to use those lapses as stepping-stones to permanent sobriety. Been clean four years now and sometimes I think I'll stop coming, but I don't feel I've entered the next phase yet, so I'm holding off."

"Very succinct, Cam," Josh said. "I think it's time you took the Facilitator's course, too."

"Maybe." Cam grinned. "Maybe not."

"If I may?" Phineas asked.

"Go ahead," Josh said with a glance at Mosi.

"In *AA*, we're taught if you slip, you start all over again. Back to zero days clean. That's not what I'm hearing here."

"No, it's certainly not. A slip should be used to forward our sobriety, not as punishment. In *SMART*, we always remember we never *lose* our clean time. It's as much a part of our past as addiction was and I mean no disrespect to you or *AA*, Phineas," Josh said with a smile.

"None taken. This is all very new to me, so I don't want to dismiss it out of hand and I appreciate that you don't speak with disrespect about *AA*. I got fifteen years clean on account of the Twelve Steps."

"Yes," Mosi interjected. "*AA's* helped many."

Phineas nodded at Mosi and Josh, but remained solemn.

"So, where do we go from Maintenance?" Josh asked, raising his brows and looking around the tables.

Anne read from her Handbook.

"Exit Stage. After a long period of maintenance, most people adopt a new lifestyle consistent with their new normal behavior. Old harmful behaviors no longer have a place in their lives."

CHAPTER TWENTY-NINE

Six months clean! It was the middle of the week and she climbed out of bed bright and early so she could have coffee before she left for work. As it was an easy bus ride and gave her an opportunity to speak with strangers as well as to Phineas, whom she liked quite well. She continued to take the bus to work though she now had her car insured. For one thing it was cheaper and meant less mileage on her tired vehicle.

Her thoughts turned to Mosi. They'd gone dancing three times to a local place that had Latin music. He'd been getting better, but would never be proficient. He seemed to enjoy it. Even though he was clear they couldn't date, they were getting closer and getting to know one another. *It's actually good that I'm not in a romantic relationship right now. I'm too busy getting to know myself. To do both at the same time might be more than my newfound sobriety could manage.* She'd seen a couple of women get clean only to relapse on account of a man. What she understood was, one could only handle so much at a time and early recovery was strenuous and for her, took most of her time and energy. No wonder people lapsed or relapsed when combining early recovery with romance, which in her estimation—which had most definitely matured in the last few months—would be very difficult. She chuckled to herself. *Having eyes for a man who's unreachable makes my choice to remain celibate easy, so it's not really much of a temptation.*

As she prepared for work, she remembered she was about to turn thirty. *Funny, being clean six months feels better and more important than a birthday.*

Her phone rang as she walked in the door to her condo after work. She dug her phone from her purse and check to see who was calling.

"Hey, Sissy," she said as soon as she answered. Her sister was still calling at odd hours, though with less frequency than she had at first.

"Hi, little sister. Still planning on getting together with your *SMART* ladies for tea and crumpets this evening?"

Emilia laughed. "More like scones, Lupe, but yeah for sure."

"Awesome! I'm proud of you and as your birthday's coming up, I thought it might be nice to get together for a birthday dinner. Mateo's willing to come, too."

I get to see Sissy's husband. Too cool. "That'd be great, I haven't seen Mateo in ages. How about the girls?" Emilia asked tentatively, hoping to see them for the first time in more than three years.

"Sorry, they're both busy Saturday."

"That's too bad, I really want to see them, and I still haven't been able to see Bartolomé or Mom and Dad."

"*Poco a poco*, little sister."

Little by little, Emilia translated in her mind. Yep, there was no other way. "I have no control over what others do and it's my own fault they don't trust me or want to see me. I know that, but it still hurts and I'm really happy you've let me spend time with you and also talk every day. It's been a real help, especially early on."

"You've only been clean six months, and that after years of addiction. It's still early on as far as your family's concerned."

"Yeah, I know and I take all the blame. I'm sure I'd feel exactly the same." Emilia's tone was sad and she frowned, though there was no one to see.

"I'm thinking seven on Saturday at the *Keg* in Surrey and

bring a friend. Maybe your facilitator friend. Mateo and I'd love to meet him."

"Seven's fine and I'll call Mosi and ask. It's kind of short notice, but I don't *think* he's got anything planned."

"Perfect, we'll see you then."

"Oh, Sissy, I forgot to tell you. I'm going to Victoria next week with Mosi."

"Bad girl! You didn't tell me you two had something going on."

Emilia chuckled. "We don't. He's been invited to give a speech to the Legislature, and Gillian Dyck's assistant wants me along for some reason. We're not staying in the same room, silly, sister."

"Damn," Lupe said. "That *is* a disappointment."

Emilia chuckled. "Actually, yeah it is a bit of one."

On hanging up with Sissy, Emilia called Mosi, as she knew he should be home by now. Her heart fell when her call went to voicemail, but he could be working late. He sometimes met individuals who gave large donations in the evenings, and stayed late for other reasons, too. She left a short message inviting him to her birthday, punched end on her phone and went to change and make a light dinner. She didn't want to eat too much as she always had a snack when her and the other *SMART* ladies met at the coffee shop on Wednesdays.

In a ratty pair of shorts and an old top she thought of as her *Sunday* top, as it was *holey* — but comfortable as all get out — she went about preparing dinner. First, she cut up the chicken breast she'd pulled out of the freezer in the morning, and tossed it in a bowl, adding soy sauce, minced ginger and garlic, sugar, vinegar and two finely sliced Thai chilies. Next, she washed and cut up broccoli, thinly sliced carrots and baby bok choy with green onions and placed them in separate bowls. When she was nearly ready she pulled out a wok she'd recently purchased. It was carbon steel with a flat bottom and worked well on her gas stove. *It was a little work to season and clean, but she's a dream to cook with.*

When the peanut oil in the wok was smoking, she drained the chicken and popped it into the pan, in two small batches, cooking it until almost done. Removing the last of the chicken, Emilia first threw in the carrots, then one minute later the broccoli and when she judged it was hallway done, in went the bok choy. When they were nearly cooked, she poured the rest of the juices she'd used to marinate the chicken and the chicken itself, stirred it constantly for another minute and a half, then turned off the burner, lifted the wok off the stove and dumped it onto a plate. Dinner was served.

She pulled a pair of chopsticks from her utensil drawer and took her plate into her home office. She'd never reconnected her cable but she now had an Internet connection and she sat in front of her laptop to read the news while she ate.

The moment she took her first bite and had her mouth full, her phone rang.

It was Mosi.

Working late was common in Mosi's profession, and this new contributor gave him a check for one million and said that she and her husband would now be giving the same each year, and to call her on her personal cell phone if any emergencies came up and they would *see what they could do.*

This was particularly useful as it was still uncertain *CCSA* would be getting their annual funding from the provincial government. When he climbed into his car after the meeting, he pulled his cell phone from his briefcase and found three voicemails—one from his mother, one from Zach and a final one from Emilia. He'd deal with Zach's later and call his mom when he got home, but he dialed Emilia immediately. He chuckled to himself at his urgency to call a woman who was, and only could be, a friend.

The voice that answered Emilia's number was so unclear he couldn't make out what it said or even who it was. He glanced at the phone screen, but it clearly said *Emilia Robles*. He was about to ask for a clarification, when Emilia's voice came through in something of a mumble, but understandable.

"Thorry, I thist thtared to eat."

Mosi laughed. "Sorry, I could call you back in a while."

A few moments past where he heard what he thought were chewing and swallowing sounds, then Emilia was back.

"No, that's all right, I just about burned my mouth on the first bite, so I need to give it a few minutes to cool anyway."

"Okay, so I got your message and I have a tennis game at five, but I'll make it earlier or cancel so it won't conflict."

"Oh, I wouldn't want to interfere with your game," she said in a tone that was clearly disappointed.

"Not to worry, this is your birthday and you only turn thirty once. I'll be there."

"That's great. My sister and her husband, Mateo, want to meet you."

"And this'll be your first family get together since you've been clean."

"Yeah, but only Mateo and Lupe'll be there. Their girls have plans and Mom, Dad, and Bartolomé still won't see me, though I think my brother wants to, but his girlfriend's not happy about it. I'm reaping what I've sown."

She sounds unhappy. "Look at it as a first step to winning the family over, not as a failure to get them to see you," he told her softly.

"Yeah, I'll try to do that." She sniffed.

"Are you crying?"

Emilia laughed. "No, I just put a lot of chili in my stir-fry and my nose is running."

Mosi chuckled. *She likes her spicy food, this one.* "Out with the ladies tonight aren't you?"

"Yeah, should be fun. Jenny said she'd be there, too. She's not working tonight."

"I'd like to be a fly on *that* coffee shop wall."

"You'd be welcome anytime."

"Thanks, but it wouldn't be the same as being a fly on the wall and listening in. I'd get an edited version of one of your meetings if I came in person."

"No you wouldn't—well yes, I guess you would, especially as you're our facilitator."

"I thought so, too. That's all right. It's good to know when participants do more for their sobriety than attend one meeting a week. Anyway, I'm in my car and haven't left for home yet, so I'll get going. We'll talk as to where and when your birthday party will be later."

"Great, sounds good."

Mosi punched *end* and could feel the smile on his face. He gave a great satisfied sigh.

Emilia's steady as a rock in her recovery. Sometimes I wish I wasn't her facilitator. No, it's too early, far too early.

His smile turned sour.

CHAPTER THIRTY

At ten minutes to closing time, Zach walked in the door. At the desk, where they were in clear de-escalation and preparations to close, he spoke quietly with one of the employees, who nodded and pointed. He nodded back and walked toward the door marked *staff only*.

He knocked on said door and it was opened an instant later by a gentleman who appeared to be in his sixties.

"Hello, Professor. I've been reading your emails. Very interesting stuff, but I'm not sure why you'd want to see me in person."

The professor gave him a solemn nod. "I do thank you for coming, Mister Robinson. I know you're a very busy man, but when you've seen the artifact in question, I believe you'll agree it was worth your time. I hope—think—believe—it will be of help to you in your ultimate quest."

Zach's brows furrowed. *What did this man know of his— quest—as he called it?* "I'm sure I have no idea to what you refer, Professor," Zach said, narrowing his eyes.

"No, no, of course you don't," the professor said, a wan smile on his lips. "Please come along, Mister Easton Aubrey Zachary Robinson." The professor gestured toward an open doorway.

"You forgot the second," Zach said, even as he followed.

"Sorry?"

"My full name's Easton Aubrey Zachary Robinson the second."

"Sorry, I misspoke. Of course it is."

Zach rolled his eyes as he followed. *The professor can't see me anyway. I don't think he got the sarcasm.* The professor led Zach down a long wide corridor to a door he opened using his ID card as a fob. It was a small, poorly lit room with three computers. Two were at small desks and the third at a large workstation, which looked to hold many stacks of papers and what might be artifacts. At one of the smaller desks sat a person who turned his chair around when they entered.

"Ah, Professor," the person said, who from his voice, was a man. "I see you've brought him."

Professor Johansson flipped a switch and the room brightened.

Zach now saw the man who owned the voice. His skin was a deep olive and his face was round, but pleasant.

"Julián, this is Mister Easton Aubrey Zachary Robinson the second."

"Yes." Julián nodded. "I recognize him from the newspapers."

"Be so kind as to show him the celt, Julián."

Julián leaned over and pulled the middle drawer of his desk open. From within he drew an ebony-colored box, placed it on the desk, and after closing the drawer with his knee, opened the box as if it were full of pearls — or nitroglycerin. *It looks like an adz, but he calls it a celt. I wonder what the difference might be.*

Julián donned light cotton gloves and lifted the celt from its container, then placed it with the greatest of care onto a felt-covered tray on his desk.

The professor lifted it as if it were an ancient piece of glass and showed it to him.

"We believe the markings on it are writing and they seem to be a different language than the Cascajal Block, and Julián and I seem to be having some success translating it," Professor Johansson said.

"I wasn't aware Olmec could be translated."

251

"It *was* an impossible task, as the only known object with Olmec hieroglyphics was the Cascajal Block, but this celt appears to date from the same period, but be written in a different, though similar language as well as what we think is the same language as the Cascajal Block. Assuming that, we've begun work to translate the celt. And if we are correct, it may be the key to deciphering the Olmec language."

"And you say with some success."

"We believe so, yes. We may have the key to the Olmec language and also in part because of four things that seemed to have verified what we've discovered."

"Please go on," Zach said, feeling like he was listening to a preacher, not an acclaimed scientist.

"From what we understand so far, it seems to be a prophecy, or perhaps it might be better to call it a future history. It appears there are to be six women of mixed ancestry, and these mixed ancestry women will somehow drive the beginnings of a new age for mankind. Of course, the Olmec understanding of mankind was likely very different from ours. But anyway, that's all we've been able to translate to date.

"I will add, however, that Julián had a very odd experience while handling the celt. He had what one might call a . . . uhm, *vision* and it included seeing six Mestiza women. This was before we were able to translate as much as we have now. He's met three of them in real life, which leads me to think these women are real and there are three left to find. One of the women was Emilia Robles with whom I believe you claim an acquaintance."

The professor coughed into his hand. "Julián and I *have* done a few—experiments—with other Latina or Mestiza women, but only the three he saw in his—*vision*—have had a similar experience. The other women saw and experienced nothing."

This was all extraordinary and Zach was inclined to

dismiss it. It seemed more than possible the professor was a bit barmy. But something held him back from coming to this conclusion. It took him a few moments for him to realize it was Emilia. Before he knew of this celt, he was intuitively certain that Emilia was an important part of his plan. Emilia was one of the three women that'd had this *vision*, though she'd never said anything to him. But why would she? He never went wrong when he listened to his gut and his gut told him Emilia was important and given that, it seemed probable that this celt was somehow intertwined with what he needed to do. His father must have an intuitive feel for this as well and that must be why he was funding the professor's studies, which was the reason Zach was here tonight. Zach was happier than ever that he'd insisted Emilia go along for Mosi's speech.

CHAPTER THIRTY-ONE

M osi had suggested they take his vehicle to the *Keg* that evening, which was fine with Emilia. She found it easier to chat while someone else had the wheel and Mosi was a careful driver, she knew from experience.

When they pulled up outside the *Keg* restaurant, she began searching for her sister's car, but realized they could just as easily come in Mateo's auto and she had no idea what it might look like because she didn't think he still drove the same SUV she'd last seen five years ago.

Once inside they told the hostess they were with the Robles reservation, as her sister had made the booking in Emilia's name. Though Emilia didn't know why, she didn't see it as an issue. The slender bleach blonde hostess led them to the far end of the restaurant and Emilia spotted not only her sister and Mateo, but their two girls. She slipped past the hostess and ran to see her nieces. She hugged them both, kissed their cheeks while tears of joy flooded hers. She turned to face Sissy, but Mateo stood between them.

Mateo opened his arms and engulfed her. "I'm so glad you're back with us, Emilia," he said, then released her so she could hug her sister. The two Mestiza sisters cried in each other's arms.

"I thought you said the girls weren't able to come tonight," Emilia said, when she was finally able to speak, although she was still sobbing.

After wiping Emilia's tears with a tissue, Sissy said, "I lied."

Emilia laughed and hugged her older sister again.

"Actually, I lied about a lot of things," Sissy said with a broad smile.

In that moment, her mom and dad came out of a hallway, followed by her brother and a young woman she didn't recognize, but assumed was the girlfriend who'd answered the phone the first time she'd called Bartolomé. The people she loved most in this world surrounded Emilia and they laughed and cried together for an entire five minutes.

Before they sat, Bartolomé introduced the woman with him.

"This is Megan, we've been together for a year and a half."

Emilia shook the glowering Megan's hand. "I'm so glad to meet you."

"Yeah, whatever," Megan said, giving Emilia's hand a limp shake.

Bartolomé frowned.

Emilia turned to search for Mosi. He was behind her, steps away. She stretched out her arm and beckoned him with a warm smile. Mosi smiled in turn and the results were as they always were and he had her entire family under his spell in an instant. Even the truculent Megan's face held a feeble smile.

"This is Mosi, he's our *SMART Recovery* Facilitator and a good friend."

"So you're the one who saved my little girl," Emilia's dad said, with warmth.

"Your daughter saved herself, Mister Robles. I just happen to facilitate the *SMART* group she chooses to attend."

"However it works and whoever's responsible, we're happy she's back," her mom told Mosi, as she looked up at him with her bright dark eyes.

They all took seats and as the group was small, they were all in easy hearing of one another, which worked well as

Emilia was pressed to tell all the details of how she'd gotten clean, the people who'd helped her along the way, her time in rehab and how things were going at work now she was sober. Every member of the family threw Mosi surreptitious glances, clearly wondering how good of a *friend* Mosi was. Each one of them listened intently when he spoke and their eyes would brighten when he smiled.

On their way home from her birthday party, Emilia's phone rang. She checked the screen and was delighted to see Bartolomés name and slid the green icon to accept the call.

"Hi," Emilia said in a cheerful tone.

"Just stay away from him. You have no idea how much you hurt him. Just go die somewhere."

It's Megan, Emilia realized. "I'm sorry, I really am and I'll never understand how much he must have hurt. What I did was awful, but that's not who I am. Please, Megan, give me a chance to make it up to him in some small way by being the sister he remembers from before my addiction."

"Fuck you. Just stay away."

The line went dead.

She turned in her seat to face Mosi. "That was Megan. She basically told me to stay away from Bartolomé and in rather vulgar language. I guess she's trying to protect him from me. Not that I blame her, I treated him like shit and tried to use him to borrow money and things all the time. But he's too smart and didn't go for my bullshit lines most of the time."

"It didn't take a genius to see Megan wasn't happy at your party, but truth be told, she didn't seem to get along with anyone except Bartolomé."

"She sounded like he didn't want to see me and I shouldn't see him."

"That's certainly not how Bartolomé acted at your party," Mosi said. "He wanted to get together with you now and do things like you used to. Is there any way you can talk to him when Megan's not around?"

"I could call him at his work."

"Why don't you try that," Mosi suggested. "Maybe you can figure out what's going on. We can't control how others think or feel. By accepting that fact, it not only helps us stay clean, but be more at peace with ourselves."

"It'll have to wait until the middle of next week 'cause we're going to Victoria for your speech on Monday and won't get back until late Tuesday."

"I'm sure it'll be fine," Mosi said, with a smile and a tone flooded with encouragement.

"Changing the subject a bit," Emilia said, "how's the speech going for Monday at the Legislature?"

"It's been done for over a month, but I read it out loud and still tweak it. My poor mom's heard it over a dozen times. Hey," he said, "why don't you let me read it to you and get some input?"

"Sure, we'd have time on the ferry to Victoria Monday morning."

"I'm not sure that's a good place to do it, maybe tomorrow if you don't have too much to do?"

Emilia most certainly didn't have so much to do that she couldn't find time to spend with Mosi.

Emilia's cell phone rang. As it was still in her hand, which was resting on her lap, she flipped it over and was surprised what the caller ID displayed.

"It's *Bartolomés* number," Emilia said, "I hope it's not Megan again."

"Only one way to know for sure, just remember, she can't say anything to upset you unless you let her."

"That's right, SMART doctrine, I'm in control of my own feelings," Emilia said as she lifted the phone and slide the answer button.

"Hi," Emilia said tentatively.

"Hi, little sis."

Emilia exhaled forcefully, her decision not to allow Megan to control her emotions notwithstanding.

"Hi, Barty, I'm so glad it's you."

"Who else could it be?"

"Well—Megan called me on your phone a few minutes ago."

"Really, the little—anyway, she has her opinion, it's not mine."

"I know, but we talked about getting together a couple of months ago and it kept getting postponed. I ah—actually thought it might be—you know—because of her."

"The truth is, it mostly was, but I'm getting tired of her trying to keep us apart. Honestly, she doesn't like me spending time with any of the family and it's growing old. I don't know what we're going to do, but she's going to have to quit trying to keep me away from my family, or it's going to end."

"Jesus, I'm sorry to hear that. Do you see her family at all?"

"Yeah, and that's the most annoying part. We see her family all the time. At first it was all new, I thought maybe she was shy or something, but she's got something else going on in that head of hers."

"Have you thought about going for counseling together? I know some couples from *SMART* do that. Maybe it'll help," Emilia said.

"No, I hadn't. That's certainly worth a try. I mean she should be willing if she wants to work it out. Thanks, little sister, that's a great idea. Who knows, maybe it's partly to do with me."

"Or maybe her past. The way we're raised and experiences we have when we're young can really have an effect on us. I've learned that from my own counseling sessions."

"You can't change the way you were raised," Bartolomé said.

"No," Emilia agreed. "But we *can* change how we think about it and how we deal with it. Knowing is half the battle, at least it was for me. Now I know what happened and why I feel the way I do, or rather did, I was able to change it."

"That sounds too easy."

"Yeah it does, but in reality it's been a lot of hard work. You have to be patient and persistent as well as go easy on yourself for your mistakes. Anyway, it's working for me."

"This is all from *SMART Recovery*?" he asked as his tone rose.

"Yeah, it is."

"It sounds more like stuff for everyday living than about recovery."

Emilia chuckled. "Recovery's *all* about living every day, and learning to live it to the fullest."

"We need to talk more about this," Barty said, "but I actually called to tell you how proud I am of you. I love you, sis."

"Love you, too, Barty."

"Okay, take care. We'll talk soon."

"Bye."

"That sounded very different from your chat with Megan. Of course I only heard one side of the conversation," Mosi said.

Emilia chuckled. "Curious, are we?"

Mosi glanced over at her with a wide grin. "I confess, I am. It just sounded so normal from your end and you didn't seem the least bit tense."

"Not once I realized he really wanted to see me but had been — well—duped by Megan."

"She wasn't overly friendly at your party. In fact, she acted like she didn't want to be there."

"Yeah, for sure. After talking to her just now, I wonder if she has some psychological issues."

"I wouldn't doubt it. It's estimated that twenty percent of

the population here in both Canada and the US, suffer from some form of mental illness. I was one myself."

"Me, too. I suffered from depression," Emilia admitted. "I still have to be aware of it, though Doctor Reshma took me off medication a few weeks ago."

"For people with addictions, it's especially common to suffer from co-occurring disorders."

"I wonder if the mental illnesses are caused by the addiction or the other way around."

Mosi gave Emilia a wan smile and a sad chuckle. "Science is working on that and from what little I understand right now, scientists haven't figured out the actual cause of co-occurring disorders, but have a number of theories."

"I was so busy dealing with my own concurrent disorders, I didn't think about what others might be going through," Emilia admitted.

"That's the way it was for me, too. I suffered from schizophrenia with my addictions and it took a while and a few lapses to find a medication that helped. My mind did eventually heal itself, and I'll never know if it was the schizophrenia that drove me to drugs and alcohol or if the schizophrenia was caused by my abuse of drugs. It's been almost five years since I needed the medication. Many people aren't so lucky and have to live with it all their lives. Believe me, that would suck."

"Now I feel lucky I only suffered from depression!"

"And I feel lucky my mind healed itself. Granted, that healing took a lot of meds, therapy and hard work, but still, many people with co-occurring disorders never completely recover and only about twenty percent get by quite well. Usually with medication."

"It feels *so* good not to be depressed or get urges to use anymore. I still get cravings, but they're not strong anymore."

"I've been clean going on twelve years and thoughts still

cross my mind. But I refuse to own them and they fly by, with me barely noticing that they passed through."

"That's pretty cool. Phineas says something very similar. He also says his addiction is out in the parking lot doing pushups, just waiting for him to slip."

Mosi gave her a thoughtful nod. "I've heard that, but I think *SMART* explains it better. We know we created an extremely strong neuropathway when we abused our drug or drugs of choice."

"Yes, I understand."

"When we quit, that pathway begins to weaken and the longer we maintain abstinence, the weaker it gets. While it never goes away, it becomes so weak that thoughts of using are laughable."

"If I may," Emilia interjected.

Mosi turned and smiled. "Sure, you've picked up a lot, let's see how well you understand this."

"So even though the old pathway is overgrown and weak, it still exists and picking up my drug of choice can light that pathway right up again. That's why people who've been clean for many years can still relapse."

"Yup," Mosi said with a smile. "You've got it."

"The things that help me stay clean the most are how much clearer my mind is and the ability to do the things I did before I was addicted."

"Like dancing?"

"Yeah, I love Latin dance moves, but also the chance to be part of my family again. I just got that back after losing it for so long and if I relapse, I'll lose them again. Maybe permanently."

"You're very lucky to have family that support you. Not everyone does. Like your sister calling you every day. That took dedication on her part and I don't think her husband was too keen on it at first."

"Mateo thought it was a bad idea at first and he was worried that I might hurt Lupe again. She really took my addiction hard. I mean my whole family did, but we'd been really close. I was raised to think of the family as number one. The family always came first. My parents not only taught us that, they lived it. It was one of the reasons I got clean and stay sober."

"I didn't have family backup like you do. My father died when I was a teenager. It was an industrial accident and Mom got some money, but not really enough to live on properly, so she had to sell the house. She started drinking right after Dad died. It was hard on her and she didn't feel she had anyone to talk to and just drowned herself in vodka for a few decades. And I was an only child, so I didn't have any support from that quarter either. Luckily when I got clean there were facilities like *Creekside*, where they have an outpatient program they call *Daytox*. That's where I heard about *SMART*."

"And now you finally have your mom back."

"Yeah, and it feels good. I wanted it for a long time. I confess I'm also proud she works in the industry helping people get clean."

"Yeah—you know I really like Bernadette. She was more like a friend than the housemother. At least to me."

"She mentioned you any number of times while you were in *Ellendale*."

"Really?"

"Oh yeah, she was particularly attached to you. She's been working there for three years now and she's never talked about anyone like she did about you. Every time I'd call, she'd give me a play-by-play update on your recovery." Mosi chortled.

"Wow, I had no idea. She did go jogging with me and brought in tortillas, let me make salsa and things like that. I guess I was still so centered on my recovery I assumed she did things like that for everybody."

"Um—no, not so much. She always pays attention to special dietary needs and things like that, but doesn't tend to treat anyone different or special. But you seem to have that effect on people."

"Me? What do you mean?"

"Well, for example, I've never seen a group of women from a *SMART* meeting get together so often and with such dedication. Under most circumstances, or at least statistically, at least one or two of them would have relapsed by now. I suspect it may have something to do with you."

Emilia laughed aloud. "Well, I suspect you're mistaken."

Mosi gave her that smile that could slay a hundred virgins and laughed. "You don't understand the effect you have on others."

Emilia shook her head. "I certainly don't see what you're talking about and have *no* idea what you mean."

"It's difficult to describe. It's like you have an aura that attracts people. You know I'm not one who believes in superstition and I try to base my life on science, so I don't understand what seems to be happening. But both men and women are drawn to you."

"I do make friends easily, and it's helped in my recovery 'cause most of my old friends had severe drug or alcohol addictions and I couldn't hang with them, not and stay clean. But that doesn't mean I have some kind of aura that attracts people to me."

"I'm not talking about a visible aura, rather something more—mundane? Perhaps it's as simple as you being an exceptional listener."

"I don't know about that. It sure doesn't seem to me that I'm especially attentive to what people say."

"It was only a suggestion, but having said that, do you feel more attentive to others now you're sober?"

"Well that's a gimme."

"Maybe because you expect to be more attentive, or because your head's clearer you don't realize just how attentive you really are," Mosi suggested, as he tilted his head.

"Has anyone said anything to you about me?"

"Truth be told, yes, on any number of occasions."

"Like what?" she said with a frown.

"Like how dedicated you are to the *SMART* tools, how well you know them . . ."

"No," she interrupted him, "I mean about some special supernatural ability to listen?"

"I was getting to that." He chortled.

"Okay, okay, sorry for interrupting. I just don't get all this. And I find it's generally not good to be impatient. Mostly it just harms me emotionally, but sometimes it's hard."

"Not to worry. Anyway, some tell me how much you've helped them during crosstalk. Explaining how you were tempted and how you used the tools to remain abstinent. I'll add you always seem to have a helpful story for anyone who's having urges or cravings."

"It does just seem normal to me to tell others how they can beat back their desires to use and what helped me in my first couple of months. So I just see myself as giving back. I'm glad it helps some of the other participants."

"And you listen."

Emilia shrugged and pursed her lips sideways, as she really didn't get what was the big deal.

"It's like you're a super listener. I've seen it in the meetings, seen you hyper-attentive. Not everyone does that, or can do that. And you do it with no effort. It just comes naturally to you. It *is* a gift, a very special gift."

"If you say so. I remember my first couple, well more like first three months. The cravings came regularly and in my third month when I hit *The Wall*, I thought I couldn't take it and almost went for a bottle of vodka."

"Yes, and you told that story. Your sister calling you at any given moment helped and so did doing a *CBA*. That kind of thing gives others hope. It's hard for me to remember what it was like twelve years ago when I detoxed and struggled. I honestly can't even remember hitting *The Wall*, because it all happened so long ago, but for you, it's fresh in your mind."

"I *do* feel a lot better and more resistant after six months, but I stay wary. Because of the way I rewired my brain through my addiction, just one drink or one pill could set me off in the ugly direction of my addiction all over again. And from what I've learned at *SMART*, if I relapse it could actually be worse than when I was originally addicted."

"Yes." Mosi nodded in agreement. "The *Kindling Effect*, where each relapse becomes progressively worse, as do the withdrawal symptoms. I know this from personal experience and I hope you never discover how bad it can be."

"Yeah, better believe I have no interest in having a worse withdrawal than I did this time. Getting off the topic a little, can I ask you a question?"

"Of course." Mosi took his eyes off the road and glanced at Emilia with a smile that lit up the auto.

"It's about the *VACI*."

"Yes, the *Vital Absorbing Creative Interest*."

"Uh huh. The thing is I'm not sure what is considered creative."

"Good question, and I think each individual has to work that out for themselves."

"Well, for example, we go Latin dancing sometimes, but I'm not sure if that's considered creative."

"In my opinion, *VACI* is more about getting a buzz out of life or relaxing for a bit in healthy ways. You seem to get a real high from dancing. It's something you truly enjoy."

"I didn't think of it like that, there's actually a lot of things

I'm not comfortable doing sober yet, so I guess I need to practice."

"As we like to say in *SMART*, it all takes practice, patience and persistence."

"It sure was hard at first and other participants, including you, kept telling me I'd get easier with more clean time and I kept thinking *hurry up clean time, I want this to be easier.* But time will move on at its normal pace, though it seems more slowly when you're in a hurry."

Mosi laughed. "I still have things I'm unsure of and I'm learning. Things that make me nervous."

"What could possibly make you nervous with twelve years clean time behind you?"

"How about a speech to the BC Legislature?"

"Wow, I never thought about that. And with possibly millions of dollars at stake for the *CCSA*."

"Thanks for that, it diminishes the nerves to almost zero."

"Oh, I'm so sorry. How thoughtless of me!" She threw her hand over her face.

Mosi sighed. "Don't worry about it, I'll manage."

"Of course you will, but I'd rather be a help than a hindrance."

"Good. Tomorrow you can give me input on the speech."

"Right, where are we going to do that? You can't very well read your presentation out loud in a coffee shop."

"No, but there's *Maccaud Park* on top of the hill or *Totem Park* on the beach. Depending on the weather of course."

"Which doesn't look promising I'll add."

"No, but that's what we get for living in a temperate rain forest."

"So, what's the plan for an alternative?"

"I guess your place or mine, unless you can think of somewhere else."

"I could walk to *Totem Park*, but I'd be happy to have you

come over and read at my place. If it's rainy and cold, I'll make coffee or tea and we can have lunch there without searching for a restaurant or going home before we're done if we get peckish."

"I could set up my laptop more easily at your place than at a park, too, and wouldn't have to worry about somebody stealing it when we have our backs turned."

"Why don't we just do it at my place, then? I have a better couch now."

"Oh, you bought a new one?"

"Actually no, I found a used one on *Craigslist*. Inexpensive, but very comfy. Also a better kitchen table and chairs. If it's nice out, I have three chairs and a small table on my deck."

"Yeah, that'd be great. I could bring something for lunch, which is the least I could do."

"Or not, it doesn't matter. I'm not scraping the bottom of the barrel anymore. Another good thing about sobriety," she said.

"Okay, that works for me. What time should I come over?"

"If you come over between nine and ten, we'd get some work done before lunch, but I haven't seen the speech. Maybe it doesn't need much work."

"I'd rather have too much time instead of not enough. If you're sure it's not too early, we could start at nine."

"That's perfect," Emilia said. Her eyes crinkled with happiness.

Mosi had walked her to her condo's door and then returned to his car. Emilia stood on the balcony and watched him drive away. She'd handled that well and was pleased with herself. No, she couldn't start dating him, not yet, but getting to know him didn't seem like it would harm her sobriety. As long as they stayed out of the bedroom, Mosi's presence could only have a positive effect.

She was so engrossed in pleasant thoughts it took her a few minutes to realize it was spitting rain.

CHAPTER THIRTY-TWO

Sunday morning Emilia awoke early. She nearly jumped out of bed, and hurried to the bathroom to pee and shower. It was because Mosi was coming over to spend several hours with her. She was also curious as to what he had in his speech. After a fruit smoothie for breakfast, she tidied up her condo, gave it a once over with the vacuum, and dusted.

She then tried to decide what to do for lunch. She had some *pozole* left, but wasn't sure if hominy stew would be palatable for Mosi, though he did seem to have broad tastes and she knew of nothing he wouldn't eat outside of avocados, which she adored. After a few moments thought, she pulled a frozen chicken breast from her small freezer, defrosted it in the microwave, and put it on to braise. That way she could offer him a choice of the *pozole*, a taco, a sandwich, or even all three. She made carrot and celery sticks, cut a handful of radishes in half, cleaned and trimmed some pea pods and finally a few broccoli florets. Though she seldom used it herself, she poured a small amount of the Ranch dressing she used on her salad for a dip. She then covered the lot and put it in the fridge. It was five minutes to nine and Mosi was a stickler for punctuality. Two minutes later her video-phone beeped and she buzzed Mosi in.

"Morning," he said with a pleasant smile.

Emilia shivered and smiled back. "Hi, come on in." She gestured with her right hand as her left held the lever handle.

Mosi was dressed down. She'd never seen him in sweat pants and a t-shirt. The white ensemble was an extraordinary contrast to his black skin and included even his socks, she saw, when he slipped off his white tennis shoes at the door. His black briefcase seemed out of place.

She turned to lead him to the living room and heard the soft pad of stocking feet on the laminate floor behind her. A few steps from their destination, that sound stopped. Emilia looked over her shoulder and saw Mosi standing still and with an odd expression on his face that she thought might be of consternation. She then stopped and turned to face him.

He spoke. "I dropped by a fast food joint for a bite of breakfast but didn't think to pick anything up for you."

"That's okay, I had a fruit smoothie and that'll do me until lunch, as long as it's not too late."

"Okay, I'll be sure to leave at lunch time."

"No need." She gave him her warmest, and she hoped friendliest, smile. "I have lunch ready. Enough for two if you want to stay."

"I didn't mean to put you out."

"It was no trouble at all, I would have made lunch for one anyway and for two makes no difference in how long it took," she said truthfully and with the warmest smile she could muster.

"Well actually, that would be great. I haven't got much in the way of groceries in the house right now and don't plan to go shopping until we get back from the Island on Tuesday."

"Good, it's settled."

Emilia went to the living room and gestured around. "I could sit on the couch and you could stand over there." She pointed to a spot near the wall opposite the sofa. "Or you could sit there." This time she waved at a button-backed armchair that faced the couch.

Mosi placed his briefcase on the armchair. "If I'm not mistaken, the armchair and the sofa are new."

"Not new, but much better than the ratty sofa I had and I

wanted something else to sit on for when I have company so I bought the chair. They don't match, but they co-ordinate and both are comfortable, which is more important to me than something brand new."

"I can't tell they're used at all. They're in great shape."

"Thank you." She gave him a cheerful grin. "So what's the plan?"

"I think I'll stand here by the armchair and you if you could sit on the sofa, that'd he great."

"Work's for me. Can I get you a glass of water before we get started? You're likely to need it with your practice speech-making."

"No thanks . . . wait, come to think of it, you're right. I'll need to wet my lips a few times I'm sure. That'd be great."

"Ice?"

"No thanks, I don't think that'll help my voice box. Room temperature would be better."

"Coming right up." Emilia went to her kitchen sink and drew a glass of water. In her new balanced lifestyle, which included healthy eating, she'd installed a filter on the faucet to help make sure any impurities caused by the chlorine's re-action to minerals in the water, would be removed. It also got rid of the chlorine taste of the water, which helped her to drink more without buying expensive bottled water.

She returned and handed him the glass of cool tap water, then went to the stack by the window and pulled one of the wooden TV trays out, set it up beside Mosi and gestured for him to place the glass on it.

"That's wonderful. Thanks so much for taking the time to help me with my speech."

Emilia gave him a satisfied grin. "You're welcome. It's no trouble at all." *Part of my VACI.*

She then went and sat on the new-to-her-sofa and prepared to put some of her mindfulness techniques into practice. She'd

271

discovered the *SMART* tools were not only helpful in recovery, but also in everyday living. Like now. Emilia would use *Mindful Observation* and *Mindful Listening* so as to be as helpful as possible to Mosi. She began to tune out everything but Mosi and his voice. It was easy to do after all her practice and with a man she adored as the focus.

After he finished reading the speech, she pointed out three places he'd stumbled, and when they went over those places again, they found they weren't clear and they rewrote them together. He read it again and they rewrote it again. They did five passes on it by lunchtime.

"I had no idea how much work it needed until I read it aloud," Mosi said with a shake of his head. "I'm so glad you helped me with it. You'd make a great speech writer."

"I don't know if I would or not, but to me it seemed intuitive to make the changes we did. But we'll know for sure how good it is when you give it to the legislature tomorrow."

"For sure."

"Are you nervous?"

"Actually, yes I am. A lot depends on this speech, like how large of a grant the BC government will give *CCSA* this fiscal year to help reduce deaths from the opioid crisis and our harm reduction work. If the attitude of the Premier doesn't change, the government will likely move some if not all of our grant to faith-based recovery groups and that would mean less access to naloxone as many of those groups feel that having it on hand would increase relapse."

"But there's no scientific evidence to support that point of view."

"There certainly isn't, but faith can be a blind spot for many people. Illegal drugs are bad and naloxone might make a person in recovery worry less about dying from an overdose, so it *must* be bad, or so many of them think."

"But when you're addicted, you don't think about that or

don't care. You want that drug even *knowing* it could kill you."

"Which is why I talk about it in my speech, that and our track record in *CCSA* in reducing deaths by overdose by using safe injection sites and how having the safe sites increases individuals getting into rehab, and getting them in quickly is well above the average."

"Yes, like me. Detoxing in the hospital was a lifesaver for me, and so was getting into *Ellendale* as soon as I was detoxed."

"I'd like to go over the speech a couple more times if you don't mind."

"Of course, but let's take a lunch break first. My stomach's rumbling. I'm surprised you can't hear it."

Mosi chuckled. It was a deep, throaty, and entirely pleasant sound to Emilia's ears. "Actually, I can hear it and was about to suggest lunch before we continued, but you beat me to it."

Emilia stood and Mosi laid the sheaf of papers on the TV tray, picked up the now empty water glass and nodded to Emilia, who headed for the kitchen with him in tow.

"Sit down." She gestured toward the kitchen table she'd recently purchased on *Craigslist*.

"Quite the upgraded table and chairs," Mosi said.

"Thanks. The other one was about to fall apart and the chairs were disgusting."

"You're being very careful with your money I've noted."

"I have some credit card debt from when I was using, so I'm busy paying that off, but I still need a little money in the bank for emergencies. So, I want nicer furniture, but I'm not in a hurry, so I wait until something I really like comes along at a great price and buy it then."

"Wise to get that debt off your back. Credit card debt is expensive."

"For sure! Happily I didn't owe too much and it's almost

paid off now. Next paycheck and I can start banking more money each month."

"Good for you."

"So, I've got *pozole,* which you could have on its own or with tacos or a chicken sandwich."

"Um — what's po-sew-lee?" He pronounced it close to the actual Spanish sound.

"It's a hominy soup or maybe it would be better translated as a stew. This one's a little spicy but I used *Guajillo* chilies which aren't very hot but give it a rich flavor and a red color. I made it with pork."

"I definitely want to try that and a taco would be great with it."

"Okay, I'll have the same as it'll save time and I prefer tacos over sandwiches any day."

Emilia prepared lunch.

She first turned on her cast iron skillet to heat up the tortillas, then pulled the *pozole* from the fridge and placed the casserole dish in the microwave to reheat it. She dug out fresh tortillas, salsa made with *chipotle* peppers, lettuce, green onions, serrano peppers, radishes for garnish, and the chicken she'd braised in the morning. When the cured frying pan was hot she dropped two tortillas into it and heated the chicken up in a smaller pan with a small bit of olive oil.

Between stirring the chicken and turning the tortillas as needed, she minced the lettuce, onion and other garnishes finely. The microwave beeped and she removed the *pozole,* stirred it and put it back in for an additional three minutes.

Three minutes later she removed the *pozole* and served it in two large bowls three quarters full. She stuffed three tortillas with the chicken and served two of them to Mosi with a bowl of the *pozole.* She served water to drink and put a pitcher of it on the table in case Mosi — *se enchiló* — had too much chili. She put the garnishes on the table with a soupspoon each and sat catty-corner from him.

"Smells great," he said. "But I'm sure there's something I don't understand about all the chopped salad vegetables on the table."

"Not to worry, I'll show you. You put the garnishes of your personal choice in the soup and the same for the tacos."

"Sounds reasonable, I'll just follow your lead. There's nothing on the table I don't like, and though I've never had hominy before, it's basically corn."

"A specific kind of corn treated in a special way, but yes, it's corn. Oh crap! I forgot to bring lemon. I'll be right back."

She popped over to the counter across from the fridge, picked out a lemon, rolled it under her palm and then sliced it into quarters. She sat again and put the lemon slices on top of the minced lettuce save one quarter, which she squeezed into her *pozole*.

"I think I'd like to try your — po-sew-lee — alone at first and then as I add each garnish, if that's not offensive."

There's not much you can do to offend me, handsome. "That's fine. Everyone has different tastes. My family all garnish it a little differently. My sister, Lupe, prefers cabbage over lettuce, for example."

Mosi picked up the spoon and took a sip of the broth. "Very robust and meaty. I like it. I think I'll add a little lemon and see if I like that."

Mosi then squeezed the tiniest bit of lemon into the broth and tasted it again. His eyes lit up.

"I can see why you add the lemon, that's really good."

He added more and tasted it again and nodded. Then he added a good amount of lettuce, tried it again, then the radish and continued adding and tasting until he had everything in his bowl except the minced chilies and salsa.

"Those chilies look hot," he said.

"I wouldn't call them particularly spicy, but I eat a lot of chili so I might not be the best judge. Your best bet might be to try the salsa instead as it'll mostly blend in with the broth, but it's very hot as it's made with *chipotle* peppers."

"What the heck are *chipotle* chilies anyway?"

"They're smoked *jalapeños*. The ones I buy are canned in a sauce. Very delicious."

"How about I just dribble a little bit into my *pozole?*"

"That's the best plan. You can always add more, but the only way to cut it is by adding more broth, and this is the last of it in our bowls."

Mosi added the quarter part of the small serving spoon Emilia had put in the salsa dish, stirred it thoroughly and tasted it once more.

"That's good, very rich and smoky. I think I'll add a little more."

Which he did, then tried it again.

"This is absolutely delightful. You taste the richness of the broth, the spiciness of the chili, the bite of the onion and the crunch of the lettuce and radishes. I've never had anything like it before."

Emilia gave him a happy grin, pulled a tortilla from the thick towel she'd wrapped them in, added a glob of salsa and rolled it up with the expertise of many years of practice. She took a spoonful of the *pozole* and then a bite of the tortilla and continued this way taking a bite of the rolled up tortilla after every few mouthfuls of the soup. Mosi followed suit but with significantly less salsa on his tortilla, which he managed to roll up if not professionally at least with some modicum of dignity.

When half of her *pozole* was gone, Emilia set her spoon down, picked up the taco and added all the accouterments including two spoonfuls of her smoky salsa.

"I forgot all about my tacos," Mosi said and rested his spoon on the edge of the bowl. He picked up one of his tacos and filled it following Emilia's example, less the quantity of salsa and took a large bite.

After chewing and swallowing his first bite, he commented. "This is the best taco I've ever eaten. It's no wonder they're so popular in Mexico! It's nothing like the ones you buy here in the fast food joints and even better than the good Mexican restaurants I've been to and the *pozole* is awesome."

"Why thank you. That's quite a compliment and I appreciate it."

"You're very welcome. You should start a restaurant."

"Thanks, no. I'm quite happy working in the healthcare industry."

"Well, I can guarantee if I get another invitation to eat your cooking it would take a major natural disaster to keep me away and even that might not work."

Emilia laughed. "That's a great compliment, but my mom's a better cook than me and so's my sister."

Mosi shook his head.

He doesn't believe me.

They finished lunch with Mosi barely touching the water, which surprised Emilia. He helped load the dishwasher and then they returned to the living room to do more work on the speech.

CHAPTER THIRTY-THREE

Reservations for the ferry had been made for them by some unknown individual who worked at the Legislature in Victoria, the capital of BC, Zach had told Mosi.

"It *does* seem odd that reservations were made on our behalf," Emilia said.

"I don't know if it's normal procedure or not," Mosi said. "What I don't understand is how they knew the color, make, and year of my car as well as the license plate number."

"Yeah, it's all a bit strange for sure," she said, as he turned to the left and drove between the white lines at the ferry terminal that were marked *Reservations Only*.

"Ten to seven," Mosi said to her after glancing at the clock on the car's radio.

"Reservations are great, because without them we would have had to have been here more than an hour ago to be sure of a spot on the ferry."

Mosi nodded and then the line began to move forward as loading of the four hundred and seventy car capacity ferry began.

Once Mosi's car was parked and secured, they walked up to the Main passenger deck, eschewing the busy elevator. They wandered to the bow of the ship and sat right at the front in order to see the panoramic view of the smaller islands en route and with a lot of luck, an orca or two.

"Wow," Emilia said. "This is so beautiful. You know, this is the first time I've crossed over to the Island sober since I was a kid and was with my parents."

"I never had the money to go to the Island when I was using."

"Me neither, but the company sent me a few times before they caught on that I was addicted to something. Of course, my addiction wasn't as bad a few years ago."

"That's pretty common, but I guess you know that."

"You mean to get deeper and deeper into one's addiction?"

"Yeah, exactly."

"This reminds me of when I was little. The blue sky above with a few puffy clouds, the sea below us, a crystalline turquoise, and the islands with evergreens shooting out of them like stillborn rockets." Emilia gave a great sigh. "I missed so much when I was drunk and stoned."

"But now, not only are we clear-headed, we've learned mindfulness in our struggle to get and stay clean. That's an added bonus that many people who never suffered from an addiction don't have. In many ways our addiction made us who we are today."

"More aware, yes, I think you're right," Emilia said, her eyes wandering the panorama before her but not really seeing it. "That reminds me. Do you feel ready for the speech?"

"As ready as I can be. It's a new experience for me to give a speech like this to a large group of lawmakers. And your help yesterday was phenomenal. I feel a lot better about it now after our edits yesterday." *She was really helpful, too, and I do feel a little less nervous.*

"Thanks, I was just glad to be able to help a little, and all we really did was tweak it a bit."

"So, changing the subject just a little, well actually more like one hundred and eighty degrees." He chuckled.

"You've got me curious." Emilia turned in her seat, crossed her arms and tilted her head, giving him a hostile look.

She's being playful. I like it . . . maybe too much.

He chuckled, then gave her his warmest smile in the hope it would break any barriers she might erect when he questioned her. *I'm asking this to help her see where she is in her recovery. At least I want to believe that.*

"What kind of hobbies do you have now you're clean? Besides Latin dancing of course. I know because you've taken me dancing several times in the last couple of months."

"I haven't thought about any other hobbies at this point. Mostly I spend my spare time either studying the *SMART* Handbook and practicing the tools, or visiting with the other *SMART* ladies. We do that every week now and sometimes I get together with Doris, Anne, or Miranda at other times. Then on Fridays I go to Doctor Reshma's *SMART* meeting, so I don't have a lot of free time. I thought that was a good thing."

"You're right, especially in early recovery, but now you've got some clean time, perhaps you should start thinking about new hobbies, or old ones that fell away as your addiction got stronger."

"Okay, I'll bite. Kindly explain why it's so important."

"As you know, our addictions create very strong pathways to our pleasure center."

Emilia nodded.

"In the short term one needs to do what you've done and re-train the brain. To slow your thoughts down and examine them when one has an urge or craving. And that's what the *SMART* tools help us to do. But one also needs to plan for the long term in order not to relapse years down the road."

"And how does one do that?" Emilia leaned closer to him and looked intently into his eyes.

"We must build new pathways to our pleasure center with hobbies, exercise, and other new things or activities we enjoyed before we were addicted."

Emilia leaned back in her chair and sighed. "That makes a lot of sense. I *have* started enjoying Latin dancing again, and thanks for your willingness to go with me."

"It's a lot of fun. I'm not good at it like you, but I have a blast."

"I've seen those adult coloring books. I could try that."

"What else did you do when you were growing up? Things you really liked?" Mosi asked, turning in his seat to face her so she'd know he really *was* attentive.

Her face brightened. "Board games. Sissy, my brother, and I used to play board games all the time! I wonder if the other ladies would like to give that a try. They could come to my place or we could take turns at each other's houses."

"That's a good idea. You could also take up tennis."

"Tennis? I don't know the first thing about the game." She shook her head.

"I play and would be happy to teach you." *And I'd get to spend time with her without dating, which could be deadly for her right now. She'd also be likely to wear a revealing ladies tennis outfit, which would look sexy on her.* Mosi smiled.

Emilia returned the smile. "Miniature golf, hiking, biking, those are all things I liked to do until the drugs took over," she interjected without preamble.

Mosi nodded and grinned. "Those are all good things and exercise releases dopamine, which makes us feel good."

"That's right, we've talked about that and I've read about it, too," Emilia said as her face lit up once more.

God, she's got a killer smile. She's already beautiful, but when she smiles, it's like an angel descended to walk on earth.

"You do have a good memory. Wait—I take that back." Emilia frowned.

"What I mean is, I've never seen anyone in early recovery whose mind's as sharp as yours. I'm not sure if you're just healing extraordinarily fast, were a genius, or some of both."

"Wow. I—I don't know what to say. That is super kind of you, but I think my mind's just healing quickly. I'm pretty sure I'm not a genius." She chuckled.

Beautiful, angelic and humble. What a combination!

"I'll let you know what I think for sure in another eighteen months," Mosi said.

"That's because—my mind will have done most of it's healing by then."

"Yes, that's correct. You seem to remember everything after you hear it once."

"A lot of times, yes, but a lot of that comes from my training at work I'm sure."

He looked directly into her eyes. "Or you got the work because of it."

"No, I don't think so. They couldn't have known I'd be so good at it." She looked away.

"Do many others at your work have this ability?"

"Oh yeah."

"Really?"

"Well actually, now that I think about it, I'm making an assumption and don't really know the facts. So the correct answer is I don't know."

"I somehow doubt many of the others have your ability. That would be an amazing coincidence, unless of course, they hire with that ability, but as you suggested, they had no way of knowing you'd be able to memorize things so quickly."

"You make it sound like I'm very special, but I don't feel that way at all."

"That you don't think about yourself as special on top of fact you have an amazing memory and ability to memorize and learn makes you particularly remarkable. Not many people who have your abilities are as humble about it as you."

Chapter Thirty-Four

From the terminal at Swartz Bay, it took her and Mosi thirty-five minutes to reach the BC Parliament buildings. Zach had told them there would be a spot for them on the street outside the Legislature, but that seemed unlikely to both, given the number of tourists who visited daily. Nevertheless, they did as Zach suggested. *He hasn't let us down yet.*

"I'm looking, but still don't see anything," Emilia said as they turned the corner off Government Street onto Superior, which would be halfway around the Parliament buildings.

"I think Zach was mistaken this time, in spite of his record for fulfilling his promises," Mosi said.

"Maybe not. Look, on the right, there's a man standing by some of those orange traffic cones keeping a spot open for somebody."

"Probably not for us," he said, as they neared the spot Emilia had pointed out.

"Think again," she said with a wide grin. "Zach's at it again."

"Oh—I think you're right."

The man by the traffic cones and who appeared to be guarding the parking spot was dressed in the uniform of a Victoria police constable and wore a bright yellow and orange reflective vest. He waved them over as he removed the first three cones, which allowed Mosi to slip neatly into the parking spot.

They climbed out of Mosi's car and the officer awaited them on the sidewalk.

"Good morning, Mister El-Hadidy, Miss Robles. Please follow the pedestrian access here on your right to the rear of the Parliament buildings." He gestured. "You'll be met just inside the door."

"Thank you," Emilia said, with a smile and nod.

Mosi nodded to him and they turned up the long concrete path toward the large rear door of the building.

"Do you think this door is usually open to the public?" Emilia asked, as she looked sideways at Mosi and crinkled her brows.

"I don't think so. From what I've read on the government website there's the Main Entrance where the general public can enter and then a handicapped door on the west side with a ramp. I didn't find any mention of this door at all."

"Well, we'll soon find out," she said, with a wink and a grin.

"That we will. You seem really excited to be here."

"I am. The Legislature's in session and you're going to speak to it. And I'll be there. I find it all absolutely exhilarating." She gave Mosi her widest happy smile.

The large door unlatched with ease and opened on silent hinges. A lady awaited them. Her shoulder-length hair was chestnut with wisps of gray scattered throughout. It was a pleasant round face with a slight sign of crow's feet around gray eyes. The eyes were bright and spoke of intelligence and something more, perhaps a certain amount of impertinence, Emilia thought.

"Mister El-Hadidy, Miss Robles, please come with me." She turned and walked into the gaping interior of the Parliament building.

Mosi and Emilia glanced at each other and shrugged, then followed the slender woman down the cavernous polished granite hallway.

How does everyone know who we are?

Their guide turned to the right and ascended a wide gray

marble staircase with stone railings and turned posts to match. After climbing two stories Emilia was pleased she wasn't the least out of breath. Working out and eating right was helping. When she was in the worst of her addiction, one flight of stairs would have ended with the need to stop for a breather. She looked at Mosi to see if he felt the same sense of eagerness she did to find out where they were going and who would guide them to the Legislative Chamber when time came for Mosi's speech. In fact, Mosi's forehead was creased and his lips held a distinct downturn. *He looks rather glum.*

They turned down a wide hallway with doors on their right and carved oak wainscoting on the left, stained in a medium dark brown. They strode to the end of the hall and entered the only open door.

There sat Zach with a middle-aged woman.

It *would* be Zach again, Mosi thought, and Ms. Gillian Dyck, a backbench member of the ruling party who was also the party's biggest dissident. *Can Zach really install her as Premier? And if he can, what does that say about our democracy?*

As if in slow motion, Zach stood, came over, and extended his hand, shaking it firmly, as was his custom.

"Welcome to the capital, Mosi, Emilia," he said, and after he released Mosi's hand, took Emilia's and looked deep into her eyes, or so it seemed to Mosi who stood less than eighteen inches away from them.

"I'm sure you know who this is with me, though I don't believe you've ever met. Miss Gillian Dyck, may I present Mister Mosi El-Hadidy and Miss Emilia Robles from White Rock. Mosi, Emilia, it's my pleasure to present Miss Gillian Dyck, Member of the Legislature."

"It's a pleasure to meet you," Emilia said as she strode forward two steps to stand before Gillian with her hand extended.

"The pleasure is mine," Ms. Dyck said, then took her hand and shook it. Gillian turned to Mosi with hers held out to him. "It's a pleasure to meet you, too, Mister El-Hadidy."

"Thank you, Miss Dyck. I'm pleased to have this opportunity to meet you, as well."

"I'm particularly pleased to talk to you because of the work you're doing with the *Canadian Center on Substance use and Addiction*. I've been working very hard on making sure the BC government grants you receive continue and are even increased. It's been a difficult struggle, but with Zach's—I mean Mister Robinson's—help, we may yet win." Gillian turned and moved to sit in one of seven black leather armchairs with seats dulled and crackled by use and age. They were in a circle facing each other with space left for one person at a time to enter the circle.

Zach motioned them with his left hand. "Please sit. We have things to discuss and someone you know, Emilia, who I wish to introduce to Mosi."

Emilia squinched her brows and frowned. She had immense respect for Zachary and zero trust in him. Zach nodded to her with his smirk of a grin that told her he was self-satisfied with whatever it was he'd done. *Oh crap, something bad's going to happen for sure.*

Mosi and Emilia sat across from Ms. Dyck. When Emilia turned to look, Zach was gone.

"Where'd Zach go?" she asked in a tone that was more resentful than worried, her arms planted firmly on the arms of the battered leather chair.

"He's gone for some doctor, I mean PhD, named—Julián, I think," Gillian Dyck said in a voice that held wonder. "Very young man to have a doctorate or else he just looks young. He brought an artifact with him. Very old, I'm told. I saw it and it looks like a stone axe. He let me touch the inscriptions on it and strange as it is, it made me feel it was important. I don't mean as an artifact, but important to me — to us — today. Right now. I know that sounds crazy, but I'm only saying what I felt, I'm not suggesting it actually *is* important."

"Did you have any kind of — vision or anything when you touched it?" Emilia asked in amazement.

"No, nothing like that."

Mosi's gaze shot back and forth between her and Ms. Dyck, Emilia saw. She looked directly at him and smiled. She was warmed by the smile he gave her in return. *Here we are two insignificant particles in the throne of power and we're connecting. Life's all about connections. SMART has taught me that.*

"Ah, here they are now," Ms. Dyck said.

She and Mosi turned their heads at the same time, Emilia could see from where she sat beside him. It *was* Julián! She wasn't sure how she felt about him. He hadn't tricked her into touching the celt, even prepared her in case she fainted or lost consciousness, which she had, but claimed he'd seen her when the celt took him — wherever it is it takes people. She sometimes felt she was a mere experiment in his strange world of ancient artifacts and prehistoric investigations. Others also had an intimate connection to a joint past with her and . . .

The ever-polite Mosi stood. She followed his lead, as did Ms. Dyck.

"As the ladies are acquainted with this gentleman, may I present him to you, Mosi? Mosi El-Hadidy this is Julián Urreiztieta. Julián, this is Mister Mosi El-Hadidy," Zach said with his *I know best* expression. He stood tall and straight, looked unblinking into each of their eyes, and gestured at each man as he introduced him. His presence owned the room. "Mister El-Hadidy is here to explain to a very confused Legislature the power of science in overcoming addictions."

"That sounds like an extremely worthwhile endeavor," Julián said. He stood motionless with his hands at his side.

His gaze flicked around from person to person, but the tone of his voice was warm and his eyes were lit like stars.

Emilia realized in that moment that Julián was a boy dressed in a man's body. *Well, he has the enthusiasm and wonder of a child for sure.*

In an arch tone Emilia asked the question that had been burning in her since she realized Julián was here. "Why exactly are you here, Mister Urreiztieta?"

Before he could answer for himself, Zach spoke up. "That's a great question and a difficult one to answer, because I asked him to come and to bring the celt with him because of a feeling." Zach's brows furrowed and he gave a great sigh.

"A feeling?" Mosi asked in a disapproving tone, narrowing his eyes at Zach.

"Yes, a feeling. May I ask Julián to demonstrate?"

A leather briefcase appeared, or seemed to—Emilia realized she simply mustn't have realized Julián carried it all along. He placed it on the weatherworn cocktail table in the center of the circle of chairs, opened it with extreme delicacy, donned a pair of thin white cotton gloves and with the care of a mother holding her newborn for the first time, lifted a black flannel bag from a molded foam compartment.

As he slipped the pouch off the object, his eyes both sparkled and glistened. He looked like nothing less than a man lost in the eyes of the woman he adores. Centimeter by centimeter the object within was slowly exposed.

Emilia took in a sharp breath and noticed the look of wonder on Gillian's face and that of adoration in the countenance of Julián. *I'm not the only one affected by the damn thing.* Mosi, she noticed, had a look of consternation and confusion.

"Mister El-Hadidy," Julián said, as he held out the granite celt as if it was a precious jewel presented for inspection. "Please take one of those alcohol wipes in my briefcase"—he nodded at his case—"clean one fingertip with it and then touch the glyphs on the celt."

Mosi stumbled back and shook his head, radiating hesitation and confusion.

Emilia stepped over and slipped a sealed wipe from the case, tore it open and handed the towelette to Mosi. "I know this is weird, but you've heard my story and what Miss Dyck just told us. *Please* do as he asks," she said, with what she thought was her most reassuring smile.

Mosi looked into her eyes like he was searching for her soul, then nodded. "I'll do it for you, though it seems silly and strange for a group of adults to be focused on an artifact like it was magical." Hesitating in spite of his words, a few seconds later he did take the wipe and cleaned the tip if his right forefinger, then ran it over the cuneiform-like marks in the stone tool. His eyes widened and his face took on a look of wonder. He kept his finger immobile but in contact with the stone for six seconds and then hauled it back as if the celt had turned into an inferno. "That-that was impossible." He stammered in a great rush of air.

"So were heavier-than-air flight and splitting the atom at one time," Emilia blurted before she even thought to stop herself. *Why am I defending this thing?*

Zach spoke in a tone of clear frustration. "I've lived my life believing in science as opposed to faith, old wives tales, and mythology, but this—rock has me thinking there might be something more out there. I find myself thinking the inscription on it, which appears to be a prophecy, is relevant to us today, right here in BC. I can't explain it and I'm not given to religion of any sort, but I feel like my life's been taken by it. It may simply be some bit of nature or science the human race has yet to discover and I'm actually counting on that, because I honestly don't feel in control of my life anymore."

That such a man as Zach was drawn to and confused by the celt gave Emilia comfort. That Mosi felt or saw *something*, reassured her that her mental faculties were intact, or at least

289

as much as was possible for a person just six months clean from a horrible addiction.

There was a short double buzzing sound. Ms. Gillian Dyck pulled her phone from her suit jacket, checked it and nodded to herself. A moment later a diminutive young woman of no more than four-foot-ten or eleven, appeared just inside the door. The platinum blonde, who was so slender it gave her a waiflike appearance, called out in a clear low contralto.

"Mister El-Hadidy, the Legislature is about to sit. Be so kind as to follow me."

Mosi turned his head to look at Emilia and shrugged, then followed the tiny blonde as requested. When he disappeared out the door, she felt a hand on her elbow. She spun her head to see Zach inches from her.

"Shall we adjourn to the Public Galleries?" he asked.

She looked around and saw Gillian Dyck striding to the door with purpose and Julián, packing the celt back into his briefcase like it was made of delicate leaded crystal rather than granite. She nodded to Zach without a word and strode off beside him the moment he removed his hand from her elbow. They followed Ms. Dyck at a sedate pace into the hall and she entered a side door. They, however, turned in the opposite direction and climbed a flight of stairs to the next floor where the Public Galleries were located, Emilia assumed.

Zach led her to front row seats directly overlooking the right hand side of the speaker's chair where they sat together with Julián, who must have followed them after repacking the celt. The sitting of the Legislature began with a procession in which the Speaker of the House followed a golden scepter down the middle of the floor to her seat. The scepter was placed on a stand in front of the Speaker and the sitting began. While moderately interesting, it was mostly formalities, but that didn't last too long before Mosi was introduced by the speaker on behalf of Ms. Dyck, in an apparent continuation of a debate on British Columbia's opioid crisis. Mosi was represented — quite correctly — as a person *in the trenches* of the province's present addiction crisis, whose organization was having enormous successes.

Mosi began with his own addiction and recovery, including how *SMART Recovery's* proven scientific tools had saved him. He then went on to discuss his work with the *Canadian Center on Substance use and Addiction* and how they were affecting the present crisis and what more needed to be done. Finally, he showed them how reducing the grants of the *CCSA* and similar organizations would cost more both in dollars and lives, but modestly increasing those budgets could have massive positive effects on reduction of opioid abuse. And end up saving the government coffers money in the long term. In particular the provincial Health Care System.

When he finished, there was a standing ovation. Mosi hung his head and lost eye contact with the house. Emilia chuckled at his obvious embarrassment. A few minutes later, Mosi was in the empty seat beside her. Though the gallery was full — and many of those present seemed to be reporters — a no-nonsense-looking lady *Royal Canadian Mounted Police* constable had held the seat Mosi took. She disappeared moments after Mosi was escorted to the chair. There were stares and surreptitious glances from all around them when he arrived.

She leaned over and whispered in his ear, "You were awesome."

"Thanks," he replied in a similarly quiet voice. "It felt — powerful."

Zach leaned forward and nodded to him. Julián had a tablet out and seemed to have missed the whole thing, as he was clearly absorbed in whatever he was doing.

Then, things got really interesting when a member of the opposition demanded a non-confidence motion against the government for its poor handling of the opioid crisis. The government, which had a handy majority, easily defeated the motion, but she heard murmurs behind and around her. The reporters were of the opinion that the Premier would soon be pushed out. The Liberal Government had to get a handle on this crisis before the next election, which was only one year away, or they were certain to lose to the New Democratic Party.

I think the reporters are right.

That evening they attended a large gathering at the *Marriot Hotel.*

Zack said, "There were over two-hundred-fifty people in attendance, which includes all the Members of the Legislature, their spouses, media, special guests including us, some of the wealthy elite in Victoria and one very unhappy Premier." Zach smiled with a glimmer of malice. "She knows it's the end for her."

In groups of two, three and more, cabinet members, caucus members and even opposition members, came to speak to Mosi and congratulate him on his work to reduce the opioid crisis. Emilia was surprised that most knew who she was and insisted on knowing her story.

"I've been clean for six months."

"Yes, it was oxycodone and alcohol I was addicted to."

"You're right, it's a very dangerous combination and I'm very lucky to be alive. The most dangerous of all were the oxy pills I purchased on the street, as they could have been laced with fentanyl, and maybe some of them were."

They keep asking the same questions over and over until I want to scream! I need to be mindful and remember that in two hours none of this will matter. The exercise calmed her and she was able to make it through the rest of the evening unscathed by the repetitive questions by people who honestly didn't understand addiction and addictive behavior.

"Why didn't you just quit?" one of the Member of the Legislative Assembly's wives asked in confusion. "I just don't get it."

Emilia, something of an expert on explaining this to her family, asked the woman, who was on her third piece of fudge a question in return. "You like fudge it seems."

"I adore it," the woman said. "I can't get enough. I won't keep it at home because I'd eat it every day. Then I'd soon weigh two hundred pounds."

"Why don't you just quit eating it?" Emilia asked pointedly.

"I've tried," the lady said. "But I just can't resist it."

"I ate a half of one piece and that was all I wanted," Emilia said in a casual tone.

"I wish I could do that, but I can't. My husband won't even bring it home, he knows I'd eat the whole box if he did."

"Take that feeling and multiply it by ten or a hundred and you'll understand why it's so hard to quit opioids, crack, alcohol and other drugs."

The lady frowned and nodded, then made small talk for a minute of two before she moved on. Emilia *thought* the woman might have understood a little better.

A man of perhaps fifty approached her with a woman on his arm who looked to be about the same age by her hair and contemporary, but modest dress. She recognized him, having seen his picture in the paper and on the news she watched on the Internet. He was the MLA from Kamloops and the lady was his wife.

"Miss Robles, it's a pleasure to speak with you." He introduced himself and his wife. "I have a question, if you don't mind. If it's too personal, please don't feel obligated to answer."

"I'll try to answer if I'm able," she said, accustomed as she now was to baring her soul at the *SMART* meetings. *This isn't anonymous like SMART, be careful what you say.*

"I understand you've been sober for a little over six months. Is that correct?"

"Yes that's right." *Not overly personal so far.*

"I would honestly like to know what you like best about being sober."

Emilia smiled. *It's nice to actually field a different and thoughtful question for a change.* "In fact, what I like best about being clean is that it gives my brain's neuroplasticity a chance to work. My head is clearer and my mind is sharp again. I still have a way to go, but from what I've been told, this healing process will go on for up to five years, but after two, most of the healing will have taken place."

"That, Miss Robles is an answer I'll remember."

"Yes," his wife agreed. "I never even thought about the damage drugs and alcohol do to the brain, and I most certainly didn't realize that the brain could heal itself. *I* think you should be voting for Miss Dyck at the caucus meeting tomorrow." Her eyes bore into her husband's.

Her MLA husband frowned at her and growled in a low voice. "That's private caucus business. Don't be discussing it in public. Besides, there are opposition members here."

The woman rolled her eyes, but nodded and clamped her forefinger and thumb together then ran them across her lips.

He gave her a curt nod. "I hope that goes no further," he said quietly with a direct look at her, Mosi, and to someone behind them.

Emilia turned to look. It was Zach. *This guy is everywhere.*

"I agree," Zach said, with a pointed look at her and Mosi. "This should stay between us."

"Not to worry," Mosi replied. "Emilia and I both know how to keep a secret. Everything that's said in a *SMART* meeting is anonymous after all."

Indeed we do know how to keep secrets. Every week and sometimes in between, I hear things that shouldn't be repeated. It's part of being a SMART *Recovery participant.* She nodded to Zach, then turned and nodded to the MLA from Kamloops. His wife gave her a charming smile, as if she'd known Emilia and Mosi would not speak of it all along.

She weathered the party well after that and always kept a glass of bubbly water in her hand in case she was asked if she wanted a drink by one of the omnipresent servers, who walked through the crowd with free drinks, finger sandwiches, and sweet treats. She *did* indulge in a piece of shortbread.

She and Mosi would catch the 7 AM ferry back to the mainland tomorrow. She wondered how Josh did facilitating the *SMART* meeting for Mosi tonight. *I'm sure he's doing just fine.* She smiled. Mosi noticed and smiled back. *He can't possibly know what I'm thinking.*

Chapter Thirty-Five

Emilia slowly opened her eyes. After a few minutes, she shifted in bed to be able to check her alarm clock. *6:45. No sense in trying to get back to sleep for fifteen minutes.* She stretched, then did a short meditation before she got up.

Listen to your breath. Breathe deeply. Listen, listen, listen. When her mind wandered, she brought it back to her breathing. In, out, in, out, in, out.

Ten minutes later she threw the covers off her body and sat straight up in bed. *Life's awesome!* She felt energized, not just by the short meditation, but from life, from living it. Every day was a wonder. Sure, shit happened. Not everything went her way, but she could handle whatever came.

And today, she was one year clean!

One whole year without picking up. I'm high on life now and have no interest in booze or drugs at all. However, thanks to SMART I now understand that in my Lizard brain, the limbic system, that part of my brain that evolved millions of years ago, is a pathway to my pleasure center. It's now overgrown and weak, but it is still there. I'll never again knowingly put alcohol to my lips, because I know that my chances of ever drinking moderately are virtually zero. I was never a social drinker in the first place, I drank for the buzz, and if booze of any sort passes my lips, that old overgrown pathway will light up like a Roman candle, and I, Emilia Robles, will be addicted again in no time. I am now free and my freedom's too valuable to climb back inside that jail cell, lock myself in, and throw away the key. I'm too important, too worthy to go down that road – ever again.

The smell of coffee wafted into the bedroom. The automatic coffeemaker had done as she'd programed it to do and she smiled at the simple delight it gave her that she almost always remembered to put on the coffee before bed. And this was just one more tiny reward for remaining clean.

She pushed the toaster's plunger down, then sat with her coffee in hand. She took the first satisfying sip and slipped into reverie. *One year clean is not enough to get Mosi to be more than friends, but in another year, my mind will be a very different thing than one year ago and even from what it is today. Then I'll make my move — if Mosi doesn't first. In the meantime, we're getting to know each other and the more I know him, the more deeply my feelings are bound to him. He's imperfect, but like me, he's continually growing, learning, and changing.*

She knew if Mosi wasn't facilitating a *SMART* group, he'd no longer be attending, which was very much what *SMART* taught. Once one no longer needed to attend, when a person's entire way of thinking had been changed, they moved on and stopped attending meetings, or at the least, went rarely.

Then there was the unofficial ladies *SMART* group that met at the coffee shop in the middle of the week and also did other group *functions*. Often on weekends. There was a 100 percent success rate among them to date and only Anne had slipped once. When her husband had called Emilia from his wife's phone, she'd rushed over right away. She called the others and they'd all gone to support her. That was months ago, and Anne had worked out what had triggered her to be sure it didn't happen again. They also had two new ladies that met with them. *How did I become the unofficial leader of this unofficial group?*

And this weekend, she was getting together with her entire family and Mosi of course, to celebrate one-year clean. *I have my family again.* She was an aunt to her nieces and she and her brother met regularly, in spite of his girlfriend who continued to try and keep him from the family. She didn't really understand the girl at all, but was always polite for Bartolomé's sake, and proud that she was able to do so, unlike her addicted self, who'd only thought of what Emilia wanted and how she could slip away from everyone to get stoned.

Then on Saturday evening, Mosi would take her to dinner in a more private celebration.

Emilia finished her coffee and toast, then headed for the bus stop, umbrella in hand as the chance of rain in the afternoon was 65 percent. She found she still preferred to use public transit to go to work. *It feels good doing something positive for the environment.*

It was almost coffee break and Emilia was pleased with her progress this morning. She was getting work done at breakneck speed. *Having a clear mind feels so good!* She heard a knock at her open door and swiveled in her chair to see who it was. It was her boss, Mr. Douglas.

"Mornin', Emilia," he said with a closed expression. "I need to meet with you after coffee in my office. Oh—and Steve's still doing great. He told me you're an inspiration to him. Thanks," he said, with a nod and a genuinely kind smile.

"You're welcome, but remember, Steve's keeping Steve clean. Crack cocaine is a tough addiction to break. I'm glad mine was only opioids and vodka."

"You don't give yourself enough credit."

"Whatever you say," she told him and then smiled. "See you after coffee." *Me, I'm very proud of Steve.*

Before Emilia even stepped through the door, she noticed Mr. Douglas had his tie done up and his suit jacket on and buttoned, both were things she'd never seen in the six years she'd worked here. The instant she passed the threshold, she realized there was a woman in the room, standing in front of one of the two chairs, which sat before Mr. Douglas' desk.

"Emilia," he began, before she even got to the second chair.

"I'd like you to meet Miss Charlene McKinley, presently our Regional Manager. Charlene, this is Emilia Robles our brightest star."

"Pleased to meet you," a confused Emilia said as she extended her hand and took Ms. McKinley's. The lady gave her hand a warm, firm, dry shake and nodded. Her lips held the barest hint of a smile.

Ms. McKinley was Emilia's height so they looked each other in the eyes. She wore a frill-less white blouse under a pinstriped vest, with a matching knee-length skirt. No high heels here, Emilia noticed, but nothing frumpy either, rather low-heeled black shoes that coordinated with the stripes on her suit.

"I'm delighted to meet you as well, Emilia. When Richard sent me your file, I was more than pleased that he'd suggested you take his place as manager."

"Take his place?"

"Yes, he'll be taking over as Regional Manager as I've accepted a position at Head Office as Vice President. You're our first choice to manage this office. How do you feel about that?"

"Quite flattered, but this is the first I've heard of it and I'm honestly quite in shock."

"You have two weeks to decide if you'll accept the position. If you do, Richard will be around for another month after that to show you the proverbial ropes."

"I don't think I'll need two weeks to give you a decision. I will give you my answer in one week or less."

"Good. I like a decisive person who knows how to make a decision when needed. I believe you'll do well if you choose to take the position, Emilia.

"I'm off, Richard. I have a ton of things to do. I'll see you in six weeks for your training as Regional Manager, and congratulations, you deserve this."

Ms. McKinley strode from the room, low heels clacking on the tile floor. Her head was high, her back straight, every motion fluid and deliberate. She exuded power. Emilia felt like she'd just come down from an incredible high. *Wow! What a woman and I only met her and talked to her for five minutes.*

"Please sit, Emilia," Mr. Douglas said, wrenching her from her thoughts.

Emilia sat and faced Mr. Douglas, who loosened his tie and undid his jacket, then leaned forward, clasping his hands in front of him on the desk.

He looks thoughtful.

"Except for the last year of your addiction, you were an exemplary manager. Even then, you managed to get by. You have one of the finest minds I've ever met. I want you to know, I hid none of that from Charlene. It turns out she has a son in *AA*, so has some sympathy with your past.

"Ultimately, the decision whether or not you will head up White Rock and South Surrey's labs, is up to you, but this is a great opportunity and I'd feel I was leaving the labs in good hands if you accept."

"Thank you, Mister Douglas."

He raised his right hand in a *stop* gesture. "Please call me Richard."

"Thank you, Richard."

Richard nodded and smiled.

CHAPTER THIRTY-SIX

Emilia had put on a dress. A rarity for her. It was red with a modest neckline, but cut five inches above the knee. Not exactly a mini-dress, but short enough for her purpose and it hugged her curves, which were now significant though hardly voluptuous. It was exactly the look she was going for this evening, discreetly sexy. She put on a bit of eyeliner and powder with lipstick to match the dress. Checking herself in the mirror, she was happy. Her black hair, which now hung to the middle of her back, shone, and the slight natural curls that had, for some reason, annoyed her so much when she was addicted, now added a hint of glamour to her ensemble, which included a black clutch and red heels, again to match the dress. She was one year clean and though she knew there was—as yet—no hope the man she'd fallen for could be hers, she planned to impress him tonight. For Mosi was taking her to dinner to celebrate her first year free of substance abuse. This was something she knew he'd never done before. Though they couldn't date—yet—she'd show what would be available in another year. That was, according to *her* plan, which was in her eyes, the best plan going. While Mosi made it clear they couldn't date, it was obvious he was as drawn to her as she was to him, so there was no doubt in her mind that when she was sufficiently healed, they could—and would—become a couple. The good thing about waiting for two years was it gave them time to get to know one another. No pressure to perform, just honest, clear communication, fun times together, and really getting inside one another's head. It was something she'd never experienced in her life, not with anyone and most certainly not with a man. A good man. In addition, she was ready to celebrate. She'd just had an offer of an amazing promotion, which she was almost certain to accept, but needed some clear-headed time to weigh the pros and cons. But celebrate no longer meant a bottle—or three—of wine with five or six oxycodone, but a fine dinner at a nice restaurant with someone who she held in the highest respect. The man she was falling in love with. One part of her screamed *it's never too soon!* But the reasonable part, the prefrontal cortex, the thinking part of her brain, which she'd empowered by getting and staying clean, gently reminded her that she needed to continue to concentrate on herself. To grow and make new healthy connections in her brain so she'd be mentally prepared for a long term romantic relationship and be able to make good, wise and healthy decisions in love and life.

At the stoplight, Mosi flipped down the sun visor in his car and checked his teeth in the mirror. He was certain he'd forgotten some small item of personal hygiene, and though he didn't tend to be hyper-concerned about that sort of thing, he was today. He knew exactly why it was on his mind and though it was usually easy to dispute his irrational beliefs, Emilia made it harder. He wanted to please her.

He tended to be more of a *let the chips fall where they may* kind of guy, but with Emilia, he wanted those chips to fall where he wanted them to fall, which was irrational because she had only one year clean and still needed to concentrate on her recovery and healing. Even when her healing would be complete at two years, she was a participant in *his* SMART meeting and dating her would be no different than a doctor or lawyer dating their client. The issue, as Mosi saw it, was the fact that in early recovery one needed to concentrate on their recovery and healing of the brain and body. A new romantic relationship, especially when sex was involved, tended to do the reverse, until the mind was well healed. Mosi had to make sure Emilia kept her eye on recovery without any avoidable distractions. There were enough unavoidable hindrances in life without adding sex at a time when someone was extremely vulnerable, as they were in the first couple of years of abstinence.

He knew he should have invited the other *SMART* ladies that formed Emilia's coffee house group, but he wanted her to himself this evening in spite of the fact they could never date or become a couple, which was what he most wanted. He'd even thought of passing the White Rock group on to Josh, who was doing well and blossoming as a facilitator, but Josh had confided in him that he would like to start a new *SMART* group in the area. There was no way Mosi would stand in the way of a new meeting, and there just wasn't anybody else ready to take the meeting yet. If he gave up the group, he'd be free to approach Emilia in another year or so when she was firmly established in her recovery. But it was one of his great desires to see the group he'd started in White Rock almost ten years ago continue.

Get a hold of yourself, you're here!

Mosi was ten minutes early and ordered a cappuccino while he waited. The moment she arrived, he spotted Emilia from where he sat. When her eyes scanned the dining area, he shot his hand up and waved. *I'm acting like a schoolboy.* He chuckled at his juvenile reaction to Emilia's arrival, but it worked and after a word with the maître d' she strode his way.

When she was steps away, he stood and walked around the table. He pulled the other chair at the small table out and sat her. She smiled at him, clearly pleased with the gesture. Her smile was enough recompense for ten times the effort he'd expended and he felt his face heat from the pleasure. He sat and they ordered dinner.

They talked trivialities until their meals arrived, then Emilia asked, between forkfuls of local salmon, "Does Zach keep in touch with you?"

His mouth full, Mosi nodded. When he swallowed he expanded. "Yes, weekly. He always asks about you. He thinks the celt, you, and politics are all mingled together."

"It seems crazy, that's for sure. I've never been much for myths or prophecies, and Zach says he never was, either, but now he's a like a religious fanatic about the celt."

"Yeah, it seems that way to me, too. He and Julián think Miss Dyck's election as leader of the Liberal party, ergo, Premier, was foretold in the prophecy written on the celt."

"Whether it was or not, her election was certainly good for the *CCSA* and there are already hundreds more people with addictions getting into rehab facilities and with seven new government facilities, there's usually no waiting time to get into rehab like there used to be."

"Yes, thank God for that!"

Emilia gave a throaty chuckle.

"What are you laughing at?" Mosi gave her what he thought was a warm smile.

"You thanking God. You don't believe there's a God."

"In theory, no, I don't. But remember, I'm agnostic and could change my mind at any given moment — with genuine evidence."

"My family's all Catholic. Many Mestizos are."

"Aren't they worried you'll go to hell?"

"Nope. I was baptized, so my original sin was washed away and I was confirmed at eight years old. I might have to spend a few thousand years in purgatory, but I'm still *saved*."

"But you don't believe any of that." Mosi cupped his chin with his left thumb and forefinger, with his elbow on the table.

"No, it's a nice thought, but there's no evidence it's true. And if there *was* a God, which is the right one?"

"When did you come to this conclusion?"

"I was fourteen, I think. How about you?" She looked at him expectantly.

"I was a bit older than that, but I remember clearly 'cause it was on my nineteenth birthday. I was raised Muslim . . . kind of. Mom was a believer, but didn't actually follow the faith or pray five times a day. She was very much a *western* Muslim, to the point she drank and suffered from addiction." He shook his head at the memory.

"That certainly isn't proper behavior for a Muslim, especially not a woman, I'd think." Emilia gave Mosi a thoughtful look.

"You'd be right. When she got sober six years ago, she re-thought her faith and is no longer a believer." Mosi stared past her, clearly pensive.

"You wouldn't have had anything to do with that now would you?" Emilia said in a playful tone.

"Oh, absolutely not." He grinned and gave away the joke.

"It can be lonely being a non-believer, but there seems a high incidence of people who reject faith in the *SMART* program." She sighed.

"I've noticed the same over the years, but there are also many people of faith in *SMART*, too. Some of them are facilitators." Mosi tilted his head and gave her a crooked smile.

"It seems like a paradox to me," she said with furrowed brows.

"We're all enigmas," he said flatly.

"Who, exactly, are *we*?" She leaned back in her chair, sipped on her carbonated spring water and looked into his eyes.

"We, Homo sapiens."

She gave him a thoughtful nod. "Yeah, I think you're right."

God, she's lovely. And I've never met a woman like her. She's — absolutely brilliant, has the charisma of a kitten and the prowess and life skills of a lioness, not to mention determination. She's one of the few I know who haven't slipped on their road to recovery. Including myself. Maybe in another year I'll stop facilitating. One can never tell what life will throw at you. Maybe there's some way we can be together. But I'll have to wait another year at least. He smiled inwardly.

"Oh, I meant to tell you earlier." *Except your smile blanked my mind.* "I was offered a promotion at work," Emilia said.

"It sounds like you didn't accept it."

"I did ask for a few days to think about it. I'm going to do a *Cost Benefit Analysis* when I get home, or at least start one. It may take a couple of days to figure out all the pros and cons, what I'll like about it and the problems it may cause," she said, with a gleam in her eye and a bright smile.

He grinned, apparently at her obvious exuberance. "So, don't keep me in suspense, tell me what position you've been offered."

"Local manager. I'd be taking over Mister Richard Douglas' position as he's being bumped up to Regional Manager and the Regional Manager's going to Head Office."

"Sounds like a lot of pressure. Do you think you're ready for it?"

"I think so, but that's one reason I'm going to do *CBA* as well as talk to some team members to see what kind of support I can expect. That may make the difference between being safe and endangering my sobriety," she said in a thoughtful tone as she twirled a lock of hair.

Mosi gave her a warm smile. "So how many offices would you be in charge of?"

"Ten right now, but they're building a new office in Abbotsford and that one would be in my jurisdiction as well."

"That seems like a lot, but you're exceptionally gifted intellectually and I've no doubt you'll handle it well. And you know how to use the *SMART* tools, not just for sobriety, but also as life tools," he said with a certainty that sounded absolute.

"Yes, thanks to you," she said as she crossed her legs and put her warmest most heartfelt smile on her face, which was unbelievably easy to do when she was with Mosi.

Emilia's smile gave him butterflies in his stomach. *I don't know if that's manly or not, but I can't say I give a damn.* Then her gaze abandoned his face and the look on her face changed to one of shock. Mosi spun his head around to look. "Zach!"

"Happy one year anniversary, Emilia," Zach said, as he brought his powerwalk to an abrupt halt at their table.

"You came just to wish me a happy anniversary?" she asked, with furrowed brows.

"Um, yes and no."

Mosi gave a strained chuckle and shook his head, "Multitasking, are we?"

"I'm not sure it's multitasking, but I *am* here on business for Premier Dyck."

"May I ask what kind of business it involves?" Emilia screwed up her face.

"Well—the Premier had a dream last night," Zach explained with his head hanging down.

"Whoa!" Mosi exclaimed. "Don't tell me you now believe in the supernatural, and that with no evidence to support it?"

"I've been thinking about what *I* saw when I touched the celt," Emilia growled, upset at the interruption of her time with Mosi. "I don't know if that would be considered evidence, except to me, and even I think it must have been something I'd seen and heard subconsciously."

"You could be absolutely right," Zach said, in an overly cheerful fashion. "But the more time I spend around the celt the greater the attachment I feel."

"*You've* seen something, too?" Mosi asked.

"Not at all. But though I've seen nothing, I've felt a presence."

"Presence?" Mosi and Emilia gasped at the same moment.

"Kindly explain yourself." Emilia growled.

"When I touch the inscriptions I often feel a small rush of dopamine. But if I have something on my mind I want to do and if it's against the prophecy, as I understand it, I get the shakes like I did during withdrawal. And if I make a plan that *follows* the prophecy, I get a huge rush of dopamine. That's what happened today. I felt Gillian's—ah, Miss Dyck's dream, though I saw nothing."

"What exactly did you feel?" Mosi asked.

"I felt the need to come back to the Mainland to prepare Emilia, Bianca, and Paola for what's to come."

"Wait one moment." Emilia lifted her forefinger in an indication to stop. "Who are Paola and Bianca, and explain *what's to come.*"

"They're mother and daughter and the celt was in Paola's family's possession for many, many generations and when they touched the inscriptions, they saw more or less what you did, according to your detailed explanations.

"As for what's to come, it would seem it's political and will happen here in the Americas. Can I count on you?" Zach asked.

Emilia nodded. "Absolutely." *I have no idea why I'm agreeing to this, but somehow . . . I need to.*

CHAPTER THIRTY-SEVEN

Emilia woke to see the sun shining through her window, as she hadn't closed the blinds. The days were getting longer. She stretched and then slipped out of bed. It was Saturday and she'd been clean two years as of today.

Emilia smiled.

Mosi was taking her to lunch.

Emilia was so excited Mosi was coming. She felt no hunger pangs and skipped breakfast altogether, though she did drink two cups of coffee. She put on a load of laundry and while it washed, she dusted. When the clothes were ready she threw them into the dryer and vacuumed all her carpeted areas and swept and mopped the kitchen and bathrooms. Before she knew it lunchtime had rolled around and Mosi would be picking her up. She was ready to get on with life. A life that included Mosi.

The buzzer let her know someone had arrived. She checked the video-phone and it was Mosi.

"Hi Mosi, I'll be down in a couple of minutes."

He smiled and nodded. "Okay, sounds good."

When Emilia hauled open the glass door, it reminded her of the very first *SMART* meeting she'd attended, but this time Mosi awaited her. He was smiling, but it was forced. *Something's happening. I'll ask about it when we get into his car.*

Once in the auto, they headed up the steep hill to eat at an Indian restaurant, but she also had a question.

"What's wrong, Mosi?"

He sighed. "Nothing really and the truth is it's good news. Josh is starting a new meeting in Tsawwassen."

"That *is* good news."

"Yeah—it's just that I was hoping to turn the White Rock meeting over to him."

"Oh, that's too bad. Are you tired of facilitating?"

"Actually, no, I'm not." He shook his head and the smile turned up-side-down. "I just wanted—never mind."

After lunch, Emilia invited Mosi up to her condo for tea, which he accepted. *Now's the time to make my play.*

"Would you like *Earl Grey* or herbal tea?"

"Hmm, what kind of herbal tea do you have?" He shrugged.

"I have *Echinacea, Lavender and Rooibos, Chamomile,* and *Ginger.*"

"*Echinacea* sounds great." He smiled, a genuine smile.

"*Echinacea* it is." She gave Mosi a warm coquettish smile in return.

As they sipped on their tea they chatted about inconsequential things until Emilia worked up enough courage to invite him to stay the night.

"Now that I've been clean for two years, I think I'm ready for a little bit of romance."

"Oh—did you have someone in mind?" he asked. His lips were compressed, he wrung his hands together, and he continually touched his face.

"Yes as a matter of fact I do."

"May I ask—"

She lifted her right hand in a *stop* motion and cut him off. "Mosi, you're the one. I kept thinking about you from the time I went to rehab, but I also learned I had to get well before I could get involved with someone else. I really enjoyed the time we spent together as friends, but now I'm ready for more."

"But I'm your facilitator, so it just won't work. I have to keep my relationship with you as well as all the other participants professional. Can't you see that?"

"No, I don't. We're all equal, that's what *SMART* teaches."

"Of course we are, but when relationships go bad, relapse is a very common occurrence, and I can't take that chance with someone from the group I facilitate. And usually it's the person with the least time sober and clean who relapses."

"Well, I'm not going to relapse. No way. I have too much to lose now. I have my family back, the other *SMART* ladies to hang with and now ten offices to run."

"I'm so sorry, Emilia, but I simply can't do it. I'm your facilitator."

"Well then, fuck you, Mister El-Hadidy." She jumped from her seat, stomped off to the kitchen and began to clean up, rattling the dishes to the point of almost breaking some of them.

Two minutes later Mosi appeared at the door to the kitchen. "I guess I should get going." He put the teacup down on the counter beside her. "Are you safe?"

"Of course I am. Why would you think otherwise?"

"I thought it possible that our discussion triggered you and I wouldn't want to leave you alone if that's the case."

"Don't worry." She huffed. "If I feel triggered I'll call Doris or Anne. I have a good support group."

"Yes, you do. Please promise me you'll call someone if you have urges."

She turned and gave him a mock salute. "Yes, sir, will do, sir. Anything else, sir?"

"No, there's nothing else and thank you for the tea. I hope to see you Monday."

"Of course I'll be there Monday. Why wouldn't I be?"

"Okay, until then." He turned and walked out of the kitchen into the hallway that led to the entrance and let himself out.

"The bastard. How could he do this to me?" She then did a *CBA* and ran through an *ABC*. As she did these tools, she began to feel better. *He didn't reject me, he's being careful so I don't relapse.* Then it struck her. *I have two years clean and can reach out and help others more than I'm doing now.* She went to her computer and logged on to *SMART's* website and signed up to take the Facilitator's course. The online course would begin next week, and last six weeks. She'd keep it a secret from the entire group . . . even the ladies.

Now, she'd need to find a church or meeting hall either cheap or free. Cloverdale would be perfect, she thought. A fifteen-minute drive north of White Rock, and there was no *SMART* meeting in that town.

CHAPTER THIRTY-EIGHT

This would be her last *SMART* meeting with Mosi and Wednesday would be the first *SMART* meeting that she'd facilitate. The ladies' group had agreed to meet on Thursdays from now on. Emilia was nervous and excited at the same time. She'd printed a copy of her certificate that showed she was now an official *SMART Recovery* Facilitator. She decided to walk to the meeting this evening as the weather was fine, the temperature warm and the sun would set late. She made sure she had her certificate and her handbook and set out on the fifteen-minute walk.

Mosi was there when she arrived and ten others. It was still early though, and some habitually came at the last possible minute. Mosi was seated in his usual spot at the head of the tables in front of the whiteboard. She walked over to him and placed the certificate in front of him, then glided over and sat between Doris and Caryn. She nodded and smiled at Phineas, Zach, Miranda, and Anne. There was no Josh this evening as he'd started his meeting on Mondays as well. Tsawwassen was almost a thirty-minute drive from White Rock and much closer to where he lived. She then glanced over at Mosi and saw a confused look on his face. She covered her mouth and grinned. Just then, seven more arrived almost treading on each other's heels, but all were laughing at the inconvenience they'd caused each other.

Mosi read the *Opening Statement* and then began check-in. Finally it came around to her.

"I'm Emilia and I now have over two years and seven

313

weeks clean."

The people around the table clapped and hooted. Emilia smiled and continued.

"I just finished taking the *SMART Recovery* Facilitator's course and found a church in Cloverdale that will let me have a meeting room for free. So, this will be my last regular meeting here. I'll still attend Doctor Reshma's closed *SMART* group, but I don't want to overdo it. That, as most of you know is the fourth point in the *SMART* doctrine. *Living a balanced lifestyle.* I need to be sure I have *me* time. Wish me luck!"

They all clapped again. Mosi, too, but he had a look of absolute astonishment on his face. Emilia smiled at him.

It was 7:00 o'clock and time to start her first meeting. Anne and Doris had come to give her support and there were six people she didn't know.

She read.

This is an open meeting of SMART *Recovery.* SMART *stands for* Self-Management And Recovery Training.

SMART's *four main objectives are.*

One, to maintain motivation for abstinence.

Two, to learn to cope with urges and cravings.

Three, to manage thoughts, feelings and behaviors.

Four, to live a balanced lifestyle.

SMART *sees addiction as a learned unhelpful behavior. At the core of* SMART *is the principal that I am largely responsible for my thoughts, feelings and behaviors, including addictive behaviors. And if I want to change the way I feel and behave, I need to start by changing the way I think.*

If this is your first time at a SMART *meeting, welcome. You are invited to participate as much or as little as you want.*

During check-in, Emilia discovered that one of the new participants was encouraged to come by his counselor, two others were mandated by the court to attend two recovery meetings per week and the forth, a woman, was trying to quit alcohol and cocaine. The remaining two men said they were not satisfied with and not very successful at *AA* meetings and thought they'd try *SMART*.

Emilia decided to do a *CBA* and divided the whiteboard into four quadrants. In the top left she wrote—

What did my addiction do for me?

At 8:30 on the dot, she ended the meeting. She signed forms for the two who were mandated, chatted with the others for a few minutes and then set the alarm and locked up.

It felt so good to reach out to people in need with a scientific program that worked.

CHAPTER THIRTY-NINE

Saturday morning Emilia slept in until 7:00 in the morning. As she lay on the bed waking up, she heard the distinct sound of a text message arriving. She reached over and plucked her cell from the nightstand and looked to see who'd texted her.

It was Mosi!

While getting together with him was *part* of her goal in becoming a facilitator, she'd discovered from her first meeting, she *liked* facilitating. It gave her a dopamine rush as well as satisfaction that she was helping people who were trying their damnedest to free themselves from their addictive behavior.

She read the message.

Hey, Emilia, would you like to go to dinner with me this evening? I was thinking Greek food, as there are a couple of nice places here in White Rock and nearby.
Let me know so I can make reservations.

She most certainly *would* go to dinner with him—*if*—he came back to her place for tea afterwards. She texted back with that condition, and he answered in the affirmative.

Emilia closed her eyes and gave a deep grateful sigh.

At 5:30 Mosi buzzed her number.

"Hi, I'm here!"

"I'll be right down."

There were a few moments of hesitation, then he finally replied.

"Okay, I'll wait right here by the front entry."

"Got it."

Emilia scurried out the door and took the elevator down to the main entry. There was Mosi waiting patiently for her. She burst through the door and found herself in Mosi's arms, his lips pressed against hers, and his tongue exploring her mouth and lips. He finally pulled away and looked deep into her eyes.

Dinner was lamb, falling off the bone, spanakopita, rice, and roasted potatoes, served with pita bread. They talked like they'd never stopped seeing each other and constantly gazed into one another's eyes. When they'd finished, they decided against dessert.

"Check please," Mosi said, then turned his head back to her and gave her a warm smile.

Emilia felt like she was wilting. "I don't mind you paying this time, but I expect us to take turns."

"It looks like you've already decided this is the beginning of a long term relationship." He grinned and rested his chin on his knuckles, looking it seemed, deep into her soul.

"Am I mistaken?" She frowned and tapped the four fingers of her right hand on the tabletop.

"Not as far as I'm concerned."

Mosi paid and they left to have tea at Emilia's condo.

Emilia prepared a pot of *Chamomile* tea while Mosi watched her every move. She found it pleasant to be admired by the man she adored and gave him a smile each time she turned his way. When the tea had steeped four minutes, she took it to the living room. Mosi followed with a tray, teacups, cream, sugar and stevia.

"This is good tea," Mosi said. "I've never had it before."

"Now you know what you were missing." She smiled and winked

"Indeed." He grinned.

They were going to have sex. It was in the air, there were no doubts. It was then it struck her. *Oh my God! I don't remember ever having sex while I was sober. Will I do okay? Will I please him? Will he be able to give pleasure to me while I'm sober?*

Emilia! This is the man you love. Most of the world makes love while they're sober. It'll be fine.

That bugaboo seemed to largely calm itself with her reasoning. She let out a gentle sigh and let herself focus on every sensation and the beauty of this moment.

This might be a good time to make sure we make love safely.

"So I did buy some condoms and have them in the night table by my bed," she said in as casual a voice as possible.

Mosi chuckled. "I brought some, too. They're strawberry flavored." He grinned.

"Mmm, sounds delish." She smiled back at him. "I'm also on the pill. I'll be starting my second month on Tuesday."

"If that's the case we could both get tested for STD's and then we can go bareback in a week of two."

"I like your plan." Emilia gave him an embarrassed smile.

With the tea finished they sat together on her sofa and cuddled, which led to kissing, then Mosi ran his hand down the back of her neck. His fingertips seemed to give off tiny jolts that sent shivers down her whole body and then back again to the tips of his fingers where another burst sent the pulses again and again. She couldn't place the scent he wore, but it was imbued with what she'd come to know as the smell of *him*. His hand gently pulled her to him and she felt her tongue on his. They entwined. She pulled back and rubbed her cheek on his roughness, then softly sucked an earlobe, tasting the slight saltiness. She pushed her hand into his short tight hair and felt his sweet breath escape his lips, warming her cheek.

She pulled out of his embrace. He frowned. Then she climbed on top of him. Her plan had been to straddle him to enhance their mutual connection, but she slipped and fell backwards.

Oh no, the coffee table!

Before her head could hit the table, she felt herself being swept back up by strong hands. She landed straddling him exactly as planned.

Almost.

"Oh crap! My foot's twisted under me," she grumbled.

Mosi chuckled and bodily lifted her straight up by her hips until she was able to re-accommodate the unruly appendage, then dumped her right back down in his lap and pulled her in.

They bumped foreheads.

"Ouch!" she cried, pushing against his shoulders.

"Sorry, I was a bit overenthusiastic," he said with a grin, bushing her forehead with the back of his right hand.

She left his hand where it was and reached forward placing her hands on his cheeks she looked him deep in the eyes. He let his hand drop where it landed with ever so much gentleness on her bosom, where he wasted no time slipping open the top button of her blouse. Then the next. She stroked his arm as his fingers slipped under her bra until they reached her erect nipple, where they halted progress and began to softly knead with finger and thumb. She leaned forward and kissed him.

In an apparent mutual understanding, they pulled away. Mosi reached back down and undid the four remaining buttons on her blouse.

He smiled.

Apparently he noticed it's a front hook bra.

She'd barely thought it he reached for the hook and undid it. The bra fell away and she felt slight currents of cool air waft around them. A moment later she felt heated breath as Mosi leaned over to suckle her left nipple as his left hand caressed the right, wafting over its plumpness and the erect nipple.

The sensations of his hand on her skin, his sweet warm breath and feeling his heart trying to escape from his chest made her giddy. She wanted to envelop him. She reached up and in quick succession undid all the buttons of his shirt, then slid her hands under his shirt and along his sides and then up his back.

A moment later he tugged her blouse off and then the bra. Except of course the bra somehow got tangled either with itself or the mostly removed top. Instead of the bra coming free the force pulled her sideways into the back cushions of the couch.

"Oh God, I'm so sorry!" Mosi cried as he reached over and pulled her back up. "Are you okay?" He held her by her arms and looked her in the eyes.

Emilia burst out laughing.

"Well, I guess you're okay," Mosi grumped with a frown.

After hauling in two deep breaths, Emilia calmed enough to speak. "Oh, my love," she grinned, "I just think it's funny how we keep bumping into each other when we're trying to be serious."

Mosi scrunched up his face. "Serious? I think of making love more as fun time together rather than being serious."

"Point taken. But let's try not to leave any bruising on me."

Mosi chuckled. "That sounds like a reasonable plan," he breathed on her neck.

She leaned her head into him and he ran his lips down until they lay on her collarbone, then he softly sucked her skin and ran his tongue over it. Light lips then worked to the front of her neck as he leaned her back from where she still straddled him. With one strong arm at her back supporting her, the other brushed over her left breast and his lips continued until they came in contact with the erect nipple of her right breast.

"That's nice," she said as he continued to draw the nipple into his mouth and then circle it with his tongue. She ran her fingers into his short curly hair, closed her eyes and enjoyed the warmth and wetness of his lips and mouth on her breast. Then he began to work his way down, first with his free hand, which caressed the outside of her thighs.

Seeing a need to re-accommodate themselves, Emilia leaned her arms, which were now around his neck, to her left. He understood right away and as if afraid he might bruise her, pulled her down beside him with amazing gentleness.

Emilia pulled her lips away from his while she tried to slide his shirtsleeve off his arm. He chuckled. "Here, let me help," he said as he lifted his torso up so Emilia could tug his sleeve off. They snuggled back down onto the sofa and they began to explore.

Emilia felt the back of his hand against her cheek as he brushed it. The hand continued down to her breast, where it fondled the whole breast and then the nipple. But this time Mosi's hand strayed lower. Upon reaching the top of her stretchy jeans, he expertly popped open the button at her waist and slid the zipper all the way down. Emilia gave a quick sharp breath when she felt his fingertips glide over her thong. The gentle strokes caused waves of electrical energy to flow through her entire body over and again.

A moment later he slipped her jeans down as she arched her torso to make pulling them off easier. He then slipped his left hand under her undies. She glanced down at him to see him look up at her with a look of surprise. That may have had something to do with the fact she'd just freshly shaved herself a few hours ago. She grinned at him and winked. He smiled back and a moment later, relieved her of her panties, which she was quite happy to lose.

She felt his heated breath on her flat belly as he eased

himself down. His every heavy exhalation produced a wave of intense pleasure flowing to all corners of her body. A moment later she felt his breath hover over her most erogenous spot, then his tongue touched it. It was an exquisite moment followed by another as she felt her clitoris being drawn into the moist heat of his mouth. As his tongue did slow circles around her most intimate spot, he ran his hands up her hips. Everywhere he touched, her body lit up with the intensity of the experience giving her powerful tingles until panting, she arched herself against his mouth in uncontrollable spasms.

She lay there for what seemed like a few minutes oblivious to anything outside the sensations of pleasure that flashed through her. When she felt something outside of her body, Emilia opened her eyes and found staring into hers, Mosi's dark hungry eyes. She reached to pull him to her. To kiss her.

As his lips touched hers, she felt the exquisiteness of his hardness penetrating her. There was a long eternity of sensations as he plunged in and out. Their bodies covered in perspiration made slapping sounds in time with their thrusts and counterthrusts. Their scents mingled, producing a new one that screamed sensuality and a oneness she'd never felt.

As they lay there in the aftermath of their love, Emilia decided that there was no doubt.

Sober sex is the best.

CHAPTER FORTY

Zach stroked the felt bag that held the priceless treasure. I'll bring Julián with me — if he'll come. We need to search for the other women and he's somehow connected to the celt. Zach chuckled to himself. The professor is really pissed with me for borrowing the celt. But even he knows I need it to find the remaining Mestiza ladies Julián saw when he held the celt. I'm not sure why I need it, but I know it will be invaluable in my quest for good government. Maybe a new kind of government. One that truly benefits humanity.

You may also enjoy the following from eXtasy Books Inc:

Quadratic Equations
Sofía T. García
January 2018

Sometimes one plus one isn't a simple sum . . .

After her bitter divorce, Paola moves to Vancouver for a fresh start. She and her twenty-three-year-old daughter, Bianca, have new jobs working at a firm owned by a father and son team. Complications develop almost immediately when Paola discovers Bianca thinks she's in love with Fritz, her fifty-year-old employer. Luckily, their relationship is platonic. So far.

Karl, the thirty-seven-year-old son, is attracted to Bianca, but hesitates to make a move because he assumes the elder pair are sleeping together. Things go from bad to worse when Paola finds herself drawn to Fritz, but won't act on her feelings because she doesn't want to hurt her daughter.

When tragedy strikes, nothing is certain, and the lives of four people hang in the balance.

Excerpt

Paola looked out the window of the commuter jet as it headed into Vancouver International Airport. She hoped Bianca was there to meet her. That was the plan, but her twenty-three-year-old daughter seemed distracted these days, and had been for months now.

Paola was starting a new life. Her husband of twenty-seven years had run off with a nineteen-year-old and tried to take everything, but she'd had a good lawyer. That wasn't by accident. Paola believed in research and references. She ended up with more than half, which in no way made up for the loss of the man she'd thought of as her soul mate. She'd then sold everything, quit her job, and with Bianca's help, found new employment here in Vancouver, one hundred and sixty miles north of Seattle.

She'd married and raised her family in Seattle, but it was time for a new start and a clean separation from her ex. She would be working with her daughter, who had followed her into the same profession and became a video game designer.

Vancouver, British Columbia, Canada, was one of the international hubs for video game design, and her new employer was known worldwide as one of the best.

Net One Co. Ltd., was started twenty-nine years ago by the far-seeing computer programmer and all-around genius, Fritz Felkner. The fifty-three-year-old and his only son, the twenty-five-year-old Karl, ran the company. It was one of the largest private companies in Canada and she understood both father and son refused to go public, in spite of lucrative offers. Much of this information came from her daughter, Bianca.

It seemed to Paola that taxiing to the de-boarding ramp had taken as long as the short flight from Seattle. She felt invigorated, with none of the jetlag from trips overseas or other long flights. After making her way through a very polite Customs and Immigration—she had all the paperwork in order, including her shiny new work visa—she followed the signs to the luggage claim area. Before she even looked for her bags, she sought her daughter.

She must have overlooked the sign three times in her excitement to see Bianca, but at last, it clicked in her mind that her name was written in black, on a large off-white sheet of craft paper.

Ms. Paola Vasquez

A bored-looking man held it, who must have been less than thirty. When she took a moment to examine him, she caught her breath. He stood a head taller than those around him, had broad shoulders, with the quintessential square chin and blonde hair of German stock. It was a young, handsome face well, actually, it was gorgeous, and attached to a luscious body in the bargain.

Yum, yum, she thought, then chastised herself, but reconsidered. She was now single, and as such had every right to look at such a scrumptious piece of manhood with as much lust as she desired. He was a boy, after all, not much older than Bianca. It's not like she would do more than enjoy the view. She strode toward him with a warm smile on her forty-seven-year-old face.

He must have realized who she was, because his eyes widened in clear surprise and his green eyes glowed as they roamed over her body. Yes, she'd put on a few pounds over the years, but her body was still something close to voluptuous. Usually the stares of men as she walked down the street annoyed her, but in this case, she felt a thrill, in spite of the fact that he was a puppy.

"Yes. I would be Paola Vasquez," she said, looking way up into those lust-filled emerald eyes.

"Uh . . . hi, I'm Karl Felkner . . . um, ah . . . Bianca was . . . um, busy and couldn't make it to, ah . . . pick you up, so Dad sent me. It's just you look different in person than from the video conference."

"Yes, I didn't recognize you at first either. I'm unhappy not to see Bianca, but you're not a bad recompense." She gave him a cheeky grin.

His eyes grew wide as saucers and then in an instant, he became the ultimate gentleman, offering her his arm. "Shall we go in search of your bags?"

"That would be an excellent idea." She smiled at him again and enjoyed his flustered look. "Bianca has seemed a little distracted the last while," she said. "She seldom answers her cell and when she does return calls, which is not often, she acts a little . . . otherworldly, if you know what I mean?"

"Ah . . . at work, Bianca is the consummate professional."

"At work?"

"After work, she lives in another world."

"What the hell are you talking about? Is she all right?"

"No, no, please don't misunderstand, she's fine. Just . . . well, acting odd for a woman her age."

"You have to take me to see her at once!"

"I'm sorry, that's impossible, Ms. Vasquez, but please let me tell you that she's fine." He gave her a lopsided smile.

Paola laughed. "Okay, but I need to see her soon."

"Of course. I'm sure that she wants to see you, too," he said.

"That's it!" she cried out as her second bag rolled around the carousel.

Both bags collected, Paola and Karl left for the parking area. After he'd loaded her carry-on and the two bags into the back of the plain white Ford van, they drove off.

"I assume you're taking me to Bianca's apartment," Paola said.

He gave a soft hiss.

"Sorry. I understand that she isn't set up for guests. I could get you a hotel room until you find a place, but I thought maybe you could stay in one of my guestrooms. I'm leaving for New York this evening on business for two weeks, so you'd have the place to yourself, and it beats any hotel you could find." Karl gave her another of his lopsided grins.

"Why's this coming up now, and what's wrong with Bianca's place?"

"She was supposed to text you and tell you," he said.

ABOUT THE AUTHOR

Sofía was born on the southwest coast of British Columbia, Canada to immigrant parents who came from southern California. In the summer she's on her bike or hiking the BC and Oregon mountains and in the winter you can find her cross-country skiing. All year and at every hour of the day and night, she can be found at her laptop working on her Mestiza series.

www.ingramcontent.com/pod-product-compliance
Lightning Source LLC
Chambersburg PA
CBHW062024170626
46813CB00001B/287